A SHOWGIRL'S RULES FOR FALLING IN LOVE

A

SHOWGIRL'S

RULES FOR

FALLING
IN LOVE

ALICE MURPHY

**UNION
SQUARE
& CO.**

NEW YORK

**UNION
SQUARE
&CO.**

NEW YORK

ISBN 978-1-4549-5946-5
ISBN 978-1-4549-5947-2 (e-book)

For information about custom editions, special sales,
and premium purchases, please
contact specialsales@unionsquareandco.com.

Printed in Canada

2 4 6 8 10 9 7 5 3 1

unionsquareandco.com

Cover design by Patrick Sullivan
Cover art by Decue Wu
Interior design by Christine Heun

To my younger self, who deserved better.

Sophie Tucker: I'm fat, and I know it, and I intend to stay fat.

Ted Shapiro: Miss Tucker, you shouldn't say fat. In the best places, they say one is "stout."

Sophie Tucker: (laughs, strokes her curves) In the best places, I'm fat.

—Sophie Tucker, vaudeville star,
"I Don't Want to Get Thin," 1929

PART ONE

THE MOTH AND THE FLAME

Armitage Gallier <ALG@gallierentel.com>
To: phoebe.blair@tmhps.org

Miss Blair,

Hello. I understand that you are the author of *The Secret History of Vaudeville* newsletter recently featured in NPR's "Jazz Night in America" program. I have a research inquiry with which I believe you are best suited to assist me. Please reply with your availability at your earliest possible convenience. I am happy to meet with you in your office at the Manhattan Historical Preservation Society, or at another location of your choosing.

Warm Regards,
Armitage Gallier

Phoebe Blair <phoebe.blair@tmhps.org>
To: ALG@gallierentel.com

Hi there!

Thanks for reaching out! So nice to hear from readers—there aren't a lot of you out there, lol! "Featured on NPR" is a very nice way of saying, "referenced in passing by a random guest on a story barely anyone heard," but I'll take the compliment. Maybe even put it on my business card!

My "office" is more of a desk in TMHPS' basement, but if you can stand the schlep downtown, it's probably the best place to meet. That way, if you need any documents pulled from our archive, I can grab them for you then and you won't need to make a special trip!

I'm in the office from 8 to 4, Monday to Friday. No need to make an appointment—I'll be there, and probably bored!

Looking forward to it!

Phoebe
P.S.—I can go ahead and start pulling documents for you now if you tell me the subject of your inquiry!

Armitage Gallier <ALG@gallierentel.com>
To: phoebe.blair@tmhps.org

Miss Blair,

Thank you for your prompt reply. I will visit your office this week.

No need to preemptively pull documents.

Warm Regards,
Armitage Gallier

Present Day

MARSHMALLOW FLUFF. IT ALL STARTED WITH MARSHMALLOW FLUFF.

I mean, it *literally* all started with a three-email exchange with a man I'd never met. But that was just preamble.

In my heart, it started with marshmallow fluff.

You see, at the Manhattan Historical Preservation Society where I worked, archivists weren't supposed to have food while on duty. But on the day Armitage Gallier finally materialized in my basement office, I was on my period, going through a brutal ghosting situation, realized that my favorite jeans didn't fit anymore, had my coffee stolen from the pick-up bar at Starbucks and—

Anyway, there I was, sitting under my desk, eating marshmallow fluff by the spoonful like a very cool, very put together, adulting adult. I didn't even consider the possibility that Armitage's "I will visit your office this week" meant "I will visit your office when it's least convenient and most embarrassing." But then, the door opened.

Shit, I thought. *Probably my boss.*

So I tossed my snack/the incriminating evidence, scrambled back to my seat, and tried to do my best to look as not-guilty as possible.

"Oh, shit."

This time, I didn't just think that. I said it out loud. Because the guy standing across from me wasn't my pinch-faced boss (*Sorry, Mr. Kaczmarek*), but . . . someone else.

Someone *unbelievably* handsome. Like, *I thought he was a hallucination conjured by a bored and lonely mind* handsome.

But no, he was real, and he was looking down his long, perfect nose at me.

Civilians never came to the archives. Researchers occasionally did, and the rumor was that Marty Scorsese visited when he was researching *Gangs of New York* (nice guy, apparently), but in all the time I'd worked there (six months), I'd only saved my isolated brain from going totally *The Shining* on everyone's ass by reading way too many books, writing a Substack that no one cared about, and developing deep and abiding parasocial relationships with the hosts of my favorite podcasts and YouTube channels.

So yeah. Seeing *anyone* in the archives would have shocked me. But then I remembered the email. Of course, this surprisingly young, surprisingly handsome gentleman caller with the surprisingly muscular forearms had to be my pen pal. Armitage Gallier, the scion of the massive Gallier Entertainment and Telecom company.

The shock was enough to make me forget I had marshmallow fluff on my face.

"Uh, hi," I said. *Be professional.* "Welcome to the Manhattan Historical Preservation Society. Can I help you?"

"I have an appointment with Phoebe Blair," he said, his deep voice gliding over my name like a sharp blade over fresh ice. He looked hesitant, almost as uncertain and surprised as I felt. "Might that be you?"

"... Yes?"

"You don't sound certain."

When I saw that email from one of the biggest companies in the world, I thought you'd be some stuffy loser. And I mean, you may be kind of a stuffy loser, but you're also a hot, stuffy loser I'd definitely try to take home if I found you at a FiDi bar on some random Tuesday. So yeah. You've thrown me off my game.

"Are you Armitage Gallier, then?" I asked, ignoring his question so I didn't say something entirely regrettable.

"That's me. Thanks for taking the time."

"Thanks for donating the entire Eastern wing of the museum."

Oof. Wrong thing to say. And in case it's not already obvious, I was always doing that, saying the wrong thing.

I tried again. "Sorry. I'm not used to having people down here. Especially not—" *Especially not guys with eyes green as Prospect Park. Especially not rich donors. Especially especially not rich donors with stunning green eyes looking at me like I'm important.* "I guess I'm just a little out of practice in the human interaction department. Not many people come down to the basement for conversation. Can I start again? Hi. Yes, my name is Phoebe Blair. Nice to meet you, Armitage Gallier. Welcome to the Manhattan Historical Preservation Society. Can I help you?"

His Ivy League good looks only got better when he was trying not to smile.

"Yes, I think you can. I hope you can, anyway."

"I'll do my best. I've been dying to know what you're looking for. Your last email was so mysterious."

"Do you recognize this woman?"

From his pocket, he withdrew a plastic baggie containing a yellowing 4 × 6 piece of cardstock. Instead of handing it over, he held it out at a distance for my inspection, as if it were too precious to pass along to a stranger. The overhead lights glared off the plastic, so I blinked.

I readjusted my glasses. Then, blinked again. This time, it had nothing to do with the glare.

"Where did you find this? Looks original."

"I believe it is. Would you mind signing a nondisclosure agreement before we proceed?"

Boy. If I had a nickel for every time a guy asked me that . . .

—=◇=—

An hour later, once I clocked out of work, I broke the number one rule of New York City singlehood. I went to a second location with a guy I'd just met.

A total rookie move. I didn't know anything about this dude except, well, that he was Armitage Gallier of *the* Galliers. Yes, I had googled him after I'd gotten his emails—I am a professional researcher, after all—but basically all I had learned was that he was super rich. In fact, the kind of super rich guy I typically hated, who seemed to spend a lot of time dressed up at galas and soirees with very thin models. Now, here I was in his car. He'd given me very little information about this assignment, and his dark eyes did totally unprofessional things to me. The whole situation had all the makings of a Lifetime original movie—the slightly sexy but potentially murder-y kind.

But when a strange guy with more money than God hands you an original 1896 Evelyn Cross *Spring Will Come* girlie card and asks you to go somewhere with him, you've just *gotta* say yes. What other choice do you have?

Near the turn of the century, Evelyn Cross was one of vaudeville's hottest commodities, a genuine star forged by the strange, American art form. A plus-size performer with scintillating yet tasteful song-and-dance numbers, she toured the United States and Europe, becoming a huge box-office draw all on her own. She counted Harry Houdini and Ethel Barrymore amongst her friends. Later, a group called Billy Watson's Beef Trust would co-opt her iconic style, billing themselves as a troupe of beautiful dancers each over two hundred pounds, and going on a hot streak of popularity spanning nearly thirty years.

Before there could be Judy Garland, Fanny Brice, Sophie Tucker, or even Miss Piggy, there was first Evelyn Cross.

Just as legendary as the woman herself was her disappearance from vaudeville in 1897. Her abrupt departure from the stage was a mystery no historian had yet been able to solve. So even without the good-looking millionaire of it all, seeing a mint-condition girlie card of Evelyn would have been enough to make me drop everything and follow Armitage Gallier anywhere.

To take matters a step further, I was a plus-size woman myself. And not one of those hot, striking plus-size women who knew how to dress themselves to show off every curve. I was a jeans and oversized sweater, half-jar of marshmallow fluff for a stress snack, insecure mess of a plus-sized woman. Evelyn Cross, with her bold, unflinching performance style and reputation for sexual conquest, had always been a particular fixation of mine. An image of the woman I could have been if I had even a fraction of her courage and self-confidence.

Back in high school, I'd been basically every fat-girl stereotype rolled into one. And when a boy pulled a mean prank on me involving prom, a date, and me showing up to the first without the latter, I'd fallen into an eating disorder spiral. I visited the pro-ana Tumblrs, I pinned thinspo to my locker, and I drank Diet Coke and chewed Tic Tacs for at least two meals a day.

For a while there, I wasn't sure I'd live to see graduation. But I didn't care about graduation. All I wanted was to disappear.

But then, while researching for a final paper in my US history class, I'd come across some photos buried deep in a local archive. These weren't the glossy pictures from documentaries or history books, and they certainly weren't glamorized stills from one of those classic MGM musicals. They were snapshots from a local theater, where Evelyn Cross had once passed through town to rapturous notices.

She was a woman who looked like me.

After a lifetime of idolizing Kiera Knightley thinness and Nicole Kidman's consumption-starved body in historical costume dramas, it was a revelation. Contrary to what galleries and textbooks and pop culture would have you believe, fatness wasn't some new concept. And people before me had lived and loved and been celebrated in bodies like mine.

I went to my counselor that afternoon and told her about my eating disorder. She got me the help I needed. I lived to graduation and beyond. All because of a few pictures pulled from the library. Proof that history was more than I'd been told. Proof that I could have a life and love without changing who I was.

That's what made me passionate about historical research in the first place: the idea that people have been erased from our history . . . and I had the power to bring them back.

And, by doing so, I got to make people feel less alone. I had the power to give other people the same revelation I was once given all those years ago.

Evelyn Cross was a chapter in that lineage. She was big, unapologetic, and a star. She wasn't the first buxom beauty, and by God, she wouldn't be the last. But she was remarkable. An undeniable inspiration.

She gave me hope. Reassurance. Encouragement that, one day, I could be like her, too. Not just a fat girl who'd survived an eating disorder, but a full-fledged *person*—one who believed in myself, loved myself, and reached out for more.

That's why this opportunity to research her for Armitage Gallier was personal, right from the start.

What I didn't know then, as Armitage's driver inched his Continental GT through Manhattan traffic, was that it was personal to him, too.

"It's not a big thing, really," he said in the quiet, rushed way people used only when they said really big things. His eyes darted this way and that, as if he expected mal-intentioned eavesdroppers under the car's seats or inside my six-year-old iPhone. "It's just that my dad is retiring to the South of France soon, and he's deciding how to split up the family properties before he goes. We opened up the old estate on Fifth Avenue—it's basically gone unused since the '50s—and when I went up to the attic, I found some old junk that I want more information about. Like I said, not a big thing."

Old junk, huh? Fucking rich people.

"Really?" I teased. "The South of France? I thought you billionaires were all retiring to space these days."

A tiny sigh. "I sounded like a total prick just then, didn't I?"

"Don't worry. I'm not sure guys like you can help it."

Our eyes locked. A look passed between us that I'd only seen in movies—at first defiant, then soft and vulnerable, then bashful at what we'd both just revealed with nothing more than a glance.

He let out a small laugh, took a handkerchief out of his pocket— *rich people*—and lifted it to wipe that forgotten streak of marshmallow fluff from my face.

I shivered and did a thing I never should have done. I decided I liked him.

"Believe it or not," he said, "I'm a little out of practice in the human interaction department, too."

⇒ ◆ ⇐

From the outside, the mansion on Fifth Avenue looked as if it'd been plucked from one of my photographs back in the archive. A copy-pasted sliver of our collective history, the sight of which made me giddy with nerd excitement.

Once inside, that excitement only increased. If there was an opposite of the Tenement Museum, this house was it. Nothing against the Tenement Museum, obviously—but I have always had a weakness for glam, and this was a perfectly preserved nineteenth-century mansion, complete with original furniture and what appeared to be a functioning gramophone.

Near the end of our tour, he tried to breeze us through the parlor, but an oil painting above the mantel caught my eye. I stopped on a rug older than most universities in this country and stared.

It looked like any other turn-of-the-century painting at first glance, John Singer Sargent in style and abruptness. A stern man in a suit standing behind a seated, button-nosed woman attired in her finest gown and jewels. He was surprisingly handsome, and she slender and lovely. Confident brushstrokes. Strong use of shadow.

I noticed the family resemblance between the two painted figures and the live one waiting in the doorway for me. Over a century had likely passed since the portrait had been made, and still, the genes ran strong. Armitage shared the man's strong jaw. His ears peeked out a little too far from his head, just like the woman's.

But there was something else that caught my eye.

"That's Thomas Gallier, isn't it?" I asked.

Everyone who knew anything about the history of New York, or vaudeville, or the history of power in the United States, knew about Thomas Gallier. I recognized his picture from the hundreds of photographs and articles about him I'd thoughtlessly catalogued at the archive.

"Yes, and that's his wife. Constance."

"They look . . ." How to say this without being rude? "I mean, they look—"

"Like royalty? We have a copy of this painting in our offices in London. My mother loves the image they project, makes us put them up everywhere. People always assume they're old royals."

"I was going to say miserable. They look miserable."

Armitage shifted, but that tiny light in his eyes telegraphed amusement instead of annoyance or discomfort. "Maybe we should go back to the tour. We're getting ahead of ourselves."

"What does that mean?"

Armitage glanced up at the couple hanging in their place of honor. "It means that Thomas Gallier might not have been in love with his wife. And after finding this in his personal effects . . ." He waved the *Spring Will Come* card. "I think he might have been in love with this woman instead. I want to know if I'm right, and I'm hoping you can help me uncover their story."

So there you have it. What constitutes the rest of this book is the story of the man in that painting and the woman on that card. Through fictionalized history, drawn from almost a full year of research and accounts of my own life while investigating and writing this book, *A Showgirl's Rules for Falling in Love* will finally and definitively reveal what happened between Thomas Gallier and Evelyn Cross. I have tried to hew as close to reality as possible—both Evelyn's and mine—and so this book features historical figures, events, locations, celebrities, newspapers, fads, and contexts that will be familiar to the reader. Each part is named for a song Evelyn Cross once sang onstage.

But, to begin. A disclaimer.

A warning, really.

If you're a true historian, you'll know what it's like to get swept up in your research, to the point that its characters become more than figures on the pages of old letters and newspapers, to the point that you wake up thinking about them and go to sleep dreaming of them. The point where their story becomes your entire life. And when that happens, sometimes the truth—the kind of truth I learned about in graduate school, the truth of facts and dates and figures and absolutes—that kind of truth isn't enough to truly capture the past, in all its richness and emotion.

So with that in mind: What follows here isn't a true story.

Not really. Not entirely.

I just wish it was.

1897

MANHATTAN

CHAPTER ONE

AT SIX O'CLOCK ON THE EVENING EVELYN CROSS'S ENTIRE LIFE changed, she wasn't opening fan mail or getting a costume fitted or sampling San Franciscan chocolates from one of her gentleman admirers. She wasn't doing anything remarkably sensational, glamorous, or otherwise befitting the woman who, at least until quite recently, had been the toast of the Manhattan vaudeville scene. Instead, she was doing one of the most unremarkable activities one could think of.

She was staring at a billboard.

The damn thing had gone up overnight a few weeks back, just around the time that her early-afternoon shows had been canceled and she'd suddenly found herself with ever-lengthening stretches of free time. Every day, she would perform her act, retire out of most of her costume, and then immediately sojourn to the fire escape outside her dressing room, where she would sit with a warm cup of tea and once more enter an unwinnable staring contest with her new, fifty-foot-tall neighbor.

In lurid color on the wall outside, a scandalously thin woman held out a corset in one disdainfully curled hand.

"I don't need this any longer," the lady-shaped image cried. "All thanks to slimming Banting's!"

Evelyn knew there was no point to this obsession of hers. Her most imperious gaze might have worked wonders on any stage manager, doorman, or chorus girl this side of 42nd Street, but it wasn't going to do much to a woman who was, in actuality, nothing more than a bit of paint on a brick wall.

And yet, she couldn't help it. As though she was compelled, she found herself going back, every day, to her elegant purveyor of gilt-edged, corset-free self-hatred.

There were two reasons for this, both of them perfectly reasonable if she didn't examine them too closely. For one thing, the woman in the advertisement didn't look so unlike Evelyn. They shared the stage-ready features of unruly blonde curls and blue eyes that could easily be spotted by the poor saps in the second balcony. Beyond that, the almost-Evelyn's image warped, as if she had been painted just to taunt her not-quite-doppelganger. The small waist. The flat stomach. The slender, dainty fingers and the figure designed to barely fill out the depressed groove in some man's mattress.

She was like Evelyn. But . . .

It was that *but* that proved Evelyn's second reason for staring.

"Here you are again," a familiar voice said from the open window behind her. "Has the old girl moved yet? The way you're watching her, I could swear she's about to charge. Thank God we have you keeping watch. I can't imagine the damage a woman like that could do to a poor, unsuspecting populace."

Jules Moreau. Even if they hadn't come up together on the vaudeville circuit, Evelyn would recognize that voice anywhere. The city's most famous female impersonator, despite wearing what he called his offstage "masculine costume," was unable to ever fully divorce himself from Julia, his alter ego.

Evelyn rested her head against the cool bars of the fire escape, listening to the sounds of Jules's balletic footfall as he settled his warm body beside her own.

"You won't be laughing when I'm the only one here to save the city from that monstrosity," Evelyn replied, her lips curling up in a weak attempt at a smile.

"You think I'm frightened of that skinny little nit? Oh, heavens, no. No matter how tall she is, smart money is on you, my dear . . . which explains my confusion at this repeat performance you keep giving out here between shows."

"She's mocking me."

"She's a painting on a wall."

Evelyn bit the inside of her lip. Now, they'd come to the second reason for her Miss Banting's obsession.

"I lost a booking today," she admitted.

"Another one?"

"Things are changing. Little Miss Waistline over there is only a symbol of it. We're a dying breed, you and me. People used to love us for being so delightfully scandalous. Now, they think we're unfashionable or dangerous or both. The moralists are coming after you with pitchforks. The slender snobs are coming after me with diet food. The conservatives are calling for Natia's arrest after she spoke with that Emma Goldman woman, the racists are going after Nathaniel because he has the gall to be ten times more talented than any white man on the circuit, and the eugenicists would rather push Annie's wheelchair off the Brooklyn Bridge than see her onstage. I talked to Lillian Russell and Eva Tanguay last week, and even they're feeling the strain. You know it's bad if those two are complaining. We're all getting boxed in from every angle. Our days are numbered. Hate to admit it, but you can't deny something staring you in the face."

"There's one across from my window, too. Not Banting's, of course, but cologne. Four rugged men in Yale football uniforms, all beaten up and muddy from their sporting. Dainty women dripping from each arm. *DeVeer's Cologne—What the Real Man Wears in 1897.* And look at this."

He flicked something in Evelyn's direction. It was a newspaper. The *Manhattan Daily*.

"Jules, you know better than to read this trash," Evelyn admonished, even as she took it in hand. The *Daily* had always been regressive nonsense, but over the last few months, it had taken its pointed disdain for anything and anyone not like its wealthy owner—one Nehemiah Alban—to new heights of cruelty. From page-long screeds advocating forced "sanitization" of "infirmed" circus performers and vaudevillians to type-faced pearl-clutching about the dangers of "ethnic comedy" to "God-fearing Christian audiences," it and its opinions were barely even fit to wrap fish down at the docks.

For years, she and Jules had ignored it when they could and laughed at it when they couldn't. But tonight's evening edition blared a headline that was too dangerous to bear either response.

NEW ROCHESTER LAW FORBIDS VAUDEVILLE ACTS OF MORAL DISREPUTE—IS MANHATTAN NEXT?

A brief scan of the article treated Evelyn to a screed about female impersonators, left-wing agitators, and scantily clad contortionists. The paper listed Julia Moreau as one of the acts whose tour had been canceled as an immediate result of the ban, and while she herself was not mentioned by name, judging from the author's disdain for "inhumanly large songstresses," Evelyn could only imagine that her own time was coming.

"Oh, Jules—"

"Don't *Oh, Jules* me. Not yet, anyway. The pity party hasn't even begun."

Evelyn dropped the paper and glanced at her friend, who somehow still managed to smile even as their careers lay in rubble at their feet. Tall, dark-haired, and slight of stature, Jules was a beautiful creature whose inner self was nearly as flawless as his outer. He still wore his full face of stage makeup but had removed his wig and exchanged the first few layers of his elaborate Lady Rebecca Crawley costume for a thick robe that covered his decidedly female underclothes.

Even on a trash heap day like today, just seeing him made her feel better.

It didn't hurt that he'd brought her a bottle of champagne.

"I thought we might celebrate my imminent forced retirement. Will you do the honors?"

Evelyn reached for the bottle, shot the cork off onto the street below, and raised it between them.

Evelyn's mother said time was like a grandfather clock, with a pendulum that swung back and forth. She'd pat Evelyn's hand and say, *Not to worry, mein kürbis, that old clock is always ticking. You only have to wait for your chime.*

But Evelyn and Jules had caught the highest point of the pendulum's arc. For a few years, Jules hadn't had to hide himself. He'd won over the public, delighting them with his chameleonic displays of womanly virtue and beauty. Likewise, Evelyn's fashionably fat figure and superlative singing voice were the toast of the vaudeville circuit. She was the epitome of immigrant success—the daughter of someone who came to this country with the clothes on her back and worked until her daughter could be a healthy, round, well-fed picture of the American dream.

Two months ago, neither of them could get a day off to sell their souls. Sold-out shows. Packed houses. The plaudits of an entire island constantly ringing in their ears. Now . . . the culture was leaving them behind.

"To changing times," she toasted.

Jules jerked his chin defiantly. "And the ones they leave behind."

Evelyn drank first, and drank deeply, letting the fizz of the champagne bubble carelessly past her lips. She then handed the bottle over to Jules, who followed suit.

Neither of them was defeatists by nature. Their level of success would have been impossible to achieve for anyone who easily succumbed to gloom and doom. Still, it was difficult to look defeat in the face—in Evelyn's case, literally—and stand tall. Sometimes, drowning the fear in warm champagne was all the world could ask of you.

Eventually, they had emptied half the bottle and Jules's cheeks flushed. His usual slightly biting, slightly warm tone cut over the hum of the carriages, crowds, and cops on the streets below.

"So. What will you do now that you're no longer *de rigeur?*"

"*Moi?*" Evelyn asked. "Oh, you know. Same old story for women like me. I'll find some fabulously wealthy man to take care of me for a few years, make some wise investments, and then live out my days as a mysterious and unconscionably scandalous toff."

"And who will be your companions?"

"Besides my endless string of lovers?"

"Naturally."

"An old dog, I imagine."

Jules nudged her shoulder with the blunt end of the champagne bottle. "That's some way to talk about me!"

"Sorry, an old spaniel. *And* you."

"Sounds like a darling little life."

"Yes."

And Evelyn knew that. To most in this wonderful misery of a city, where she watched thousands of the forgotten fight futilely for a better life, the future laid out before her seemed rather nice. Safety. Security. Glamorous, no. But certainly lucky.

So why was it that every time she considered it, her forehead began to sweat and her throat closed up? Why, at such a young age, couldn't she look on a happy retirement as a reward for years of hard work and relentless hustling?

As if reading her thoughts, Jules said, "But we both know that's not how you'll end up."

"And why do we know that?"

"Because you've done everything you could to escape having a little life. You won't give up on that dream now."

He said it with such an air of finality that she didn't even bother to protest. Jules knew her, after all, better than just about anybody. And wasn't the beauty of having a friend never having to lie to them?

"What about you?" she asked. "What will you do when they finally manage to take everything you have?"

He shook his head, his pale skin catching the last pinks of sunset and glowing from their touch. "There's nothing worth anything that they can take away from us. You would do well to remember that."

More silence, at least between them. Down below, audiences with their two-bit tickets rushed the theater's entrances, elbowing each other for the best seats in the house. Clearly not everyone read the *Manhattan Daily*, at least not in this less desirable quarter of town. A familiar knot of excitement tightened right at the place where Evelyn's heart met her stomach.

They were here, those strangers out in the cheap seats, and they were here to see her. Her fame might be fleeting, but for now, she would hold on to it with both hands.

Inside, the company bell rang. Jules shook out the champagne bottle a few times, hoping for any last droplets.

"Back to the mines," he said, though he made no move to stand.

Evelyn didn't budge either. "Should we just ride off into the sunset together? Rob a train? Start a new life out west?"

"West? I thought you always wanted to go to Paris one day."

"The manager at the Moulin Rouge *did* write me again recently."

"And you said?"

"That I was grateful for the offer, but what lies between my legs has *terrible* stage fright, therefore becoming a can-can dancer and putting it all on display is simply not for me."

"Shame. You'd look quite at home in a Toulouse-Lautrec painting."

Another gallows laugh.

"What do you say, hm?" she asked, only half joking. "Let's go on the run."

"No. We should make them sad to see us go. Give them a great swan song. Remind them of what they're missing."

"You're right. As usual."

In a sweep of skirts and feathers, the two of them started back for the theater. Evelyn made a point of stepping on Nehemiah Alban's *Manhattan Daily* as she went—a small protest.

"Evelyn?" Jules asked as they slipped through the open window.

"Yes, sweet?"

"What is it that you want? *Really* want?"

The answer to that question was a simple but impassable roadblock. The reason she couldn't just wander off into the green pastures of a nice, safe future. The reason she had spilled years of sweat and glitter and tears into this career, this life she'd built herself. The reason she'd left her tenement childhood behind. The reason she'd never go back.

"I want to be undeniable."

CHAPTER TWO

THOMAS GALLIER WAS A MAN OF LISTS, RULES, AND ORDER. Control. Discipline. He prided himself on being precisely correct in his posture, behavior, manner of dress, speech, approach, and even thoughts in all respects and in all situations.

But as he sat in the structurally dubious opera box of the shabby Theatre Unique on 14th Street, waiting for the evening's vaudeville program to commence, he couldn't help but see the appeal of a little misrule.

What he wouldn't give to throw a big, old-fashioned dust-up. To actually *feel* his feelings—like the bustling crowd below him did with unabashed relish—instead of categorizing them and filing them away in a sealed vault somewhere in his darkest depths.

And yet, as he waited for the houselights to dim, the humming audience to still, and his companion for this evening to settle in beside him, he resigned himself to flexing and clenching his hand. A small, totally inadequate expression of his current frustrations. The only external sign that he was distressed in the slightest.

He was a man with his world set to collapse. And here he was, sitting at a vaudeville show.

Control and discipline indeed.

"Do you wish to discuss it?"

The voice came from his companion, Dr. Andrew Samson—a tall, refined, fair, bespectacled man in his early thirties.

"Do I wish to discuss what?" Thomas asked, feigning confusion.

"The imminent destruction of your entire life, I should think."

Thomas's hand clenched in a final fist. He'd been called out on his most private fear and his most pressing current worry—*damn it.*

"Or the weather, if you'd prefer," Andrew offered, ever observant.

No sense in dancing around it. Not when this was—when it had to be—little more than a temporary setback. "Destruction isn't imminent. I have a plan."

"Is that so?"

"For a man who's seen me conquer every challenge I've faced on the path to opening my Empire, you have so little faith in me, Doctor."

Andrew cleared his throat. "While I've seen you conquer challenges, I've never seen you conquer a major backer withdrawing ten thousand dollars from your Empire just over a month before opening."

There. They came to it. The truth of why they were here. Thomas Gallier, the impresario behind the sprawling pleasure palace known as The Empire on 34th Street, stood at the cliff's edge of disaster. In six weeks, he was meant to open his grand masterpiece, an attraction that was, in part, meant to house the greatest vaudeville theater in the history of mankind.

But despite months of searching, he still hadn't a headliner. It wasn't for lack of trying. He had held auditions, scoured practically every theater in Manhattan, even brought in a director from France, for God's sake. And yet, nothing was good enough. Not a single act lived up to the promise of The Empire. He had delayed the announcement of the vaudeville bill for so long now that his stratospherically high standards had become something of a citywide punchline—to everyone but Thomas, that is.

Well, everyone but Thomas and Mr. George Westinghouse, who'd told him at a party this very evening that he would be withdrawing his investment from The Empire. He was tired of waiting on Thomas to find a headliner for his act, especially when the *Manhattan Daily* was turning more and more members of their prospective audience against vaudeville in the first place.

So here Thomas was, in one of the last theaters he hadn't already scouted, begging the fates for a change in his fortunes.

One star. That was all he needed. One star on which to hang his entire universe.

"I'll ask once more," Andrew prodded after a prolonged silence. "Do you wish to discuss it?"

"Why should I wish to discuss it? I have a plan. I will put it into action. By this time tomorrow, all will be set to rights again."

"How?"

"Mr. George Westinghouse is a spectacularly singular brand of imbecile, and The Empire is better off without him. He doesn't know a damned thing about the entertainment industry, and he was always poking his nose where it didn't belong. A man who could be persuaded to withdraw his money from a surefire investment like The Empire by something as silly as one of Alban's newspaper articles isn't someone with whom I wish to continue associating anyway. I will simply replace him with someone more worthy of this opportunity. I'll find my vaudeville star, inform the papers—though certainly not Alban's; E.W. Scripps's, maybe—and before tomorrow night, the city will be begging to hand their money over to me."

"Sounds simple enough." Andrew nodded thoughtfully. "What can I do to help?"

"Your *job*. Nothing more."

"And what exactly is that job again?"

"To reassure my investors and the public that I'm of perfectly sound mind and body. And, I suppose, to act as my personal physician, advise me on all matters related to my well-being, that sort of thing."

"As I thought. In which case, I need to inform you that this pathological need for control is extremely unhealthy."

This again. Andrew meant well, but ever since Thomas had retained his services, he had dragged them back time and time again to this battlefield. Thomas's need for control, Thomas's unwillingness to share responsibility, Thomas's desire to be solely in charge of every aspect of everything related to the building, outfitting, or opening of The Empire and all it would contain. In the last six months, Andrew had cited this as a reason for Thomas's headaches, his insomnia, his lack of romantic entanglements . . . It was a most annoying lecture to endure for months on end.

Thomas straightened, subverting his nearly overwhelming urge to lower himself all the way down to the floor and let it swallow him whole. He was a gentleman. Gentlemen didn't sulk. Or slouch. Or scowl.

They did, however, snark.

"Fascinating. And, in your professional opinion as my personal doctor and advisor, at what point in this conversation am I justified in flinging myself off the Brooklyn Bridge?"

"Come now," Andrew replied dryly. "Rich men don't kill themselves by jumping off bridges. They drink and whore themselves into an early grave as is fitting of their station. Besides, medically speaking, it should take at least fifteen more minutes, and by then, the show will have started."

As if on cue, the lights lowered and the orchestra blared to new life, filling the hall with a grand, jaunty tune Thomas recognized from a thousand other shows just like this one.

It was promptly followed by three acts nearly copied note-for-note from a thousand other shows, too.

By the time the intermission neared, Thomas felt a swell of despair coming on. But he clung to his last shreds of hope, gripping his fists until his knuckles went white. *Just one star. I only need one star. My entire future depends on one star.*

It was this desperation that kept him pinned to his seat. And this desperation that apparently led Andrew to whisper:

"May I ask what you're even looking for? You've been searching tirelessly for months and still, you've come up empty. A hint at what you require might help me contribute to your search."

This was not the kind of question to which Thomas usually gave an answer. But he was so out of sorts, he deigned to make an attempt.

"I want something . . ."

At that moment, his vision caught on the illuminated stage. The world snapped into focus. Suddenly, everything—Andrew, the box, the dingy theater—it all disappeared, and there was nothing but *her*. He barely breathed the end of his sentence.

"Something undeniable."

At center stage, a blonde beauty stood in a gown constructed entirely of flowers. She was a woman of Amazonian height, sturdy-legged, and proportioned like a goddess of bounty. Perhaps the most beautiful creature he'd ever beheld.

Soon, she began a song in dulcet, sensual tones, her eyes downcast like a shy lover, drawing in the crowd with her demure softness.

It worked. Thomas was enraptured. Just how secure *were* those flowers covering her generous curves? Were her cheeks as pink up close as they were from a distance? The flowers sewn into her gown seemed to burgeon under the rapt attention of the audience. Thomas wondered how they would smell if he brought his face to that blooming carnation at the center of her bosom.

And when she sang of spring coming . . .

He wasn't sure she was *entirely* speaking of the season.

She wasn't like any of the doe-eyed chorus girls dragged in front of him these last few weeks. They'd all had talent, yes, but this one? She had *spark*. That electric ability to trap strangers in the palm of her hand—and making them grateful they'd let her do it.

Soon, her croon faded out, the lights in the hall shifted, and as quickly as the song had begun, the orchestra kicked into a lively dancehall upbeat, the kind that gave her a good excuse to, in one swift motion, rip her gowned skirt from her hips, revealing a short dance costume of soft petals beneath.

That's when the performance *really* began, he realized. The rest had all been preamble. An invitation.

Now, exposed in a way that would have been indecent if not for her beaming, unashamed smile, she let the music move her full body. Those wide hips and thick thighs twirled in perfect circles that proved more effective than any hypnotist's watch.

She was chaos. Disorder. Thoroughly incorrect.

And against his better judgment, maybe before he could even consciously understand it was happening, Thomas was struck.

"Oh, Thomas," Andrew muttered. "I don't like that look."

"She's—"

"Don't say it."

"—she's undeniable."

Andrew cursed, but for what reason, Thomas couldn't immediately fathom.

The way she danced, the way she sang, the way she angled her body to soak all of the spotlight up as if she were made of stardust . . .

Thomas wasn't the only one enthralled, either. When he briefly managed to steer his gaze away from her magnetic figure, the rest of the audience appeared similarly enthused.

In his mind, he heard the clinking of coin registers over the sound of her clear, strong singing voice.

"Who is she?" he asked.

"Evelyn Cross. She was quite popular for a time—a real gem of the stage door set."

"And why haven't I seen her before?"

"In the time since you've begun looking for acts, she's become extremely unfashionable. You understand how fickle audiences can be. Their tastes change."

A bitter taste coated the back of Thomas's teeth. "You mean *Alban* has told them that their tastes have changed." Suddenly he saw Evelyn not just as a commodity—but as someone with whom he might have something in common. An ally.

Well aware that they were still very much in the middle of the show, Thomas rose decisively, ready to march back to her dressing room and offer her a job on the spot.

The movement must have drawn her attention, because no sooner had he stood than her golden curls bounced in his direction, and their eyes met across the glimmer of the stage lights.

Blue. Her eyes were blue. The melted blue of a painter's favorite shade.

The orchestral break swirled around her, she raised one delicate hand to her lips, pressed her fingers to them, and blew a kiss that reached him all the way in his box seat.

He wasn't sure what possessed him. He wasn't a man taken to flights of fancy. But he knew in that moment, he was as good as gone.

"I must have her," he muttered.

Andrew snorted. "I imagine you're not the first man who's ever said that about Miss Evelyn Cross."

"I mean for the show. I'm going to meet with her. Sign her immediately. We haven't a moment to lose, given the circumstances."

"Thomas. You can't be serious. She is not the woman who will change your fortunes."

"Yes. Yes, she will be." He spoke with the easy certainty that guided all his business dealings, and yet he felt something stronger still.

Andrew shook his head. "Did you hear what I've just told you? She's losing bookings, she's already on Alban's bad side, and her audiences are moving on to other acts. How can you possibly imagine that she is the best choice to convince doubters like George Westinghouse that your Empire is destined for success?"

A fair question. One of the reasons that Thomas relied on Andrew was that he knew Manhattan society, its conventions and whims. If Andrew said hiring Evelyn Cross was a bad idea, he should have believed him.

But . . .

He couldn't remember the last time he'd *felt.*

The last time he'd felt *anything.*

No matter the risk, Thomas knew he couldn't turn his back on that. Not yet, anyway.

"Because if I can make an audience feel for her even a fraction of what I do in this moment, then The Empire won't be a pleasure palace. It will be a money printing factory."

A NOTE FROM THE HISTORIAN

A man coming absolutely unglued the second he encounters the woman of his dreams. We love to see it. That was sort of Thomas Gallier's whole thing. In public, with his business associates and the media, he was cold and imposing and tightly controlled. But around Evelyn, he unraveled—and he couldn't help himself.

So how did Thomas get there? How did he, a would-be entertainment deity, come to teeter on the brink of disaster?

Let us turn to the newspapers of the day, which spared no ink in chronicling that very journey:

THE SUN,

FEBRUARY 16, 1895 (New York, New York)

REAL ESTATE

A strange business was conducted today when, in the office of J. Peabody Russell, a deed of sale was signed for the property spanning one entire block of 34th Street. The amount paid? An astounding sum of nearly 400,000 American dollars. This fantastic sale—a fool's purchase, some say, is all the more confounding when it was reported that this transaction had been initiated by a stranger to our shores. One Mr. Thomas Gallier, born in France, raised in England, lately of No. 820, 5th Avenue. More will be reported as it is available.

THE WORLD,
MARCH 1, 1895 (New York, New York)
AN EMPIRE OR A FOLLY?

More on the affair of the 34th Street land sale—which is to say, no more news to report. It appears that this Thomas Gallier has no connections to this city—and even fewer friends. Not much can be discerned of his past, and though he has inserted himself in upper circles of the city, he has persistently failed in his efforts. Rumors, none yet verified, persist that he seeks funds for what he calls "The Empire on 34th Street," and what his detractors call "Gallier's Folly," a pleasure palace said to rival P.T. Barnum's own attempts. Only time will tell if this unknown quantity may prove successful where the great master once failed.

THE MANHATTAN DAILY,
NOVEMBER 15, 1895 (New York, New York)

Further reporting on The Empire on 34th Street. To be built Italian Revival in style. Included, among others: seven restaurants of international fare and taste, a motorcar racing track, ice-cream parlor, live animal menagerie, sanctioned boxing ring, racket courts, dancehall suitable for dignified ladies and gentlemen, seventy statues in the Michelangelo style, aquacade, shopping district, and central theater to host the most extraordinary talents of the modern vaudeville stage. All seem unlikely, as Gallier has failed in several funding attempts. Symptoms of impending nervous breakdown apparent to all who meet him.

THE MANHATTAN DAILY,

APRIL 29, 1896 (New York, New York)

Situation for The Emperor of 34th Street—construction proceeding as planned, construction crews less than enthused by Emperor's exacting demands. Financial situation increasingly bleak. The Emperor has "bet the farm" on his pleasure palace's success. Will be ruined, disgraced by its nearly certain failure. Monied families of the city watching the situation with great interest, as may be opportunity to finally see an irritant Emperor defrocked.

THE MANHATTAN DAILY,

OCTOBER 15, 1897 (New York, New York)

More reports from The Empire on 34th Street—one might think it more rumor mill than pleasure palace. Performers desperately needed for the vaudeville. Emperor exercising usually impossible exactitude upon selection of the bill. Success or failure is said to ride on this show.

THE MANHATTAN DAILY,

OCTOBER 15, 1897 (New York, New York)

Evelyn Cross, fallen star from vaudeville firmament, announces new engagement at the Theatre Unique on 14th Street. Fellow degenerate Jules Moreau also on bill. The moral watchers of the city keep careful watch on these two.

The tl;dr, for anyone who skips over my beautifully curated primary sources (how dare you?): Thomas entered New York society with a splash . . . and an aura of mystery. The city was skeptical of the outsider, with no connections and seemingly no past. He needed their money, and once he had it, he was on the hook to prove his enormous theatrical gamble would pay off.

Thomas's position in New York was precarious. His proximity to power, fame, and money were all equally so.

Meanwhile, Evelyn was on the decline—a liability. He shouldn't have wanted her. She was no longer fashionable. She was big, loud, fearless. Notoriously outspoken at a time when women were expected to demur.

I don't know why what happened next happened.

However.

As a historian, my job is to color between the lines of fact in order to paint a full picture of the past.

When it comes to Thomas Gallier and Evelyn Cross, I only know one thing for sure.

Maybe they shouldn't have wanted each other.

But they needed each other. Desperately.

CHAPTER THREE

THE MAN FROM THE OPERA BOX WAS THOMAS GALLIER. SHE WAS certain of it. Sure, there might have been about fifty yards and a hell of a lot of stage light between them, but it was her job to know where her next meal could come from, and if what she'd read in the papers was true, Thomas Gallier looked like a twelve-course dinner.

Blowing kisses was one of her signature moves. She didn't originate the practice, certainly, but she'd learned over time that men couldn't resist being singled out in a crowd. They all, without exception, had a pathological belief they were somehow exceptional, an obsession with being the one and only chosen out of an endless stream.

So it didn't surprise her when there was a knock at her dressing room door. In fact, she was waiting for it. Expecting it. She would have been disappointed—maybe even devastated—if it hadn't come.

"Hey, Evelyn," a gruff-voiced stagehand called. "You've got a visitor."

For a moment, she considered how to play this. She'd entertained plenty of men in her dressing room before—men who would go on to buy her furs, take her for dinner and dancing, or introduce her to other men who could get her bookings. On those occasions, she'd played it all very cool, very coy, very refined—almost aloof. But lately, those meetings took up less and less space on her social calendar, and she couldn't remember the last time any of them had wanted to continue their dalliances in public.

Of all the men she'd met, none of them had ever been in a position to help her quite like Thomas Gallier. And considering the holes in her stockings and the sprawling emptiness of her future . . .

She didn't have time for subtlety.

"A handsome gentleman caller, I hope," she crooned.

A beat of assessment from the other side of the door. "Meh. He's alright."

Evelyn knew *that* wasn't true. Thomas Gallier was one of those rare creatures of the Manhattan jungle—a genuinely good-looking man of means. Most wealthy men, Evelyn would classify as "interesting" to look at. They were fine enough on their own, but it was the gleam of gold watches and pearl cufflinks that really made their features shine. Thomas Gallier, on the other hand, would have been the handsomest ditch digger just as easily as the handsomest millionaire. There was a marble quality about his tall and built frame; his smooth features, too, were worthy of Michelangelo. His dark hair hung slightly roguish across his forehead like a painting of a tempting devil.

"Well, can the gentleman wait? I'm afraid I haven't got a stitch of clothing on."

A lie. With a robe thrown on over her costume, she was as close to fully dressed as she got backstage. But no harm in giving him a little bit to chew on before he entered her den.

A moment later, she crossed to the door and peeked it open, intending only to give him a brief look at her to heighten the suspense.

Unfortunately, something infinitely more devastating occurred.

She realized he was even more handsome up close than from afar. A little tired, maybe. But with crystalline green eyes that could make you believe he loved you and only you, right there on the spot. The kind of handsome that made knees weak. The kind of handsome that could be very, very dangerous to a woman like her.

"Miss Cross. It's a pleasure to meet you—"

He started out innocently enough. Cordial. Refined. Even professional. That deep English accent of his didn't hurt matters. But
then, his eyes traveled down, down, down the nearly bare curve of her
shoulder, and southward to more exotic locales.

"The pleasure's all mine, Mr. . . . ?"

"Gallier," he said, his eyes snapping up and his body coiling in
that practiced rigidity so common in the higher quarters of society.
"Thomas Gallier."

"That's right," she said, ushering him in. "I think I read something
about you in the papers."

Gallier chuckled. Nice smile, though she wasn't sure it was particularly genuine. "I can assure you, anything you're reading there is
a pack of lies."

"Oh? Even the ladies' column about you being . . . what was it they
called you? *A handsome man with a constraint of passion that leaps
like flame into desire?*"

"They wrote no such thing."

"No, you're right. I must have read that in a book somewhere. But
it describes you quite well. You can understand my confusion."

This was a dance she knew well, the steps so rehearsed she could
do them in her sleep. She would flirt a little. He would assess her
legs—in the year of their Lord 1897, if your legs held a man's attention, he was as good as yours—and then they would get down to the
particulars of their exchange (her *company* for his help) in a polite,
roundabout way that left both of their consciences clean.

But Thomas Gallier didn't fit the mold, not the way she wanted
him to. Standing near the door as if waiting to bolt, he stood out like a
gray rain cloud amidst her wardrobe's frilly feathers and palette hues.
And as a partner in this dance, he stumbled, never quite committing
to her tempo or letting her lead.

Strange, that. Men were often so happy to be lured to their own destruction.

Gallier cocked his head. "Do you think you're flattering me?"

"Is it working?"

"I can assure you, it's not necessary."

"Flattery isn't ever necessary, Mr. Gallier. But I find it's a bit like alcohol. Good for lubricating *all sorts* of interactions."

Not her most subtle of approaches. The man cleared his throat and averted his gaze from her, taking sudden interest in a virginal white gown dipped in red hanging from her dressing screen.

"Speaking of alcohol," she said, when it became clear he'd lost his words, "maybe we could celebrate your visit with a glass of champagne."

"I am not one to drink."

"Shall we sit, then?"

"I would prefer to stand."

Damn him. Now he was making *her* stumble. Time for a new approach.

"Well, then, do you mind if I sit?"

"By all means," he said, flat but polite.

With his attention elsewhere, he freed Evelyn to situate herself on the chaise longue stretched across the far wall.

"The long and the short of it is this, Miss Cross," he began, still directing his speech at the gown instead of her.

Did he know she'd once gotten a ticket for indecency for performing in that gown? That her writhing in the role of a sensual Salome had popped one of the pearl buttons down the front, exposing her, um, superstructure to the entirety of the Atlantic City Theater's audience? Surely not, or he wouldn't have been trusting it to keep his eyes pure.

"The Empire Theatre is opening in three weeks. I've my pick of performers, mind you, and there is plenty of remarkable talent in this city, no doubt about it. You should see them, coming in and out all the time, audition after audition, acts of the highest caliber—"

"I have no doubt."

His gaze flickered to the mirror, which lined the room's longest wall and gave a full view of everything he'd been unable to see with his back turned. His words fell out in a tumble then, rushing to end this interaction before he could fall into her trap.

Poor thing. Didn't he know the only way to defeat temptation was to succumb?

"But after some deliberation and a considerable amount of thought, I believe you would look just fine on The Empire's marquee."

"*Just* fine?"

"As I said, I have my pick of performers, so I won't be hard-balled, but if you're interested, I could offer you a fare wage, top billing, and— *why are you sitting like that?*"

In a blur of man, he turned on his heel to give her just what she'd wanted. His full attention.

His full, lustful, frustrated attention, focused squarely on her body. Arms raised over her head in a lazy repose, she propped herself up on a pile of the chaise longue's pillows so her generous breasts— straining against her corset—were the most pronounced part of her. Everything else, from her bare wrists to her stocking-clad legs, was sprawled and open, ready to receive.

She didn't flinch from his gaze.

"Because I want you to see me sitting like this," she said.

Wordlessly, his eyes traced her waiting form, then made the return trip back to her lips, where they settled.

"Miss Cross . . ."

That was a question.

"Mr. Gallier."

That was an answer.

"I've offered you what you want," he said, words shaking from some unseen effort deep inside of him. "You don't need to do this."

"In my experience, a man's promises aren't worth anything until *after* the glow of seduction is gone."

It was the truth. Listening to lovesick men was a hereditary sickness, a sin of the mother passed down, and one to which she'd never succumb.

She needed something from him. She was going to do what she needed to get it. Simple as that. If those facts bothered him, so be it.

And, indeed, bother him they did. He flinched. His face turned to stone.

"Miss Cross, I should like to make one thing perfectly clear: I do *not* mix business with pleasure, no matter how I may want to. Tomorrow, I will be at The Empire Theatre on 34th Street with my associate to see your act promptly at noon. Is that understood?"

She blinked. "Sure."

"And one more thing."

"Yes?"

Maybe she imagined it, but she was certain the lines in his face softened . . . just barely. Just enough for her to notice. Just enough to give her hope. "This isn't you. I don't know who, exactly, you are, but I do hope *she* shows up to The Empire tomorrow instead of . . . whoever *this* is."

With nothing else to say, the man departed. Evelyn listened to the sound of his footsteps carrying down the hall, then she raced to the window to watch his figure eventually exit the theater below and enter a waiting carriage.

It was only when that carriage disappeared into the sea of Manhattan streets that she finally slumped, letting her mask slip.

At first, there was anger. How dare he lecture about who she was when they had only just met, when he didn't have any idea of her life or her character outside of a few moments on the stage? She was used to patronizing men, but somehow, Thomas Gallier's condescension particularly stung.

But it wasn't just his condescension, she realized, looking up at that cursed Banting's advertisement, now lit by a pair of spotlights in the night. Because under her anger, there was pain.

He didn't want you, that pain said. *He rejected you because he didn't want you. Just like everyone else in this city lately.*

She reexamined every moment of their encounter, scanning for anything she'd done wrong, any misstep she'd taken. But it all came back to that insecure little thought.

He didn't want you.

That was . . . until she remembered something. Something she'd missed during the first run of their little drama. Something that made her think all hope wasn't lost for him—for *them*—after all.

I do not mix business with pleasure, he'd said, *no matter how I may want to.*

CHAPTER FOUR

SHE WAS SMART.

He had to give her that.

He couldn't be upset that she tried to manipulate his masculine urges for her own gain. They were similar creatures in that regard, it would seem. He had been known to do the same thing—working people to get what he wanted.

However . . .

He was upset that she'd thrown him. That his carefully crafted control crumbled to nothing at her sharp tongue and the sight of her perfect, grabbable legs.

Once their encounter ended, he fled to the safety of his carriage and ordered his driver to return him home. He had a list of tasks to complete at The Empire, but he elected to forgo the lot of them.

It would have been impossible, after all, to attend to any of those tasks with the impressive erection straining against his trousers.

Present Day

"YOU'RE NOT PUTTING *THAT* IN THE BOOK, ARE YOU?"

Armitage Gallier was reading over my shoulder again. Like a kid trying to sneak a peek at a present before Christmas, he was peering down at the worn notebook where I'd been scribbling Thomas and Evelyn's story.

I hadn't expected much extended interaction when I took this side hustle. I imagined I'd keep working at the Manhattan Historical Preservation Society by day, and then spend nights in my studio apartment poring over Armitage's collection of Thomas Gallier's personal ephemera and papers.

It wasn't like that, though. Armitage surprised me.

In more ways than one.

The first surprise was the treasure trove of boxes in the attic of the Fifth Avenue house—basically a historian's fantasy in the form of hundreds of letters, ledgers, and newspapers that had never before seen the light of day. I could understand why Armitage wouldn't just let me pack hundred-year-old letters into my ratty Strand tote bag. But I was used to archives that were only open from 2 to 4 p.m. on the first Tuesday of every month. I certainly wasn't expecting him to invite me to work in the house whenever I needed to make full use of the materials.

Surprise #2: Instead of giving me a key and leaving me to my own devices—or giving me a heavy ivory business card for some secretary who would relay messages to and from the man himself, Armitage took my phone and typed in the number for his personal cell. He told me to text him. He even used the box and ancient scroll emoji as we exchanged messages about my next research session.

Then, when I showed up for my next research session, and the research session after that, and the research session after *that*, Mr. Titan of Industry didn't just let me into the house and leave me to sift through Evelyn and Thomas's story. While he was clearly attempting to feign disinterest, he hovered, pretending to work on his own projects while watching me with great interest from over the edge of his laptop. Questions would come casually, almost offhandedly, and the sound of his voice traveling across the fireplace-warmed room always left me with goosebumps.

I couldn't tell, not then, why he wouldn't just buzz off. Why he averted his gaze every time I caught him looking at me across the room. Why he always brought me tea just the way I liked it.

I thought maybe it was that he didn't trust me. That I was a stranger in his house, in his past, and he thought he could protect both by monitoring my every move.

That had to explain why I kept catching him reading over my shoulder as I scribbled notes about the story I would one day write for him. Right?

That day, a shadow crossed over me, and his cologne—a mix of vanilla and petrichor and vetiver (rain and sharp smoke for all you non-romance readers out there) announced his presence.

"We agreed that you weren't going to read my research until *after* it was entirely complete," I sing-songed, not looking up from my notebook, determinedly not swayed by his sudden proximity and nice smells. "We can't keep having these little study dates if you can't respect the process, Mr. Gallier."

He scoffed. "'Study dates.' We're not—"

"If you say so."

"I'm supervising my employee."

"Sure."

"Minding my investment."

"Uh-huh."

"And it's a good thing, too. Because"—he pointed to the line I had just written, which, as you recall, described the status of Thomas Gallier's dick—"you can't be putting that in the research."

I laughed. He now stood in front of me, so I had to crane my neck to see his slightly flustered expression. "Why not? It's not like anyone's going to see this. *You're* not even supposed to see it until I've finished writing."

"Still. It's not—he's dead, Phoebe. More than that, he's a *Gallier*. We have an image to protect. My family would die if they knew Thomas was being talked about like this."

"Talked about like what? Like he had a big dick?"

"Small point of order, but you didn't mention size."

"You're right. I should go back and add that. *Prodigiously impressive* erection has a nice ring, don't you think?"

"I think you can agree that it's not appropriate."

"Who decides what's appropriate?"

"Me," he snapped. "Because I'm paying for it."

The whiplash of his sudden sharpness threw me. I'd thought we were joking around—you know, *you're the flustered uptight boss and I'm the lovably impertinent scamp you hired to sort your family's dirty laundry, aren't we a funny pair?*

But I guess I'd read it wrong. Sure, he was paying me way above asking rate for work like this—enough money that I had started considering a move to a slightly less shitty apartment and following eBay auctions for early twentieth-century jewelry I definitely didn't need.

But I had felt sure that we both understood that this was not just a business transaction—this history was something we both cared about, even after just a few nights spent looking through those boxes and making notes.

If I were Evelyn Cross, I would have stood up right then, tossed my chin, and stormed out of the room with some line about how my silence couldn't be bought. But I wasn't Evelyn, no matter how much I might have wanted her confidence.

No, I was all bark and no bite. A few quips here and there, sure. But in the end, I just got quiet and muttered:

"Well. At least I know where we stand, sir. Sorry."

Folding in on myself, I rifled through my bag for an eraser. There had to be one in there somewhere.

The fireplace crackled. The shadow over me moved. "It's just that I read your dissertation—"

"You read my dissertation?"

"—and you're excellent. Very talented. Smart. Exceptional, really."

My heart throbbed right at the top of my throat. He'd read my dissertation. *No one* had read my dissertation except for the adjudicators, and they hadn't particularly liked it. Armitage, though, thought I was "very talented." He thought . . .

I went back to rifling around for that damn eraser.

"As exceptional as anyone can be when they're writing about sweating to death in Louisiana in the 1700s," I muttered.

"Don't do that."

"Don't do what?"

"I don't waste my time on anything but the best. And you are."

He was the kind of man who could have anything he wanted. Anyone he wanted. The best, just like he said.

And over everyone else, he'd chosen me.

I gave up looking for the eraser. I wouldn't need it.

"Good." My smile returned. "Let me have the erection thing, then?"

He threw his hands up and dropped into the nearest chair.

"C'mon, Mr. Gallier," I goaded. "No one's ever going to see this but you and me. Give me a *few* creative liberties. I won't even describe the size if that makes you feel any better."

His lip tugged in the tiniest smile. The kind of smile that felt like a secret. "Just . . . I want to know the truth here. Don't add anything that will change the story. Alright?"

Lifting my pencil, I held it across my heart. "You have my word."

When he left, though, the interaction stuck with me, leaving me to chew on it like a Tootsie Roll caught in my molar. One minute, he was snapping at me about my work, and the next, he was telling me how brilliant I was. Every time I thought he had his guard all the way up, he shocked me with a bolt of vulnerability.

It reminded me of Thomas and Evelyn, really. Like he didn't want me close but couldn't stand to push me away.

I could read into that, I supposed. Make wild guesses about why that must be. But he'd literally just told me not to go guessing about Thomas and Evelyn. Speculating about him *had* to be off-limits too.

My thoughts turned back to my research. If I wanted to assert the boner conclusion (great band name, by the way—I totally call it), I had to support my "Thomas Gallier hard-on" contention with evidence.

The first and slightly less compelling bit of evidence was simple inference. Who amongst us wouldn't get hard in the presence of an absolute plus-size goddess like Evelyn Cross? My lady boner is throbbing just thinking about her. Maybe I wasn't the kind of big girl who inspired erections in men, but I knew Evelyn was. It only made sense that Thomas's first meeting with the woman would awaken some desire in him.

However, the second piece of evidence was far more concrete. I was able to locate the below note from the log of the butler at Thomas's residence, dated the night Thomas and Evelyn met:

Half past ten in the evening—dispatched by M. Gallier to the back room of DF Datton's shop. Requested card of Miss Evelyn Cross in "Spring will Come Again" dress. Urgent. Returned within half hour. M. Gallier retreated to quarters for the rest of the night.

Hm. Sending your butler out in the middle of the night to one of Manhattan's seediest literary institutions to "urgently" acquire a copy of some half-dressed woman's girlie card? Interesting.

One can only imagine what he needed such a thing for.

PART TWO

CAN YOU TAME WILD WOMEN?

CHAPTER FIVE

EVELYN WAS NOT MUCH INCLINED TO MATHEMATICS, BUT AFTER meeting Thomas Gallier, she spent the entire walk to her boarding house doing arithmetic—namely, subtracting her expenses from the money she had saved.

She was confident she wouldn't go hungry, at least. She'd never met a man she couldn't talk out of a dinner or a bag of donuts—even in her current state. Housing, though? That was another matter entirely.

She had been living at the Matterly Ladies' Theatrical Bath and Boarding House for so long that it didn't seem right that a little thing like lack of funds could force her to leave it. The boarding house wasn't particularly expensive. For four dollars and fifty cents a week, one was treated to a room, hot water for bathing, two square meals a day, and companionship from other like-minded professionals. Still, if tomorrow's audition with Thomas Gallier didn't result in a paycheck, she might not be able to remain in her little room. The thought nettled her. Bea, the founder and matron and her best friend besides Jules, would doubtless extend her charity, but she wouldn't take it. She was too proud for that. However, she didn't need a crystal ball to imagine her future nights spent shivering in the street—or worse.

As she made her entrance, she found the usual gang assembled in the parlor. She spotted some of her old faithfuls—among them, fluffy-cheeked, redheaded Rose McKinnon with her French horn; Annie, the ambulatory wheelchair user whose skills as an illusionist helped her escape a lifetime of bilking suckers in her father's so-called faith healing ministry; and Natia, the stout Georgian radical of their group. Busy with tuning their instruments and stitching their costumes in between illicit sips from the flasks tucked away in their cases and sewing baskets, not a one of them seemed to recognize Evelyn's flush and fluster, which still lingered from her encounter with Thomas Gallier.

Usually, Evelyn was a professional. She left her craft—stage and otherwise—outside of the boarding house doors. Tonight, he'd made her break that streak. Damn him.

"Hiya, girls," she greeted, forcing a smile just like she would have if she were in the spotlight. Which, in a way, she was. "What's good?"

"The Mission down the street if you don't have your rent paid on time," Rose snarked, waving a valve brush dismissively in her direction.

Evelyn's pride bristled, but she tried to keep her tone light. "Who says I haven't paid rent?"

"I'm no snitch."

"Can it," Annie snapped, making a show of brushing Rose away with a thick handful of lace. "No one's said anything, Evelyn. Work's just . . . well, bookings are just hard to get all around, you know? Even Nathaniel can't find work. Too many whiteys corking up and singing about plantations."

The room went silent then. Nathaniel Fry was a friend of theirs. A colored man who'd left Wilberforce University when he discovered his passion for tap dancing, he was one of the greatest performers of the modern stage. A genius, really. Anyone who saw him dancing wasn't just witnessing art; they were being given a gift. They were getting to see the very act of heavenly creation in person, with their own eyes.

For him to be losing gigs—that was a sign that things were not as they should be.

"It's their loss," Evelyn ventured, as though that made it any better. "How dull and boring and artless and *pathetic* their lives will be without us."

"We were just wondering if you were having the same trouble, Evelyn. That is all," Natia interjected, her accent curving the corners of her words like a splash of bathtub *chacha*.

"I mean, look at me!" Annie cried, trying to inject some warmth and cheer back into their bleak futures. "I'm wasting away over here. My stomach's near enough to touch my backbone, that's how hungry I am."

"No, you've just got your laces tied too tight."

"Yeah, the lack of air is getting to your brain."

"Lay off her, or I'll show you what it's like to *really* stop breathing—"

It didn't take long for conversation to devolve. It never did. Idle chat gave way to an incessant overlapping of self-satisfied jokes and gallows humor. Everyone was hungry. Everyone was broke. Everyone's looks were fading and their acts were stale and their social calendars were barren for want of a date on their precious one night a week off. But somehow, in the middle of the verbal slings and arrows, the knots in Evelyn's shoulders unwound and all thoughts of Thomas Gallier slipped from the forefront of her brain. She settled into the safety of this place—the sanctified air of her messy, chaotic, wonderful home.

Until, inevitably, the conversation shifted back to her.

"So, Evelyn," Natia prompted. "We return to the point. How is it for you out there?"

A shadow crossed the doorway and a new player entered their drama. Beatrice Matterly, to whom Evelyn hadn't paid rent in three weeks, raised one eyebrow and asked dryly, "Oh, yes, Evelyn. Do tell us."

Evelyn chewed the inside of her cheek. "As it happens, I might have gotten a job offer today."

"Might have?" Annie feigned shock, then wiggled her eyebrows lasciviously. "Did Miss Evelyn Cross not manage to seal the deal?"

Evelyn gave what she hoped was a coy shrug. The whole room knew she was usually a professional when it came to games like the one she and Thomas Gallier had played tonight.

Usually.

"Well," cracked Rose, "I guess there's a first time for everything."

"The gentlemen of Fifth Avenue are weeping. Ash and sackcloth as far as the eye can see. Evelyn Cross has lost her sensual touch," said Natia.

Bea huffed a sigh and reached up, clanging the curfew bell a full three minutes before the nearby clock would have agreed with her. "All right, ladies. That's quite enough. This is the sort of conversation for which the Manhattan Board of Female Social Hygiene would not stand. Don't lose me my license, now. To bed—all of you."

Groans and shuffling, but no real argument. As the rest of the women retired, Evelyn and her landlady withdrew to the small office where they so often spent their evenings. The two women had been friends for years. They understood one another. Beatrice, for all of her hard-nosed respectability now, had once been rather like Evelyn. Not a performer on the stage but, instead, of a different kind. As a wealthy man's mistress, she'd been gifted this very house as a love nest. However, after the panic of '90, she'd ditched the now-broke man, kept the house, and opened her doors as a boarding house. Evelyn had been her very first boarder.

Beatrice's office was the sort of tidy space one might expect of a headmistress. Stacks of paper and piled books covered the surface of an expensive, but not ostentatious, desk. Shelves covered in respectable knickknacks and walls lined with miniature portraits. Dark curtains. A few chairs on either side of the table. Modest lamps for late-night reading.

However, it was to a hidden decanter of brandy that Beatrice marched the second they entered that room. She helped herself to a generous measure.

"Settling in?" Evelyn asked, dropping herself into a chair.

"This sounds like a good story," Beatrice replied. "I want to make sure I enjoy it."

Then, she fixed Evelyn with one of those stares. The kind that could just as easily have belonged to one's best friend as much as one's landlady.

"I met Thomas Gallier today," Evelyn started.

Bea choked. "Thomas Gallier? *The Emperor and His Little Empire* Thomas Gallier?"

"One and the same."

"And what was he like?"

Disgustingly handsome. Strict. Disciplined. Principled, even. I couldn't have been more available if we were in the midst of coitus and yet . . . he would barely look at me, much less do anything with me. He was confusing and stoic and professional and clearly a masochist and I can't stop thinking about what it might have been like if he'd let me have my way with him tonight and—

"Tall."

"My, I *do* hope the coppers don't call you in to describe a suspect. They'd never catch their man."

Rolling her eyes, Evelyn recounted the night—seeing him in the opera box, welcoming him into her dressing room, the proposition, the rebuff . . .

Oh, the rebuff. She wasn't necessarily making it common knowledge, but she'd had more and more of those lately. She was used to being scandalous—men had always hesitated to be seen in public with a vaudeville star—but they had never objected to having her in their beds, their carriages, or on the available surfaces of her various dressing rooms. It seemed Alban's newspaper screeds and advertisements like a certain Miss Banting's had contaminated the waters of her pool of eligible suitors.

And now that she considered it, maybe it hadn't been Thomas Gallier's principles that had held him back. Maybe he was as repulsed as the rest of them. But that didn't make sense, did it? He'd as good as *said* he wanted her.

Was it better or worse if he was simply a devotee of convention, willing to sacrifice what he really wanted on the altar of other men's taste?

It was at this point in her train of thought that she caught Bea's expression out of the corner of her eye and realized she had stopped talking a full minute before.

Dash it all.

Evelyn crossed her arms. "Why are you looking at me like that?"

A dimple appeared in Bea's left cheek. "Because you have the chance of a lifetime waiting for you tomorrow at noon and yet all I've heard you talk about is how the man wouldn't take you on your dressing room floor."

"I'll have you know I've gotten many a job on my dressing room floor."

"Oh, I know. And that's what I'm afraid of."

"What, precisely, is that supposed to mean?"

Sipping at her brandy, Beatrice only shrugged. "It's just that I can't remember the last time you spoke to a man who wanted you for something more than your body. Could be a dangerous thing."

A NOTE FROM THE HISTORIAN

In the history of vaudeville, there are few friendships more confounding than that of Thomas Gallier and Dr. Andrew Samson.

As the newspapers of the time suggested, when Thomas Gallier arrived on the rock known as the island of Manhattan, he had no connections—not just in high society, but anywhere. His money opened certain doors, but after micromanaging his contractors to the point of alienation, engaging in protracted fights with every creditor in the city, and facing rejection from quite a few society circles fussy about his connections to the scandals of showbiz, it quickly became apparent that he needed some assistance if he was going to make inroads with the circles he longed to join.

Enter: Dr. Andrew Samson. You may recognize the name. The Samson Library? The Samson Wing of NYU's Medical School? The Samson Ramble in Lower Manhattan?

In the early 1890s, Andrew had thoroughly shamed his family by entering the medical field. It seemed, for a time, that he was estranged from them for this reason—but by 1895, when Thomas Gallier came to town, he'd returned to the family fold, formally hung up his stethoscope, and begun apprenticing under his father to one day inherit their various businesses.

As for Thomas Gallier: while there were plenty of reasons one might disparage the man in the early days of The Empire's development, no one could suggest that he wasn't a dogged worker.

In records from the time, those who knew him noted his visible lack of sleep, his anxious refusal to take meals, and his single-minded devotion to his work.

Devotion that led to disaster when, at the conclusion of an investor presentation, Thomas collapsed on the mercifully plush carpet of his host's morning room.

Andrew, who had been shadowing his father that afternoon, leapt into action. Dr. Samson's early forays into the medical field were primarily charitable in nature, and while ministering to street rats was not deemed acceptable by polite society, the room didn't mind taking advantage of his expertise now that there was a body on their floor. He roused Thomas, assured the assembled investors that their investment was not in jeopardy, and whisked his new patient away.

After a small, private meeting between the two men, an agreement was struck: Thomas would appoint Andrew as the theater's resident physician—a position that would not only allow Andrew to monitor Thomas's health, but that of their staff and performers as well, truly a revolutionary boon for a workplace at the time. In return, Andrew would assure the public that Thomas wasn't going to expire before seeing The Empire to its triumphant opening night.

This arrangement wasn't met with enthusiasm in the Samson home. However, Andrew eventually convinced his father that he was only returning to medicine in the interest of protecting his family's investment in Gallier's theater. Meanwhile, by Andrew's account, he and Thomas became fast friends. Though prickly and determined to keep his employee at a distance, Mr. Gallier treated Andrew as his only close confidante.

Andrew made himself invaluable not only by providing public relations support vis-à-vis his boss's health, but also by acting as a charismatic countermeasure to his brooding, exacting new associate. By morning, he could be setting a stonemason's broken arm at the construction site, and by evening, he might be smoothing Thomas's way through a high society party. He was always on hand for coffee, for negotiations, for cocktail hours, and to be the friendly ear it seems Thomas Gallier never had.

Thomas Gallier tried to refuse that friendly ear. He made repeated attempts to keep his and Andrew's relationship strictly professional. However, Thomas Gallier could not remain an island forever.

Certainly not with a man like Dr. Andrew Samson in his life.

And certainly not when Evelyn Cross walked through the doors of The Empire.

CHAPTER SIX

THE THEATER WAS A MARVEL. A TRUE WONDER. NO CONSTRUCTION as grand had been attempted since the first cornerstones were laid at the Taj Mahal, and after, only fantasies would be so elaborate.

Or rather, it would be all of those things once it was finished. For now, as Thomas situated himself in the primary lobby facing the bustle of 34th Street, the entire building shook under an endless onslaught of construction. Walls trembled and electric lights flickered as hammers and drills worked their incursions into the building's facade. Every once in a while, a sprinkling of dust would rain down from above, a side effect of the carnage.

All of it added to the fraying of his nerves, externalizing frustrations he wished to keep buried.

As he sat on a workbench and sipped the last of his fourth cup of coffee, he gave orders to the two men in front of him—one, a dark-haired freelance newspaperman named Smith; the other, Emile Deschamps, the fine French director Thomas had hired to direct his vaudeville show.

"Shall we review the plan again?" Thomas asked, helping himself to another cup of coffee. He needed it after last night—it had been positively sleepless.

Smith and the director shared a sidelong glance.

"It is not complicated, sir," the newsman said, answering for them both.

Thomas clapped his hands together. Though Andrew always scolded him for "excessively and needlessly" instructing his "already extremely capable employees," he didn't care. Anything to ensure success. "Clocks aren't complicated either, but we still tune those, don't we? Now, Emile, when Miss Cross arrives, you're to present your concept for her new act. And Smith—"

"I'm going to make it into a story. Or try, anyway."

"You *will* make it a story," Thomas amended, handing him the first half of his fee in a small envelope.

A snort from the other man. "Sure. One big, fat story."

Thomas didn't appreciate the joke or have the energy to feign a laugh, so he changed the subject. "Don't you have flashbulbs to polish?"

He must have—or the dollars in his pocket made him biddable— because he disappeared, leaving Thomas behind with his director and his director's fine European mustache.

"I wouldn't worry, monsieur," Emile purred, petting his facial hair with a flourish. "Mademoiselle Cross may not be the draw she once was, but I, the great *Emile*, can turn even a dress-wearing pile of cream puffs into a surefire hit."

There it was again. That condescension toward Evelyn and her looks. Thomas swallowed his disgust.

"Yes. Well. Please. Don't let me keep you from preparing."

A moment later, Thomas was totally alone in the lobby. Perhaps he could review his notes for the afternoon's meetings? But when his attention kept slipping to the clock, he rose from his chair and began to wear a path back and forth across the freshly laid carpet. Pacing and checking the grand clock on the wall—rumored, at least when he paid an outrageous sum for it, to have been smuggled out of Versailles during the French Revolution—he knew he must look like he was going mad . . . but he couldn't help it. There was only so much nervous energy one could bear before it had to be expelled somehow.

"Thomas, as your medical advisor, I feel it is my Hippocratic duty to inform you that you have had entirely too much coffee today."

At the sound of the doctor's arrival, Thomas's steps stuttered. "Good morning to you too," Thomas scowled, determinedly ignoring the twitch of a smile on Andrew's lips.

"Good morning, Thomas. Shall we?"

The good doctor waved him over to the bench. Thomas knew better than to protest. This was their morning routine, after all. And at least it gave him something to do other than pacing.

With the kind of ease that could only be learned at a prestigious medical school, Andrew touched his fingers to Thomas's pulse, keeping count on the pocket watch in his free hand. Checking his vitals.

"Care to enlighten me?" Andrew murmured.

"On what?"

"On whatever it is that's got you tied up in knots. Pacing, Thomas. I've never seen you pace. *Really*. You thought that wouldn't concern me?"

Thomas didn't answer asinine questions like that—not even from his doctor.

Andrew continued without being prompted. "Does it have anything to do with what went on in Miss Evelyn Cross's dressing room last night?"

Thomas's thoughts skipped like a scratch on a phonograph vinyl. "I don't know what you're implying."

"Not implying anything," Andrew said, too casual. "Merely observing that when I said her name, your pulse jumped."

"More innuendo. I won't listen to another word of it."

"Alright, then. What happened last night?"

What happened. Facts. Thomas could handle facts. "I offered her an audition. She's coming here today at noon. Emile is going to pitch her an act. Smith is going to make a story of it. By the time the evening edition of the paper hits the streets and the news of our star hits the populace, The Empire will have several new investors, George Westinghouse and his withdrawn funds be damned."

"Rather a lot of words to avoid telling me what *really* happened, don't you think?"

"I told you everything that happened."

Andrew was quiet for a moment as he withdrew a sphygmomanometer from his kit. Hoping they had reached the end of the doctor's line of questioning, Thomas took the liberty of relieving himself of his jacket and rolling up his sleeve. But once Andrew began tightening the cuff around Thomas's biceps, the questions came back with such offhanded casualness that Thomas choked.

"Did you take her to bed?"

"Andrew."

"It's just a question, which I ask out of an interest in your health."

"Of all the—Last night, you seemed thoroughly opposed to the idea of her."

"Yes, well, the way you spoke about her, the way you ran off after her last night, the way you've thundered around here this morning . . . it made me reconsider."

Andrew pressed fervently on the pump end of the air line, causing the device to clench Thomas's flesh painfully. He then continued: "You, my friend, are what we in my profession call *severely repressed.* I've never been worried about you losing your marbles as the papers suggest, nor have I been worried about the health of this professional enterprise of yours. But I have been worried about this . . . *inability* you have to connect with—"

"Showgirls?" Thomas snapped.

"Anyone," came the solemn reply.

Thomas's jaw tightened. His *inability* to connect with people . . . a wholly inaccurate diagnosis. He had the ability. He knew that. But he also knew better than to allow himself the pleasure.

The cuff around his arm felt tighter than usual.

"I thought last night might have changed that," Andrew confessed. "That's all."

"Well. Nothing changed last night. And I wouldn't have—what you suggested I did with Miss Cross."

"But you wanted to."

There was no judgment in Andrew's tone. That didn't change the fact that having his love life picked apart by his personal physician was nearly as humiliating as having it picked apart by all of Manhattan's newspapers and gossip rags.

Heat spread across the back of his neck. He ripped the cuff from his arm and shot to his feet—just out of the doctor's reach.

"It wouldn't have been appropriate," he said, fussing with his shirtsleeve, returning himself to visual, unrumpled perfection. "She'll be my employee soon enough."

"Most men in your position would have pressed their advantage. No matter the business hierarchy," Andrew pointed out.

"Just because most men would doesn't mean they should."

"True. Was she willing?"

Willing. She hadn't just been willing. She'd been *luring.* A plush, warm, delicious treat laid out for him, waiting to capture him between those bitable, thick thighs of hers.

She was perfect. Which, of course, made her the worst sort of temptation.

"She was confounding," Thomas said. "A hurricane of a person. I've never met a woman as thoroughly unsuitable—brazen and unchecked and wanton. I repeat: even if I was in a position to *press my advantage*, as you say, I wouldn't have."

"Despite the fact that you are clearly attracted to her."

Thomas replied before he could consider the consequences. "*Due* to the fact that I was clearly attracted to her."

Andrew glanced at him from over the rim of his gold spectacles. "Care to elaborate?"

"No."

Evelyn Cross presented an existential threat to a man like Thomas Gallier. He trusted his initial assessment. She *was* a hurricane. And he had been a man desperately clinging to a rock beneath her.

Dr. Samson didn't need to know any of that.

"It's just business, then? That's what you've chosen to claim?"

"Just business. That's the truth."

Andrew, understanding that the daily physical was over, tucked his instruments back into his bag.

"Do you want my professional advice?"

"I didn't hire you for your professional advice. Not really," Thomas said. "I hired you to keep the papers from questioning my health."

"Well, I hope you'll forgive me if I give it to you anyway. I have never met a man with as much drive as you. You are endlessly determined. Formidable in every respect. But I have also never met a man as empty. When I say I'm worried for your heart, Thomas, I don't just mean that we have to keep it ticking. I also mean that we must keep it from rotting due to lack of nourishment. You do not need to control everything. Everyone. And you also don't need to insist on doing so alone."

Thomas straightened his cuffs. Andrew was being obtuse, as usual. "I *don't* bear it alone. I have an army of employees at my disposal."

"That's not what I meant."

"Then what did you mean?"

Andrew sighed, heavy and solid. "If you're not careful—"

"If he's not careful with what?"

The room stopped. Thomas's heart stopped. Time itself, even, seemed to stop. Because a third had joined them. And she was just as stunning in the daytime as she had been by stage light.

No. Even more so.

"Miss Cross," Thomas said. "What a pleasure to see you again."

CHAPTER SEVEN

GROWING UP ALONGSIDE CENTRAL PARK, THE BROOKLYN BRIDGE, and the Statue of Liberty, Evelyn had seen plenty of wonders. In a year, the state would incorporate Brooklyn, Queens, Manhattan, the Bronx, and Richmond County into one New York supercity. She had barely turned twenty when Ellis Island first opened its doors five years ago. She'd been witness to the inventions of the telephone, the electric lightbulb, the gramophone, the zipper, the escalator, and the motion picture machine.

However, from the moment she approached its teeming mass on 34th Street, Evelyn knew that The Empire Theatre was the most beautiful, no, magnificent thing she'd ever seen.

It may have been covered in construction materials now, but the block practically glowed with potential. Through the scaffolding and ladders, she could spy everything the papers promised—the grand, Romanesque columns, the freshly tiled mosaics, Tiffany glass windows. If she blinked away the dust and tuned out the shouting builders and noisy street, she could almost see it. The future.

And damn, if the future didn't look gorgeous.

Once she stepped *inside* the building, her assessment only cemented. She'd been in nearly every theater in the city, and plenty more around the country, but she'd never seen anything quite so miraculous. Gilded clocks and flawless mirrors decorated hand-painted fresco walls. Every furnishing was finely appointed and either old enough to be fashionably antique or so new she could still smell the fresh lacquer. The carpets were the color of perfect rose petals and twice as soft and lush.

And the man at its center? Even more promising.

"Miss Cross. What a pleasure to see you again."

"Mr. Gallier. The pleasure is all mine."

He adjusted his cuffs, looking everywhere but at her.

She waited for him to speak. Something. Anything. To ask her about the weather or her act or inquire about her sheet music or her journey here or how she liked The Empire's progress. But he didn't. As if he were afraid of what he might say if he opened his mouth again.

In situations such as this, Evelyn generally reached for a lurid joke or quip. But over brandies last night, she and Beatrice had talked the whole thing over. The seduction, the rejection, the business proposition, the ultimate realization that he *had* wanted her the whole time, his invitation to be herself in his presence . . .

Evelyn generally did *not* do sincere, not in public. There were so many Evelyns, sometimes it was hard to keep track. Firstly, and perhaps most importantly, there was Performer Evelyn, the greatest star of the Manhattan stage. Then, there was Business Evelyn, the temptress who'd talked many men out of their wallets and relieved even more men out of their clothes. And finally, there was, well, Evelyn Evelyn.

She only had the pleasure of being this last—the *real* Evelyn—in private. At the boarding house, with her friends, when there wasn't anyone to impress, when she allowed herself to be a person instead of a perpetual climbing machine, she was still bawdy and dramatic and painfully ambitious, yes, but there was more to her than that, too.

She was strong-willed and determined, sharp-witted, with a dry sense of humor. And in contrast to her public persona, which was singularly unflappable, in the safety of her friendships and her own room, she felt things. God, did she feel things. Too big and too much and too deeply. Sometimes, it felt like she would collapse under the weight of all her feelings. Drown beneath the tide of her own emotions. Her upbringing had shaped her like this. On the street, she had to be tough and unflappable. A survivor. A scrapper. But back home, with her big-eyed, big-hearted mother, she'd been able to laugh, to cry, to scream at the unfairness of it all. She'd relished those moments when the tenement doors would close, and she could fist at her mother's skirts, drop her head in her lap, and wail about the brokenness of the world.

To, for a little while, at least, *feel* instead of perform.

Evelyn couldn't be like that. Not here. Not around Thomas Gallier.

But she could try to let a little of the real Evelyn show. It was just that she was so out of practice that all that came out was:

"Well."

Thomas echoed her, still fiddling with his cuffs. "Well."

"I must admit, I've rendered many men speechless before, but never *before* the formal audition."

"You're looking . . ." He gave her the quickest of once-overs, polite and pure. Then, he paused, giving Evelyn enough time to guess what his next thought might be. *Decent? Close-legged? Clothed?* "You're looking eminently sensible."

Today, she'd dressed in one of her more conservative ensembles, one she might have usually reserved for the confines of the boarding house and the few nearby blocks where she conducted her day-to-day. A white puff-sleeved top, complete with a high neckline, tucked itself neatly into the black woolen skirt. A black onyx gemstone—or so the man who'd gifted her had called it; she'd never had the piece valued—sat neatly at the base of her throat, drawing attention to her simply dressed face. Pale lips, barely darkened eyes, her simple blonde bun tucked beneath a straw sun hat decorated with a black bow. Her sturdy coat completed the look and protected her against the occasional winter chill biting on the edge of the early afternoon's autumn breeze.

She was nothing like the Evelyn he'd seen yesterday, and yet, she'd followed Thomas's suggestion. She'd come as herself. Still bawdy and brassy and thoroughly determined to get into his trousers.

The question was whether he'd like that. Whether he'd like *her*.

"A day of firsts, then. I've been called so many things in my life. Alluring. Stunning. Outrageous. Scandalous. But sensible? No."

"I happen to admire sensible. It suits you."

There was her answer. He *did* like her.

"Mind yourself, Mr. Gallier. That was very nearly a compliment."

Their eyes met, and she searched his green depths for any hint of a genuine reaction fighting toward his polished exterior. Before she could find it, though, someone cleared their throat and reminded them both that they were not alone.

Thomas sparked to immediate life—any softness that had accidentally invaded him once again hardened to marble.

"Where are my manners? Forgive me. Miss Cross, allow me to introduce my business associate, Dr. Andrew Samson."

"Hello there," Evelyn said, reaching out for the doctor's hand, who took it with enthusiasm. He, apparently, had none of Thomas's trouble expressing emotion.

"An honor, miss. I'm quite a fan. Jules Moreau is an old friend of mine, so I've seen rather a lot of your work."

Evelyn brightened. "You know Jules? Darling Jules?"

Before the doctor could answer, Thomas cut in—all business. As if he didn't want any kind of familiarity or congeniality in his vicinity.

"Shall we begin?"

His strange abruptness caught her off guard, but Evelyn recovered as best she could. "By all means. I would love a tour."

A tour, however, was not in the cards. Thomas was walking much too fast for it, and would have left her a step or two behind if she hadn't been determined to match him stride for long-legged stride.

He had a direct, professional way about him that she admired. She could see already that he was not humorless, not unkind or unfeeling, but he was properly committed to his work.

It made her want him all the more. Now that she knew she wasn't just his casting couch conquest, she found herself toying with ways to make him *her* conquest.

"Am I the only audition today?" she asked.

"Yes."

"You must have the rest of the bill settled, then."

"No," he replied smoothly. "I am here to find a north star. I will wrangle the rest of the constellation after that."

The implication that *she* was that star made her heart flutter. She offered, "I know a great number of simply spectacular performers. I'd be happy to make recommendations—"

He stopped short at two carved wooden doors depicting a series of satyrs and naiads at the water's edge, performing a song with lyres and flutes. Suddenly, she and Thomas were very close. She swallowed hard. Being near him was like standing near one of those sideshow electrode generators—mere proximity threatened to shock her.

"The offer is very much appreciated, but with all due respect . . ."

Trailing off, he threw open the doors before them, ushering her into the grand new world of The Empire Theatre.

". . . this is *my* project, Miss Cross."

Unlike the rest of the pleasure palace, the theater was nearly completed. If one ignored the sawdust accumulating in unswept corners or the dust settling into the crimson stage curtains, one might imagine a performance going up this very evening.

Designed to look like an Italian courtyard, the theater was surrounded by grand facades inset with columns and fountains and statues of the muses. The seats were genuine red-crush velvet, unlike the imitation most of the theaters used. Live trees had been planted upon the false balconies topping the facades of House Left and House Right, filling the air with the scent of sprouting olives and fresh lemon. The ceiling was painted a deep, endless blue, and small electric lights had been installed to give the impression of a starry night sky.

The grandeur of the theater drew her deeper down its aisles. Her companions followed.

"As you can see, I've done quite well, building The Empire on my own. I'll be the one to make the programming decisions. I trust myself in all things, just as last night, I trusted myself when I decided you belonged here."

He was right—arrogant beyond belief, but right. At least, her vanity said so. She could imagine herself standing there at center stage, singing to the twinkling stars as lovers swooned in the opera boxes and gentlemen fanned themselves down in the orchestra.

"You're flattering me so I'll drop the subject," she flirted.

"I'm not in the business of flattery, Miss Cross. Surely, you learned that last night."

"I'll be a gentleman and pretend I didn't hear that, Thomas," Andrew said, reminding Evelyn for the second time that they weren't, in fact, alone.

Right. The audition. Her livelihood. Her future.

At the foot of the stage, she gestured to the attaché slung over her shoulder, her sacred, worn leather case that held the music that had made her famous.

"In the spirit of such generosity," she said, nodding to Andrew, "let's get to brass tacks, shall we? If you point me to a piano, I can favor you with a song, or—"

"No," Thomas said. "That won't be necessary."

Surely, he meant that to be flattering, but the muscles in Evelyn's back—the ones that might have curled in anticipation if she were about to outrun a predator—only tightened. "Oh?"

"Your reputation and last night's act spoke for itself. So I contacted the one and only Emile Deschamps—our resident director. He's worked with the great Enrico Caruso, Maud Allan, so many stars; a few years ago, he even directed the main stage performances at the World's Columbian Exhibition. I've elected to have him develop an act for you."

As if summoned by magic, a spindly man with an enormous mustache emerged from the wings, carrying an easel covered with a sheet. From his stage-polished boots to the hat deliberately placed at an attitude upon his balding head, he looked every bit the micromanaging villain Evelyn knew many "directors" to be.

Something about all of this was very, very wrong. Vaudeville wasn't the kind of art form that typically *had* directors. Each performer was their own auteur.

"Mademoiselle," Emile greeted from the stage. "It is a great honor for you to meet me."

Translation error from his native French tongue? No, Evelyn didn't think so.

"Charmed, I'm sure." She nodded up at him, then turned her attention to another man setting up a camera near the stage's left wing. "And who's this handsome fellow?"

"Just the newshound, miss," he said, completely immune to her charms.

She swayed her hips a bit—just enough to test his resolve. "Make sure you get my good side."

He didn't budge. Evelyn felt a little of her inner light dim.

This was not going to end well.

CHAPTER EIGHT

SHE WAS A TEST ON THOMAS'S RESOLVE. A STRAIN TO HIS WILL-power. But he would not fall. He would *not*. They would get on with this little publicity stunt, she would sign a contract, and then he would have his star—and no further reason to be anywhere close to her. After this meeting, she would be a theatrical property to be assessed and managed, not a very beautiful woman with perfume like tuberose and hair like summertime sun.

At least, that's what he told himself as he began the proceedings.

"Smith, make sure your camera is ready."

"What do you think you're paying me for? To sit here on my hands? Calm down, old man."

Thomas opened his mouth to protest but Emile stamped his cane twice, calling the room to order. "If you gentlemen are quite finished!"

Appropriately chastened, Thomas took a seat beside Miss Cross in the audience . . . and focused his attention on the stage so as not to dwell on her closeness.

Fortunately, Mr. Deschamps proved somewhat distracting, speaking and bounding back and forth in front of his concealed easel like some sort of deranged scientist before a wicked experiment.

"Thank you. Now, last night, when Thomas requested I develop an act for Miss Evelyn Cross, I spit on the idea. It cannot be done. Evelyn Cross cannot be a star. She has been cast onto the ash heap of the artistic world, a passé delicacy. Even I cannot make her beautiful—no more than I could blot out the sun. Impossible."

Thomas frowned. He could hardly believe that any man didn't find Evelyn Cross beautiful. Onstage, Mr. Deschamps was still monologuing, with a sense of drama that could only be described as very French.

"Then it occurred to me, like a light from the heavens itself, a message from God almighty: We shall *not* make Evelyn Cross beautiful. We shall make Evelyn Cross a clown. Not a real clown, no, but a clown in spirit. As the public embraces the Gibson Girl, women like Evelyn are going to become the new bearded lady. A woman like *that*? Dancing? What a sight. We will tell the joke about our star before audiences have a chance to tell it for us. She shall be a novelty."

A metallic tang coated the back of Thomas's tongue. A joke? This ridiculously mustachioed man wanted to turn Evelyn Cross into a joke?

"A great number of our potential audience members look like Evelyn, mind," Andrew pointed out.

It was a point, Thomas thought, they would do well to consider. Manhattan and America at large were filled with women like Evelyn. Turning her into this spectacle . . . was it really the right play to make? Certainly not.

Surely not.

And yet—

"No one comes to the theater to see themselves up onstage. They go to *escape* themselves," Emile snapped. "And to this end, I created a storm in my brain. A storm of ideas. First—consider our heavens. What do we see most when we survey them? The moon. A big, bright blot on our night sky. I thought first that Miss Evelyn Cross could be that moon, clumsily struggling across the sky amidst the firmament of petite stars. But then, I had another idea: an act *entirely* comprised of eating. She's Queen Marie Antoinette, surrounded by food she devours, becoming increasingly violent and tyrannical as she demands the servants bring her more and more."

When the director paused for breath, Thomas started to object. But Emile beat him to it, charging forward to his grand finale.

"But then I thought—no, these ideas are no good! This act of ours—this remaking of our leading lady—requires something funnier. Bolder. *Bigger.* So, without any further ado, please allow me to introduce you to The New Miss Evelyn Cross."

With a flourish, he withdrew the cloth over the canvas, at last revealing the artwork beneath.

The image was of a woman—a woman who, if one squinted, looked something like Evelyn—standing in the center of a charcoal-drawn stage. However, upon closer inspection, the image was not of a woman at all. The figure beneath the words INTRODUCING EVELYN CROSS . . . only had a woman's head. Her torso and legs had been replaced with that of a hippopotamus on two legs, its form made vaguely female by a loose-corseted dance costume inlaid with jewels and more ruffles than one woman could possibly wear.

Across the bottom of the image read THE WORLD'S FIRST DANCING HIPPOPOTAMUS.

A lightning bolt slammed right down Thomas's spine. This was *not* what he had asked for. Not what he wanted. He rose from his seat.

"Emile—"

A small, gloved hand gently brushed his arm, holding him in place.

"Oh, no, Mr. Gallier. Please don't say anything. I should like to have a closer look at this . . . conceptual rendering . . . before we proceed."

With that, Evelyn abandoned her chair and made for the stage. Struggling to keep up and play the gentleman, Thomas followed behind and offered her his hand as they ascended—a gesture she ignored altogether.

At center stage, the men watched as long, manicured fingers removed their gloves and reached out to smudge the face of the dancer in the poster's center. Emile, who had clearly anticipated rapturous praise for his brilliant work, looked on with some disgruntlement.

"Now. What do you think of it, Mr. Gallier?" Evelyn's voice betrayed none of her thoughts.

Internal conflict, at least where his work was concerned, was not an emotion with which Thomas engaged very often. He was decisive. Direct. Dictatorial in his opinions, even. But here, he found himself at odds. If he told Evelyn the truth—that he hated it—and she actually liked it, then he might be out a director *and* a star. But if he lied, and it turned out that she found Mr. Deschamps's idea as awful as he did, then she might be angry or offended.

With nowhere else to turn, he chose the path of least resistance. The path of cowardice.

"Emile is one of the finest directors of our age. And you are one of its greatest performers. I'm sure together, you two could turn this into something spectacular." And then, when Evelyn remained silent: "I confess I've always cared more for the company of facts and figures than feather fans and frippery."

"Quite a poetic evasion, sir," she replied.

"If you have any ideas for improving upon Emile's ideas, please," he encouraged, doing his best to make her feel at ease, "do speak up."

A pause. Evelyn pocketed her gloves as a delightful blush crept past her collar and all the way up to her cheekbones—exactly, incidentally, the path Thomas had kissed for her in one of his dreams the night before.

"Come to think of it, I *do* have an idea . . . But it's only . . . It's only that it's so very scandalous. I'll blush to even say it out loud."

"We're all grown men here," Emile replied. "Whatever you have to say, we've likely heard it before. And besides, if you're going to perform whatever it is you're dreaming up, you'll be doing more than *talking* about it."

The woman in question dipped her head in a demure gesture that was a far cry from the woman Thomas had met in Evelyn Cross's dressing room. She pressed her hands together almost as though in prayer and glanced up at Thomas through long, fluttering lashes.

She couldn't truly be shy, could she? Not after the way she had acted the night before.

"Could I . . . Could I just tell it to *you*, Mr. Gallier?"

His own cheeks went hot. "Me?"

She stepped closer to him, picking up the canvas as she did so.

"You seem such a *trustworthy* sort."

His skin hummed. Was she going to touch him? God, he wasn't sure what would happen if she did. "Well—"

Another step closer.

"The look of a real *champion*."

"I wouldn't say that—"

She touched him. A small hand on the edge of his jaw, tipping his head down so deliberately he feared—*hoped?*—a kiss was next. "You could be *my* champion. Couldn't you, Mr. Gallier?"

He spoke before he thought it through properly. "Yes. Of course."

"Alright. Here's my idea."

In full view of director, photographer, and doctor, Evelyn's hand slid from Thomas's neck to his lapel, which she used to tug him down to her height. Once there, she whispered to him, with such vehemence that her tongue darted out against his ear every other word.

"My idea is that I burn this entire theater to the ground and dance naked in the demolished grave of your dreams, you spineless fraud."

Thomas barely had time to process just what had happened when she stepped back, lifted the poster high, and smashed it over his head, letting the frame hang limply from around his neck.

Then, she turned on her heel and marched straight to the stage door, only pausing for the briefest of moments to shout behind her.

"This audition is over."

A NOTE FROM THE HISTORIAN

In academic circles, the highly technical term for what happened between Thomas and Evelyn that day is "A big yikes."

Alternatively:

"Not a good look."

"0/10, would not recommend."

"Not his best work."

But this is such an interesting interaction between Thomas and Evelyn. I can't believe I almost missed it when doing my original research pass.

Robert Smith, the newspaperman—well, it turned out that even Thomas's money in his pocket didn't keep him from taking a fantastic photograph of Evelyn smashing the drawing of her as a hippo over Thomas's head and marching it to one of the most dangerous men in all of Manhattan.

That man was Nehemiah Alban. The owner of *The Manhattan Daily*. The moralistic one-man anti-vaudeville campaigner who had already been nothing but trouble for both Thomas and Evelyn. The man who would not hesitate to print a story that could thoroughly humiliate them both.

It was a juicy tale with an eye-catching photograph to go right alongside it. And would you believe copies of the paper with this sensational story were even printed, ready to hit the streets by the next morning? If there are any editions of this paper outside of the Gallier Institute's collection, I have not been able to locate them. The copy *within* the Gallier Institute has been ripped up (*curious*), leaving some pieces completely illegible, and others (including the photograph of Thomas and Evelyn mid-fight, too delicate to reproduce here, as photocopying or photographing might jeopardize them in their delicate condition) barely so. It's a shame, but let's recall, these are old documents—this one, in fact, is about forty years older than the invention of the chocolate chip cookie.

The only words visible are as follows:

THE MANHATTAN DAILY,
OCTOBER 17, 1897 (New York, New York)
AN EMPEROR REJECTED

It gets more interesting from here because, despite this sensational headline and its accompanying photograph, not a single copy of this edition of the paper was ever sold.

Instead, an alternate version of *The Manhattan Daily* went out—identical in every respect to the original version, except that the story about Evelyn and Thomas was notably missing, replaced by a racist cartoon about recently escalated Cuban-Spanish tensions.

The reasons for this adjustment will become clear soon enough. But I've got to hold some things back to keep you interested, don't I?

For now, I'll just share one more tidbit. In his daily ledger, where he kept single-line entries regarding the activities, appointments, and decisions of his day, Thomas Gallier wrote only this:

Today, I disappointed a woman.

CHAPTER NINE

EVELYN WOULDN'T CHARACTERIZE WHAT SHE DID NEXT AS *FLEEING from The Empire*. Nor would she describe it as *avoiding returning to the boarding house in abject shame after failing to keep her promise to land the hottest job in town*. She would simply describe it as *arriving, red-faced and justly enraged, to her appointment with Jules—several hours early*.

Make no mistake: Evelyn was righteously and thoroughly pissed off, and, though she'd never admit it to anyone, emotionally injured by the whole spectacle. They wanted her to be a hippo. Not even a beautiful one, either—Evelyn believed any creature could be beautiful. She was living proof of that truism—but one to be laughed at.

She'd arranged to meet Jules at their favorite little Tin Pan Alley drinking spot that evening, and so made her way downtown.

This evening was originally meant to celebrate her successful negotiations with The Empire. But now she'd have to tell Jules of her failure. She didn't mind. Of all the people in the world, she knew she could trust him with her disasters.

At least, she *believed* she could . . . until she threw open the door to Jules's Tin Pan Alley studio to discover that not only was Jules also early to their quiet tête-à-tête, but he'd expanded the guest list as well.

"What in the devil is this, Jules?"

She wasn't surprised to find Jules with company. Nearly anywhere he went, his loyal companion and costume designer, Akio, was sure to be close at hand. Ever since he'd picked him up on tour in San Francisco, the two had been inseparable, to the extent that Evelyn counted the second-generation Japanese American alongside Jules as one of her closest confidantes. And indeed, that afternoon, when Evelyn opened the door to the small room where they'd often meet for coffees and rehearsals between gigs, Akio was there, hand-sewing away on a length of extravagant silk.

However, Akio was not Jules's only companion.

"Ah, Evelyn," Jules said. "How kind of you to finally join us."

"Finally? We weren't supposed to meet for hours yet." She paused, remembering her manners, "Hello, Akio."

Akio nodded in acknowledgment, his gaze never leaving his intricate stitchwork, as Jules waved vaguely, as though to brush her question away. "I had some extra time on my hands this afternoon. And who should arrive at my door today, looking for my counsel, but this handsome young gentleman?"

Evelyn turned, resigned, to the final member of their happy little quartet.

Dr. Andrew Samson.

Friends with Jules or not, this was *not* the sort of place a man like Dr. Andrew Samson—one of Manhattan's wealthiest sons—belonged. It was odd for him to look so at home here, sitting on a chair-height pile of sheet music and smiling up at her.

"Hello, Miss Cross—" he said.

"Akio," Evelyn said, cutting off the doctor and turning her attention to her deliberately oblivious friend. "Would you like to join me for cocktails? Dinner, perhaps? I fear the air in here has been soured by the stench of a *traitor.*"

"Now, Miss, if you'll allow me—"

"I will not."

Jules tossed his hands up, exasperated. "He only wanted to check and see if you were alright, Evelyn. Gracious, always with the dramatics."

This notion stopped Evelyn in her tracks. She blinked.

"You did?"

Dr. Samson nodded. "That display back at The Empire was ghastly. I wanted to talk to you. See if you were well."

A fine and lofty goal. Or it would have been if Evelyn believed it. Which she didn't.

"And?" she prompted.

"Well," the doctor replied, removing his spectacles and cleaning them on a handkerchief—a nervous habit if Evelyn ever saw one. "I tell you this in confidence, but Thomas does not come from the same world that I do. It's given him a chip on his shoulder. A boulder, really. He's desperate for the real elite of this city to take him seriously, to finally show him some respect. I do not know the details, and even if I did, they wouldn't be mine to tell. But one thing I can say is that you have awakened something in him, something good, something that I've never seen in him before. And as his friend, I should hate to see him lose that so soon after its discovery. So, really, I am here to beg you to give Thomas another chance."

Evelyn let the silence in the wake of Dr. Samson's little speech settle for a moment, trying not to dwell on just what kinds of feeling she might have made Thomas feel. Finally, she determined she had let the good doctor fidget long enough and threw back her head with a not-very-ladylike scoff. "Of course I'm going to give him another chance."

It was Dr. Samson's turn to blink. "Beg pardon?"

"He's the biggest vaudeville promoter in the world at present and his money is going to make me a star again. I am enraged and insulted, Dr. Samson, but I am an enraged and insulted woman of business. I'll have to reserve judgment on the man himself, but I have every intention of at least giving his theater and his money another chance."

What manner of woman did he take her for? One who would run away weeping the first time her pride was insulted? Especially when her dreams were on the line? No. Absolutely not. Her dramatic exit today was one thing. A punishment for her mistreatment. But she would be back tomorrow—her career depended on it.

Still, Dr. Samson's face twisted.

"Please, Miss Cross. Thomas is a dear friend of mine. I believe in this wild dream of his. I want him to succeed. But I also want him to remember that he's more than a money-minting, publicity-chasing machine. Help me—help Thomas. Give the man another chance too."

Help Thomas. Help the most powerful man in all of show business, one of the richest men on this entire island. Help a man who could buy, sell, and buy her again with the loose change jingling, discarded and forgotten, across the floor of his motorcar?

Not likely, the hardened, cursed part of her resolved.

But . . . she'd always had a marshmallow where her heart should have been. It was her greatest flaw. She knew the world was a cruel, unkind, unfeeling place full of people who would never give her the time of day if she couldn't do something for them in exchange.

But still, she loved those people. Especially the forgotten, the grown crooked, the abandoned, the lost.

She addressed Akio and Jules. "How do you know this clown?"

The couple shared a glance, as if coming to a silent agreement. Then, they both looked at Dr. Samson, who nodded once, his face soft and understanding. At length, Jules answered:

"The good doctor runs a *gratis* and discreet service for certain members of the community for whom medical care may not be immediately possible."

And then it hit Evelyn: *that's* why the man had looked familiar.

Jules Moreau was no stranger to illness and misfortune—some of his own making, some of pure rotten luck. On the occasions when he'd arrived at the back door of the boarding house with black eyes and split lips, Evelyn had been the one to stitch him up.

But there had been a time last winter, a time when Jules had turned away all visitors and canceled his bookings. It took Evelyn a week of built-up annoyance and worry to finally climb through Jules's window, where she caught a glimpse of a man with a doctor's bag leaving in a hurry through the bedroom door . . . and Jules lying limp in the bed.

In that moment, crouched in his window, Evelyn had been so certain she'd never see her friend again. Death embraced him like a very familiar lover.

Now, searching his eyes, she realized that he was only sitting there, alive and pink and happy, because of Dr. Andrew Samson.

"So he's a good man?" she asked, as though he weren't in the room.

"One of the best," Jules assured her.

During a lifetime of friendship, Jules had never once led Evelyn astray. She trusted him with her very soul. And if he vouched for Dr. Samson, and that man vouched for Thomas . . .

"Fine, then. But I'll warn you, Dr. Samson. He lost much of my respect today. If he wants it back, he's going to have to earn it."

"How?"

Finally—he was asking the right sorts of questions. Evelyn chewed it over, her fingers running idly through a discarded pile of sheet music, until an idea struck her with the force of a moving streetcar.

She had a boarding house full of friends with no work. Jules had no work. Thomas needed a bill of performers . . .

"Tell me. How badly does Thomas want me for The Empire?" Evelyn asked, addressing the doctor.

"Desperately," Andrew said.

Excellent. Because she would probably need a bit of desperation to get what she wanted.

"What do you think he would give me? If I said I could give him the greatest show in Manhattan?"

A warm smile stretched across Andrew Samson's face. And for a moment, she glimpsed the first hints of mischief in his gaze, too. "Everything."

CHAPTER TEN

THIS DAY HAD NOT GONE TO PLAN. AND IF THERE WAS ANYTHING Thomas despised in this great, wide world, it was a day that had not gone to plan.

His calamitous meeting with Miss Evelyn Cross set a snowballing chaos into motion. First, there was the matter of the newshound—who Thomas had tried and failed to track down after he'd run off with the photographs of the portrait incident. Then, he'd had to fire Emile Deschamps—their visions of The Empire's show were at irreconcilable odds. After that, the day was a blur of half-remembered meetings with contractors and inspections and accountancies—in short, the *rest* of his daily to-do list all fogged by the memory of Evelyn Cross's devastated, furious face.

The fog was broken that evening. He hadn't wanted to go to a party at the home of one of Manhattan's elite, but he'd accepted the invitation some time ago, and he could not be seen as a man who didn't keep his word. So there he was, standing on the outskirts of the night with a seltzer water in his hand and (almost certainly) a scowl upon his face.

Thomas had lived in slums. He'd eaten out of garbage cans. As a boy, he'd listened at the feet of wounded soldiers as they recounted the bloody atrocities that they'd committed on the fields of Awadh and the Cape Coast. He'd known hunger. Suffered abuse. Done shameful things on his journey from the gutter.

But nothing—absolutely nothing—was worse than a ball.

It was a shame, really. Thomas spent so much of his time and resources angling his way into these parties. He'd expended a great deal of social capital so that he might be accepted by this lot, the Rockefellers and the Stanfords, the J.P. Morgans of the world. It wasn't enough to be rich, famous, successful. He knew all too well that true power could only come from being recognized by *other* powerful men.

And yet that didn't mean that he failed to realize the sham of it all.

He'd spoken to men who'd gone on safari to Africa, and the scene of a high society ball in Manhattan rather reflected their stories. Mothers on the prowl for prospective mates for their children. Fathers keeping watchful eyes on their packs, ready to pounce at the first signs of danger. Young bucks and cubs scanning the horizon for prey to devour. Mothish girls blending in with the wallpaper and preening peacocks getting noticed.

Thomas, for his part, was a human, theoretically at the top of the food chain who, standing amongst these wild creatures, felt very much like someone's next supper.

Before long, someone pounced, flanking him from the left and trapping him in a corner.

"Ah. Just the man I wanted to see."

The voice wasn't unfamiliar to Thomas, and it instantly sent cold sweat down the back of his neck. He turned to spot a towering reed of a man who sported a silver walking cane in one hand and a cocktail in the other. Mr. Nehemiah Alban. The newspaper magnate.

Newspaper magnate was probably too small a word to describe him. Magnate implied enormity, but not absolute power. Titan was more accurate. Along with Hearst and Pulitzer, his compatriots and competitors in the journalism game, Alban wielded that power with great authority. He'd gotten McKinley elected in 1896. He orchestrated the arrest and sensational trial of Annie Besant and Charles

Bradlaugh for publishing a book on contraception. He turned the nation against its favorite vaudeville performers. If he had his way about it, he was going to single-handedly get the nation into war with Cuba.

And now, he'd turned his attention on Thomas Gallier.

"Mr. Alban," Thomas said, doing everything in his power to maintain a civil tone and keep his fisted hands at his sides instead of swinging them at the man's jaw. "Always an honor."

Alban smirked. "I must admit, my boy. I'm surprised that you've graced us with your presence." Casually, he emptied his cocktail in one swallow, retired the crystal to a passing waiter, and withdrew something from his pocket. "Losing one of your investors and now *this*? Really, Thomas. It's no wonder we all worry after your health."

It was only years of practiced calm that kept Thomas from crumbling when Nehemiah Alban passed him a copy of *The Manhattan Daily*. The ink stained his gloves, leaving behind ghosts of the photograph of him being assaulted by Evelyn Cross. Alongside ran a new story decrying the recent failures of The Empire and its proprietor.

God, he would be ruined. This would be a step too far for any investors he had left to tap.

"Has this gone out?" Thomas asked, in a voice too small.

"No, but it might tomorrow morning."

"Might?"

All around them, the party swirled into a cacophony of joy that seemed to exist solely to mock Thomas's present circumstances.

"Will you join me in a drink?" Alban asked, his tone still cajoling in a way that surely concealed darker intent.

"No, thank you, sir. I never touch the stuff."

"Nonsense. Have a drink with me."

"I'm afraid I must decline."

"Unfortunate. I have a confession to make, and some liquor might have made the whole messy business go down a little smoother."

"Oh?"

"Despite myself, I've come to admire you. I have thrown everything I could at you and your little Empire and dammit, if you haven't knocked every curveball right out of the park."

The baseball analogy was lost on Thomas. But so, too, was Alban's true meaning.

"I'm not sure I follow."

"We're both men of business. Out to get what we want—by any means necessary. For a time, I didn't think you were on my level. But the more I see, the more I think you may well be more than I bargained for. Which is why I've come to decide that it would be more advantageous if we work together rather than at cross-purposes."

Thomas swallowed hard and pocketed the newspaper.

"You want to call a truce?"

"Make an alliance, let's say," Alban gently corrected.

It was impossible to halt the swell of relief that gripped Thomas. If Alban were to cease his attacks on The Empire, then the possibilities were endless. He could secure further investors, he could curate his vaudeville bill in peace, he could actually attain the success he always dreamed of. Without *The Manhattan Daily* constantly slinging awful press his way . . .

He might have a chance.

And yet.

"Forgive me if it sounds too good to be true," Thomas replied.

Something shifted in Alban's gaze, as if Thomas had passed some test he hadn't known to study for. "Do you see that girl over there?"

With the silver-tipped end of his cane, Alban pointed at a stunning, slender, button-nosed blonde in a white gown, who twirled gleefully in the arms of a portly, fair-haired gentleman in diamond cufflinks.

"The one with Edward Langmore?"

"That's my daughter. Miss Constance Alban. And Langmore . . . he has been an inconvenience."

"Ah." The Langmore family had once been amongst the most prosperous and well-connected in the city. But rumor was they'd fallen on hard times after several bad deals, which meant that now, the only virtue they had to their name *was* the name itself. Edward Langmore had little to offer the Alban family, at least the way Nehemiah would figure it. All of which was not to mention the man's appearance, and the way this quarter of society had recently come to see anyone who didn't fit the trend for lithe limbs and trim ankles.

No. It was no surprise that Alban would object to Langmore as a match for his daughter. The real shock came when Alban spoke again.

"I'm sure a handsome, clever, accomplished young man such as yourself could succeed in turning my daughter's head. You English always seem to have such a way with the ladies on this side of the Atlantic."

Locking his jaw to mask a wave of emotion, Thomas prompted, "And?"

Alban continued smoothly. "And I'm sure that my papers never turn their ire against my own family. In fact, they would do anything in their power to ensure my family's continued success. Do you understand my meaning?"

Only a fool wouldn't. The terms were simple enough. *If you woo my daughter away from a man I no longer find suitable . . . then I will help The Empire survive—no. Thrive.*

"Perfectly."

"You don't seem convinced."

He trusted that Nehemiah Alban would be true to his word—the man seemed like someone who would pride himself on that sort of thing—but what he couldn't quite accept was Constance as a kind of chess piece. From where he was standing, Constance Alban looked perfectly happy with Edward Langmore—*more* than perfectly happy. She practically glowed in his arms. Breaking up a romance such as that? The thought sat in his belly like a turned fish.

And then . . . he couldn't help but think back to Evelyn Cross and her striking eyes, her perfect legs, the way her lips curled around a precisely timed quip at his expense. The way he, too, felt as though he glowed when she was near.

But just as quickly as those barriers erected themselves, he swatted them down. This was business. This was his plan. His future. He would not turn his back on it now. He'd sacrificed too much to get here.

"I could be persuaded."

Smirking, Alban picked up another cocktail. "As a show of good faith, check the papers tomorrow, why don't you? See that I'm serious. We'll speak again soon."

Thomas tried not to think about how much those last words sounded like a threat as the man disappeared into the crowd.

⇒◆⇐

So it was that a few hours and one miserable carriage ride through the rain-drenched streets of Manhattan later, Thomas stumbled into the dark of his sitting room, thoroughly drained. He'd lost his star. And gained the chance to save his Empire from ruin.

He could do this. He could—

The moment he opened the door to his sitting room, the sight of the roaring fireplace caught his attention.

"Byrne, old man," he called out to his butler. "I thought I told you that I would be out. That you were to take the night off. Shouldn't you be halfway into a whole heap of trouble by now?"

"Well, I've been exceptionally good at staying out of trouble lately, Mr. Gallier, but I'm happy to indulge if you haven't."

That voice.

Thomas staggered. Like a siren emerging from crystal waters, Miss Evelyn Cross rose from his high-backed leather chair and stepped around it to face him.

"Miss Cross," he managed, but just barely.

How was he meant to draft coherent thoughts, much less articulate them into actual sentences, when Evelyn Cross stood in his library, uninvited and unescorted, in the *middle of the night*?

Oh, and she was completely soaked through, as if she'd just walked through the night's abysmal rain to get here. Her clothing molded to her, leaving no hint of her body to his imagination.

Besides the fabric sticking to her skin and her hair hanging limply across her lovely face, she looked fundamentally no different than she had this morning at The Empire or the night before when he'd first seen her onstage. Soft, pink lips. Bright, clear eyes. A figure meant for all manner of sins. A series of curves that conjured fantasies of stripping her *out* of those wet things.

His mouth went dry.

He checked the clock. Nearly midnight. What was he meant to say to a woman in his private rooms at midnight?

And how the hell was he going to get her out of here before he made several errors in judgment?

"You . . ." he began. "You are dripping on my floor."

"Please accept my apologies. I needed to speak with you and considering the rain, I couldn't even get a cab to run me over, much less carry me here. I did my best to dodge between the raindrops, but as you can see, I wasn't entirely successful."

It was a mistake to ask her any follow-up questions, he knew. The closest he should have gotten was *May I call you a cab*? But curiosity got the better of him.

"You needed to speak to me? And it couldn't wait until more sociable hours?"

"I happen to do most of my finest work during *un*sociable hours, Mr. Gallier. Don't you find the same?"

"I won't be much of a host."

Abrupt. Short. Unwelcoming.

In his pursuit of greatness, Thomas had taught himself to don the costume of a gentleman. Not just a suit and a top hat from the finest ateliers, mind you, but a physical and mental costume as well. His posture, his attitudes, his turns of phrase, the way he interacted with and treated people were all part of it, various accessories that marked him as the man he wanted to be.

But that costume didn't fit him very well. If he moved indelicately, it was likely to split and reveal the real man behind it all.

So when an occasion arose that threatened to rip him at the seams, he stood very still, spoke very little, and deferred to a cold, almost awkward, state.

One that could be seen as rude. One that should rid him of complications such as Evelyn Cross.

Should. But Evelyn didn't spook. She began a slow, deliberate circle around the room. Her focus was not on him, but on the walls around her.

Unwilling to take his gaze from her for even a moment, he turned slowly in place, his eyes following her path. He was dull Earth to her brilliant sun, trapped in the pull of her gravity.

"I don't need a host," she replied plainly. "I need you."

"You made it clear to me today that I'm the last person you need. If you've come for an apology—"

"Would I get one, if I asked for it?"

Yes.

"You assaulted me," he said instead.

"You deserved it."

Yes. He supposed she was right on that score, too. He should have stood up for her. Should have done what he did best—made himself a nuisance of everyone who worked for him and gave his brutal, unfiltered opinions. He should have protected her.

"But as it happens, no," she continued. "I'm not here to flagellate you—thrilling as I believe you might find such an activity. No, I'm here because our business isn't concluded. And because your friend Dr. Andrew Samson intimated that you might not be quite as fickle and weak-willed as you've shown yourself to be thus far. In fact, Dr. Samson tried to tell me you're a *good man.*" She pronounced the words as though they had been taken from a foreign language. "As far as I'm concerned, a good man is like a mermaid at a carnival sideshow—surely fake, but still, a rare and singular attraction not to be missed. How remarkable to see one in person."

He both admired and hated how she could make even an insult glitter.

"More to the point, he said you were a good man so enamored of me that you could deny me nothing. Which puts me in an excellent position to negotiate, vis-à-vis our unfinished business, particularly after the disaster you forced me to endure this afternoon."

"He's wrong," Thomas said, once again attempting to wrest control of this situation. "I could deny you a great deal."

"You're assuming I don't *enjoy* being denied, Mr. Gallier," she taunted.

What a mental image. His lips twitched upward, but he ran his hand over his mouth to hide the gesture. Laughing at her jokes was halfway to enjoying her company, and enjoying her company with his clothes on was nearly halfway to enjoying her company with his clothes *off.* And dropping his clothes was halfway to dropping his pretenses and guards, and that was more than halfway to seeing his life crumble before his eyes.

Quite an imaginative journey from point A to point Z, he realized, but he could take no chances.

"What is it you want? Why have you really come here?" he asked.

"I will save your Empire," Evelyn said magnanimously. "I will make its vaudeville show a success. I will put it on the map. I will be your star. I will pack the houses every night until every last one of your bills is paid and you're the king of Manhattan. Oh, and I'll forgive your atrocious treatment of me this afternoon. But I'll want a return on my investment."

"What is that?"

She smirked, and he knew that part of himself was lost forever to her in that moment. "Everything."

A NOTE FROM THE HISTORIAN

If this were a real history book, or if I were still trying to impress the puffed-up tweedy professors who deigned to grade my graduate school papers, this would be the part where I dryly printed the contract that Thomas Gallier and Evelyn Cross signed that fateful early October night. I would then quote legal scholars and experts to give the full context for what that old-timey handwriting said, and what it might have meant for the early days of Thomas and Evelyn's relationship.

If I were feeling especially cheeky, I might have thrown in a half-innuendo about inkwells and pens or *binding* contracts or the *body* of law, but only in a subtle, understated way so none of my stuffy old professors could fail me.

I'm sure this is where Armitage would have wanted me to go the stuffy and boring route here, rather than the "imagining what Thomas Gallier's dick was up to" one I took earlier.

Two small problems with that, though.

One? I don't want to. The best thing about not being in grad school anymore is freeing myself from the tyranny of the *Chicago Manual of Style* and any lingering shame I might have felt about wanting to give history a little glow-up.

And two? I don't *have* the contract. I know that one existed. It was referenced heavily in contemporaneous materials, and a signature page does survive. But the rest of the contract has been lost to time.

That means this is one corner of the history where I can let my imagination fill in some of the gaps. Given what I know of Thomas, given what I know of Evelyn, and given what I know about where their relationship and their professional partnership went after this point, I imagine what transpired between them that night went at least something like this . . .

CHAPTER ELEVEN

"I'm gratified you decided to see reason," Evelyn said as Thomas led her into a stuffily appointed dining room. It was becoming increasingly clear to her that this mansion on Fifth Avenue wasn't a home. Instead, it was just another part of Thomas's facade—a big old pretender, which, as far as Evelyn was concerned, could also be said of the man who lived there.

"Yes. You'll make a fine addition to The Empire's staff. Please," he said, pulling out her chair like the gentleman she knew he only pretended to be. "Be seated."

"Mr. Gallier. You're acting positively professional. You wound me."

"Heaven forbid a man should want to speak to you vertically."

A small chuckle escaped her lips. "Was that a joke? If it is, you're surprisingly funny. If it's not, then you're an absolute tragedy."

He tidily took his seat. "How so?"

"Because I rather enjoy it when men wish to speak to me in *any* direction."

What he said next surprised her. But not nearly as much as the concern that tinged every word. "Always?"

"No. Not always," she muttered, shocked into telling the truth. Strange. She didn't like telling the truth around men. If she'd learned anything from her mother, it was that information was ammunition to men, and no woman should ever willingly disarm herself. Quickly, she backpedaled into a more comfortable state—flirtation. "But I believe I would with you."

"If you're quite finished, please. Take a seat."

The rebuff stung and she reminded herself, again, of the reasons why she was in this man's dining room. She owed Dr. Samson Jules's life. She had the power to save her career and the livelihoods of her friends. She could become famous again. Beloved. Wealthy. Wanted. Undeniable.

But at the same time, she had to admit that it was that mystery of him, the promise of Thomas Gallier, that had ultimately made her come to this house this evening. That had pushed her here, to this place, with this man, staring down the barrel of this future. He was a puzzle she was figuring out—a game she was playing—and by God, she wasn't about to let him win.

"I prefer to negotiate *vertically*, if you don't mind. Power positions, and all that."

"Whatever possessed you to believe this is a negotiation, I'll never understand. You will be my employee."

"So, under you? Directionally speaking, that is."

"No—"

"Quite right. Because I won't be your employee. I'll be your partner."

There was no mistaking the way the muscle in his jaw tensed. Interesting. "I don't *do* partners."

"Not yet, you don't. We haven't even *begun* our negotiations."

"Of all the presumptuous cheek—"

A flash of sincerity struck her. "You can't do this alone, Mr. Gallier. No matter how much you may wish to."

Their eyes met across the table. He said nothing. An admission.

"Now," Evelyn proceeded. "As you pointed out so helpfully when I arrived, these are not exactly sociable hours. If you wish to sleep before sunrise, I suggest we commence. Yes?"

"Your salary, then."

He threw out a number quadruple her current pay. She would have taken half as much. Not that he needed to know that. Or suspect it.

"I'm afraid that doesn't quite meet my expectations," Evelyn said. "I won't be underpaid."

"Underpaid?"

"What you've proposed there is a *star's* salary. Fine enough for someone to tread the boards, certainly. Generous, even. But now, I'm a star *and* management. I propose a twenty percent increase on that number there."

"Fifteen percent. But I'll make you earn that salary, Miss Cross. I'm a difficult boss to please."

She smirked. "I'm counting on it."

He ducked his head, a nervous habit that delighted her. Every time he did it, she tasted the sweet heat of victory—and perhaps something else? She shook the thought from her mind. That was a matter for her to consider later.

This, she could handle. A man enamored of her. As long as the feelings went that direction and none other, she was safe.

"And I want three shows a day instead of four."

"Very well, but no Mondays off."

"Mondays off, but four shows on Sunday instead of three."

"Done."

With one of those newfangled ballpoint pens, Thomas took down notes, which she watched with a keen eye from her place across the table. Her heart told her this was not the kind of man who would deceive her in negotiations, but still . . . one couldn't be too careful.

"And I'll want a cut of the box office of course," she said, shamelessly pushing. "Three percent should be acceptable. It is my show and my name on the marquee, after all."

"Three percent on everything left after the bills are paid."

Evelyn glanced his way. He should have looked ridiculous sitting alone at the impossibly long table—his greatness minimized by the empty stretches all around him.

But he was perfectly at home. In control. Regal, even.

She needed to pull her head out of the sentimental slop bucket. She pressed harder—reaching for anything that might keep her on track.

She'd come here in the middle of the night to catch *him* off guard, not vice versa.

"I'll trade my three percent for the ability to unionize and strike," she blurted.

That caught his attention. He peered up at her through dark, hooded lashes.

"Unionize?"

"The unions that already exist are for white men, which means many of the performers I have in mind have no real protection against their employers. I want The Empire to be a union of their own. And I mean *real* unionizing. No strikebreakers. No union busters."

"That could cost me a fortune. I would have to light this contract I'm writing with you on fire the moment you decide—"

His attention was sharp. Undivided. And if there was one thing Evelyn knew how to do, it was use a man's attention.

She went for her wet glove and took to slowly peeling it off her skin—like a striptease. With satisfaction, she noted how Thomas catalogued every millimeter of skin she revealed.

The glove dropped to the table. She went for the second one. When that joined the first, she started for the button on her coat.

Unable to break his hypnotized stare, Thomas licked his lips. Had he even noticed he'd done that?

A thrill shot through Evelyn's body.

"What are you doing?"

"Getting out of my wet things. You don't want your star to catch her death, do you? That streptococcus is going around. Now, we were talking about unionizing and striking."

Button—pop. Button—pop. Button—pop. Button . . .

The final button on her coat *popped* open, and Evelyn dropped it to the floor in a puddle of ruined velvet. She hadn't been able to seduce him last night—fine. But she knew he wanted her, no matter how he tried to hide it.

She would just have to use that to her advantage.

The more flesh he feared she'd bare, the faster he'd be inclined to negotiate.

"Fine," he conceded.

The one saving grace for Thomas—or curse, depending on how you looked at it—was that women's clothing was so damned cumbersome. Evelyn gracefully slipped out of her overvest next.

"And sick pay."

"Yes, yes."

Her cuffs.

"Integrated dressing rooms?"

"Mm-hm."

Her rumpled collar.

"Every other Sunday off."

Her overskirt. This time, just a nod of the head as his eyes remained trained on the table before him.

"New sets."

Her first boot. Another nod.

"A new wardrobe."

Her second boot. Another nod.

By the time Evelyn—her only proper clothes her opened blouse and underskirt—collapsed into a chair, the man was a bundle of shaking nerves. His hands clenched so tight she worried his ballpoint pen would burst into a geyser of ink any second.

Yes. She had him right where she wanted him. Time for the grand finale. Lifting her legs, she placed one shapely ankle on the table, and then crossed the other over the top of it. Her skirts cascaded up her thighs, revealing sumptuous, stocking-clad legs.

She was well aware, as he must have been, that he'd seen her in even less clothing than this just last night. But the act of taking it all off for him, the closeness of his bedroom just upstairs, the understanding that there was no one in this house to catch them if they fell . . .

It proved intoxicating. Even to herself.

Her hands traced slowly up her thighs. She toyed idly with the bows linking her stockings to her bloomers.

"And you and I are partners in this. Fifty-fifty on all decision making."

"Miss Cross, I've already told you. I don't *do* partners."

Surely Thomas had meant for that to be a firm declaration of terms. Instead, he chose that precise moment to finally change a look at her, only to find Evelyn slowly working her silk stockings down her legs.

His own voice broke. And he stared, slack-jawed, at her bare flesh within stroking distance.

"And how has that been working out for you so far, hm?" she asked, barely louder than a whisper. "All of that control, and where has it gotten you?"

She lay the stocking out across the table between them—her line in the sand. Then, she dragged her skirt up to reveal her other leg.

Heat built between her thighs as she became certain that's where his attentions were traveling. God, she wanted this man in her bed.

And it felt indescribably powerful to feel him want her—especially now, when she was beginning to worry she'd lost her touch.

"Very well," he breathed. "I will want something else in exchange, though," he managed, his voice barely above a growl.

"I'm listening."

This was it, she believed. The moment he would give in and tie the two of them in a simple knot of sin.

Instead—

"I won't see you outside of work hours."

She dropped the bow on her second stocking. Her first fumble of the evening. "You don't want to see me outside of The Empire?"

She didn't do a winning job of hiding her surprisingly potent hurt.

He watched the rain against the window as if it were more appealing than she could ever be. That stung, too. "We're going to be business partners, Miss Cross. For the sake of our work, we should restrict our relationship to those hours only. Friendship, fondness, affection, these things can complicate a partnership."

"My, how I envy the woman who gets to marry you," she deadpanned.

A wince crossed his face so fast she almost didn't catch it.

"What about Dr. Samson? You're friendly with him outside of working hours, aren't you?"

"With his familial connections, Dr. Samson provides me access to certain sectors of Manhattan society from which we new money tramps generally are barred. He makes me look respectable. Ensures the populace that I'm not going to suffer a mental collapse any moment. Therefore, our social hours and calls *are* part of our work. You and I, on the other hand, will have no reason to interact outside of the walls of The Empire."

"And why is this so important to you? Are you so ashamed of me?" she asked, passing off a genuine fear as a joke.

"No—"

"Ah, so you're terrified that if you have a taste of me, you'll never stop begging for more?"

"I—"

"Say no more, sir. I understand. You wouldn't be the first man who's had to tie himself to the ship's mast to keep himself from falling prey to my charms. Fear not. I won't darken your doorstep ever again."

"I didn't say there would *never* be occasion to see one another, just that I will be otherwise engaged and it wouldn't be appropriate—"

"No, no. Don't try to spare my feelings. You've been quite clear on this point. We'll maintain a respectful, professional distance from one another. If I see you walking down Fifth Avenue, I'll turn and walk the other way. I'll steal a police horse and ride it all the way down to the Bowery, where I'll hop on a boat to South America. I'll—"

There he went again, ducking that head of his. But he was too slow this time. She caught the laughter in his eyes. "You're teasing me, aren't you, Miss Cross?"

Warmth blossomed in her heart, unbidden. "Tease you? My *business partner*? Sir, I've never heard the like and I won't sit here and be insulted by such spurious attacks on my character."

They settled into a companionable quiet. What a pair they made. A surprising fondness itched at her heart, and firmly, she turned her mind back to their negotiation.

"If," she said, "you will not be seeing me outside of work hours, I will require a trade-off."

"And that is?"

"If your nights are yours, then your days are mine."

The second stocking met its mate on the table. Thomas visibly gulped as Evelyn went to the bottom button on her blouse. His breathing went ragged.

"'Yours'?"

"If you'll have me."

"What need could you possibly have for me?"

She smirked. "Besides the obvious?"

"Please," he croaked.

Button. "If we're meant to be partners, then the intricacies of our labor should be shared, yes?" *Button.* "There will be costumes to design, sets to approve, visits to our competitors, programs to lay out and print. In short, I will need you for everything. Just as you need me."

Her hands stilled. A thought gripped her. And against her better judgment, she told him the truth.

"I think I like the idea," she said softly. "Not working alone any longer. What do you say to that?"

"I say if it's best for The Empire, I will do it. *During work hours.*"

Their eyes met. And suddenly this whole charade—the stripping, the cajoling, the half-hearted attempt at seduction—all felt terribly silly. Every time he looked at her like that, she felt naked enough.

Gripping his nearby pen, she hastily signed one of his papers, a scribble to serve as her mark. She then shot up, scrambling into her clothes and fighting her boots back onto her feet.

"Excellent. With all of that settled, then, I'll leave you to draw up the legalese, yes? Send a copy to my home—Beatrice Matterly's, home to all the lady stars. I'll be terribly busy this weekend, so I'm afraid I won't be able to see you again until Monday. A shame, that! Well, you know what they say, good things come to those who wait! That's what I always say, anyway . . ."

She prattled the entire way through dressing, leaving not even a breath of time for him to interject. It was only moments later, when she reached for the front door handle, that he finally got a word in.

"And what about the bill?"

"Oh, don't worry. I'll send you *all* of the bills, Mr. Gallier."

"I mean the bill for the show," he deadpanned.

"Leave that to me," she rushed, trying to drown out the sound of *leave, leave, leave* roaring in her ears. "I'll have everything arranged by Monday morning."

With that, she moved to swing the door closed behind her and once again submerge herself in the deluge outside. But a firm hand gripped the door before she could manage it.

Thomas lingered in the doorway, neither moving to pull her deeper into the house nor shove her outside. Her breath fluttered.

"Is there something else I can do for you, sir?" she asked, her voice low. Wanting and not all at once.

His hand flexed around the doorframe.

"I . . . I *am* sorry for what transpired this afternoon. You aren't a novelty act, Miss Cross. You are a wonder. A devil, too, I think. But a wonder all the same."

Her usual impulse would have been to tease him or twist it into an innuendo of some kind. However, words failed her. All except: "Thank you, sir. I look forward to working with you."

"And you."

The warmth of the house and him beckoned her back. But she couldn't let herself. Sex was one thing. But to let him smile at her and apologize and tell her she was a wonder?

No. The rain was preferable. She stepped out into the night.

"You may keep those stockings, by the by," she called over her shoulder. "A small token of my appreciation."

A NOTE FROM THE HISTORIAN

x *Thomas Gallier* ✗ *Miss Evelyn Cross*

That was all it took. The only element of the original contract to survive, it was two little signatures on a few leaves of paper—one so simple, one so flamboyant—that made everything else come to pass.

At this point, Evelyn Cross wanted Thomas—and as far as their relationship went, that was the beginning and end of it. She would do anything to conquer him.

Surely, his influence, his wealth, his power attracted her. She was never one to back down from a challenge either, and he represented a hell of a challenge to her. But it feels like it was more than that, too. Something to do with the flash of lightning she couldn't help but feel when she caught him looking at her.

That was the real risk, the seed that was planted the moment she opened her dressing room—and her life—to him. And Evelyn thought that the best way to inoculate herself against that risk was sex. The kind of transactional but pleasurable sex that she knew all too well at this point in her rollicking vaudeville existence. If she conquered him, if she got him into bed, it meant that he was just another in a long line of guys she banged—not someone to consider romantically or to, horror of horrors, actually fall in love with.

So she had one goal, which she would pursue single-mindedly: getting some Thomas Gallier dick.

On the other hand, Thomas couldn't fall prey to Evelyn's charms. He didn't do casual. He didn't do sex. He didn't do anything that he might find even mildly enjoyable. He had a big, big secret. And he worried that letting anyone get close to him would result in that secret getting exposed. All of that means sex and romance were firmly off the table, especially with someone who captured him like Evelyn Cross did. He controlled his life tightly to keep his secrets safe and his plans on track, and he couldn't let Evelyn jeopardize that. Not to mention the fact that he had to keep his options open where Miss Constance Alban was concerned—another reason that he and Evelyn becoming an item was a non-starter.

So he would try to single-mindedly pursue his own goal: keeping Evelyn Cross out of his pants.

But, c'mon. There's only so much you can do to avoid the undeniable.

Present Day

WHEN WE FIRST STARTED WORKING TOGETHER, ARMITAGE KEPT the attic, where all of Thomas's old relics were kept, under firm lock and key. He was the keeper of the records, and when I needed something, he would bring it down to me in the study, one box at a time.

It was infuriating, sitting beneath all that history, day in and day out. So close, yet so far. I hated being drip-fed information, and I hated the nettling feeling that he was keeping something from me.

I was also annoyed. Because reconstructing history one banker's box at a time did not exactly make for timely work.

So, one day, I resolved to do something about it. I was the historian here. Armitage was the money. I would decide how this historical research would go, thank you very much.

"Ah, good morning, Phoebe."

"Good morning, Armitage."

It was a random Tuesday, with our normal greetings. He continued working behind his desk, pretending to only half-notice my existence, as I dropped my things off on the leather couch where I'd taken to doing my reading.

But then, instead of plopping down into it like normal, I strode across the room, past his desk, and swiped the brass key from its home next to an antique inkwell, never once letting my usual, cheerful grin slip from my face.

I was halfway up the nearby servants' staircase by the time he realized what I'd done.

Tough luck, Mr. Gallier. That's what happens when you pretend not to pay attention to the help.

"What are you doing?" he asked, catching up with me breathlessly as I ascended.

"I want to see the attic."

"What do you need?" he asked, double-timing the steps and cutting me off at the second landing. "I can get it for you."

When he reached for it, I held the heavy brass key behind my back, out of his reach.

"That's alright. I'm good to get it myself."

"I'd be a terrible host if I let you go up there. It's a mess—"

"Armitage. I don't just want something out of the attic. I want to *see* the attic. You can't do that on my behalf."

With that, I tucked the key into my pocket and skirted around him. He wasted no time in pursuit.

"I just don't know what you'd want with it. I mean, it's just a bunch of dusty old boxes. Nothing interesting."

"In my experience, I've found that dusty old boxes usually hold the most interesting stuff in a house like this. And you must think so too, considering how much you're paying me to go through them."

We went back and forth like that for three more flights of creaking stairs. When, finally, we reached the white-painted door of the attic, he stood in front of it, blocking my entrance.

All this time, I'd kept my cool. I was levelheaded and breezy. How strange it was to feel in control when he was so clearly out of it.

"C'mon, let me through," I said with a resigned sigh. When it looked like that wouldn't happen, I tightened my grip on the brass key. "I mean, why won't you let me see it? What's the big deal?"

He shifted his weight from one foot to the other.

"I'm just not used to giving someone this much . . . access."

A pang of sympathy struck me. I'd thought this was about control. About needing to feel big and powerful, even over something as simple as a locked door. But now, it felt like something else. Like he was afraid of letting someone in.

Literally.

That sympathy, though, didn't eat away at my resolve.

"I think you'll live."

"But—"

I waved the key. "Step aside, or I'm leaving right now. Forget your research. Forget Evelyn and Thomas. I'm not working with someone who doesn't trust me."

"You wouldn't do that."

"I'm learning how to drive a hard bargain."

It took him a minute to catch my meaning. But when he did, he couldn't hide the small lift of his smile.

The last few workdays had been occupied by reconstructing the particulars of Evelyn and Thomas's contract. Though the contract itself was missing, I'd taken plenty of circumstantial evidence and pieced together a rough idea of what they might have agreed on in that fateful document.

Thomas and I had been joking that Evelyn missed her calling as a negotiator.

Now, it looked like I was following in her footsteps.

"Ah. Evelyn's rubbing off on you, then?"

"Yes," I said, playfully narrowing my eyes. It was fun to channel her boldness until it felt like my own instead of something borrowed. "You've been warned."

He heeded the warning and stepped aside. I slid the key into the lock. It groaned from disuse as it turned. But then, it opened.

"Oh, *wow*."

I never could have prepared myself for what I found in that attic.

It was a treasure trove. An intimidatingly stacked playland of history. Overflowing boxes of handbills and posters. File organizers of papers and documents. Steamer trunks, jewelry boxes, discarded furniture.

A lifetime in ephemera, all hidden away.

Without further ado, I began scrounging through it all. Armitage's stare over my shoulder was piercing, but I didn't care. After a few minutes, I forgot he was even there. These were *genuine* artifacts, touched during the last hundred years only for dusting.

A historian's dream.

My dream.

I bubbled over, unable to contain my excitement. I found postcards from Steeplechase Park and handwritten sheet music. Rough-draft design plans for The Empire with Thomas Gallier's personal notes on them in careful pencil. Newspaper clippings and a Jules Moreau poster in full *Vanity Fair* costume. Gramophone records of some of vaudeville's hottest stars.

"You should take some of this stuff downstairs," I said. "Think of how cool the house would look if you decorated it with all of Thomas's original stuff."

"Oh, no. Nothing like that. I'm going to throw it out when this is all over."

"But you can't," I protested.

Armitage shrugged. "No one's needed this junk for years. I don't think anyone's going to miss it when it's gone."

On that point, we would have to disagree. However, before I could make my stand, I stumbled across a stunning hat. One I recognized.

It was one of Evelyn Cross's hats. She'd been photographed and sketched in it dozens of times, with its distinctive confectionary swirl of pink feathers and paste diamonds.

With shaking hands, I picked it up and inspected it. The years had not been kind to this hat, but it still held a kind of magic—at least, to me.

I'm sure I looked as silly and awed as I felt. Again, Armitage's opinion of me was the furthest thing from my mind, even as his stare burned, reddening my cheeks.

Then, he reached out for it, gently wresting it from my grip.

My heart sunk. I'd gone too far. Touching the old papers was one thing, I guessed, but coveting antique millinery must have crossed one of those invisible lines he was always drawing.

But to my surprise, he softly asked:

"You want to try it on?"

"I couldn't—"

"Like I said. Everything's getting thrown away when you finish your research. It's just old junk. Come on," he said, parroting my earlier words back to me. "What's the big deal?"

I nodded and gestured for the hat. I'd expected him to hand it over and let me sort it out myself. But instead, he closed the space between us and settled the hat atop my head, perfectly perched above my messy low bun.

His fingertips brushed my ears. I told myself that my speeding heart was just, like, from the excitement of the historical finds or whatever. Nothing else.

"How do I look?" I asked, once he stepped away.

He opened his mouth to say something. But he had a terrible habit of self-editing, so instead of sharing that thought, he closed his mouth, reconsidered, and then finally landed on, "See for yourself."

Whipping a velvet drape off a gilded mirror tucked away in the corner of the room, he revealed its oxidizing face. I shuffled over to it, inspecting my reflection.

I'd often wondered what it was like to be Evelyn Cross. To walk down the street knowing that everyone wanted you—even if they pretended that they didn't, or even if they'd never admit it out loud. And yes, she was beautiful. Yes, she was talented. Yes, she'd fought to build a life for herself that no one could take away.

But she also had this hat. This hat that made me feel like I was wearing a cloud and a halo all at once, like I was a heavenly body gracing this sordid earth with my luminous presence.

I'm sure I didn't look beautiful. But *damn*, did I feel it.

And the feeling couldn't be contained. As I inspected myself, I began to sing one of Evelyn's famous songs, preening this way and that, jumping into a little dance when the energy carried me away. I was only brought slamming back down to earth when I nearly tripped over a stray cigar box and had to steady myself against the mirror.

My eyes slid to Armitage, standing over my shoulder. His expression was completely unreadable. Every muscle in his body was rigid. He looked . . . well, I don't know how he looked, exactly. I just knew that the laughter died on my lips. I fiddled with the moth-bitten ribbons dangling down past my shoulders.

"Are you regretting it?" I asked with a self-effacing smile.

He blinked, as if suddenly remembering where he was. "Regretting what?"

"Getting stuck with me."

A considering silence.

"I'm one of the most powerful men in this entire city, Phoebe. Do you think I can get *stuck* anywhere?"

I snort-laughed. Attractive. "Okay, *brag*—"

"I'm just trying to say . . . if I'm somewhere, it's because I want to be."

The dismissive humor left my body. There was nothing else in my world but the sincerity of those words.

He *wanted* to be here. With me.

"Keep the key," Armitage said, by way of goodbye. "And the hat, if you like it so much. Someone ought to enjoy all this old junk."

Then, he was gone. Leaving me alone with a big, empty room full of his family's secrets.

PART THREE

I JUST CAN'T MAKE MY EYES BEHAVE

CHAPTER TWELVE

By Monday morning, Thomas was ready to acknowledge that he had made a terrible mistake. There was a reason that he worked alone. If he was both master and commander of his fate, then all successes and failures were his own.

So why had he allowed himself to pass off his most important work, the staffing of The Empire's bill, to Miss Evelyn Cross? Why had he agreed to take her on as a *partner*?

"She seduced you, then?"

"*Doctor.* What a thing to say—and so close to the press."

Thomas cast a look around at the gaggle of reporters who were scattered throughout the audience, waiting for Miss Cross to debut the full range of their new performers.

Andrew simply shrugged. "I beg your pardon, but unless you've suddenly turned into an H.G. Wells character and had your brain replaced or some other such nonsense, it's the only explanation."

Thomas sighed. Yes, he supposed it did look that way from the outside. But Thomas had his reasons, reasons he answered for in equally hushed tones, lest any of the reporters nearby was tempted to eavesdrop.

"I spoke to Nehemiah Alban last night," Thomas confessed.

"Yes, I noticed one of his reporters here." Andrew smirked. "A stunning reversal from your previous policy to *shoot all* Manhattan Daily *reporters on sight.*"

Choosing to ignore the jibe, Thomas shifted his gaze to the crimson velvet curtains concealing the stage. "He's agreed to help raise The Empire's profile as we approach the grand opening next month."

"That doesn't sound like him. What does he want from you in exchange?"

Thomas kept his gaze stubbornly on the stage before them. "He wants me to pursue his daughter."

At that, Andrew's usual good humor seemed to dissolve.

"And how do you feel about this?"

"Less than enthused," Thomas said.

The understatement of the century. The longer he thought about it, the more distasteful the entire business seemed—for a multitude of reasons, including the one Andrew had the audacity to call him on.

"I should think so. It's a hell of a thing to court one woman when you're fixated on another."

"I am not fixated. Miss Cross is a real talent, and her reach through the Manhattan theatrical community is unparalleled. She will bring us a fine bill, and if the papers are to be believed, she has even more of a knack for publicity than I do."

"I'm inclined to point out that I simply said *another*. I didn't say that you were fixated on Evelyn Cross specifically. You're telling on yourself here, friend."

Damn. Andrew had him there.

"Miss Cross and I have agreed to keep our relationship strictly professional."

Another fact about which Thomas found himself less than enthused. But he certainly wasn't going to say as much to Andrew.

He also didn't tell Andrew how, that morning, Evelyn had arrived at the theater when he did—at six thirty, hours before anyone else was due. As much as he had designed The Empire to surprise and delight, these were feelings that he rarely felt, but that was the only way he could describe his reaction to her arrival in his office doorway as the sun was just beginning to peek through the surrounding buildings outside. She was a human kaleidoscope, dazzling him at every turn.

And yet, the warmth of those first minutes had quickly dissipated. Over coffee and pastry in his office, she informed him briefly of her plan to present the bill this morning, and then, as soon as she'd wiped the last crumbs from her skirt, she'd disappeared into the theater, not to be seen again until Thomas and Andrew and the reporters arrived for this very appointment.

It was a brusque, professional encounter. Not unkind or cold, mind you. But focused. Disciplined. Thomas should have been thrilled.

And yet, when he eventually arrived in the theater for Evelyn's little spectacle, he couldn't find the strength to unclench his jaw or relax his hand from its fist.

Strange, that.

Oh, sure, he greeted the newspapermen with his usual restrained friendliness and helped them all to their seats with promises of a fine preview, but still . . . he was nettled by Miss Evelyn Cross. Despite the fact that he had no right to be. Despite the fact that he'd orchestrated their entire contract to keep himself from feeling *anything* for, toward, or about her.

When the clock struck twelve, Andrew and Thomas took their seats in the third row, behind the reporters. The doctor lowered his voice. "So you roped her into this far-fetched contract, under which you think you'll be safe from her charms? Safe, I mean, to pursue a sure-to-be-lucrative dalliance with Constance Alban. All while you and Miss Cross are business partners?"

"That's the idea, anyway," Thomas said, reminding himself that this was for the best. That their arrangement would pop these bubbling feelings between him and the woman who so fascinated him.

"It won't work," Andrew said.

"And why not?"

"Because rules like that are made to be broken. And I imagine Miss Evelyn Cross will have a very, very good time doing just that."

If he'd had the time, Thomas would have protested. But just then, the woman in question appeared onstage—and the unveiling of The Empire's acts began.

"Good morning, gentlemen!" Evelyn stood directly at center stage, with an ease that told everyone she belonged exactly there.

Finding himself marveling at the sight of her—and the feelings that sight invoked—Thomas flipped through a stack of notepaper in his lap as though this were all some tiresome formality.

If Evelyn noticed this, she didn't have time to comment.

She raised her hands and clapped twice.

Showtime.

At once, an electric spotlight encircled Evelyn's fine form. The orchestra pit roared to happy life . . . and the show commenced.

"To begin," Evelyn called in her best announcer's tone, "let me introduce you to our orchestra."

The limelight slipped down to illuminate the pit below her, where seventeen musicians sat in white gowns, with deep black bows in their hair. They struck up a rousing rendition of "Grand Ole Rag," filling the theater with explosive crashes of cymbals and blaring horn counterpoints.

"Not only is this Manhattan's premier band, but take a look, gentlemen. They are also the world's first, and only, band made up entirely of ladies."

Chills ran up and down Thomas's spine—and they had nothing to do with the snickers of the journalists who peered into the orchestra pit for a better look. A flash of uncertainty crossed Evelyn's face, but she recovered, continuing in spectacular fashion.

"And now," she continued, "to our bill. You'll find no greater collection of acts anywhere in Manhattan, these United States, or the wide world."

"This ought to be good," one of the other journalists muttered, making no effort to lower his voice. "If she opens with a lady band, I can only imagine what other plagues she's wrought."

The song shifted to something more driving and insistent. Evelyn reached for a great gold braid at the edge of the stage, gripping it for dear life.

"Humble denizens of The Empire . . . I present to you, our Sacerdos of high art and entertainment!"

A cymbal crashed deep in the orchestra pit, and, with a great heave of her arms, Evelyn pulled the curtains open.

The stage behind it was, to Thomas's shock, empty. But Evelyn relished the obvious jolt she'd given the men, before a figure quickly filled it.

"Nathaniel Fry," she called with a grand gesture as a tall, slender black man in a perfectly cut tuxedo sliced his way across the stage on silver-tipped shoes, his percussive steps joining with the drums of the band's song. "The greatest dancer the world has ever known."

"Julia Moreau." *Vanity Fair*'s Lady Rebecca Crawley floated to center stage, where she triumphantly ripped off her white-powdered wig and presented the very male head underneath. "A female impersonator of great renown."

"Annie Parker." A chained woman in a wheelchair. "A world-famous illusionist and escape artist."

"Melvyn Sorrel. The human joke factory."

"Alejandro Cansino. Cuba's finest opera singer."

"Tyrone Furthman. The Human Twister."

"Betsy Washington. The Maravian Medium."

Thomas wasn't quite sure what to make of the commercial prospects of this lineup of outcasts and misfits. His eyes flickered to the stage and the journalists, hoping to gauge their reactions, but what he saw wasn't precisely promising. If the laughter and chatter was any indication, then this chaotic assemblage would not pass muster amongst most fashionable audiences today.

However.

Thomas didn't lose heart. He should have. But he didn't.

Because for the first time since he'd started building this wild fantasy of his, he wasn't bored. He wasn't dreading each new body that stepped out onstage. He didn't taste the metallic sting of failure in his mouth.

He was excited. Hopeful, even.

It occurred to him then that the reason he hadn't found that "undeniable" he'd been seeking for so long was that he hadn't *actually* been looking for it. Undeniable implied a kind of oneness, singularity, uniqueness, but all he'd been searching for was pleasing, inoffensive, acceptable. Whatever the press agreed was *de rigueur.*

His respect for Evelyn Cross grew once again. It had taken her all of two days to realize that which he'd been oblivious to for years. She'd created undeniable out of nothing but her own indominable spirit and her thirty closest friends.

"And finally," Evelyn called, setting herself at center stage, finally joining the performers. "May I present a new act of my own creation. Evelyn Cross and The Dancing Dozen. The first dancing troupe in this or any other nation made up entirely of beautiful, talented, and deliciously plump women."

From the wings, twelve dancers—six on each side—shuffle-ball-changed their way out to center stage, their matching red skirts frilling about their white-stockinged knees. They were graceful and elegant in a simple, understated way—the kind of artistic flair that one often saw in a working-class dance hall instead of the Russian ballet.

They were a magnificent constellation of big, beautiful women. And Evelyn was their lodestar. Just as he'd dreamed.

Yet . . . the newspapermen didn't clap. Not a single one of them said a word. Instead, they laughed.

And in that moment, Thomas's esteem for this show and this bill collapsed at his feet.

He might be delighted by the show onstage, but the tastemakers of the media did not see what he saw in this assemblage of talent. Thomas Gallier was confident, but he wasn't foolish. He needed the newspapers on his side if The Empire was going to be a success.

That's when he realized he had two choices. The first: fire Evelyn, dissolve their contract, and go back to the bland, palatable entertainments that had previously sashayed and sung their way across his stage. The second: keep this bill exactly as it was—and take up with Constance Alban.

CHAPTER THIRTEEN

FOR THE NEXT HOUR, THE EMPIRE WAS LESS THEATRE AND MORE zoo. For all their initial disinterest in Evelyn's bill, the newsmen came alive when the performers left the stage and began to walk amongst them, posing for pictures and answering all manner of intrusive questions. For her own part, Evelyn resisted the urge to drape herself across Thomas's lap—it would make for *such* a scandalous newspaper front page, and he was *so* stiff and stoic in that chair of his. Instead, she positioned herself on the edge of the stage, where the photographers could snap the choicest pictures of her legs and call up queries from below.

Once they were gone, however, Thomas called her to his office: a bare, intimidating space situated on the second floor of The Empire.

She rolled in on a wave of triumph . . .

"I think that went very well." She beamed.

. . . And immediately crashed into the impenetrable wall of him.

"You do, do you?"

He offered her a cup of coffee. She accepted, careful to let their fingers brush. He pulled away almost violently.

"Gracious, Mr. Gallier. You'd think you'd never seen journalists at the theater before. Are you sure this vaudeville thing is right for you? You'll need far more nerve if you wish to survive this game. They're all like this. I've never done a preview for the press that didn't go exactly like that. Or worse."

She sipped her coffee, unable to break her long-ingrained habit of seductively licking her lips as she returned the cup to the saucer.

Thomas's brow curved, clearly uncertain if the tic was genuine or a part of the same game she'd been playing with the little striptease she'd performed at his home a few nights previous.

"Do you think this is the correct decision, what you're doing here with this bill you've put together?"

"Yes."

"Awfully certain of yourself."

"Awfully certain of my friends. Do you have any idea what this vaudeville show of ours represents? Sex and scandal and titillation and outrage. A whole crew of the best performers this side of the Mississippi River—all in one place because no one else wants to touch them. Because they're all afraid of what moralists might say. But *you* are brave enough to do this. And *you* are going to have absurd returns for your trouble. Those reporters may have seemed like cold fish today, but they are going to write your Empire into a phenomenal success. Mark my words."

She desperately wanted to say *we. We are brave enough to do it. Our. Our Empire.* But given the way he seemed intent on keeping them as separate, discrete quantities, she bit her tongue.

"No," he said decisively. "You're enough scandal for one show. We will tone down the rest of the acts. You'd still be the star, of course. Don't you worry about that—"

"I won't."

"Excellent. I shouldn't want you to trouble yourself."

"You misunderstand. I won't be your star without them."

If she hadn't been listening intently, Evelyn might have missed the hitch in his breath. Or the way his big hands twitched.

"And why not?"

What a foolish question. "Because there's no use in having power if I keep it all for myself. I negotiated our entire deal to get these people working again. I won't go back on that because you're frightened of a few reporters."

"I'm not frightened of them," he retorted, though everything about him screamed the opposite. "I have this well enough in hand."

The temperature in the room rose, the tension along with it. Under such pressure, Evelyn might have retreated, but she couldn't. Not when it meant abandoning the people she loved.

"Trust me," she said, her voice low and certain.

"I don't trust anyone," he replied. He vacated his chair behind the desk and took to pacing. "It's why I'm still here. And you should do the same. I can't believe you would risk your career for those people—"

"Every day of the week and twice on Sundays."

"They could ruin you. They could ruin *me*, The Empire—"

"They won't."

This wasn't like any of their previous conversations. Every time they'd spoken before, she kept her sensuality between them, only occasionally peeking past it, then darting away again with a pretty pout or a flutter of lashes. Now, in her simple working clothes, she stood on her principles instead of her passions.

And she felt all the stronger for it.

"Please, Miss Cross," he implored. "Reconsider."

"No. This is what we do for people we love. We share the bad so we can share the good. No matter the cost or consequences."

"Do you think they would do the same for you?"

"Yes."

"Really?"

"*Yes*," she repeated, more forcefully than before.

Thomas lorded over her now. She got the sense that he wasn't fighting against her bill, but something else. Something he didn't care to share with her. "Those people would leave you and take everything you care about. This is a harsh world. Bitter and cruel and deceptive."

"You don't think I know that? I know that better than you, Mister Silk Top Hat."

He didn't so much as flinch. "Then why won't you see reason? Be my star, dismiss that motley crew you dragged in here this morning, and go about your life having saved your own skin."

Checking the watch in her dress pocket, Evelyn feigned a yawn. "Is this all you have to say to me? It's growing tiresome."

They had a contract. He couldn't fire her. She was disinterested in a fight, especially about something so serious to her as her friends, but what did interest her was getting under his skin. He was stuck in this with her, and if he thought his little "daytime" clause would protect her from breaking into that shell of his, he was as foolish about this as he was about vaudeville. "Just a question, if I may, Mr. Gallier. You say my friends could ruin me. That I shouldn't trust them. But considering that *I* could ruin *you*, why am I here?"

"We are not speaking about us."

"I'll answer for myself, then. My friends are here because I love them. Each and every one. To cut them off would be to lose parts of myself. I don't know why you would want *me* and not *them*, Mr. Gallier, but without your answer, I can only assume that your answer might be closer to mine than you would ever admit."

It was a challenge. *I know you like me. Confess.*

When he didn't, she just shrugged. "I won't stay here without them. If you fire them, you will lose me, too."

Their eyes met. An emotion she didn't recognize crossed his. Something like resignation.

Or regret.

"Very well, then. I will ensure that the press spins this bill of yours appropriately. No matter what it takes, I'll make it work."

Such a simple thing to do, and yet, he said it with the resignation of a man signing his own death certificate.

She would circle back to that. But for now, she had to take her victories where she could.

"Lovely. Now, are you ready, Mr. Gallier?"

He blinked. "Ready? For what?"

"We have an agreement," she said, marching for the door. "Your days are mine."

PART FOUR

THE BAND PLAYS ON

CHAPTER FOURTEEN

THOMAS SHOULD HAVE LET HER GO WHEN HE HAD THE CHANCE.

The proposition in her dressing room, the late-night negotiations, this morning over coffee—he had so many opportunities to be rid of her. Any one of those opportunities would have saved him from the dangers of being near her.

If I could ruin you, why am I here?

He'd convinced himself it was safer, keeping her close, but barricaded by their contract.

Now, he knew what a fool he was.

There was still nearly a month until the opening of The Empire. Nearly a month he would have to endure her persistent closeness and the brush of her honey perfume as it danced against his cheek and the delicious crumple of her gowns as they cinched over her river-bend hips.

Nearly a month to resist her. More like a lifetime. More like an eternity. More like an impossibility.

"So, Mr. Gallier. My place, or yours?"

"I beg your pardon?" he asked, pausing at the top of the spiral staircase leading them both away from The Empire's executive offices and toward the main arcade.

"I'm sure we *both* have business matters to attend to," Evelyn amended, fluttering those damn long lashes of hers as though she hadn't *just* intentionally flirted. "Shall we attend to yours first, or my own?"

"You mean you didn't have a reason for taking me from my office?"

"I didn't have a specific reason for pulling you out of your second-story monastery, no. I don't require one. Not according to our contract. The sun is up. The timecards have been punched. You and I are officially on the clock. We'll conduct the day's business together, as we agreed."

Thomas bit the inside of his cheek. She was trying to fluster him. It was working.

"Besides," she continued, flouncing down the steps, "I've never conducted my *business affairs* in an office, and I don't intend to begin now."

It took a full moment for him to recover from the shock of that particular quip before he was able to chase her down again.

She stood in the center of the Grand Arcade, staring at the magnificent scenery all around her. If he didn't know better, he might have thought the sight took Miss Cross's breath away. The way her soft, pink lower lip dropped ever so slightly instantly drew his entire attention.

He hated how his chest puffed at her approval.

"How about a tour?" she asked, at last.

"Of The Empire?"

"I'll be working here, won't I? Or are you too afraid of what I might think?"

A challenge. She made a sport out of riling him. This time, he didn't retreat.

This was work. Business. He could handle that.

"No," he said. "A tour is a capital idea. May I?"

"*Capital idea*," she scoffed.

"It's an expression. It means—"

"I know what it means. I also know that people haven't used it since the last time you lobster backs went to war with the French."

He smothered a smile. "I'm sure I don't know what you're implying."

"Just making an observation," she mused. Yet the look on her face reminded him of a detective in a play, discovering a clue that unlocked a grander puzzle.

He offered her his arm. Merely the polite, gentlemanly thing to do.

Even the weight of her hand on him, the heat of it, the soft, gentle shift of her body against his, inspired spectacularly impolite, ungentlemanly thoughts.

At every turn, window painters applied gold leaf lettering to the shop windows. Muralists transferred their designs onto the half-moon relief gaps between the walls and ceiling. For the first time since embarking on this project, he was too distracted to find fault in their work or micromanage from over their shoulders.

Together, they carried on for a spell, with Thomas narrating the sights and pointing out the building's wonders. When Evelyn slipped from his touch to bend over a wrought iron specialist—a Haitian artisan brought all the way from New Orleans—as he shaped metal for a nearby gate, Thomas shook his head.

She was *purposefully* bending over like that. Drawing attention to her fine—posterior.

"May I make an observation?" he asked.

"Certainly. So long as it's thoroughly complimentary," she replied idly.

"You scandalize on purpose, don't you? I thought, perhaps, it was second nature. A product of your time in show business, so normalized it became almost a tic. But I've come to reconsider that. You actually enjoy making a man squirm, don't you?"

She raised a flirtatious eyebrow. "You're damned right I do—"

"I heard it as soon as I said it. Please disregard."

She laughed—heartily and freely, a sound that made Thomas nearly weak with envy. "If you must know, Mr. Gallier," she began, leaning on that singular ability she had to say his name like it was an invitation to take her clothes off, "I don't enjoy making *all* men squirm. But you? I happen to enjoy making you squirm very much."

"Even though there's no need? Even though you've already gotten everything you could possibly want from me?"

"Oh, I haven't gotten *everything* I want from you. Not yet."

He didn't have the strength to ask any follow-up questions. Instead, he nudged her forward on the tour. The Grand Arcade led to the vaudeville theater, which she'd already seen, so Thomas diverted to one of seven birdcage elevators that cut straight through the heart of the building. The marble staircases would have been good enough, but perhaps he was showing off.

Just a bit.

The elevator was forged by bars of pure decorated steel, and its floor was an elegant marble cut across by a handwoven carpet of countless imported threads. Traveling twelve stories high, it was a miracle of engineering and a feat of elegant design. He was proud of it and didn't mind showing her so.

"An electric elevator," he announced as he busied himself engaging the doors, locking them into the contraption together. "Have you ever ridden in one before?"

"I've never had the pleasure. The pleasure of riding in an elevator, anyway."

"The first ride is always a thrill," he said.

Leaning against the far wall, she licked her lips ever so slightly, giving no doubt of her scandalous train of thought. "I bet."

Perhaps the stairs would have been better after all. The confines of the elevator now felt like a cage—too small to share with her. Her perfume clouded his senses.

He grasped the control lever firmly, as he'd been taught by the elevator's designer upon its installation.

"You'll want to hold on to the railing, Miss Cross. It's not dangerous, but it can be discombobulating."

With that, he threw the lever and the elevator buzzed to life, pulling them downward at a racing speed of twenty feet per minute. It was at this point in the proceedings that he usually gave a speech about how he acquired the elevators, but when the elevator jolted—

"Miss Cross!"

A body, warm and welcoming, stumbled into him, pinning him against the elevator door. Arms wrapped around his shoulders for stability. And when he blinked, Evelyn Cross's lips hovered just over his. She was on tiptoe, curving into him. Tantalizingly close.

She didn't even have the decency to pretend it was a mistake.

"You've been in an elevator before, haven't you?" he asked, careful not to let his mouth move too animatedly—if he did, there was no doubt they would kiss. That's how close they were.

Evelyn only hummed her reply. Smug. "Mm-hm."

They were alone. They were close. He wanted her. The math worked out to one simple conclusion.

Kiss her.

Instead, their world rattled as the elevator reached its terminus. This time, the force was enough to genuinely knock Evelyn—away from him this time, rather than toward him. He took advantage of the distance and continued with the tour as though nothing had happened.

The basement aquacade was designed with the stampeding horse fountain of Versailles in mind, and he repeated his usual precis of the design's architectural inspiration with practiced coolness. If she noticed the occasional waver in his voice or how he tripped over his own feet not once, but twice upon exiting the elevator, she had the decency not to say.

He was determined to let their brush with the carnal pass by unremarked. But as she leaned down to brush her bare fingers along the furnace-warmed water, his resolve gave way and he foolishly mused:

"I don't understand you."

"What's there to understand? I'm a fairly simple creature, all things considered. I like fine clothes and applause and money and my friends and you. Or, at least, I think I would like you if you took those clothes off long enough for me to judge fairly."

"See, that's what it is. You insist on making a spectacle of yourself. It baffles me."

With a tap of her fingertips in the smooth surface of the water, she muddied her reflection.

"At the risk of scandalizing you even further, attention is currency for women. Particularly women like me. If I'm not a spectacle, I'm invisible. And invisible women can't earn a living."

"You're not invisible," he said. "You never could be."

Realizing how that sounded—*almost like a compliment*—he hastily added, "Because sometimes, it doesn't feel like you're doing all of this to promote yourself. Sometimes, it feels as though you're using yourself as a weapon."

She flinched. He'd struck true. With a small, secret gesture, Evelyn raised one wet finger to her barely smiling mouth—*shhhh*. When her hand dropped to her side, she licked the droplets from her lips. Another one of those gimmicks to distract him. "A lady never tells."

As they made their way through the rest of the building, Evelyn had the good sense to ask so many questions that he had barely any time to further plumb the depths of her inner life. How do you intend to secure the aerialist's rigging in the acrobatics pavilion? The boxing ring—will medical staff be on hand in case of predictable emergency? The hall of wonders and oddities—how often will exhibitions be changed to encourage repeat visits? Were *nine* restaurants of international flavors from Italian to Chinese really necessary? The Racket Hall—will gentlemen be required to pay extra for admission and will ladies need a chaperone? The moving picture show—isn't that just a fad? The racing car course on the roof—the view is fine, but that seemed like a poor bit of planning, didn't it, considering the cars will need to be lifted by crane to reach the track?

On and on the questions went, partly fueled by genuine interest and partly, he suspected, by her desire to avoid any more of his questions. Thomas allowed them because they flattered his vanity—and kept her mouth busy far away from his own.

However, Thomas realized, he hadn't put much thought into the conclusion of his tour. As a result, it proved quite anticlimactic.

They stopped in a great empty hall that occupied two full stories of the palace.

"What is this?" Evelyn asked, tilting her head in such a way that a curl slipped free of her sensible bun. Thomas fought the urge to tuck it back into place.

"The zoo—sorry. The menagerie. That's the proper word."

"I don't know a single person who knows what the word *menagerie* means."

"You know Andrew and me," he pointed out. "And yourself."

"You spent so much time earlier asking me about why I make a spectacle of myself, and here you are doing the same thing."

"I don't know what you're talking about," he lied, his throat tightening.

Despite the room's emptiness, Evelyn took a turn around it. So casual, and then—"That accent of yours. It's fake, isn't it?"

"I beg your pardon?"

His throat wasn't tight now. It was properly closed. She'd destroyed him with a single question.

A single, very astute, very dangerous question.

"I've been in the business a long time," she said, shrugging. "I've heard every faker the good Lord ever put on this earth. In the early days of my career, in fact, I traveled with *Lady Prudence Evergale*, whose entire act consisted of nothing more than being a 100 percent bona fide English lady—at least, that's what the marquee called her. In reality, she was just a girl from Sweet Water with a mouth of straight teeth, a fantastic accent, and a country of rubes happy to buy her lies. Accents are sort of a specialty of mine, you might say. Is yours real? And if it's not, who are you trying to fool?"

Thomas's cheeks burned, but he adopted a teasing smile that he hoped reached his eyes. *Evade. Don't let her see you sweat.* "What was it you said earlier? *A lady never tells?*"

She tutted. "If you'd been any kind of clever, you would have replied, *But neither of us are ladies here.*"

"I have nothing to hide, Miss Cross."

Evelyn searched his face. Then, her lips curled into a smile—soft and sweet.

"I *nearly* believed you there. But you should know one thing about going into business with show people, sir. We can always spot one of our own."

She whispered that last bit, taunting him. Thomas offered her his arm, deliberately turning the conversation back to work.

"Shall we return to the tour?"

CHAPTER FIFTEEN

AFTER THEY RETURNED TO THE THEATER, THOMAS RECEIVED A letter and excused himself to read it, promising to rejoin her once he'd done so. But he never did.

Just when they were getting somewhere.

Disappearing act or no, Evelyn was a determined sort. Life on the vaudeville circuit had taught her that. So as the afternoon drew to a close, she went hunting for him. Despite the size of the place—the tour had shown her that The Empire was even vaster than she had initially imagined—she eventually found him tucked on the floor behind one of the great doors in the central atrium. Having relieved himself of his jacket and braces, he had rolled his sleeves up to the elbows, exposing some unfairly chiseled forearms. His mussed hair hung lazily in his eyes as he attended to his task.

Replacing . . . screws? That's how it appeared, anyway. That he was taking out screws and replacing them with nearly identical ones, set apart only by a half-shade difference in color.

For a moment, he was so absorbed in his work that Evelyn had time enough to properly drink him in. As they had yesterday, his handsome face and figure struck her down to the core, awakening a hunger in her she hadn't felt in some time. But it was the careful, attentive work to which he set himself that brought a smile to her face.

She wasn't sure she'd ever met a man like Thomas Gallier. A man who owned a theater like this—the kind used to seeing his name in the paper—was not the sort who would roll up his sleeves and sweat over screws. Yet, here he was.

It added to her conviction that Thomas Gallier was a myth. A workingman in a rich man's clothing.

He was hiding something, of that she was absolutely certain.

She shouldn't have cared. She didn't need to know the truth of him to fuck him or get what she wanted from him. But what she wanted was to fuck him *and* know his truth.

Evelyn was used to finding ways to get what she wanted.

"You've done a remarkable job of avoiding me, Mr. Gallier."

At the sound of her voice, he started, attempting to scramble to his feet like any gentleman would in the presence of a lady. "Miss Cross—"

"No, please. Don't get up on my account. The view is exceptional from up here."

He ducked his head, as though mouthwatering shoulders rippling through a slightly sweat-damp shirt were something of which to be ashamed.

"Tell me," she said once he'd gone back to his screwing . . . sadly, she thought, the construction kind, not the fun variety. "Do you always do your own carpentry or only when you need an excuse to evade your business partner?"

"Shock of shocks, Miss Cross," Thomas said, not exactly unfriendly, though not its opposite either, "but not everything is about you."

"Don't you have people to do this sort of thing for you?"

"Considering the *people* were the ones who installed it improperly in the first place, no."

There it was again. That brilliant flash of dictatorial control. He really *didn't* know how to let go. Fascinating.

"I'm surprised you even know how to operate a screwdriver, considering what a fine-bred, absolutely genuine English gentleman you are," she teased, reminding him of how she'd called out that phony accent of his.

With a grunt, Thomas tightened one of the last screws. Although she suspected he wished to continue ignoring her, his pride got the better of him. "Well, as it happens, once when I was in France—"

He stopped short, blood draining from his face, and she was shot through by the peculiar sense that she had stolen something from him. She didn't know what that was, precisely, but she took note of the moment all the same.

"When you were in France . . . ?" she prompted.

Every movement twitchy and unsure, he wiped his palms on a nearby handkerchief and returned his tools to their case.

He reminded her of an automaton who, having stuttered out of its trained choreography, suddenly clicked back into rhythm.

"I forget myself, Miss Cross. You carry me away sometimes."

"Oh? To where?"

His eyes were sad, tinted with something like simmering anger. "To someone I haven't been for a very, very long time."

Was that a confession? Or merely as close to one as he would ever get?

A million thoughts and questions and desires bubbled to her breathless lips, each one fighting so fiercely to be freed that none of them ever quite made it. Thomas, all traces of introspection and confession erased, leveled his gaze at her.

"Was there something you needed? You have . . ." He withdrew a chained brass watch from his vest pocket and inspected it. "Ten, nine, eight . . . seconds until our business today has concluded."

Evelyn scoffed. "Surely you don't mean to hold to that silly rule."

But he could. And he did. First, he snapped his jacket from the floor, causing a crumpled, golden invitation to slip from his pocket. She only just noticed its watermark—the flourished letters NA—when Thomas whisked it again out of sight. Straightening, he gave her one of those little bows to which she'd become so coldly accustomed.

"If you'll excuse me. I have an engagement. Enjoy the rest of your evening."

"Mr. Gallier, you really *are* avoiding me, aren't you?"

His hand went to his pocket, once again joining the invitation he'd just hidden there. The letter he must have gotten that took him away from her this afternoon. "I merely wish to hold to the terms of our agreement. And my engagement this evening is important. Vital for our business. Farewell."

He was gone before Evelyn realized he'd said *our.*

Our business.

A NOTE FROM THE HISTORIAN

That evening, the following notice appeared in Nehemiah Alban's paper next to an inset sketch of the "winsome" (read: fashionably slender) Miss Constance Alban:

THE MANHATTAN DAILY,
OCTOBER 19, 1897 (New York, New York)
JILTED: THE EMPEROR

Last night, a coup was attempted by The Emperor of 34th Street—upon introduction from Dr. Andrew Samson, he made overtures to Miss Constance Alban, daughter of Nehemiah Alban, newspaper magnate. This first meeting did not go to plan. Miss Alban was not impressed by her latest suitor, clearly finding him to be a bore. However, this *Manhattan Daily* reporter has been reliably informed that Mr. Gallier indeed intends to try his luck again with the pretty heiress.

That's right. Thomas met the woman he needed to impress, royally screwed it up, and Alban's *Manhattan Daily* had to publicly nudge him to try again at a later date. Not quite the auspicious start to a relationship that would come to define his life.

Meanwhile, Evelyn Cross, who made it a rule to avoid reading the dross published by the *Manhattan Daily* whenever possible, was more concerned with another newspaper item:

THE NEW YORK SUN,
OCTOBER 19, 1897 (New York, New York)
MR. BRIGMAN'S ANIMAL AUCTION

Mr. H.A. Brigman, of 39th Street, is delighted and proud to present the largest sale of wild, trainable animals that the fair city of Manhattan has ever seen. To be in attendance: alligators, exotic fish, elephants, tiger cub, a company of minks, egrets, and perhaps a unicorn. Animals are highly trainable with the help of Mr. Brigman's Authentic Guide to Animal Husbandry and Tutelage. Animals acquired legally in their countries of origin, all animals authenticated and checked for fleas. Inquire at Lower Manhattan Parade Ground tomorrow.

After the brush-off the day before, a lot of women in Evelyn's position probably would have been cowed. I would have. I *have*. As a "woman of size" or whatever ridiculous euphemism we're using lately to describe north of Rubenesque, I know there's nothing quite like the slap of rejection. Suddenly, even if you usually like everything about yourself, you become convinced that every bad thing in your life—but especially that rejection—was because of your weight. Something that is so second nature to you, your own appearance, suddenly becomes your enemy.

But Evelyn didn't fall for that shit, which I guess is part of the reason why I love her so much. Evelyn was fearless. Evelyn was without self-consciousness. She could not be scared off or deterred from what she wanted. In a world that kept telling her no, she found new ways to make people say yes. All people wanted to do was deny her. Deny her star power. Deny her existence.

Deny her beauty. But she was undeniable. And she did every-thing she could to make sure people knew that.

Maybe I'll be like that one day. Maybe we all will be.

A woman who wasn't undeniable probably wouldn't have given Mr. Brigman's Animal Auction a second thought.

Not Evelyn, though. Never Evelyn.

CHAPTER SIXTEEN

Thomas's first meeting with Miss Constance Alban had been an unqualified disaster. He'd barely gotten a word out. There was so much on the line that his already-feeble social graces had abandoned him completely. If he didn't convince her father that his attentions were sincere, if he didn't succeed, then The Empire . . . it could fall under the heavily weighted type of Alban's headlines.

His nerves hadn't been the only thing to get the better of him. There was also the matter of Evelyn. During his introduction to Miss Alban, he'd not been able to restrain himself from comparing the two women—and Miss Alban, despite her good breeding and status, simply could not measure up.

Still, Thomas resolved to redouble his efforts with the newspaper heiress. Meanwhile, he would also withdraw from his acquaintance-ship with Evelyn Cross and devote himself to any part of The Empire's final preparations that might keep him away from her.

Like this morning, for example. After managing a few smaller projects on-site, he left for an abandoned parade ground in Lower Manhattan. Once home to a military installation that had eventually fled for the greener pastures of Brooklyn's Prospect Park, this patch of dead grass and rain-rotted wood benches now played host to working-class Sunday picnics, the occasional game of stickball, and—every so often—a real spectacle.

It seemed that this abandoned waterside property was one of the only places in an ever-crowding Manhattan with enough space to host wild animals, the kind that populated the sale Thomas Gallier was about to attend.

Without Evelyn.

Or, that was his intent, anyway.

Because when he stepped out of the carriage, she was already leaning against a tree, biting into a hot and generously sugared donut from a crumpled and greasy paper bag.

She beamed. His jaw dropped. That only made her smile all the wider.

"Mr. Gallier. Fancy meeting you in a place like this." She extended the bag. "Cruller?"

"Hello again, Miss Cross," he said, quickly composing his features into their usual tight politeness. "I suppose I shouldn't be surprised that you're here. Or that you're early."

Business. Think of business. Do not think about kissing that cinnamon sugar from her lips.

"Nothing I do should surprise you any longer."

"Too right. But don't you have a rehearsal to attend?"

"Beatrice is measuring for costumes and Andrew is performing those medicals we discussed." She met his gaze. *"I'm all yours."*

He opened his mouth.

"Professionally speaking," she amended.

Heavens, he didn't stand a chance. She was a sharp-witted wonder, always keeping him on the knife's edge. He wanted to whisk her away and revel in that delightful repartee of hers for hours—and then do something *else* with her for hours.

He ground his jaw. He couldn't let himself think of that. Not when he needed Constance Alban. Not when he needed the papers on his side.

But now that she was here, refusing her would cause a scene. He offered his arm and tried not to shiver when she tucked herself into his side.

"Very well, then. Shall we?"

The parade ground had been transfigured into a cross between a market and a circus. Lines of metal cages and tanks of varying sizes were arranged to create straight, perusable aisles, and in the center, a fenced-off square dotted with inspection blocks served as a center ring of sorts. Each exhibit was a creature available for both personal use and commercial sale. As top-hatted gentlemen of business strolled the selection, rough-faced, large-boned men with calloused hands and baker boy caps stood sentry outside each animal's enclosure.

Thomas pulled Evelyn into his side as he eyed up a mountain lion. Closeness like this, with her warmth and her scent so near, should have been out of the question, but he worried with the wild beasts nearby.

"So. Enlighten me," she said. "What, precisely, are we doing here?"

"About a year ago, I laid down a sizable amount of money for a pack of tigers for The Empire. And yet for reasons unknown, those tigers never arrived. After some negotiation"—here, he cleared his throat meaningfully—"my money was returned, and I now have carte blanche to select new creatures for our menagerie by way of restitution. It can be quite dangerous here amongst the animals, so I thought I would allow you to remain at the theater and work. I'm sure you understand."

"I'll do you the favor of not calling you on that lie, sir. You clearly just didn't want to suffer my presence." Was that a flicker of hurt in her tone? If so, she smothered it with a smile before he could fully appreciate its depths. "Allow me to turn the conversation to more pleasant topics. What are we looking for?"

Together, they strolled the aisles, taking in leopards and piranha alike.

"Something that will draw the attention of the papers."

"They might as well run our operation, mightn't they?"

He could practically hear the roll of her eyes. Thomas hated how easily she cut to the truth of matters—always. His humiliating attempt to court Constance Alban last night was proof of the power of the press. He wouldn't have done it without Nehemiah Alban's threats looming over him. "More than you know."

"You're frightened of them."

"Aren't you? They could destroy The Empire. They *have* destroyed you."

"Not yet. I've still got some tricks left. Besides, they can't take anything from me worth having. Not really. You would do well to remember that."

Thomas didn't like the sound of that. He also didn't like the familiarity with which she spoke to him—not like a seductress now, but almost like a friend.

They arrived at the edge of a fenced paddock, where a few elephants lingered. They were a family, five in all. Two couples, and a calf with ears so big they tripped her as she splashed around in a water trough.

Struck by the sight of them, arrested by their size and beauty, Thomas quite forgot himself. He watched them with outright wonder.

A small tap on his shoulder distracted him. He turned, assuming it was Evelyn who had done it. But when he looked, it was a large trunk—an elephant trunk. At the same time, another elephant took advantage of his distraction and snatched the top hat right from his head.

He tensed, scanning for anyone who might see this silly breach of etiquette and protocol. But when he realized there was no one except

Evelyn to spot his slip-up, he stroked the trunk of the baby elephant, warming to it until, at last, the mother returned the hat (crookedly) to his now-mussed hair. He gave her trunk a small, friendly pat, too.

"They like you. Good judges of character, they are," Evelyn muttered.

Thomas winced a smile. "If they like me, that guarantees they *aren't* good judges of character."

Looking up at the great gray creatures, he felt a kinship with them he couldn't quite explain. Given the chance, he might have stayed there indefinitely.

In companionable silence, they lingered by the great animals until an approaching crowd caught Thomas's attention. The crowd marched straight for them.

No, not them. For *Evelyn*.

"What is this?" Thomas hissed. He recognized many of them at first glance. Reporters and photographers.

"I just called in some favors. You wanted the press's attention, sir? You've got it."

How dare she. He hadn't sanctioned this. It all would have infuriated him before, but given his current tenuous situation with the press and all he was doing to buy their favor, it made him *livid*. "Miss Cross—Miss Cross, we are leaving."

"Oh, no you don't," Evelyn said, twirling to catch his hand before he could run. Her words contained a trace of a girlish giggle. "We still haven't tested the merchandise! Elephant rides are *all* the rage, you know."

"I will *not* make such a fool of myself. I cannot afford the negative publicity—"

But Evelyn wasn't listening. She ripped her coat from her shoulders, surrendered her shawl beneath, unpinned her own *directoire,* and practically tossed them all to Thomas. In exchange, she collected his top hat and set it atop her curls.

To say the look didn't appeal to him would have been untrue. A lie of the first order.

He wondered, briefly, how she might have looked with fewer of her clothes and more of his. Her own stockings and one of his tuxedo jackets, perhaps?

Clearing his throat, he tried again. "I have *not* approved this. Are you really doing this for The Empire? Or because you think you'll get a rise out of me? You are completely mistaken, out of line even, if you think—"

But then, her gentle hands came to settle on his shoulders. Her eyes bore into his. And an unfamiliar sensation of peace settled in upon him. "*Thomas*. For once in your foolish life, trust someone else. Trust me."

When he didn't say anything, when they both felt like the moment had been too sincere, she winked saucily and added:

"Or, failing that, give me a kiss for good luck."

That, she said loud enough for the onlookers nearby to hear her, but her grip on his shoulders assured him that this wasn't for the crowd—not entirely.

Thomas merely shook his head, laughing as if to reassure everyone, including himself, that it was nothing more than a tease.

"Fine," she said. The reporters had closed in now, and the cameras were at the ready. She was in full performance mode. "Final offer: give me a boost."

With all eyes on them, Thomas knew he couldn't refuse.

He slipped one hand to Evelyn's stockinged ankle and one to the ball of her foot—giving her an indecent boost to the elephant's back. He burned where they touched. Too intimate. Too addictive.

As soon as she was safely aboard the creature, Thomas stalked away, collecting his feelings. His wants. Himself.

He already wanted her so badly, and yet this very afternoon would almost sign his fate to marry Constance Alban. He would need her father after this show hit the papers. He couldn't handle Evelyn Cross right now. Couldn't indulge this ridiculous stunt of hers . . .

And yet, a few minutes later, Thomas found himself cornered near an amphibian tank by the very journalist who'd snapped them fighting that first day at The Empire. Smith.

"I've gotta hand it to you, Mr. Gallier," the man said, his usual disinterested grimace rising into a grin. "I didn't think much of this Evelyn Cross bit when you first floated it, but . . . you might have something here."

Smith's gaze then traveled across the parade ground to the center ring, where Evelyn rode the elephant as easily and languorously as a queen carried on a litter. She giggled and flirted and blew kisses and encouraged *everyone, simply everyone* to come and see her at The Empire in three weeks' time for its opening. The crowd of journalists turned into a mob of fans, all ready to break with the decided tastes of the day to fall at her feet.

She was not just beautiful or lovely. She was all-consuming.

And so out of Thomas's reach.

Or very *in* Thomas's reach.

If only he would unclench his fist and hold his hand out for her.

⇒◆⇐

Half an hour later, Thomas set off in his carriage with his star.

He was too lost in thought to say anything to her. Her spectacle had drawn plenty of attention, and no doubt, it would make the papers tomorrow. But he was stuck on the last sight he'd seen before ducking into this carriage.

The elephants returning to their cages, shrieking for one another as they were separated.

All their life, they'd been poked and caged and forced to perform. Just like Evelyn.

Just like him.

"The alligators." Evelyn eventually tutted, oblivious to his wandering mind. "Of all the things you chose from that sale, you chose the alligators."

"We'll build them a swamp," Thomas said, thinking of the albino alligator and its more camouflaged friend, both of which he'd just purchased. "Add turtles. Fish. Maybe some exotic flightless birds. Make it feel like home. The menagerie is big enough for that. The elephants are all very well, but we don't have the space to build them an entire enclosure at The Empire."

And I wouldn't want to, even if I could.

"But you *did* buy them."

"Yes," he conceded, carefully. "One of their handlers knows a fellow who looks after retired circus animals out in Nebraska. The elephants will make an appearance at The Empire's grand opening, then they'll settle there. Live out the rest of their lives without being herded into tiny boxes and forced to do tricks for the masses."

He'd meant to only think that last bit. But it came out—bitter and true.

"Careful now, Mr. Gallier. You may be developing a soft side. And what's worse, you're letting me see it."

Thomas checked his pocket watch. "It was a practical decision. Strategic. If I buy them, no one else in town can."

"So ruthless of you. Smart. Very calculated."

She said it with such sincerity, he knew she had to be mocking him.

Streets rolled by. Those elephants and their lifelong servitude to the greedy public made him consider something else.

"I notice you haven't wanted to talk about my performance. Was it really so awful?"

He fiddled with his top hat, brushing circus straw from its soft surfaces. "May I ask you a question?"

"Sure thing."

"How do you do it?"

"You'll have to be more specific."

The carriage clattered against the cobblestone. Newsies screamed the headlines. He had a thousand concerns that should have absorbed his time and energy. And yet, all he could think about was her.

"How do you make everyone love you?"

"Is this a skill you're hoping to acquire?"

"Tell me."

Tell me it's a trick so that I can defend against it. Tell me how to claw my way back from the brink of you.

The sardonic twist in her expression slipped away, leaving only sincerity in its wake. For a moment, it seemed as though neither of them were performing any longer. Thomas wasn't sure he liked the sensation.

"I suppose I just love people. Care for them. Care *about* them. And let them love me back. Not a very complicated system."

He cracked a smile, small and self-deprecating. "Impossible for me, then. I don't love, I don't want to be loved, and I don't have any qualities worth loving."

"Don't want to love? Sir. Love is practically the only thing that makes life worthwhile. Hasn't anyone ever told you that before?"

No. He didn't suppose anyone had. And every time he'd experimented with the practice before, all parties involved had failed miserably.

As though sensing an opening, Evelyn continued, more earnest than he had ever seen her. "It doesn't have to be romance—God knows that has its risks—but love? The love we have for our friends, for the people we really care about. That's the good stuff. Trust me on this. I know it's not easy, but most of the best things aren't."

As the carriage beneath them lurched onward, Thomas wondered what it might be like to trust Evelyn Cross. To trust her not just with their work, which she'd proved already today that she could handle . . . but to trust her with *himself*.

Miss Cross straightened and, into his silence, spoke again.

"And on your last point, I must disagree. You do have qualities worth loving. It's just that you're like a fine magic trick. All of the true wonders are hidden. And only those who pay the closest attention can see."

A NOTE FROM THE HISTORIAN

Evelyn's impromptu elephant show bought them pages upon pages of publicity. The stunt was too good to ignore, the headlines too easy. But they're all cruel, and I'm the fat lady writing this story, so I get to cancel culture the newspapers of the 1890s.

Fatphobic commentary aside, Evelyn wasn't wrong: the press from the auction was useful in an *all press is good press* way, contributing to a general sense of anticipation around The Empire's impending opening night. Between that and the sudden shift of *The Manhattan Daily*'s attitude toward Thomas Gallier in its columns, Thomas found himself invited to more and more parties. All parties where Constance Alban would no doubt be among the guests of honor. But after the elephant incident, Thomas Gallier didn't attend a single one.

There's no clear explanation for this change. Just the breathless retellings of Evelyn's elephant ride and then the sudden drop-off of Thomas's attendance at the gatherings of Manhattan's elite. Strange, considering how hard he'd worked to get into them.

If I were the kind to speculate (which we've established I definitely am—sue me), I would say that Thomas believed Evelyn's knack for greasing the publicity machine had produced a way out of his little "court Constance Alban" dilemma.

Whether or not he was right about that assumption? Who's to say. But what interests me is what small indulgence he allowed himself when he thought he wasn't going to have to marry the daughter of the most powerful man in Manhattan. What he did with that glimmer of freedom.

Wonder of wonders: he took his best girl to a theme park.

CHAPTER SEVENTEEN

EVELYN CROSS LOVED CONEY ISLAND. IT WAS IMPOSSIBLE TO GO and escape un-delighted. Whenever she had more than a fifty-cent piece in her pocket and an afternoon to herself, she would grab anyone even mildly interested and head straight there. Both titillating and ephemeral, its mass entertainments appealed to her as a woman of the people.

Coney Island was her scene.

It was not Thomas Gallier's.

One could only imagine her shock, then, when she mentioned the possibility of them sneaking out one afternoon to Steeplechase Park . . . and he immediately took charge of planning an outing for them.

"It's purely for research purposes, you understand," he reminded her as they stood at the end of the pier leading down to the park.

Protesting a bit too much, she thought.

"All of this Coney Island nonsense is competition for The Empire," he explained for what felt like the thousandth time. "I've got to know how to beat them, and I'll never know that if I don't experience it for myself."

"Certainly. And you've taken me along . . . ?"

"It's working hours. You're obliged to join me. Just as I was obliged to join you at that costume fitting yesterday."

Evelyn couldn't help but laugh at the memory of his blush and hasty exit. She took the opportunity to tease him—just a little bit. "That reminds me. I *must* apologize. I didn't realize those stitches were so tight. You can't fathom my shock and horror when the skirt split as I bent over to collect that hatpin." He'd been more amenable to her teasing over the last few days, ever since their great success at the elephant sale. She relished their newfound ease.

Still, if she hadn't been doggedly watching for it, she might have missed his right cheek twitching in an almost-smile.

The bastard. He *did* still want her.

He was also, it seemed, still trying to deny that want.

But today promised a wealth of opportunities to break his resolve.

"You're an expert in these cheap amusements, aren't you? You'll make a fine guide," Thomas explained.

"And the disguises?"

He'd meticulously planned the afternoon's excursion down to their clothing, and now, Thomas held his arms out and inspected them both. He'd exchanged Evelyn's usual fading furs and finery for shabby, simple afternoon clothes, and as for himself? Well, she'd seen him in less than a full suit just once, and even then, he'd lost only the jacket and braces. In this workaday costume of his, with its thin material stretched over broad, muscular shoulders and a tailored jacket that drew her eye toward his tight belt and even tighter trousers, he looked . . .

Ordinary. Rugged and handsome. Absolutely perfect.

Although the dark-rimmed sunglasses and the oversized hat did much to conceal that fact.

"Is it all too much?" he asked.

"I think you should have asked Bea for costuming advice. These sunglasses—" She gestured toward them, resisting the urge to brush his cheek as she went. "They don't suit you. And the hat has to go."

"Why?"

Wasn't it obvious?

"Because they hide your face."

"That's rather the point. We can't be discovered doing this," he said, his voice suddenly gripped by a note of genuine worry. "The papers will have a hot time if this gets out. *Thomas Gallier, spying on the competition.*"

"Or *Thomas Gallier, caught with secret lover at Coney Island,*" she crooned.

All around them on the pier connecting the front gate of Steeplechase Park to the body of the fairground, couples strolled arm in arm, curling into one another oh-so-innocently to defend against the chill wind snapping off the Hudson. A thrum of jealousy battered Evelyn at the sight of these comfortable pairs.

But that jealousy quickly melted to surprise when Thomas spoke again.

"We'll need to adopt new identities today. Naturally. We're just a young couple of no ones passing a lovely day together on the shore."

She blinked. Could it be that *Thomas* was teasing *her*? This was a new development, unexpected but nevertheless welcome. "You never cease to surprise me."

"I can assure you that's not my intention."

"I wouldn't have imagined a man as controlled as you should like to play pretend."

There was a moment of silence, and all at once, she became startlingly aware of her words, and how they cut deeper than this game they were playing. If her suspicions of him were right, then his life was a game of pretend. One that never ended.

He cleared his throat. "I don't like it. It's simply . . . necessary."

"Why is it necessary?" she asked, though she shouldn't have. Knowing the truth of him would just pull her deeper, and she certainly didn't need that.

The wind whipped around them, drawing her a step closer to the warmth radiating off his body.

"Because the real me does nothing but hurt people."

"Come now, Thomas." She tutted. "I thought you were beginning to trust me."

He ducked his head and offered her his arm. And just like that, the game of make-believe began.

"Very well, then, darling. What shall we do first?"

⟫◆⟪

He'd never been to Steeplechase Park before. It was a place for sweethearts and saps and people all too willing to spend their meager wages irresponsibly. It was *not* a place a man of his station should be going.

But as he and Evelyn wandered the fairgrounds, he couldn't help regretting that reality. When he took her in hand, he felt the knots in his shoulders loosen. The pretensions he'd spent most of his life honing dropped away. Rather than thinking of himself—his responsibilities, his business, his secrets—he accounted for the world around him. A roaring mechanical amusement ride. Laughter from children. Whispered declarations of lovers. The scent of popping corn and sweet nuts. The illicit burn of cheap liquor in steel flasks. Warm sunshine and sharp river air on his cheek.

Thomas threw himself into the role of doting lover. It was an absurd exercise, to be sure. But if he was going to waste his time and potentially risk his reputation—and he was going to do so while wearing the borrowed, ill-fitting costume of a nobody—he might enjoy Evelyn Cross's seductive closeness for a few hours.

She, too, had no trouble playing along with their fiction, cuddling up to him so brazenly he wondered briefly if they'd get thrown out for indecency. Her cheek brushed against his shoulder. The scent of her freshly washed hair encircled him. Her hand gripped his arm—why the devil didn't this woman ever wear gloves? And her breasts . . . well, he did everything he could *not* to think about their spectacular weight teasing his side.

Yes, absurd indeed. But as they strolled around the various amusements, taking in the sights and sounds that the park had to offer, he couldn't help but memorize every detail. Here, it felt like anything was possible.

And maybe it was.

In the guise of someone else, he glimpsed the freedom to finally be himself. To have everything he'd ever desired. If only for a day.

"You're enjoying yourself."

The gentle accusation pulled him from his thoughts and when he resurfaced, he did so to the sight of Evelyn holding out a box of Cracker Jack and a sarsaparilla bottle in his direction. He glanced at the latter curiously. She shrugged.

"I remembered you're not one to drink. Couldn't exactly come back with beer now, could I? As for the Cracker Jack, well, you simply haven't lived until you've tried it. Coney Island delicacy."

The thought she'd put into the sarsaparilla was too much to accept, so he took a few kernels of Cracker Jack in his hand, inspecting the sugared sweet.

When was the last time he'd had a sweet?

When was the last time he'd had *anything* just for the pleasure of it?

Indulgence was not his modus operandi. He popped the dessert into his mouth, biting back a groan so Evelyn wouldn't know how good it tasted.

"I'm simply marveling at how much the common man will spend on amusements like this. And women, too. With so many young ladies leaving the home to pursue work—a trend we only expect to see increasing over the coming years—the days of pool halls and pubs cornering the entertainment market are over. Women will have their own money to spend, and as you can see here, they will spend it on safe, socially acceptable entertainments. I wish to be at the forefront of that movement. I intend to be a very rich man, Miss Cross."

"Yes," she said, calling his bluff by very much *not* calling it. "I'm sure it's all about the money, Mr. Gallier."

"Tom," he said before he could think better of it. "Call me Tom today. Tom Gallagher. Just for now."

"Alright, Tom."

A shiver traveled down his spine. When was the last time anyone had called him that?

To ward off the feeling, he steered Evelyn toward one of the park's signature attractions—a naphtha-driven "Venetian boat ride" through dark scenes of romantic Italy—and bought them tickets. It wasn't until they were both in their little dinghy, puttering along a carved canal on a simple boat, their bodies tucked into one another for lack of space and their eyes adjusting as they traveled from the external bay into the show building, that she spoke again.

"Do you want to know what I think, Tom?"

"Always."

A false Italy sprawled all around them. It was a bit rough at the edges, to be sure—nothing like the splendid craftsmanship of The Empire—but somehow, in the quiet, in the dark, it was too romantic for words. And so, they were silent. Their breathing matched. The boats to the bow and stern of them were mercifully empty, and Thomas could almost imagine that this was their own world. A world where Tom Gallagher and Evelyn Cross could be something.

Until, in the dark, she spoke truth to him.

"You're a pretender," she said. "Not just today, but always. And I don't think you're honest when you say you're opening up The Empire for money. I don't think you came here today to scope out the competition. Or to corner the market on women's spending."

"You're right," he conceded, honest as he was able, hoping the confession would end her probing. After weeks of practice now, he could just about handle her constant attempts at seduction. But when she acted like a person instead of a mattress, he didn't know what to do with himself. He liked what he saw behind her walls. "I also wish to be recognized—not just in our time, but hereafter. I wish to be important. Undeniable."

In the darkness, he felt her staring at him. Her legs even drew closer to his. Heat crept beneath his collar.

"And?"

"And what?"

As the boat traveled past a poorly plastered mock-up of the Doge's Palace, Thomas caught sight of two young lovers tucked behind the *scenae*, having abandoned their boat to take advantage of the dark seclusion of the ride. He envied them their freedom.

"And I believe the reason you chose vaudeville, the reason you chose *cheap entertainments*, the reason you spend your time surrounded by fairy tales and frippery and foolishness is that some part of you—a small part, maybe, but one you can't ignore—wants the magic to be real. The illusion."

The truth of her words was nearly enough to shatter him.

"You want *this* to be real," she breathed, practically against his lips. Once again straying from her honesty in favor of something carnal. Although maybe that was real too—he certainly felt it in in his body as her soft hands rose up to his collar, drawing him closer, as she situated herself nearly in his lap.

Here in the darkness, under a name from a lifetime ago, in this sprawling fake world all around them, he had the strength to tell one small, impossible truth.

One that might make her understand. One that might end this torment of their mutual desire.

"Miss Cross. In the spirit of being *real* . . . I do feel I owe you a confession. It might help things along in our"—he paused, catching himself before he said something even sillier than he was about to—"professional relationship."

"I'm listening."

She was listening *and* brushing a stray curl from his forehead.

"I have a great many character flaws," he began, "but chief amongst them—"

"You're controlling. You're a liar. You're a masochist who won't give in to my irresistible charms."

"I *am* controlling. But I don't have a choice. I have to manage everything, keep myself in perfect order, because if I don't, my desires get the better of me. They always have—and with disastrous consequences for me and those I have cared about. It's my worst flaw."

He took a shallow breath. Even that was a paragon of understatement.

The truth was that he wanted everything. *Everything.* He wanted everything so deeply sometimes he thought it would smother him. He wanted friends and alcohol and wealth and acceptance and a future and status and control and power and love, love, love, love, and—

"It's why I don't allow myself indulgences like . . . this. I don't drink. I don't smoke. I don't let my true self show—not to anyone. If I begin, and if I like it, I have no way to stop myself from spiraling out of control. And I *must* be in control. Always."

"Why?"

Why? What sort of question was that?

Oh, yes. The question of a woman who hadn't seen what his losing control looked like. Or what disasters such behavior wrought.

He continued. He needed her to understand so that she would let him go.

Not to the arms of Constance Alban. It wasn't about her now or even about his business prospects. It was about the gale force winds of his desire to ravish Evelyn in this dangerously flimsy boat, his desire to tell her all his secrets—and his knowledge that he couldn't, not without bringing them both to ruin.

"We both have too much at stake. Even the smallest slip-up could destroy everything I've worked to build, including your show. This is for both of us."

"And that's why . . . you and I . . ." she breathed, the words dancing on his lips as her hand rose to cup his cheek.

Thomas leaned in, despite himself. The businessman in him bargained, offering a deal he couldn't resist. "We can have today," he said. "Today, I'll play at what I think we both desire. But that's all I can give you." Today, he told himself, would have to sate this hunger he had for her. It would be his one chance to play-act at giving in.

He took another calculated risk.

With a deliberate gentleness, he brought his lips to hers . . . and kissed her as if he had been put on this earth to do nothing else. Her body awoke at his touch, surprised at first by the contact and then enthusiastic in its reply to him. The kiss was not a promise. It was a greeting and a farewell. She held him as though he were real, as though, perhaps, he was the only real thing in her world—and he held her just as resolutely, sharing her breath until they became one body.

He wanted more. No, not just more. All of her.

And if he had only one day to treasure her, he could not let himself stop at just a kiss.

He pulled away for a breath, instantly regretting the loss of her taste—lingering salt and caramel. "Have you ever wished to visit Florence?"

She blinked for a moment. Then, she understood his meaning. Their boat was approaching the Florentine section of the ride—a ride that he did not want to end.

Carefully but quickly as they were able, the two of them stepped out of their boat, leaving it to drift, riderless, down the watery track.

Tom knew how the boat felt. Out of control. Drifting without any guidance.

Totally free.

Evelyn took his hand and guided him, giddily. Her hand squeezed his with just the right pressure—a reassuring kind of want. The heat of this interaction buzzed beneath his skin, desperate to be loosed on the woman he'd been lusting after since the first moment he saw her. Behind the towering papier-mâché Duomo, its soaring arches giving enough cover to hide two lovers in the dark, they slipped into the shadows.

Once they were safely ensconced, they pounced on each other once more, threading themselves into each other's bodies like they were afraid coming up for air would shatter the illusion. Like this moment was no more real than the fake Italy all around them.

But it was real to Tom. The sensation of her cheeks between his hands was perhaps the most real thing he'd ever felt. It grounded him to the very Earth after a lifetime of merely suspending above it.

He traveled the expanses of her body with his hands, trying to memorize it, relishing this touch after so long denying himself.

Without unspooling themselves, they sunk to the floor, kneeling together as they kissed.

But when she reached for his trousers, he finally pulled back.

"No, Evelyn."

Yes, he wanted all of *her*. But he could not let her have all of *him*.

It was a line he couldn't cross. He knew that the moment she touched him, he would be hers—irretrievably emigrated to the country of her heart.

For the first time, she didn't push him. Instead, she returned her hands to his shoulders and asked, "What *do* you want then, Tom?"

The truth was . . . he hadn't gone into this with a plan. No endgame. Just the pleasure of his hands upon her, the brief indulgence of letting himself have this moment.

He considered this strange woman who'd blown into his life like a nor'easter. As much as she proclaimed she loved sex—and he firmly believed that she did—he'd gotten the sense that sex hadn't always been easy for her. She'd been used more times than she'd used, and she'd learned that the fastest way to avoid that was to strike first.

He didn't want that for her. He wanted her to feel adored. To be the center of someone else's world—even if just for a few moments.

"Come here," he murmured, maneuvering her until she was cradled in his lap, sprawled between his legs. Her back to his chest, he couldn't see her face, but he could sense every breath and every movement she made.

"What are you—"

He hushed her, bringing one hand to cup beneath her breast. She took in a sharp breath.

Then, with the other hand, he reached around her and began moving her skirts up slowly. Up and up her body until they rested at her waist, he dragged the fabric to reveal her stockings and knickers.

He kissed the well of her neck, hand drifting down to the simple material covering her sex. She moaned, finally realizing what he was doing to her.

That small sound drove him nearly to surrender his goal. His cock hardened against her back. She arched against it, adding pressure to his already throbbing member. Sex with her would be heaven, he knew, and every fiber of his being wanted it.

But he'd had a lot of practice at self-denial. And besides, how could he resist *this*? The perfect woman writhing beneath his touch.

One by one, he slipped her buttons open. Her hips rolled, desperate for him to dive between her legs.

He moved slowly, relishing each sensation. His hand lowering down her mound, running along her slit.

"Please," she breathed.

And he could not deny her.

When he dipped his fingers between her lips, it was his turn to moan. She was dripping wet for him. Her bud hard and aching for him.

Holding her closer with his free hand, wishing the corset wasn't separating her perfect breasts from him, he focused his attentions on her center, circling as she panted with every touch.

There were so many things he wanted to tell her. That he hadn't done this in years. That he wanted more of her. That she was so beautiful in his arms. But all that came out was,

"I have dreamed about this moment, and those dreams could never compare to this."

She shattered into pleasure against his hands, warbling out his name. His *real* name.

"Tom!"

He clung to her through the shockwaves, gritting his teeth against the pride and the want coursing through his veins. Her hips shuddered. Her breathing went erratic, and she gripped his thighs like they were the only thing keeping her from soaring up into the heavens.

"And now, is it your turn?"

"We can't. We just can't."

She was immediately crestfallen. But he couldn't relent. No matter how much he wanted to.

She knew why. He'd explained as much before this whole escapade. Offering her his arm, he shot her a sad smile.

"We should get back to the amusements. I'm sure we don't want to be found."

He helped her back into her clothing, righting her and then guiding her to one of the many empty boats. They slipped into and, for a moment, silently bobbed through the ride's final scenes.

She brushed her hand against his. He wanted to take it.

He didn't.

The final scene of the boat ride slipped away from them. The doors at the far end of the ride cranked open, flooding Thomas's vision with bitter sunlight.

"If my life weren't what I've made it, we would have a lifetime of days like this one, I think." He tried to make his voice light, joking, but his attempt at a laugh just echoed in the last of the dark.

If anyone had seen him blinking away tears, it was because of that. The shock from the sudden blast of sunshine. Nothing else.

They left the ride without exchanging any further words or, more importantly, any further embraces. Thomas's legs were unsteady beneath him, but he couldn't be certain if that was from the boat ride or something more internal.

"Are you quite alright, Evelyn?" he asked when he could stand it no longer.

"You know how they always say be careful what you wish for?"

"Of course."

Her smile was watery. "I wish I hadn't wished for you to be honest. I suddenly can't bear it."

CHAPTER EIGHTEEN

THOMAS WAS RIGHT. THERE *WAS* A CERTAIN CHARM IN PRETENDING. In pretending she hadn't been deeply wounded when he'd told her they had no chance. In pretending he wasn't totally transfixed. In pretending that their tryst hadn't lit her entire world aflame. In pretending that she could leave the feelings he'd awakened in her behind. In pretending that maybe she did want something more from him than his body on top of—or perhaps under—hers again.

"The games are *rigged*, I tell you!" he said as they conquered the stairs to The Empire's upper offices. "What a brilliant money-making scheme. Perhaps I should add a few to the second-floor saloon—"

"Rigged? You wouldn't be calling it rigged if *you'd* won and I hadn't. By the by," she said, tapping the new bulge in his breast pocket, "I hope you appreciate the *genuine* silver watch I gave you as a token of my affections, good sir."

"I shall treasure it always."

"And may your affection for me outlast the metal from which it's made."

Once on the second floor, she breezed into his study. Leaning in the doorway, she blocked his path inside.

"This is generally the portion of the program when the lady gets a kiss," she flirted.

All traces of good humor vanished from his face. His voice went sweet and soft. Apologetic. Somehow, that wounded her worse than the rejection that followed.

"Evelyn, I don't know that that's wise."

"And then we could go to supper," she suggested. "Prolong the day. I know some places with dark and private booths with *extremely* discreet waiters."

"That's not in our agreement. We promised that we would go our separate ways in the evenings. You *know* this."

"Hang the agreement. I'm not satisfied with ending things in a false Florence. I want the entire Grand Tour. Why shouldn't we live? Really live, not just play pretend at it? *Live for one day.*"

Half plea and half command, the words spilled out of her with a surprising desperation. The stolen moments they'd shared together at Coney Island sparked something within her, something real and raw and unfamiliar. That something could not be allowed to continue. She needed to bury it. But to do that, she needed Thomas to succumb to her charms. Because she knew, if she didn't get under him soon, there would never be getting over him.

"The day is almost done," he said, moving toward his desk and its piles of afternoon mail, sounding more like he was convincing himself than her. "We shouldn't—"

"But do you *want* to?"

When he spoke, he did so into his letters rather than to her.

"I had a lovely time."

"And?"

"And . . ."

Hope fluttered in her chest—he would now dive into bed with her so they could firmly settle their relationship into the category of *business partners with plentiful benefits*. But he narrowed his eyes down at a letter in his hand. Everything changed as he read. His inner light extinguished completely.

"And . . . it wouldn't be appropriate. You should go. Our agreement is clear on this point. Do not attempt to break it."

"Our agreement also didn't include cavorting at a public amusement park," she pointed out. "It did not, as I recall, include you pleasuring me to world-shattering completion."

"A mistake I will not make again, I can assure you."

Evelyn held her ground, confusion gripping her. She felt her tone shift to something harsh, mocking. "What is this? Have I struck a nerve?"

"My nerves are none of your concern. Dr. Samson will tend to those."

"You seemed to be perfectly happy to endure my company not twenty minutes ago. Not *two* minutes ago. What has changed?"

Whether or not he realized it, his eyes flickered down to the note in his hand. Another note just like the one she'd seen him tuck away that afternoon when he'd been fixing those screws—one marked with a golden NA.

"You are my employee, Miss Cross," he addressed her coldly. "This is how I treat my employees."

"Like dirt?" .

"Like they work for me. Since meeting you, my life has turned into a battlefield from which I can never declare victory. I'm calling for an armistice."

"Please, say more," she retorted, her emotions rising at an unhealthy rate. "I'm liable to swoon."

"I don't need you to swoon. I need you to have some compassion and release me from this *fixation* of yours. I feel as though I've made my sentiments on your intrusions upon my life quite clear. There are affairs, Miss Cross, and there are business affairs, and in my life, never the twain shall meet," he hissed.

"Except for today. When you were a few buttons from burying yourself inside me."

A strong hand crumpled the letter, and Evelyn's eyes immediately went to it. He hadn't been so set against her until he'd opened the note and read its contents.

"What's that?" she asked.

He threw it in the waste bin. "Nothing."

In one swift movement, she plucked the letter from the depths. Thomas protested and shifted into action, pursuing her as she skirted the edges of the room while attempting to uncrumple the damn thing.

"Is it a love letter?" she taunted. "Good sir!"

"Miss Cross—"

"Mr. Gallier, have you been stepping out on me? Is that the purpose of our *agreement*? To keep me separate from your strings of lovers? Are they the ones who taught you how to pleasure a woman so well?"

"Evelyn!"

The walls nearly shook with the force of his bellowing voice. Evelyn's vision blurred as she stared down at the odd piece of wrinkled paper in her hands.

"What . . ." she asked, her voice weak, "what is this?"

Thomas cleared his throat. "It appears to be a draft article about our little escapade this afternoon. I will find Nehemiah Alban and sort this out. Make sure it never gets printed."

Evelyn stared down at the page in her hand. "Our photograph on the pier looks lovely." Her voice had gone quiet, almost wistful.

But Thomas seemed to hardly notice. He plucked the page from her shaking hands and resigned it once again to the waste bin.

At his brusque manner, Evelyn's tone shifted to indignant. "What's so wrong with a photograph like that appearing in the papers?"

"I must control The Empire's image. We're in a fragile enough state as it is."

Oh, she saw how it was. After all this, he was still worried about what the papers might say if he was seen with her.

Anger and hurt in equal measures wrapped their cold, bony hands around Evelyn's throat.

"You aren't controlling The Empire's image," she accused. "You're letting the press control *you*."

"That isn't true."

"Then let them have the article. Let the world know that the most eligible man in New York City was seen cavorting around an unsavory amusement park with his unsuitable, *fat* sideshow attraction. Come to dinner with me. Take me home. Take me here in this damn office, if you want. But whatever you want, let yourself have it, damn the consequences. Play the world instead of letting it play you."

She'd wanted it to come out as a command. Instead, she might as well have been begging.

Thomas didn't even have the decency to look her in the eye. "I cannot."

It was a rejection. He was just like the rest. Turning her down, even in private, because he was afraid of what the rest of the world would think about them together. She should have been hurt or angry, but in that moment, all she could feel was pity for the man.

He controlled every aspect of his life—romance, drink, sex, business, and God knew what else. For what? To blend in with men like Nehemiah Alban?

"You want me, and you're giving me up just to please *them*. How pedestrian. How predictable. How positively ordinary of you."

"Miss Cross—"

Brisk enough to vacate the premises before any hasty tears made an appearance, Evelyn charged for the exit. She paused only for a moment in the doorway. "If this is the real you, then . . . you were right. He does nothing but hurt people. Including himself."

Present Day

IT WAS SORT OF NICE. ME AND ARMITAGE GALLIER.

There was a shift between us. A recognition that things could never go back to the way they were, all polite distance and the occasional kind word or glance.

Like Thomas, he'd made a mistake. He'd shown me that he cared. Even a little bit.

Everyone says that billionaires get to be billionaires by working hard—endless hours, jet-setting business trips, nights spent debating in the boardroom and mornings poring over "the numbers," shouting "have it on my desk by five," whatever.

Armitage didn't do any of that. Instead, he sat with me like it was his job. Not hovering anymore, because he'd been serious about our deal that he wouldn't read my research until it was done, but like we were two strangers working side by side in a beautiful old library.

That is, if one stranger always silently brought the other a cup of tea and the other always tried to make ridiculous, ice-breaking jokes that never seemed to quite land.

"There's not a dress code for hanging out with me, you know," I said out of the blue one night. "I mean, do you even own a T-shirt?"

It wasn't that I hated seeing him in collared, elbow-rolled button-ups and Savile Rowe trousers perfectly tailored at the ass. But still, it always seemed so surreal, looking up from pictures of Thomas Gallier in full suit to find his descendant, frowning over a newspaper in an outfit not entirely dissimilar.

Like seeing an echo of the past.

"Why would I need to own a T-shirt?"

"Because you're a human on the planet Earth in the twenty-first century."

"My father would drop dead if he caught me in one. I'm a Gallier. We aren't T-shirt people."

"You're not T-shirt people? What does that even mean? Who doesn't own a T-shirt? I mean, what do you sleep in?" Then, a thought caught me. "Holy shit—do you sleep in those old-timey silk pajamas? Do you wear a little sleeping cap and carry around a chamberstick so you can see at night?"

I hadn't ever expected a man like Armitage Gallier to blush—but I wouldn't call what happened to Armitage's face then *not* blushing, either. He ducked his head behind his newspaper.

Oh, how delicious. "You do, don't you?"

"Well," he said, after a brief pause. Was that a smile I heard in his voice? "Not the sleeping-cap thing."

So, anyway, that's how I ended up at the Fifth Avenue residence a few days later, carrying a Target bag stuffed with T-shirts.

If I was lying, I would have said, *Oh, no, I have no idea why I did that. Life's funny that way. Such a mystery. People are weird and do irrational stuff, huh*?

But I knew exactly why I did it. I wanted him to like me.

And like Evelyn with Thomas, I wanted to know the real him. I wanted to *like* the real him. And I wanted the real him to like me.

Weird, right? Armitage Gallier was so out of my league we might as well have been different species. Not just in social standing, but in looks, too. What would a guy who could have anyone want with a woman like me? He was a Gucci Nine; I was a solid Walmart Four. He was Saturday-morning runs and green smoothies; I was midnight movies and milkshake dates. He was runway. I was *run away, it looks like the fat girl's going to ask you to dance.*

At least, that's how I saw myself back then. Like I wasn't beautiful. Like there was something wrong with midnight movies and milkshake dates. Like the problem was with me, not the assholes who made fun of me when I asked them to dance.

I didn't have that Evelyn Cross *pop*. I didn't have *seduce a man on a Coney Island ride* energy. So when I was interested in something . . . I had to nudge it out of someone. I never came out and asked for anything; I wasn't ever forward. I just dropped crater-sized hints.

Like the T-shirts.

And I'll admit this wasn't the first time I'd done something possibly ill-advised for the sake of a guy. My track record in this area was . . . not great.

In high school, I cut class to get the boy I had a crush on some throat lozenges because he had a cold (and I found the still-full bag in a trash can an hour later). In the hope of catching the eye of the cute violin player on my hall freshman year of college, I baked cookies for my entire dorm (and still didn't get invited to the party where everyone ate them). I worked up the courage to send a drink over to a guy at a bar once (only to have the drink returned to me by a very embarrassed bartender because the guy hadn't wanted to "lead me on" by accepting it).

As a historian, I knew history repeated itself. Yet still, my problem was always thinking this time would be different. Always thinking I'd be the one to defy the odds. Always thinking that someone would look past my insecurities and see the person I was beneath them.

All that said, I should have known better than to try the whole T-shirt gambit on Armitage Gallier.

"Did you bring your dinner tonight?" he asked, nodding to the bag as I emerged onto the back terrace. He'd suggested we work outside to take advantage of the unusually nice weather, flashing a shy sort-of smile that I was trying to ignore entirely.

"Actually, this is a gift," I said, plopping the bag down on the table in front of him. So proud of myself.

He blinked up from behind his glasses, eyes seeming larger than usual. "You got me a gift?"

"Yeah. I know guys like you usually want *donations to a socially conscious charity of your choice* in lieu of gifts or whatever, but I couldn't help myself."

I bounced on the balls of my feet as he fumbled with the plastic. It was clear this guy had never touched a Target bag in his life—and his jerky movements only got more pronounced when he held up a package of maroon fabric.

"It's a T-shirt," he said, voice unreadable. "It's a *bag* of T-shirts."

"For the man who has everything," I practically crowed. I might as well have posed and said *ta-dah!*

His face clouded. His hands fisted in the material, bringing it down into his lap, where he stared at it like it was a map he couldn't decipher.

"I thought . . . Do you not like it? Was this stupid? I'm sorry. I thought maybe —"

I stopped bouncing. Oh, God. It was high school all over again. Not only was I not Evelyn Cross, I wasn't even capable of something as simple as this.

"Why did you do this?"

The question came on such a small voice that even the gentle wind over New York City almost drowned it out.

"Because you don't have any T-shirts," I said.

"I could have bought my own."

"You weren't ever going to, though, were you?"

"I don't need them."

No. He didn't. But in a million years, I'd never thought they would *offend* him, either. I figured maybe he would do a polite *ah, thank you* and throw them in a forgotten drawer, never to see the light of day again. Indifference, vague appreciation, polite dismissal? Yeah, sure. But not *offense*, which seemed to be what currently wracked him.

I rushed to explain myself, hating the warbling panic underscoring each word.

"Right, but it's, like, a gag gift. This is what friends do. I was at the store and saw them on sale. They made me think of you, so I bought some. It's not a big deal. I can take them back if you want. No harm, no foul. Here, let me—"

He shoved the T-shirts back in the bag like the very sight of them rankled. He did not, however, hand them over.

"Really, I'm sorry." God, *I* was blushing now. Stammering. "I mean, I know we're not friends. I get it. This was . . . I'm just an employee. I'm . . ."

The sentence trailed off into nothing. For a moment, I thought he was going to protest. Tell me it was okay, that he got the joke now, that it was a sweet gesture. Instead, he just said:

"It was unexpected."

I had no idea if that was a good thing or a bad thing. It *felt* bad in the moment, but later, I wouldn't be so sure.

"Anyway," I said, "I'm sorry."

"Don't be." His cheeks lifted in a half-fake-smile, half-wince. "How about we move back into the house, hm?"

We did just that. A few awkward minutes later, we found ourselves back in the library, back to work beneath the watchful, painted eyes of Thomas Gallier and his wife.

PART FIVE

WORDS OF LOVE TOO LOUDLY SPOKEN

CHAPTER NINETEEN

OF ALL THE OUTWARD SIGNIFIERS HER DARLING JULES USED TO KEEP society from speculating about his true nature, Evelyn always thought this was the funniest.

Boxing. Men held it up as the ultimate masculine activity, but from where she was sitting—a front-row bench on the south side of a hastily constructed boxing ring—she just saw sweaty, half-naked men grunting and colliding their slick bodies against one another for the enjoyment of other, generally intoxicated, generally single, men.

To female eyes, it seemed decidedly other than heterosexual.

But still, Evelyn loved the fights.

The back floor of a dockyard warehouse reeked of stale, melted sugar and the crowd was not what one might have called genteel, but in the warm embrace of the run-down, rusted building, crammed between Akio and some unenthused burly man with a thick push-broom mustache, she barely remembered Thomas Gallier or her bruised heart or how much it would sting to face him again.

The silver flask of cheap gin Akio freely shared certainly didn't hurt matters, either.

The two undercard fights had been entertaining matches, but when a heavyset Irishman in rolled-up sleeves stepped onto the elevated canvas of the ring to announce the final bout, the crowd rang out with cheers. Evelyn added her voice to their din. Everyone knew that this was the fighter they'd really come to see. Jules Moreau.

"Gentlemen and ladies of ill repute . . ." the man called in a brogue so thick, Evelyn was certain half of the spectators wouldn't understand him. "This is the moment I know you've been waiting for. The fight of the night. The . . ."

The Irishman went on, waxing poetic about the fighting styles of the two men in opposite corners of the ring. Though the alcohol racing through her bloodstream fuzzed the edges of Evelyn's awareness, she leaned forward, glued to the drama about to unfold in front of her.

Akio, on the other hand, had no such focus. He knocked an elbow into her side.

"Evelyn?"

"Mm-hm?"

"That man beside you. Have you seen him here before?"

Confused, she shifted her gaze to the man in question, who didn't seem the boxing type. Face featuring what she could only describe as a push broom of a mustache, his brow was too furrowed, his shirt pressed too cleanly, and he didn't appear to have any booze in him whatsoever. An oddity in this scene.

Evelyn returned her gaze to the fight.

"No, I don't think so. Why?"

"He's very . . . *still*, don't you think?"

Evelyn chuckled. "Not everyone is as animated as I am, Akio."

That didn't placate him.

"There's something wrong here."

"And what do you think that is, exactly?"

"These affairs aren't precisely legal. You know that."

As his whisper dissipated into the air like steamship smog, Evelyn's entire attitude changed.

"You think he's a cop?" she asked, lowering her voice to match Akio's.

"It could be a raid. The bulls could come in any second and tear this place apart."

The prospect cut through Evelyn's tipsy buzz. That couldn't be allowed to happen. In years past, their position at the top of the vaudeville circuit and their cozy connections with the upper class had protected Jules and Akio from the Manhattan Police Department. But now that they weren't fashionable—now that the eyes of the city had turned elsewhere—there was no telling what an overzealous cop might do to a couple of famed "eccentrics."

"What do you think we should do?" she asked, her eyes never leaving Jules. The crowds around them cheered and leapt to their feet as he successfully dodged his opponent, but Akio and Evelyn remained frozen, coiled in their seats. "Leave?"

"And abandon Jules? No. Under no circumstances. If we could get him out of the ring, maybe, but there's no chance of that—"

As childhood friends scraping to make a living on the circuit, she and Jules had often run gambits around the food stalls in their neighborhood and on the road. With Jules's natural grace, he made a quick and effective thief. And as for Evelyn?

She'd always been good at playing the distraction.

"I wouldn't be so sure," she muttered, rising to her feet and straightening her skirts.

"What are you doing?"

"Getting you two out of here."

CHAPTER TWENTY

A RESPONSIBLE WOMAN WOULD NEVER GET BETWEEN A ROWDY group of drunk dockworkers and their beloved boxing. But rare was the occasion that anyone ever accused Evelyn Cross of being responsible.

Without a second thought, she barged toward the ring, stomped down on the ropes so she could enter, and snapped up the bell, smashing its hammer three times to both stop the fight and draw the attention of the room.

A wave of protests crashed against her, but Evelyn pretended she could not hear them.

"Gentlemen and ladies of ill repute, I regret to inform you that due to a scheduling conflict, your previously planned diversions of the physical arts are no longer possible!"

Boos. Someone threw a beer bottle. Evelyn deftly ducked, giving Jules a slight nudge into his corner of the ring.

"What the hell is this about?" Jules hissed, blood and spit flying. "I had him!"

Evelyn lowered her voice. "Get out of here."

"What?"

"There's a raid. You have to go—"

Another beer bottle joined the first one, and this time, Evelyn didn't so much nudge Jules as she did shove him . . . directly into the waiting arms of Akio, who'd collected Jules's bag and hastened him out of the doors at the far end of the warehouse.

Now she was alone, in the center of an angry crowd that threatened to foment into a mob.

Well, she'd had worse audiences.

"I know you came to see blood and destruction, but never fear! Every man needs a little culture in his life, and I'm going to give it to you."

Whether you like it or not.

After all, it wasn't enough for her to just get Jules and Akio out. She needed to get everyone else out, too. Protect as many folks from the undercover bulls as she could.

When she and Jules used to run this gambit, she'd gotten good at reading a crowd—sometimes, a well-placed offensive song was just the thing to turn away threatening persons. But here, tonight, she decided to take a different approach, one she hadn't employed since the last time Jules had run out on some bad debts at the racetrack.

Swallowing back her fear, she wet her lips and sang out in a strong, clear voice a familiar song from her childhood. A direct poison for any boozer.

"I am so glad that Jesus loves me!"

The boos grew in intensity below her, but Evelyn's courage strengthened when she saw a handful of defectors lose interest in the spectacle and start for the door.

"Jesus loves me, Jesus loves me!"

Remaining spectators lined the ropes on every side, but Evelyn paid them no mind. After all, the first escapees grew in number.

"I am so glad that Jesus loves me, Jesus loves even me!"

One hand grabbed the ropes, meaty and threatening. Evelyn knew this would not end well for her. But she forced herself to continue, forced herself to keep her breath steady . . .

Until shrill whistles cut across her tune.

Cop whistles.

The effects of such a sound were instantaneous. Though Evelyn kept singing as though her life depended on it, the once-angry mob scrambled into hasty terror, running each other over to escape the four coppers who'd suddenly revealed their badges and billy clubs.

"When we see Jesus, we'll sing and shout the victory . . ."

Evelyn should have run too, but she knew that, as the distraction, the coppers would want her the most. Running with four flatfoots on her heels would cause Jules and Akio trouble if they happened to be outside waiting for her.

Indeed, when the crowd proved too numerous to pursue, the cops all, inevitably, turned on Evelyn at the center of the ring.

Her voice died only when the four of them joined her there—one at each corner, cutting off her escape routes.

Fighting her internal panic, she continued to play her part as the first one, Officer Push Broom Mustache himself, approached her with a wicked glint in his eyes and one gold tooth in his smile.

"Hello, gentlemen," she crooned, though she felt as if her own voice were choking her. "Enjoyed the number? There's more where that came from in just a few weeks when The Empire opens uptown—"

"Give me your hands."

"Unfortunately, these are my only two. I didn't bring enough to share—"

The rest of the quip warped into a whine of pain. Officer Push Broom snapped her up by the wrists and pinned her arms behind her back, holding her firmly in place even as she struggled.

Her fight-or-flight instincts kicked in. Her breathing grew erratic. Especially when he pulled on her cuffed wrists and molded his body to her backside.

"What's a nice girl like you doing in an illegal, immoral place like this?"

"I think the real question is why *more* nice girls aren't to be found in illegal, immoral places like this."

Not the answer he wanted to hear. With one swift motion, he knocked her legs from beneath her, sending her crashing to her knees on the unforgiving mat below. He circled until he stood in front of her. "Who organized this fight?"

"No one *organizes* a fight," Evelyn snapped. "Men just can't help themselves."

A gloved hand slid down her face. "I really don't want to have to bust up that pretty face of yours. Maybe I wouldn't have to if you told me where to find someone else to throttle."

"See?" she spit. "Men just can't help themselves."

Again, wrong answer. That gloved hand reared back before closing down on the side of her face.

Pain exploded between her eyes. Evelyn doubled over to the mat. Breath ragged. Thoughts scrambled. Ears ringing.

None of the coppers looked her in the eye. Of course they didn't. She shouldn't have expected anything from these men. Coppers protected each other, and they wouldn't ever speak up if one of them was acting like this. None of them would be the brotherhood's Judas. None of them would do the right thing.

Hands behind her back, Evelyn tried and failed miserably to right herself again. At the sight of her struggle, the officer gave her the helpful assistance of a swift boot to her stomach.

In her haze of hurt, she almost laughed. At least he wasn't abusing her face too much. She'd still be fit to headline a vaudeville show.

"Your friend," the officer said, raising his voice. "The degenerate. The lightfoot and his little Chinese friend. Where'd they go?"

"He's Japanese, you *fucking* moron—"

Another kick to her stomach.

"Where'd they go?"

"Why?"

The question was both *why should I have to tell you* and *why the hell do you want to know*? As far as she could see it, the entire affair had been supremely peaceful until the "law" had shown up.

With a grunt that came from disused limbs accustomed to sitting behind a desk, the officer crouched down in front of her, so close she could see the pretzel crumbs and tobacco still stuck in his mustache. He tapped his badge with the blunt end of his club.

"Because this badge means I get to keep the peace. And sometimes you get that only when you're knocking some pretty little boy's head into the concrete."

Evelyn couldn't help herself. Throwing her head back, she smashed her skull into the copper's, sending him topping back in a haze of limbs and blood.

It hurt like hell, but she didn't care. No one talked about Jules that way and got off scot-free.

If her hands weren't tied, she might have killed him.

Once he found his feet again, the copper brought a hand to his mouth, wiping away the blood as one might wipe away the rain.

"That's assaulting an officer," he muttered.

"Well spotted. Want to see me do it again?"

Before he could reply, she jerked her legs, smashing into his and knocking him flat on his face.

The last thing she heard, before the billy clubs swung and knocked her lights out, was the cackle of her own laughter.

A NOTE FROM THE HISTORIAN

That particular night in Manhattan, according to records, was a busy one. While Evelyn was protecting Jules and Akio from the bastard cops, several other things were happening.

Jules and Akio were running to the Arcadia Hotel down the street. The only hotel in the vicinity that, as far as they were aware, had one of those newfangled working telephones.

Moments later, back at the Matterly Ladies' Theatrical Bath and Boarding House, another phone rang.

And somewhere farther uptown, in a mansion on Park Avenue that smelled like cigars and oleander, Thomas Gallier was dancing with a button-nosed stranger.

CHAPTER TWENTY-ONE

AFTER LEAVING THE EMPIRE THAT EVENING, THOMAS HAD SLIPPED into a tuxedo and top hat and joined Dr. Samson in some grand mansion near the park, where the polished floors reflected his own pale face back to him and the electric light shone so painfully on the room's gilded finishes that he could barely see for the glare.

And he'd danced. Between chatter about horse racing and the attributes of various hunting rifles, he'd swept the room and collected women, gliding them across the parquet floor as though he were born to do just that.

He was a success. A charmer. Remote and aristocratic, yes, but the people forgave him that considering his fine English breeding. He threw all he had into this fiction, into thinking of nothing but the next dance step or bits of idle talk before him.

The clipping from a test printing of tomorrow morning's *Manhattan Daily* was as good as a threat. If he didn't follow through with Constance Alban . . . her father would see to it that Thomas's life crumbled all around him.

He was right to hurt Evelyn Cross. To leave her. To devote himself to earning Nehemiah Alban's good graces. This was all that mattered. Not the broken expression on Evelyn's face, not the scent of her perfume disappearing on the air as she fled his presence, not her cruel but accurate assessment of him.

As his entry on Constance Alban's dance card approached, Thomas excused himself from the ballroom. He required a moment alone to think and compose himself. In the quiet of the hallway, he inspected himself in a looking glass. He adjusted his tie, smoothed his copper hair—

"Don't worry. You look fine enough for this rotten crowd."

A vision in green silk materialized beside him.

He started when he realized the figure was a familiar one. Her pointed scowl, too, had become a regular sight around The Empire lately.

"Miss Matterly?"

Thomas understood the woman's reputation. She'd been something of a fixture at parties just like this one, once upon a time, as the mistress to some long-faded tycoon. It wasn't hard to see why. Even without the benefit of servants to set her hair or a wealthy escort on her arm, she set the rest of the party to shame. Her gown clung to her and, in another time, if she were out on the dance floor, she would have been the toast of the night.

But that didn't explain her presence. According to Dr. Samson, who collected gossip like stamps, once she'd spurned her last lover and converted their love nest into a boarding house, she'd vowed never to step foot in a mansion, much less a party held in one, ever again.

Something was wrong. Very, *very* wrong, perhaps. A woman of such obvious conviction as Miss Beatrice Matterly didn't go back on her word without extreme provocation.

"I thought you'd left this particular social scene," he said.

"Yes, so did I. But don't you worry, I plan to leave this viper's pit just as soon as I speak with you."

"What is it?"

"Evelyn has been arrested."

Arrested.

"Where is she?"

"Seventh precinct. Pitt Street. By the old synagogue."

Thomas opened his mouth to reply, but the sound of his name distracted him.

"Mr. Gallier!"

Turning on his heel, Thomas came face-to-face with Mr. Nehemiah Alban. He straightened and did the usual bow, though he could feel the muscles in his face were unusually tight.

In his periphery, Thomas almost missed Beatrice Matterly vanishing into a nearby closet.

"Mr. Alban," he said. "What a pleasure it is to see you again."

"I'm grateful you found the time in your busy schedule to partake in a little extracurricular excitement," Alban replied.

"I wouldn't have missed it, sir," Thomas lied with a smile. "Not for all the world."

"And you're dancing with my daughter, aren't you?"

"If she'll have me."

"I'm sure she will. And once you're done, please," Mr. Alban gave him a companionable slap on the shoulder, "do come and see me. We'll talk business."

"Thank you, sir. I'll be there."

Mr. Alban returned to the ballroom, leaving Thomas reeling. This was what he'd wanted. He'd left Evelyn today to protect The Empire. He'd denied his own feelings for her to secure this dance and Mr. Alban's esteem. Tonight, he could secure his theater. No more distractions. No more entanglements. No more fixations. Just him and his brilliant future.

But a sharp, betrayed voice behind him knocked him back.

"What the devil do you think you're doing?"

195

"Miss Matterly—"

A ferocity surfaced in her. "Evelyn could be fighting for her life as we speak, and you're—what? You plan to remain here and dance quadrilles with Constance Alban?"

Thomas swallowed. That was the choice before him, wasn't it?

He found himself torn between the man he wanted to be and the man he was behind his mask. He *wanted* to help Evelyn. But he *needed* Alban.

"There isn't anything I can do for Miss Cross at the moment," he said at last.

"Untrue," Miss Matterly said. "And you *know* it."

Thomas tried to assuage Miss Matterly. And his own conscience. "The police commissioner is here. He's just in the next room. Perhaps Mr. Alban will introduce us and he can help—"

Her rage twisted into disgust. "I was right about you."

"I beg your pardon? What could you possibly know about me?"

"Evelyn's told me all about you, I've seen the way you act at The Empire, and now I've seen you in your natural habitat. You are a spiritless coward. Just like the rest of them."

"And what makes you say that?"

Something in the air told him there were many answers she could have given to that question. But the one she settled on was the most devastating of all.

"Because you're willing to throw people away if it will put even a penny more in your pocket."

CHAPTER TWENTY-TWO

THOMAS RETURNED TO THE BALLROOM IN A DESPERATE STATE. THE gentlemanly costume he perpetually wore chafed against his real self. He struggled to keep up appearances.

But he endured. Miss Cross would take care of herself. She didn't need him. Perhaps, even, she needed him here *more* than she did at the police station. After all, if he lost The Empire, then she lost her employment, and then where would they be?

It was on this possibly tenuous logic that Thomas found himself playing Prince to Miss Constance Alban's Cinderella as her father beamed, and her current suitor, Edward Langmore, grimaced from across the dance floor.

It was becoming clear that Miss Constance Alban was a very lovely woman of very few words. She had gone rod-stiff in his touch. Was she frightened? Aloof? Annoyed? He couldn't tell. But after a full sixteen measures of silence, he attempted to change that.

Not necessarily because he wanted to, mind. But because this was all a game, and if he didn't play it right, her father might toss the board.

"I'm gratified that you favored me with a dance, Miss Alban," he said as they executed a perfect turn. Her face was as impassive as ever—bored, even.

"Yes, I suppose that makes sense."

His heart tugged. That sounded like something Evelyn might say.

No. He couldn't think about her or where she might be at this very moment. He had other matters—more important matters, surely—at hand.

"Quite confident of your charms, then," he said. "I'm glad for it. Most women wouldn't dare admit that they know how fetching they are."

It was a light flirtation, but a false one all the same and he hated himself for it. He didn't care about Constance Alban. She was a means to an end—impressing her father.

"No, it makes sense that you would want to dance with me. There's a reason I'm always the most popular young lady at parties, Mr. Gallier, and it's not because I'm particularly skilled at the waltz."

She nodded in her father's direction. Thomas lost a step, but recovered as best he could, well aware that a room full of people watched them with great interest.

"You don't have much faith in yourself, do you?"

"I am a realist."

"Are you this forward with all of your partners?"

She hesitated. "Only those I think may have real potential."

A burden lifted from his shoulders. It was almost confirmation that choosing this dance over saving Evelyn had been worth it.

"And I do?"

"My father likes you. I don't think you're so bad. Not as bad as I was expecting, anyway, given how tongue-tied you were during our first meeting."

That slight, even-toned insult sank under the weight of a million unasked questions and unleveled accusations. He marveled slightly at the ease with which she spoke of matters he'd never heard a woman comment on in polite company.

Constance saw this dance just as he did. As an extension of his father's interest in him.

"And to think," he said with a dark, humorless chuckle, "I came to this dance planning to be quite romantic."

"Dancing isn't about romance. These parties aren't, either. They're just boardrooms and offices—by a different name and with better lighting, perhaps. If men treat this space as a place of business, then so must I."

He didn't know what to say to that. He wasn't sure he ever would.

"If you think you're here for love, Mr. Gallier, you're going to be terribly disappointed. Life doesn't work that way."

Her eyes drifted, and when the dance carried them into a spin, he realized what caught her attention. Or rather whom. Edward Langmore—the portly, unsuitable man her father despised.

Yet it was clear from Miss Constance Alban's expression that she thought he hung the very stars in the heavens just for her.

Thomas suddenly felt quite dizzy. And this waltz's twirls had nothing to do with it.

He was a realist, too. Despite how terribly he'd wanted it, he knew he could never marry for love. She was right. Marriages were a contract.

A lifelong.

Inescapable.

Contract.

But was he really going to sell his life, his forever, his *bed* to the highest bidder? Denying his heart because it might make him a little richer or accrue him a bit more power?

Was he really going to let Evelyn rot in a jail cell so he could ally himself with Mr. Alban?

And what about love?

Was he really going to endure the rest of this lonely existence without it? Or even the possibility of it?

Evelyn's words from this afternoon rattled around in his mind. *You're a coward. You're letting the press control you.*

If this is the real you, then . . . you were right. He does nothing but hurt people. Including himself.

And then, of course, there was Miss Matterly.

You spiritless coward. You're willing to throw people away if it will put even a penny more in your pocket.

He was a coward, wasn't he?

Or . . . he *had* been. He didn't have to be anymore. Not if he made different choices.

"And I've shocked you," Constance Alban said, after a long silence.

"No. I just . . ."

The music stopped. There was polite clapping, more chatter, bodies moving all around them, but Constance and Thomas lingered.

"I believe you've opened my eyes to something," he said.

"Really?"

"Yes." He smiled down at her, certainty settling in him. "Thank you."

"I . . . I'm happy to have been a help, sir. Until we dance again."

"Oh, no, Miss Alban. I hope you and I never dance again. I believe there is a partner much better suited to you than I."

She returned his smile, but there was something different about it now. Maybe he'd opened her eyes to something, too. Giving the smallest of bows, he immediately exited the scene. Without farewells, he fled to the front entranceway and called for his coat.

He should have known better than to think he could get away so easily.

"Thomas?" Dr. Samson called, following him to the front door. "Where on earth are you going? Alban will surely want to speak to you after that display. Miss Alban seemed quite taken with you—"

"Something's happened to Evelyn. I must go to her."

"Are you certain? This could mean the end of this little alliance of yours with Nehemiah Alban."

Thomas gazed at that fuzzy line on the mansion's second stone step, that place where the false light of the fine home met the seductive night. Andrew was right. He should return inside, secure Constance's hand, accept her father's help, and go on with his happy and prosperous future, uncaring of Evelyn Cross and all the mixed-up ways she complicated his life.

But there was no going back. Not now.

"Yes. It most likely will. But it will also mean the start of something much, much greater."

And with that, he descended the steps and let the night welcome him.

Present Day

AFTER THE GREAT T-SHIRT INCIDENT, I DECIDED TO KEEP MY DIS-tance from my boss. Not literally, of course. The boxes kept in the Fifth Avenue residence were the basis of my entire research, and he was always hanging around the house. Physical proximity was just part of the job description. But otherwise, I was polite, distant, and kept my friggin' mouth shut.

It wasn't easy. Sitting in stuffy rooms with Armitage, saying nothing, watching slanting nineteenth-century handwriting blur on the pages in front of me as I tried not to think of how he'd set my gift aside like someone getting macaroni art for Christmas, hating the fact that he still brought me tea and kept the nearby plates filled with fresh cookies from some bakery down the street, wishing he would be the one to break the silence and prove me wrong, prove that he actually did like me and he'd just been awkward about the shirts . . .

But at least Evelyn had the benefit of *knowing* Thomas liked her, even if he worked his ass off to keep his distance. He'd been obsessed from the start. With Armitage, I was totally in the dark. Did he even like me? Did I dare think it could be even deeper than that, something like want? Or was I some needy, lonely girl he tolerated only when he had to?

I didn't know. I couldn't know. And I didn't suspect he'd ever tell me.

Do your work, I always thought to myself. *The sooner you finish, the sooner you can put Armitage Gallier out of your mind forever.*

I wasn't anything to him, I told myself. He shouldn't be anything to me.

That's why I didn't think anything of it when I came down with a cold. The day I woke up with an obliterating headache and swollen eyes, I groped blindly out from beneath my quilt, scraped out a message to Armitage about staying home because I was sick, and immediately went back to sleep. No harm, no foul. He was going to some gala that night anyway, so it wasn't even like he'd miss me.

Not that I thought he would miss me otherwise.

But then, I woke up to the sound of banging on my shitty, barely lockable front door. Not just annoyed DoorDash driver banging, either. Biblical, *knocking on the gates of Heaven* knocking. As well as I could with my joints screaming to return to the merciful haven of bed, I shuffled to the front door, opened it . . .

And immediately became convinced I hadn't woken up at all but was still in a literal fever dream.

"What the hell is this?"

At least, I think that's what I said. I mostly just slurred—maybe this cold was more of a flu situation. Maybe I was dying. Maybe I'd *already* died.

What else would explain stick-up-his-ass Armitage Gallier, standing at my front door in a white-tie tuxedo, hair in total sweaty disarray, collar wrinkled, shoes muddy, holding a giant tub of wonton soup in one hand and a mega-pack of orange Gatorade in the other?

"You're sick," he said, obviously. Like *I* was the weird one for not getting it.

"That doesn't explain anything. Do you think that explains anything?"

Polished shoes squeaked as he shifted from left foot to right. My head swam. It was a little like being irretrievably drunk—foggy and fuzzy and exhausted and heavy-eyed and without rules or manners.

Armitage cleared his throat. Looked anywhere but at me. "Well. You don't have anyone to look after you."

That was true. I'd told him how I'd left my family back home in Cleveland, and how I hadn't yet made a ton of friends—read: any—here in the city. I *was* alone.

I just didn't think he'd care about that.

"And the tux?"

"I was at the British Ambassador's Ball. I left."

"Why? Because you think I might die from a cold and take my valuable historical insights to my grave?"

It was at that point my knees decided keeping me upright was no longer in their job description. They buckled, nearly taking me on a one-way trip to the unforgiving laminate floor.

But Armitage caught me. And I don't know if it was my raging temperature or the brain fog or what, but when I looked up at him, he seemed to glow. Like he was meant to hold me like this.

A moment of contact. Of stillness. Of breathlessness. And then, he launched into action. To me, it was a headachey blur, but thinking back on it, the pieces kind of come together. Checking my forehead with big, soft, snow-cold hands. Shuffling me back inside. Leaning me against him for support. Tossing aside his jacket and white scarf. Dropping off the supplies. Feeding me two large flu gel caps from my medicine cabinet. Reaching for a nearby rag and turning on the kitchen faucet.

"You're burning up."

"Who died and made you a doctor?"

"I don't think you can inherit an MD."

"Shame. That's the only way a guy like you could get one."

"Why? Too stupid?"

"No. You just don't have any bedside manner. Zero out of ten stars."

He folded the cold compress he'd just made in my sink, then nudged me onward.

"You need to get into bed."

"Alone?" I joked before I could think better of it. Evelyn was wearing off on me. All that wishful thinking about becoming more like her, and I'd just inherited her worst traits: impulsivity and yearning instead of courage and confidence. Not to mention that my fever had clearly burned off the increasingly flimsy sense of inhibition that lately kept me from saying anything too ridiculous.

"Trust me," he said, pulling back the covers. I got under them without complaint. My body hummed at the familiar comfort. My eyes drifted closed, and he laid the cold compress across my forehead. His voice was barely more than a whisper. "When I work up the courage to get into bed with you, you won't have to ask. You'll know I want to be there."

"Hell of a thing to say to your employee," I mumbled.

A breath—a sigh or a laugh? I wasn't sure. "I'm not worried. That cold medicine is pretty strong stuff. You'll forget any of this ever happened."

"Doubt it," I breathed.

How was I ever going to forget this? Armitage Gallier sweeping into my home because I needed someone. Taking care of me like he wanted to, like it was a law of the universe that he would, as natural as the sun coming up. Me accepting it.

It didn't make any sense.

"Even if you *do* remember, you're under an NDA," he said. "You'll never be able to tell the world that Armitage Gallier just might have a heart after all."

Vaguely, I heard the kettle whining across my tiny studio. The sound of hot water being poured. The scent of bergamot. The weight of a large body just barely sitting on the edge of the bed.

A trembling hand, brushing hair away from my forehead.

"Armitage?" I asked.

"Hm?"

I know you have a heart now, I wanted to say. *Why do you try so hard to hide it?*

But I dozed off before the words could make their way out.

CHAPTER TWENTY-THREE

THIS WAS NOT THE FIRST TIME EVELYN HAD SEEN THE INSIDE OF A jail cell. Growing up with the streets for a father, she'd tripped onto the wrong side of the law—that law being *don't be poor*—more times than she could count.

But this was the first time she'd been brutalized into one. Bruised face. Chafed wrists. Ribs only saved from breaking by the boning in her corset. Blood dried around her mouth. Scraped knees. Aching shoulders. Hair missing from the base of her skull. And, to top it off, mud and prison grime of indeterminate origin caking one of her favorite dresses.

Not that Evelyn would have taken it back. Jules and Akio were safe. That was worth any price, as far as she was concerned.

What was a little prison time and a little—or quite a lot of—pain, when her friends had been in danger?

There were dark quarters of her heart that told her she hadn't done this for entirely altruistic reasons. Facilitating Jules's escape was one thing, but goading four police officers during her arrest? That was a new level of foolhardy, even for her. But the pain kept her from examining that thought too closely.

If she'd done this to punish herself for failing with Thomas—

If she'd done this to punish herself for dancing on the edge of more-than-lustful feelings for him—

If she'd done this to exorcise her emotional pain into something real and manageable—

She simply did not wish to know.

Tucked away in the back of the crowded cell of whores and pick-pockets so the passing guards wouldn't decide her face *was* worth ruining, she barely heard the voice that called from the other side of the bars.

"Cross! Evelyn Cross!"

"Yes?"

The cell immediately broke out into titters of excited conversation and gossip. In retaliation, the copper—Mr. Push Broom Mustache himself—slammed his billy club noisily against the bars.

Silence answered. Evelyn's jailcell compatriots went quiet at the sound.

He jerked his veiny neck. "Come here to the bars, Cross. Hands behind your head."

Dread bundled in her stomach, and if she were to judge from the faces around her, her cellmates had the same thought she did. *This is going to be very, very bad.*

Maybe she'd gotten out of her first encounter with this man mostly unscathed, but now that she was here, in a holding cell where there was no one to protect her but the equally terrified, equally helpless women around her, there was no telling what kind of abuse she might have earned.

In the piss-colored light at the far end of the holding cell, with only the metal bars separating her from the officer, she squared her chin. If she was going to get beaten within an inch of her life or worse, she was at least going to do it with some goddamned dignity.

He took her in—from the bloodstain on her lips all the way down to her muddy boots. Then, he spit on them.

"It's a goddamned shame, you know that?"

"No," Evelyn said, barely opening her mouth. "But I'm sure you're going to enlighten me."

"It's the ones like you, the ones who have no respect for the law, the ones who take us for granted, that always have the connections."

"Connections?"

"Someone's gotten you out."

Her heart lifted. Someone had come to her rescue.

"Who?"

"Don't know."

She mentally flipped through her list of friends. Bea would do it, but she couldn't afford to pay anyone off without calling in favors she would not want to cash in. Jules and Akio would, too, but neither of them had the scratch either.

Officer Push Broom Mustache made no move for the ring of keys at his waist. Evelyn made a show of lowering her hands from her head and tapping her foot in anxious, annoyed anticipation.

"Well. If you don't mind, I'd appreciate it if you could let me out of here. Teddy Roosevelt would positively die if he saw the way you treat your female prisoners."

Invoking the name of the current police commissioner was probably a bit much. When she reached for the bars, he once again slapped his club down on them. She only barely rescued her fingers from the assault.

"One moment, Cross. I'm not done with you."

"Oh?"

Glancing over her shoulder, no doubt at their audience cowering in the shadows, he invaded her breathing air with the foul stench of saliva and cigar. "You might have gotten away tonight, and so did your little queer friends. But don't expect your luck to last forever. It's going to run out. And when it does, I'll be there. I have powerful friends too, you know."

And he said it with such conviction that she shivered.

It wasn't a threat. It was a vow.

⸫◆⸪

The police released her into the precinct's main office—a proud wooden-paneled room laid with a marble floor. The place was absolutely lousy with blue-backs, each of them crammed shoulder-to-shoulder around someone Evelyn couldn't see. The character was visible only by the crown of his silk top hat, which stood out around the sea of coppers' caps swirling around him.

Evelyn made her way toward the exit. Cops only got that excited for real bigshots—exactly the kind of person she *didn't* want to run into tonight. Surely whoever had come for her would be waiting outside where it was safe.

But then, as if God himself had reached down and parted the crowd, the coppers shifted, giving Evelyn a clear sightline.

"Mr. Gallier?"

Blue eyes met green. And for the first time that evening, she felt safe.

He looked nothing like the stone statue of a man she'd encountered in his office this afternoon—*this afternoon . . . had it really been just a few hours? That encounter felt a lifetime ago.* Now, the muscles in his face relaxed and he suddenly appeared ten years younger, worry and relief and a mess of vulnerability gripping his handsome features in equal, devastating measure.

Shouldering past the coppers separating them, he reached for her, gripping her shoulders in his strong, warm hands.

A storm cloud passed over Thomas's face when he noticed the blood smearing her mouth like cheap red lipstick. His entire body shook with rage. "What the hell have they done to you?"

"I'm fine—" she said, more out of force of habit than anything else.

He wasn't appeased. He spun on his heel, unleashing the full curse of his rage onto the nearby cops. Evelyn had never seen him like this, so unbridled and so passionate. So *emotional*.

A thrill went through her, unbidden. He'd been worried about her. He was *still* worried about her. Angry for her.

She'd unraveled him.

"Who did this? I demand to speak to the arresting officer. I was at dinner with the police commissioner tonight, and I'm sure he'd like to see what kind of rubbish he's employing—"

Evelyn nearly snorted at that. The police commissioner probably knew *exactly* what kind of "rubbish" he was employing. If he swept up all the rubbish, there'd be no Manhattan Police Department left.

The coppers quickly made themselves scarce because, well, of course they did. They were all very happy to do the head-bashing when no one was looking, but none of them wanted to be the ones with *their* heads bashed in once someone bigger and badder and more powerful came along.

Thomas kept shouting, his eyes wild and unfocused.

Evelyn reached for one of his hands, which was grabbing at the only copper left in striking distance.

That was all it took. One touch, and he stilled. His breathing didn't calm and his eyes didn't return to their usual, intelligent passivity. But at least he'd stopped trying to throttle the police trainees.

"Please?" she asked. "Can we just go?"

CHAPTER TWENTY-FOUR

FOR SOME REASON, HE HEEDED HER REQUEST.

The man was normally so un-suggestible, so stubborn, she could hardly believe it when he took her hand and led her outside to his idling carriage.

The carriage was one of those small numbers, a two-seater usually reserved for single gentlemen or married couples. Normally, Evelyn would have relished the chance to get this close to him, to toy with him by brushing her knees against his and *accidentally* jostling into his lap when the slow-moving carriage hit a bump in the street.

But she was so tired. Exhausted past her throbbing flesh and down to her bone marrow. Not just in her sore body, either. In her emotions. Only this morning, they'd been laughing their way across Coney Island. This afternoon, he'd thrown her over for some newspapers and convinced her that she meant nothing when weighed against his career and image. Then, there had been the fights, the beating, the arrest, the imprisonment . . .

And Thomas, for his part, looked even less willing than usual to entertain her teasing. So she kept her legs firmly tucked to the side and her hands to herself, even when Thomas wordlessly reached below his bank seat, withdrew a small canteen, splashed it out onto a handkerchief emblazoned in bright thread with his monogram, and handed it over to her like a peace offering.

Hesitantly, she accepted it and lifted the cool fabric to her swollen, split lip. The blood stained his expensive *mouchoir* and her fingertips.

"Quite a spectacular way to breach our contract, sir," she muttered at last.

Thomas blinked as if he'd been asleep for a long time and was only just coming back to consciousness. "I beg your pardon?"

"Work hours concluded some time ago," she reminded him blankly. "And here we are. Together."

"Unbelievable. I've just gotten you out of a jail cell and *that*'s what you're thinking of?"

"What's unbelievable was that you didn't leave me in that jail cell until open of business tomorrow," she muttered bitterly as she crumpled the bloody handkerchief and tossed it carelessly aside.

Thomas said nothing. Anger burned through Evelyn, singeing everything it touched. He'd made it very clear that they were no more than colleagues, that they never would be anything more, and that her *fixation* needed to be put to an end.

Well, she'd done that. She'd gotten the sentiment for him beaten right out of her. And yet, here he was, confusing everything.

"That's all we are, aren't we? A business affair," she reminded him.

A muscle in his jaw flexed. "What the devil happened tonight?"

"I picked a fight with the wrong people," Evelyn said. Her lips smarted from the fresh bruising, but still, she smirked. "Or the right ones, depending on your view of things."

Thomas shot her an exasperated look. "Will you ever stop your nonsense?"

"It seems ever so imprudent to borrow someone else's nonsense when I have such a vast store of my own."

In the dark of the carriage, it was nearly impossible to get a good read on the man. He seemed to be all nervous tension, but she couldn't decide from where that tension originated. Was he angry with her for getting herself tangled up with the law? Was he genuinely concerned for her safety? Why was the usually calm, controlled Thomas Gallier now flexing and clenching his gloved hands and darting his gaze around and breathing erratically? Why did it seem as if he were fighting against his very skin?

Not that Evelyn cared a whit for his discomfort. Not after he'd shown such careless disregard for hers this afternoon. And so, she goaded him.

"What? No laughter? None of those poorly hidden smiles that show you're trying not to be charmed by me? My, my, Thomas. It's a wonder you didn't leave me in that cell *forever*, never mind business hours tomorrow. You would have been well rid of me."

His eyes flashed, and something in Evelyn's heart cracked.

It all made perfect sense now.

"Ah. I see. It *is* business, then. You couldn't lose your headliner entirely, so you had to collect me at some point. You couldn't have me bloodied too bad—then I wouldn't have been any good onstage. You didn't break the rules because you care about me. But because you couldn't afford to lose your investment." Every word she spoke was like a fresh billy club blow. But better to feel the pain than delude herself any longer. In spite of herself, she'd believed so deeply in Thomas Gallier. And she had been disappointed at every turn. "We're a sufficient distance away from the precinct now. You can leave me here. I'll walk the rest of the way back to my boarding house, thank you."

She reached up to knock on the ceiling of their buggy and alert the driver to stop, but Thomas captured her hand in his, holding it fast. The warmth of him seeped through their gloves, making her wish she could feel that bare warmth on the rest of her.

Their eyes met. He was a man at war with himself—the evidence was written all over him.

Yet when he spoke, it was with a devastating clarity of purpose.

"You are not just an investment, Evelyn. I understand the terms of our agreement. And I understand that I've broken them. If you wish to get out of this carriage this minute, then I will oblige. Freely, if not happily. But I cannot allow you to leave thinking that you are merely an obligation."

Evelyn's breath hitched. It was as if he spoke those words onto the very fabric of her heart.

"I didn't come tonight to protect The Empire," he continued.

"Why did you, then?"

He opened his mouth once, then twice. "I'm afraid I can't answer that question directly. Not yet."

Evelyn rolled her eyes and turned once more toward the carriage door. Thomas tightened his grip on her ever so slightly. Pleadingly.

"But I would like to try," he said, his voice quieter than she'd ever before heard. "If you'll let me. And if I can find the courage."

"Courage? Why should you need courage?" What an odd thing to say. And so appropriate, considering she'd called him a coward just this afternoon.

He drank in a rattling, uncertain breath, still never letting go of her hand. "Because we cannot continue until there are no secrets between us. It wouldn't be fair. So . . . May I tell you something? Can you keep a confidence?"

If only he knew how silly that question was, he wouldn't have asked it. She'd gotten herself beaten and thrown in jail tonight to protect the secrets of two of her dearest friends. She could keep whatever Thomas had to throw at her. "I can."

He squeezed his fingers around hers, as if holding on to something he was desperate not to lose. "My name isn't Thomas Gallier."

The air thickened. A thousand emotions crossed Thomas's face, and she catalogued each and every one in turn. Fear and trepidation and hope and affection and so, so, so much shame.

When he opened his mouth again, gone was that English accent of his. So posh. So perfect. So aristocratic. So foreign. In its place, his voice rollicked with an Irish lilt much more familiar to Evelyn's ears. It was the music of the docklands, the rhythm of Five Points, the cadence of her backstage fellows.

It was his voice. His *real* voice. A little rusty and worn from disuse. But she didn't care. Because he was sharing it with her. And despite her still simmering frustration with him, she couldn't help but soften at the sound. It was beautiful.

"My name is Tom Gallagher. Just Tom, by the way. My mother— God rest her—was quite specific on that point."

That was the name he'd played under during their trip to Coney Island.

"Tom," Evelyn repeated, greeting him with this new name as if they were just meeting for the first time.

And maybe, really, they were.

A NOTE FROM THE HISTORIAN

In the year 1881, a story rocked the scandal sheets of London. Allow me to present a few headlines:

SCANDAL!

AN IMPOSTER IN THE GREAT HALLS OF LONDON!

A COMMON LAD'S DEFRAUDING OF A DUKE'S DAUGHTER!

This was certainly not the first such story to captivate the public's attention. There was Perkin Warbeck. Alexander Wood. Christian Gerhartsreiter. Stories of fakes and imposters and their rises and falls.

In fact, the more history I study, the more I see how everyone has their secrets. Everyone pretends to be someone else—at least a little bit. We hide ourselves, our motives, our feelings. Masking until we're sure we've convinced someone of our own fictions.

This story from the scandal sheets, though, concerned three men:

Tom Gallagher.

The Honourable Clement Fitzhugh Ridley, heir to the barony and viscountcy of Blagdon and Blythe.

And finally, Thomas Gallier.

CHAPTER TWENTY-FIVE

THOMAS DID NOT REALIZE HOW TIGHTLY HE WAS CLUTCHING MISS Cross's hands in his own. He only knew that she did not flinch or shy away. She held on to him nearly as fast.

He'd fought for years to keep this secret. To finally force the words out, to confess his truth to another human being—an action that every private molecule in his body rejected—proved difficult. But something was changing tonight. He couldn't proceed—he *wouldn't*—with lies. He'd done that for too long.

"My parents were Irish domestic staff in the service of the Viscount and Viscountess of Ridley," he said in a rush, the only way he knew how to speak this evening, it seemed.

"Sounds like a high time," she quipped.

"You may laugh, Miss Cross, but believe it or not, I had one of those rarest of British experiences. A happy childhood."

Thomas felt his lips curl in a smile.

Although his family's status had been lowly, his memories of his childhood had a kind of blessed, golden glow to them. His father had risen to the humble rank of assistant land manager while his mother worked as a kitchen servant with a talent for baking bread. No two people had ever been so in love. And no two people had loved their child as much. They were churchgoing folk, determined to teach their son the value of hard work, honesty, integrity, and laughter. His father taught him to read in the evenings, while his mother had a habit of singing softly to herself—songs that still lingered in the back of

Thomas's mind whenever he sat in the back of a vaudeville theater and heard funny tunes about love and summer afternoons.

His parents loved each other. He loved them. And they loved him. That should have been enough.

"I grew up alongside the Viscount and Viscountess's son. The Honourable Clement Fitzhugh Ridley, heir to the barony and viscountcy of Blagdon and Blythe."

A small laugh from his audience of one. "What a monogram he must have had."

"Please, Miss Cross. I am attempting to . . ." He swallowed hard. If she kept going with these interruptions, with these little jokes, he would lose his nerve. "This is a story I've never spoken aloud before. Please. Share it with me."

"Y-yes. Of course. By all means."

"Clement was sickly from the day he was born. A weak heart, they said. The Ridleys refused to take him out in society—they said it was because they feared for his fragile constitution, but they were ashamed of him. His parents were conventional, and even if Clement had been healthy, he would never have fit their ideals. Prone to fits and fixations, unable to navigate social situations, even as a young boy. He wasn't a suitable son, so they hid him away. I suppose they were just misguided. Waiting for the day he magically transformed into a son worthy of them. Someone the rest of society could accept. That day never came." Thomas swallowed back a wave of bitterness. Emotion was just like Evelyn—if he let himself have even a taste, he would want to drown himself in it. "I took after my father. Big, broad, strapping. I never wanted to be inside. I never had clean trouser knees. My shoes were always scuffed and I was always chasing some bird or bug or dog or another. I could speak to anyone about anything, charm the skin off a rabbit, navigate any crowd, be they rich or poor. I was everything the Ridley boy was not. Yet, unlikely as it was, Clement became my best friend. My brother, really."

In the reflection of the paned glass window, Thomas caught sight of Evelyn's jaw dropping slightly.

"Don't look so surprised, Miss Cross. I was a mere mortal once. Capable of such things."

"I'm not surprised," she replied gently. "You've always been mortal to me."

Thomas cleared his throat. "On his eleventh birthday, we escaped the house and snuck into town. A regiment had just arrived from a tour in Ireland, and they were parading. Two weeks later, Clement was dead. And so were my parents. And so were most of the other staff. Typhus, we were told. Ran through the entire estate like a wind of death. I can still feel it, you know. The way the whole house seemed to shudder when Clement's eyes closed for the last time."

"Thomas, I'm—"

"As it was," he continued abruptly, "I was a child without parents, and the Ridleys were parents without a child. Everything slotted together quite tidily, indeed. After all, it was easy to fire the remaining staff and bring on a new one, introducing me as the future viscount. I'd already picked up Clement's accent. No one outside of the Ridleys knew Clement, so no one knew I was an imposter. They buried him under a grave with my name on it and never visited. I was, from that moment on, their son. I was Clement."

It had all seemed so simple back then. Righteous, even. They told him this was what Clement would want. They told him this was best.

Now, he knew better. His life, his agency, his future—not to mention Clement's memory—they had all been sacrificed on the altar of the Ridleys' vanities and ambitions and longings and shames.

"They painted me in family portraits and I was given extensive lessons in elocution and sums and history. I went to Eton. Summered with dukes. Chased long, pretty silk skirts. Answered my adopted father and mother when they addressed me by a name that was not my own. Learned how to sneak enough drinks from their wine cellars and liquor stores to dull my pain away."

"And eventually, when I looked in the mirror, I did not see Tom Gallagher, the son of a landman and his songbird baker of a wife, but Clement Fitzhugh Ridley, the heir to all he surveyed. The older I grew, the more resigned I became to my fate."

His breath rattled in his chest, threatening to fail him. A small squeeze of hands in his spurred him on.

"And by the time I turned eighteen, it was as if my younger self never existed. I graduated from Eton with high marks and was meant to go on a Grand Tour—that's what aristocratic sons did, after all. Before that, though, a schoolmate invited me to a house party at his family seat. There, somewhere in my alcoholic haze, I met his sister."

He could still picture it in his mind's eye. The image of her was always a little distorted because of the amount he'd had to drink—it was common at that time, for him to awake in the morning with but a blurred recollection of the previous night's events. But still. She was a silly, sophisticated nit in a sunset-pink dress. Years ago, he'd shoved her in a drawer in the back of his mind. Thinking of her now was an ice pick to the sternum.

Eliza Jane.

"You loved her, didn't you?" Evelyn asked, at length.

"She was a duke's daughter. Wholly unsuitable for me, viscount's son or no."

"But you loved her all the same. Didn't you?"

Yes. Or as close to love as a foolish, drunken eighteen-year-old boy could manage. From the moment her brother introduced them, he was hers. She was precisely what Clement Fitzhugh Ridley should want. And he did.

Thomas winced and shrugged. What else could he do? He'd been determined to tell Evelyn Cross the truth tonight. And this was the center of that truth. The only way out now was through. "Perhaps you were right. Perhaps I have always been merely mortal, somewhere deep down. No two people were as in love as my parents. Living in the cold clutch of the viscount and his wife's dead, resentful, booze-soaked marriage for as long as I did only heightened the beauty of that love's memory. I'd spent a lifetime growing into another man's existence. I thought, perhaps, I could allow myself this one thing of my own. My own love. I've yearned for it all my life. And for a moment, I believed I had it."

He would never forget the delicious burn of that romance. Being near Eliza Jane was like his best memories of childhood, before the typhus had changed everything. It was like walking the grounds of Blagdon House at sunrise with Clement at his side—as if everything was at his fingertips, no matter how impossible.

"On the last night of the house party, more than tipsy on champagne and claret and anything else we could get our hands on, I declared myself to Eliza Jane. We fell into one of those entanglements men and women so often do when they find themselves beneath starlight . . . And in her euphoria, she cried out . . ."

Clement. Oh, Clement.

Even now, the echo of that sound was enough to send a shudder through his entire body. It had spoiled something so beautiful, awakened him from a dream.

He wanted her love. But he would not have it like that. His romance would be true, or he would have none at all.

He could not spend his entire life pretending. Not in everything. Not in love.

"I drew the assignation to a swift end. I loved her. I wanted her love in return. I could not live the rest of my life with another man's name *and* another man's love. It wouldn't have been right. It wouldn't have been real."

Real was a joke. But he'd spent his entire life searching for its punchline.

Nothing in his life was real. His name, his personality. Hell, even his line of work was theater—illusion.

"So when it was over, I cradled her in my arms and told her everything. I told her the truth—about my origin, about my parents, about the real Clement and the real Tom Gallagher. A fool's mistake."

"It wasn't foolish," Evelyn whispered earnestly.

Thomas wasn't sure he agreed with her. But he couldn't change the past now, even if he'd wanted to. Which, more and more lately, he was beginning to think he didn't. "Once I'd said my piece, she fled. A day later, every scandal sheet in England had the story, and in a day, I lost my position, my family, fake though they were, my friends. Everyone I'd loved betrayed me, abandoned me. I was a laughingstock in every room where I'd once been champion. And I didn't even have love to show for it."

She leaned forward. "What happened then?"

"The Viscount and Viscountess had liquidated many of their assets in preparation for my Grand Tour and to set me up with a house and a wife once I returned. I will never understand why, but they gifted that money to me. A few years later, when they died, I inherited everything else."

"You weren't *totally* abandoned, then."

"Guilt is a powerful thing, Miss Cross. And even monsters feel it every so often, I imagine. I won't pretend I didn't benefit from the decision, just as I benefited from their decision to make me into their son. I've never gone hungry, never lacked for creature comforts. But you know there's more to life than that.

"Anyway, I was suddenly an incredibly wealthy man with no name and no prospects and no plan. I went to France for a few years. At first, I went to their vaudeville halls and the Folies Bergère for escape. They were places a man could waste a great deal of time and money drinking and whoring himself into a stupor. But in the few, quiet moments of sobriety I allowed myself, I learned a great deal from that world. I learned how to make an illusion real."

"And how do you do that?"

"By making the world a stage. By never allowing anyone to see that it *is* an illusion."

That, he knew she could understand. They both lived by that simple axiom, didn't they?

"That was my mistake, after all. I had gotten out of control. I'd been drunk and reckless and trusted someone with my secrets. I'd let my affections drive me out of my senses. I'd been so addicted to feeling good, to feeling loved, to being myself, that I'd let it rob me of my future. So I took control of my life. I swore off women. I never touched liquor again. And I reinvented myself for this new, American stage, determined to win back a life for myself. I changed my name from Tom Gallagher to Thomas Gallier—Gallagher was too Irish, of course, and if I was going to make it anywhere in America, I knew that was the last thing I could be. I re-trained myself in the ways of an English gentleman. I made a vow to re-conquer society. To claw my way to the top again."

"Why?"

"Why what?"

"You could have done anything. You were a wealthy man. You could have stayed in Europe. You could have lived out the rest of your days in perfect comfort. You didn't need to become one of them again—"

His pride flared. "They rejected me. I was molded and shaped into one of them my *entire life*. My real self was thrown into a shallow grave at eleven years old with the body of my best friend and now, I am this. I wanted their acceptance. I wanted to be so powerful they could never deny me again."

Undeniable. That's what he'd wanted to be.

"So I hid everything I could of my past. I became a performer—or, I suppose I became one *again*. I controlled every aspect of my life. I never let anyone see past the mask. It was the only way to secure my future, you see."

Her gaze pierced him. "Yes, I see. I see an incredibly lonely man with the world at his feet and nothing in his heart."

Yes. He supposed that was true.

"You've never told anyone any of this?" she asked. "Never?"

It was then that he realized her hands had never left his.

She knew the truth of him . . . and she wasn't leaving. She wasn't pulling away or running to the scandal sheets.

"No. Not until this moment. Not until you."

CHAPTER TWENTY-SIX

EVELYN HAD ALWAYS KNOWN. OTHERS MIGHT HAVE BEEN FOOLED, but she had a professional eye, and it had noted every crack in his mask and loose thread of his costume. Still, to finally know Tom Gallagher in fullness . . .

It destroyed everything she'd thought of him to this moment.

Or, perhaps, not of *him*. But of what the two of them could mean to one another.

Until this night, she'd fancied the possibility of a dalliance. He was unconscionably handsome, and good in a way she wasn't used to. He respected her. He treated her well. Their tryst on Coney Island had given her a taste of him; she wanted more. She had thrilled at the thought of unraveling this tightly bound-up man. And perhaps bedding him, so powerful and so coveted, would have helped her overcome the self-consciousness that had been haunting her ever since Miss Banting's had gone up outside her dressing room window. All this alongside the fact that they had true chemistry, the kind that didn't come about every day.

Yes, the reasons for wanting to fuck this man—controlling and remote as he could often be—were plentiful. They were never far from her thoughts, either.

But here, on this night, with this revelation, she knew it was possible for her to want more. That he was *offering* her more.

And that could not be allowed.

Evelyn pulled in a shaky breath. "Why have you told me this?"

"Tonight, a very appealing offer was made to me. An offer that might have fulfilled all of my hopes. All of my ambitions. However, it came with certain . . . strings attached. Strings that made me look down the barrel of my future and hate what I saw loaded for me there. After a lifetime of seeking control over my destiny, I found myself on the brink of trading that for a bit of good press and a place at a powerful man's table. And I finally saw in myself that cowardice of which you spoke this afternoon."

He laughed. Evelyn did not. The carriage rattled on.

"Tonight, I saw the possibility of a future with someone else. A life of cynical social climbing. A life without laughter or warmth or wonder. A life that mirrored the one I'd left back in England. A life . . . A life without you. And I couldn't bear the thought of it. So when I heard you were hurt, I knew I had to make a decision. And this was the one I made."

"And you told me about yourself—?"

"Because I am not content with our current agreement, and I couldn't imagine changing the terms of our relationship without you knowing the truth. I needed you . . . I *want* you to care for me. Not who I have pretended to be."

The carriage pulled to a sudden, steep halt. Evelyn blinked the past from her eyes and found herself once again in Manhattan, far away, but not as far as she would have liked, from the pain of the man sitting across from her.

Their hands were still interwoven.

To her relief, the carriage driver afforded her a few minutes to collect her thoughts and harness her feelings before he opened the door, lowered the step, and ushered her down onto the street outside Thomas's house.

Thomas's house, she noticed. Not her boarding house.

If the mood between them hadn't been so uncertain, she might have made a joke of it, might have raised her eyebrows when he quietly murmured a request for her coat, might have started for the stairs instead of his sitting room when he removed it from her shoulders.

But, as it was, she felt she not only stood on his floorboards but also on the brink of a thousand-foot drop. She couldn't allow herself to fall.

"I didn't wish for you to return to the boarding house in such a state," he said, by way of explanation. "I don't know much about your friend Miss Matterly, but I imagine she would have had my head if you didn't at least receive some medical attention. Given his family's feelings on his medical career, Dr. Samson uses my back parlor as a clinic on occasion, so my supplies should be sufficient to clean you up."

With that, he opened the French doors of the sitting room, where a roaring fire illuminated tasteful and utterly plain furniture towered high with what must have been every pillow and blanket in the house. A small rolling bar had been retrofitted with nearly a dozen medical supplies in various shapes and forms—scissors and needle and thread (thoughtful, but unnecessary) and medicines in glass vials and rags and hot water bottles and real, honest-to-goodness *ice* and—

That's when she knew for certain that he hadn't been lying. This rescuing act of his wasn't about the show or his business or their various agreements.

It was more than that. Far, far more.

He wanted to care for her. Something, it seemed, he'd never done for anyone.

She didn't have the first clue what to do with a man like that.

Hand hovering over her lower back but never quite touching it, Thomas guided her to the makeshift hospital bed and propped her up on the pillows. Wordlessly, they set about the work of playing doctor and patient. She sat still as he positioned the hot water bottle against her ribs, as he wet a rag and washed the last of the blood from her lips, her eyes, the column of her neck.

With his every touch, she felt as if he were not only fitting the fragmented pieces of her back together, but fitting *them* together, too. Here in the halls of his home, they were both stripped of their performances and pretensions and suddenly, finally, *actually* alone.

Just Tom and Evelyn.

In his silence, she heard a thousand questions he couldn't bear to ask her out loud. He'd just bared his soul and she'd not said a thing. He must have taken it as a rejection, condemnation.

"I understand," he said, at length, his voice trembling as badly as his hands, "if you wish to draw our association to a close. I only hope you'll let me finish looking after you now."

"Why would I want to do that? Leave you, I mean."

"You know who I am now. What was done to me. What I've done."

"Yes," she said, meeting his gaze firmly. "I do. And I'm still here."

The fact that she was exerting all her self-control to keep a wave of warm, romantic sentiment from overtaking her was reason enough for her to leave. To run down the street, out of the city, across the ocean, and never look back.

But when the light of the fire danced in his eyes and he tipped her chin upward with one gentle finger, she knew she wouldn't be leaving.

"So you are. And if that is going to remain the case . . . ?"

He asked for confirmation with his eyes, and she nodded. She was Evelyn Cross. She could salvage this. She could keep this wonderful man in her arms *and* her heart firmly protected. She'd never faltered before. Surely, Thomas Gallier would not be the first man to break her.

He grinned. So did Evelyn. It was decided.

"I think we should court," he said, at the exact same moment Evelyn declared, "We should have an affair."

Present Day

I DON'T THINK THAT, AFTER THE WHOLE "SLEEPING OVER AT MY house to make sure I didn't die of the flu in my sleep" thing, it was a particular secret that I liked Armitage.

Okay. Let's be honest. It probably wasn't a secret from the beginning, either. But it *definitely* wasn't after that.

More shocking, though, was that he didn't keep his feelings a secret anymore, either. At least, not from me.

Our relationship was almost assumed. Easy. Our affection incidental. Domestic. As we worked together, it was like we'd been doing it all our lives. I'd gently tease him. He'd try to parry back, but never as well because he wasn't used to being liked enough to be teased. He'd bring me tea and go out for waffles at a place I'd mentioned loving one time. I'm pretty sure he rigged a ticket contest after I'd talked about never having gone to a Yankees game. After work, he'd ask me out to the terrace for a drink or up to the observatory to watch the sunset over Central Park. We'd tuck ourselves in the window and people-watch. Sit close but never touch. I'd think about kissing him, think the moment was right, but never make a move.

We talked a lot, but never about anything important.

Or perhaps, what I should say is that we talked about some stuff that was *very* important to me, but probably not to him. And I always tried to keep it casual so that he wouldn't know just how much I wanted to know the answers to the questions I was asking in a carefully lighthearted, almost ironic tone.

Do you have a girlfriend, Armitage? No. *Boyfriend?* No. *Partner?* You're my research partner. Does that count?

Have you ever written a love letter? No, and I've never had the urge to, either. Not yet.

How was your date last night? I saw that picture of you in the society pages. It wasn't a date. She was barely dinner conversation. Just something my father set up so I wouldn't look ridiculous sitting next to an empty chair.

We never talked about our feelings. We just danced with each other around them. Afraid that it all might burst if we so much as breathed on each other wrong. But to me, whatever was going on between us was like finding a life raft in the middle of a stormy sea.

The night that everything changed started with grilled cheese. He'd had food poisoning for four days after attending the wedding for a Getty or a Rockefeller or a Kennedy or something, so when he found himself on the mend, I decided it was the perfect recovery food.

Harmless enough, right?

"I can't believe you've never eaten a grilled cheese before," I said, slathering butter on two big pieces of cheap white bread I'd grabbed from the bodega around the corner. "It's like, an American delicacy."

"That explains it. They don't teach the fine art of grilled cheese at Swiss boarding school."

"No grilled Swiss cheese?" I made a ba dum tss sound and faked hitting a drum kit rim shot with the butter knife. He flattened his stare. I surrendered. "Sorry. Bad joke."

His shoulder brushed mine as he gingerly placed the cheese— puzzle pieces to a picture he hadn't ever seen before. "I happen to like your bad jokes."

"Oh, boy. Then we've definitely got to get you out more. What do you say? Comedy show tonight? I know a great place in the Village."

A gamble, asking him out like that. The grilled cheese sizzled in the pan.

"Yeah," he said at last. "I think I'd like that."

"Really? Like a . . . like a date?"

Okay, *that* was pushing it.

Still—he blinked at me over the stove.

"Isn't that what we've been doing? Dating?" he asked.

My jaw dropped slightly and I totally botched the grilled cheese flip. "I thought we were doing more of an unresolved workplace sexual tension thing."

"I see."

"It's not that I don't want to date you. I just didn't think—I mean, I never thought that you would—"

"Yes, I would. I really would." His face shifted and I could tell he was going to take one of his rare stabs at teasing me back. "Because there's one American delicacy I've been desperate to try, and it's not the grilled cheese."

My stomach fluttered, but I rolled my eyes anyway. "Now *that* was a terrible joke—"

All of a sudden, the air in the house shifted and a great *thump, click, click* rang out. The sound of the aging front door opening and closing again, its heavy lock-latch clicking into place. Armitage and I jumped away from each other, surprised by the sudden intrusion.

No one ever came to this house. It was our retreat. A sanctuary. Our own private world.

Not anymore. A deep, booming voice called out: "Armitage?"

Everything in his demeanor changed. His spine straightened. His face fell. His eyes clouded. He took another step away from me, and ran a hand through his hair, trying to arrange it out of the mess it had been in all day.

"I—" he whispered. "Will you go into the next room?"

"What?"

"It's my father. Please. He doesn't know about—about the research."

Everything in me wanted to ask, *What are you, twelve? What does it matter if your dad sees me or knows about what we're doing here?* But this was the first time I'd seen anything even approaching panic in Armitage's handsome face, so . . . "Sure. Okay."

Quick as I could, I stepped through the nearest door, which turned out to be the pantry, and closed it behind me. Darkness washed over me, cut through only by the tiniest shaft of light across the floor from the kitchen. Heavy footsteps from expensive shoes accompanied Mr. Gallier's entrance.

Yeah. I eavesdropped. I couldn't help it. It wasn't like it was a noise-canceling pantry.

"What the hell are you doing in here?" a dismissive voice asked.

"Just . . . cooking."

"You? Cooking? What are we now, poor?"

"No, sir."

"And what is this? A sandwich?"

"Grilled cheese."

"You're joking. That shit will clog your arteries."

A *swish* of the trash can signaled the sandwich's immediate and final end. My heart panged. Not because of the gesture, but because of how quickly Armitage followed the order.

"We aren't grilled cheese people, Armitage."

"Of course not."

"What are you doing in this fusty old house anyway? People will start to think something's wrong with the penthouse. Can't have them whispering. That building cost a fortune and we still need to move four units on the seventh and eighth floors."

"Just trying it out. I'm thinking about moving here, actually. It's beautiful."

"Absolutely not. It's a relic. You should get rid of it. Sell it. You'll make a fortune—and not a small one, either. One of the last mansions left on the Avenue. The Duke Mansion sold for eighty million last year, and that place was an absolute shithole."

I knew about the Duke Mansion. Shithole was not a word I would have used to describe it. Ever. But Armitage flatly replied:

"Yes, sir. Great thinking."

"I didn't believe it when your secretary said this is where you'd been working lately. I was having a hell of a time trying to find you. Wanted to check and see that you were still alive. You haven't been answering my calls."

"Alive and very well. Sorry about the calls. Been working on a project."

"Anything you want to clue me in on?"

"No, sir. Just a small side thing. Not worth your time."

"Then it's likely not worth yours, either."

My chest tightened. So did Armitage's voice.

"Sure."

There was another ten minutes or so of conversation. Well, not so much conversation as a diatribe from the older man on everything from worry about Armitage's diet—apparently, he also spotted a bag from our last waffle truck visit in the trash—to the idiocy of the CEO of the company they were about to acquire, to the weather (aka the only thing a man as wealthy as Mr. Gallier couldn't control). There was much *mm-hm*-ing and *yes, sir*-ing from Armitage, who suddenly sounded nothing like the warm, quietly funny man I'd been falling for these last few weeks.

Eventually, Mr. Gallier left. I gave it a few minutes before I emerged from my hiding place. Armitage sat at the kitchen table, staring ahead at the wall, face blank and expressionless.

I sat next to him. Hands on the expensive wood grain of the table's surface. Wordlessly at first, and then:

"Why are you so afraid of him?"

"I'm not afraid of him." Fingers reached out and brushed my own, then laced through. He pulled my hand up to his lips, pressed the smallest kiss I'd ever been given into my skin, and breathed: "I'm afraid of you."

I didn't know what he meant then. And the moment was too fragile to break. I let it go.

I shouldn't have.

That night, Armitage asked if we could stay in instead of going to the comedy club. He looked so small, so sad, that I couldn't think of any reason to say no.

There it was again. The funny feeling that he was playing *go away, closer.*

Just like Evelyn and Thomas. Always on the knife's edge of disaster and hope.

We were everything, and we were nothing.

Just like them.

CHAPTER TWENTY-SEVEN

Thomas's mind blanked.

I want to have an affair.

I think we should court.

"I beg your pardon?"

But Evelyn was equally confused, a fact that only perplexed *him* even further.

"I beg *your* pardon?" she asked.

"I said I wanted to court you. And you said—"

"That we should have an affair, yes."

Still, they stared at one another as though they were speaking different languages without a phrasebook to help them translate.

"What do you mean, an affair?" he spluttered.

"You're a grown man, Thomas," she said. "I hardly think I need to explain the mechanics to you. You certainly didn't this afternoon at Coney Island."

Considering how long it had been since his last full, pre-Evelyn indulgence, a refresher wouldn't go amiss.

"Besides," Evelyn continued, "I don't know why you're looking at me as though I've just proposed a murder. Or worse, as though I've just proposed that we *court*."

"It's not such a ridiculous proposal as murder," he said, an incredulous laugh bubbling to the surface.

"You're right. It's worse."

For the first time in his life, he wanted partnership—not a dalliance on one hand or an alliance on the other. Yet here was the one woman with whom he could see himself taking on the world, and she had no interest in being anything but his own personal featherbed.

"Miss Cross—"

"*Really*, I think if we're going to embark on an affair, we should call one another by our Christian names, Tom."

"I never agreed to an affair."

Oblivious to his inner turmoil, Evelyn fluttered her eyelashes, the minx. "You're going to hurt my feelings. Don't you *want* to hop into bed with me?"

God, yes. He'd wanted her from the first moment they'd met, and that desire had only become more potent with every minute they'd spent together. The more she talked about it now, the more carnal images his mind conjured, the more he yearned for their connection from this afternoon, and the more he thought of that, the harder refusing her became.

And the harder he became.

"That's not the point."

"And what is the point, exactly?"

"That I don't just want to . . ."

Make love to her? Bed her? Fuck her? He couldn't get the words out; they all seemed too intimate, too forward. Well aware that most other men in his position would have taken her in their beds the moment she so much as suggested she was amenable to it, Thomas tried not to shrink in embarrassment as he held firm to his convictions.

"Courtship has rules. It has guidelines and structure. It's safer for both of us if we proceed from this point with caution."

"Safer for whom? Yes, courtship has rules and guidelines and structures, Thomas, but it also has an endgame. Marriage."

Marriage. Yes, he supposed courtship did imply such a commit-ment. It was one he wasn't ready to make, not yet, anyway. Filing that "yet" away for later contemplation, he focused instead on what marriage meant. Not just financial and legal bonds, but emotional ones, too.

If his parents' marriage, the one by which he judged all others, was any indication, to be married was to be one's entire, unashamed self. It was vulnerability. It was trust. It was to be truly known. And to take the broken pieces of yourself, join them to someone else, and become whole again in the process.

Maybe he and Evelyn would never be married. But the *promise* of marriage? To be seen after a lifetime of hiding? To feel un-alone after a lifetime of solitude?

"I shouldn't wish our relationship to be purely physical. And I sus-pect that desire is shared. You have always said you could see through me. But I see through you, too, Evelyn."

She shuddered. He continued.

"You use sex as a shield. Whenever you think you're in danger of exposing your heart, you put it between us. I couldn't bear the thought of being just another conquest. I didn't expose myself tonight so you could remain concealed. I won't be another body you've used and thrown away in your eternal quest to keep yourself safe from . . . Well, I don't rightly know *what*, exactly, you think you're protecting yourself from."

Her physical attitude didn't change, but something in the timbre of her voice did. It still danced musically as usual, but now, the sound rang hollow. "If we're doing story time tonight, I may as well tell you. But don't go falling in love with me just because I spilled a few secrets, you hear? I'm only telling you so you'll let me get into those trousers of yours."

Another evasion. Another clever use of sex to keep him from getting too close.

"Understood."

She rushed into her speech. The sentences stumbled over each other like clumsy chorus girls unable to fall in line. "It's an old story, my parents'. My father was a top hat, you know? Rather like you, but with even more money and a family name as old as time. My mother was a new immigrant fresh off the boat from Germany, so new her clothes still reeked of pretzels and sauerkraut. She finds employment as a lady's maid, meets a man who promises her the moon, gets her pregnant, and then immediately abandons her. Fires her from his household staff, too, just to add insult to injury."

The scoundrel. In his time spent around high society, he'd met too many men just like Evelyn's father. They acted selfishly, completely oblivious or uncaring to how their actions might echo. If he had been born with what he had now, he might have become one of those men.

He and Evelyn—and their stories—couldn't have been more different. But at the heart, they were the same.

An old tune sung with new lyrics. Both shunted between the upper class and the lower. Both haunted by bodies and lives that didn't belong to them. Ambition fueling them. Pain never quite leaving them. Hearts big as the whole outdoors hidden behind matchbox firewalls.

"Anyhow, my mother raised me on her own and she never took another man. She loves that bastard who left her even to this day. Even after what he did to her. She's dying a very, very slow death of a broken heart."

During the length of their acquaintance, Evelyn only ever peered out from behind her internal defenses. At turns bawdy and brassy and absurd, and then sentimental and loving, she was always putting on a show, holding herself separate from her audience. But now, as she was talking about her mother, Thomas thought he finally saw her in fullness. In all her beautiful and biting and realistic and fantastical glory.

"Everyone who knew my mother before she met that man said she was a brilliant, vibrant woman. I wish I could have met that woman instead of the one who raised me. I bought her a little farm up in Queens. Pay her an allowance. Give her all the comfort and care she deserves. She's sweet. But she could have been so much more."

The sadness in her eyes was nearly enough to break him.

"What happened to him? Your father, I mean."

"He was killed. One of his other conquest's fathers found out about their dalliance and shot him dead in the middle of Park Avenue."

"A tragedy," he remarked dryly.

"Only tragedy is that I wasn't the one to pull the trigger."

They wallowed in the delicious filth of that comment for a few silent moments.

"And that's why you won't indulge in romance. Your past experiences have cured you of the affliction," Thomas said, in summation.

"Precisely. See, you understand."

"No, I don't."

And he truly didn't. She *did* love many, many people. She loved more deeply and with more passion than he'd believed possible. Theoretically, what was one more person to love?

"I'm never going to give some man the power to hurt me like my mother was hurt. Affairs, I can handle. They are physical matters. Sex is about power and pleasure. I always know what I am putting into it, and what I expect to get out of it. But courtship? Feelings? No. I won't have it. If your addictive nature and your need for control are your biggest weaknesses, then my heart is mine."

"It's not—"

"Fine, then. My biggest vulnerability. A massive, gaping hole in my armor. I have lived my life with one rule. One *simple* rule. *Never* fall in love. I won't risk breaking that rule. It's best for all parties involved."

They really were more alike than he ever could have imagined. Two cynics who had spent their entire lives clinging to rules—trying to light out the long shadows cast over them.

Thomas had half a mind to end things there. He shouldn't push her. He shouldn't pressure her. If she didn't want this, then, fine.

But he couldn't hold back. Not when she shivered even in his warm room, not when she looked as though she needed someone to wrap their arms around her and whisper that everything would be alright.

"Things can be different, you know. It won't always be like your father and mother's story. The world, people, the times. They can change."

"Oh, I'm well aware," she replied with a big, sad grin. "It's just that they usually change for the worse."

A beat passed between them. He had nothing to say to that. He'd experienced enough of society to see how it treated anyone deemed different or lesser. He thought of Clement, of those poor elephants, of his younger self. Maybe she was right.

When Evelyn was finally finished cleaning her wounds, she rose to her feet, brushed at her ruined skirts, and squared her jaw in his direction. The attitude told him this was either the end of things or the very, very beginning.

"An affair is what I'm comfortable with. It's what I'm offering. If you don't want that, I understand. I'll still be your business associate. And, if you'd like, your friend. But intimately, you can have me like this, or you can have me not at all—"

He didn't hesitate before crashing his lips to hers.

They were two people bound by rules. *No contact outside of working hours. No recklessness. No love affairs.* Rules, rules, rules.

Perhaps it was time to see how it would feel to finally break them.

A NOTE FROM THE HISTORIAN

Now, this is probably the part of the story where you're bracing yourself and wondering, "Oh, God, wasn't the 'fingering her at Coney Island' thing bad enough? Is she really about to give us a fully realized sex scene between these two?"

And to your question, yes, fuck you, I'm writing a sex scene, and with God as my witness, if I hear one more peep of complaint, I'm going to make the rest of this story nothing *but* sex scenes.

CHAPTER TWENTY-EIGHT

ALL HER LIFE, EVELYN HAD KNOWN EXACTLY WHEN TO EXPECT A kiss, how to position her face to perfectly accept the gesture. She knew how to anticipate. She knew how to outplay. That was the only way to win the game, after all. To be better at it than the men with whom she played could ever hope to be.

But when Thomas's soft, inexperienced lips met hers, her entire body awakened with the surprise of it. This was not a performance, nor was it desperate and stilted as that first kiss at Coney Island had been.

This was the real thing. And suddenly, as his hands cupped her face and drew her deeper into it, she felt as inexperienced and new as he must have.

A flush of lust overtook her, and she grabbed him by the front of his tuxedo, dragging him onto the couch with her. It may have been more appropriate to trip up the stairs together, pinning each other against the walls and stealing more of these hot, breathless kisses along the way, but she didn't care.

She wanted him. Here. Now. Like this.

They moved like one body, rolling against one another as intimately as their excessive clothing would allow. Her bruised ribs and aching muscles protested at the jostling, but the rest of her couldn't care less. His touch was as healing as it was destructive, and she would walk through fire if it meant she could have more of him.

Hands moving from her face so he could brace himself on the back of the couch and hover above her, one knee settled between her thighs while one foot balanced his weight firmly on the floor. As she moaned into his kiss, Evelyn rolled her hips against his knee, relishing the delightful pressure.

She was perfectly wanton. Already begging for him, practically. This afternoon hadn't been enough. She wanted *all* of him.

But just that simple motion seemed to smash Thomas back into something resembling reality, because no sooner had she done it than he resurfaced from her with wide, worried eyes.

"I really feel as though I should apologize."

"And I really feel as though sex doesn't need this much conversation, thrilling as the conversation may be," she said, raising her hands to slowly slip the tuxedo jacket from his shoulders. It fell limply to the floor. She began, then, with his shirt buttons, slowly slipping them out of their placket until that, too, fell to the floor.

His body was hard to her touch. Firm and solid and impossibly strong for a man with a build as slight as his. But what really struck Evelyn was the hammering of his heart, which she could feel even as she grazed his chest ever so carefully.

She dragged her hand against his undershirt until her palm rested against that throbbing muscle in the left side of his ribcage. The epicenter of his fear.

"It's just that I haven't done this in quite some time and when last I did—"

"Thomas."

His heart didn't slow beneath her hand.

"Tom."

Ah, there it was. The rhythm steadied. So did his erratic breathing. He looked up at her from beneath dark eyelashes, and in those eyes, she suddenly saw the young boy who'd had his life stolen from him. A boy whose entire existence had been spent yearning for the approval of others. A boy who hadn't ever had the chance to become his own man.

She knew the look because she saw it in her own mirror so often. She'd been fourteen when a man first had her—a booking agent who said he could take her out of the chorus and get her a full twenty-five-cent raise if she just did a little *private dance* for him in his office.

Ever since then, she'd had sex because she knew it could get her things. Sometimes, she enjoyed it. Sometimes, she didn't. Sometimes, she *really* didn't.

But this . . . This was different. She and Tom were equals now. And the only thing she wanted from him was, well, him.

"I just don't want to disappoint you," he said softly.

She brushed a stray lock of hair away from his forehead. "As if such a ridiculous thing is even possible."

"But—"

No. The two of them had spent too long at the mercy of others' whims. Too long trading their very essences for the satisfaction and help of others. Tonight, they would, for maybe the first time in their lives, have something that was just theirs.

A stolen moment for themselves in a lifetime of moments stolen from them.

She would never love Thomas Gallier. *Could* never love him. Couldn't allow it of herself. But she could give him this. They could *share* this.

"Do you want me?" she asked, breathing the question against his lips.

"Yes. Since the moment I saw you."

"Likewise. So, then. Let's have each other."

She could almost feel his lips quirking upward in a small, hesitant smile. "Just like that?"

The smallest of nods she gave him brushed her mouth against his. A suggestion. A welcome. A question. "Just like that."

But Tom didn't answer. He hesitated.

So Evelyn began to kiss her way down his throat, reveling every time he shivered at the contact.

"You know," *kiss . . . shiver,* "once I told you that I never trusted a man's promises until after he'd bedded me." *Kiss . . . shiver.* "A person's words can lie, but his actions never do." *Kiss . . . shiver.* "If you really want more for us than just sex . . ." *Kiss . . . shiver.* "Tom," *kiss . . . shiver,* "then I think it would be prudent for you to show me. Entirely, this time. Not just part of the way like you did this afternoon." *Kiss . . . shiver.*

That was all the permission he needed. After far too long, Tom threw himself into the moment, bringing his own mouth to her soft skin and working his way down, down, down from the top of her throat to the place where her breasts swelled against her corset. Ripping away her topcoat and shirt—almost certainly ruining them in the process—he fought the coarse boning of her stays to withdraw her breasts without loosening the laces.

Between her legs, his hardness pressed against the fabric of her skirts, stroking against her center. She rocked her hips against him, groaning in pleasure as his mouth found her nipple and began to pleasure that, too.

They were a mess of hands and mouths, cries and hisses. Somehow, Evelyn managed to get his shirt over his head in a brief reprieve between his campaigns upon her breasts, and once his skin was finally revealed to her, she couldn't help brushing her own hands over his nipples, just to see him writhe from the sensation of it.

From his chest, it was now her turn to descend, relieving him of his trousers in a fit of buckles and buttons. His shoes and socks followed. Once they were gone, all they had left between them were the folds of her skirts, her combination, and his undershorts.

Lifting her from the couch, Thomas easily unbuttoned the back of her skirt, and the fabric fell away. The combination went next . . .

And then, she was lying before him much as she had the first night they'd met. Only this time, there was nothing on her body but a pushed-down corset. Her open legs revealed her wet center. Her breasts were on full display.

She was ready for him. Waiting. And from the growing hardness straining against his underclothes, she could tell he was too.

For a moment, though, he looked at her from the bottoms of her feet all the way to the top of her head and then back down again, drinking in the fullness of her every curve and valley.

She flushed. When was the last time anyone had looked at her like this? Had anyone *ever* done so?

In that moment, under his scrutiny, she wasn't just being observed. She was being *adored*.

"Do you like what you see?" she asked, if only to break the tension. "You know, when you turned me away all those times, I believed it was because you were like the rest of them. Disgusted by me. Or at least pretending to be so that you could fit in."

His tongue darted out across his bottom lip. Hungry. There was no doubt his lust was genuine. "I've never seen anyone so beautiful."

Likewise, she wanted to say, but she didn't have the time. The word was replaced with a cry of ecstasy. Because when she opened her mouth to say it, he bowed down between her legs, took her clit in his mouth, and gave it the same treatment he'd given his bottom lip only a second ago.

She arched her back, desperate to get closer to his touch. He obliged, tasting deeply of her, reacting to her sounds and movements as she made them, coaxing more of them out of her with every passing second. The dizzying high of a climax approached with the speed of a streetcar—

But just when she thought she might get struck, she laced her fingers through his hair and pulled him away from her.

"I want you inside of me," she said, breathless. "Please."

"But—"

"Not to worry. I fully intend to finish what you started."

It took a moment to navigate the use of contraception. Thomas, not imagining himself a man who would have an affair, did not keep any on his person or even in his home, while Evelyn, who generally did just that, had suffered her bag being taken from her at the police station. It had not been returned—another reason to curse those cops—but she was hardly inclined to spare a thought for them at this critical moment. It was Thomas who thought to avail themselves of Andrew's makeshift medical ward, which—thank goodness—had sheaths to spare, and soon enough, they returned to the moment as though they'd never taken a reprieve in the first place.

Once again, Thomas brought his lips to hers and they crashed into one another. The taste of herself on his tongue sent her nearly to madness, and she rocked her hips against his, drawing the hard length of him fully inside her in one smooth gesture.

They cried out together this time, and found their rhythm together—slowly at first, and then with increasing need and intensity with every passing moment. Thomas guided her along him, and she tightened with every stroke inside of her. Gripping onto him with one arm, she lowered her other hand down between her legs, rolling her fingers along her clit and once again bringing herself toward the peak of her pleasure.

She could feel it. They were both close. They were both so, so close.

"Thank you," Thomas whispered against her skin, burying his face in her neck.

And that was all it took. Evelyn toppled over the brink, shattering in a climax that sent fireworks exploding behind her eyes. She tightened around him, and before she knew it, he reached his own apex, too, crying out her name with every reckless thrust.

They each breathed their recovery for a few seconds, staring blearily into each other's eyes as they came down from their shared height.

When they returned to earth, Evelyn couldn't help but smile. Something in her smile must have triggered something in Thomas, because he returned it and before either of them knew how or why, they were both laughing.

Evelyn had never laughed like that before. Not with any man. And she wondered if it could be like this always. If she could feel this way forever.

If this was what love felt like.

And if it was . . .

How was she going to keep herself from falling for him?

CHAPTER TWENTY-NINE

LATER THAT NIGHT, THOMAS DRIFTED OFF WITH EVELYN IN HIS arms. In that hazy gray space between the waking world and his dreams, a single urge slipped into his consciousness as easily as thought.

Good night, he wanted to say. *I love you.*

The thought opened his eyes and banished all thoughts of sleep.

Love.

He loved her.

The revelation was first shocking, then natural. Obvious.

Of course he would love her.

He knew it with striking clarity. He was a romantic, and as much as he might have tried to deny it, he could no longer ignore the love-starved part of him that still carried his parents' wedding portrait in the false bottom of his trunk. That demanded more love songs in The Empire's piano players' repertoires. That watched young couples strolling through the park with piercing jealousy.

For years, he'd cast aside all romantic notions because he knew himself: once he had a taste—of strong drink or strong feeling—he always wanted more. And he knew how deeply he'd wanted to love someone.

Now, he did. He loved Evelyn, body and soul. And that changed everything. No longer could he allow himself to be driven by the whims of newspapers or financiers. No longer could he bend to fit the small-minded attitudes of men who would never allow themselves the luxury of such an unsuitable lover.

It would be complicated, of course. Allowing Evelyn into his heart this way. There were practical considerations about their future, The Empire. Taking himself off the marriage market would surely cause a stir. Alban would need to be dealt with. And Evelyn would need convincing that their love wasn't an *affliction* for her to fight.

The course would not be smooth or simple. But if a man truly wanted control over his own destiny, his own life, he did not begin by selling short his own heart.

Let no one say that Tom Gallagher was not a man of his word. He had made the choice. He would now love her with everything he had.

With that settled, he sank back into his bed and tightened his grip upon Evelyn. The lullaby of her soft breath against his chest sang him to sleep.

PART SIX

SHE IS MORE TO BE PITIED THAN CENSURED

Present Day

EVEN WITHOUT A LABEL, I REALLY DIDN'T SEE A REASON NOT TO
date Armitage Gallier. He was handsome, single, into me, and unless
the Buddhists were right—I was only going to live once. Why not date
the guy who looked at me like I hung the moon every time I cuddled
into him on the couch?

Still, after that whole scene with his dad, I wasn't about to push
him. We fell back into familiar patterns. Spritzes on the terrace. Long
drives through the city. Extravagant take-out dinners from his favorite
restaurants—the kind that wouldn't ever do take-out unless a Gallier
ordered it.

It wasn't wild. It wasn't whirlwind. It wasn't like what I imagined
Thomas and Evelyn's courtship had been like—at least, the parts that
I could piece together. Our whatever-it-was was just . . . nice. Pretty
much everything I ever could have asked for.

The only thing that was missing was sex. Well, labels too, but
labels didn't really matter to me, not when he made me feel so good.

And, to be honest, when you're not confident, you don't think
you deserve labels. Who was I to think I should be Armitage Gallier's
girlfriend?

For a while, I entertained the possibility that he wasn't into sex—
maybe ace or somewhere along that spectrum. But then I remembered
that during my flu thing, he'd said those fateful words: *When I work
up the courage to get into bed with you, you won't have to ask. You'll
know I want to be there.*

So I knew he wanted to have sex. And I knew he wanted to have sex with me. But unlike America's Top Nineteenth-Century Seductress Evelyn Cross, I had not yet worked up the courage to make it happen.

I'd had sex before. I wasn't a virgin or anything. Maybe I wasn't an Evelyn at all. Maybe I was a Thomas, one of those dreamers who thought sex should mean something, so when Armitage never broached the subject—never even kissed me—I didn't dare ask.

I mean . . . what if he said no? I believed that there was something real between us, but what if he was just lonely and using me for company? Or what if we ended up having sex and then I realized he was just using me for sex? Or what if we *did* have sex and he *wasn't* using me but it still ruined everything?

What if I was just delusional, and he wasn't attracted to me at all? What if he said that stuff about wanting me in bed in the heat of the moment? What if, as he'd spent more time with me, he'd realized that I wasn't desirable? Or what if I did manage to take my clothes off and he was so disgusted with my body—round and soft and too much, just like the rest of me—that he sent me packing? Or had sex with me just to be nice and then never spoke to me again?

The catastrophizing about sex never stopped. And honestly, I didn't know which of those scenarios would be worse. So to protect myself, I stayed in our safe stasis, taking what little of him I could get.

Then, one night, my umbrella broke on the way to the Fifth Avenue residence.

He opened the door when I rang. I dripped in the hallway as I entered, bringing the storm in with me.

"Rain," I explained simply.

His lips twitched. "I can see that. You couldn't run between the drops?"

"These are New York raindrops. They don't know how to stay in their lane."

"You could have called a cab. I would have paid for it. You could have called *me*."

"And what, you would have picked me up from my shitbox apartment in the Rolls?"

"No, of course not." He sniffed. "I would have sent the helicopter."

This time, it was my turn for my lips to twitch. He was becoming funny, this weird, tense man.

Hitting a pocket of drafty air, though, I shuddered from the cold.

"Come on, now," he said, gesturing me toward the staircase.

"Where?"

"You're going to freeze. You need a shower. I don't want you catching your death."

His hand went to the small of my back, strong and sturdy but forgiving and gentle, and he led me up the stairs to one of the guest bathrooms. Since his conversation with his father, he'd been sprucing up the house, moving in and making it feel more modern and lived-in. I guess so he could follow orders and sell it one day.

As we moved deeper into the house, I became very aware of the reality that I was about to be naked. That should have scared me, but it didn't.

For one thing, I *wanted* to be naked here. And I wanted Armitage to be naked with me. Despite my reservations, despite my fears that it would ruin everything—I wanted him. And if Evelyn Cross taught me anything, it was that a woman should get what she wants. Damn the consequences.

And two: I thought maybe the quiet care of *You're going to freeze. You need a shower. I don't want you catching your death* was as close to *I love you* as a man like Armitage Gallier could get.

So he left me alone in the bathroom. I stripped, dropped my clothes in a soggy pile on the floor, and was fully ten minutes into a hot shower before I realized something.

I didn't have any dry clothes.

Shit.

Scrambling out from under the spray, I helplessly checked my bag—which wouldn't have helped even if I *had* put clothes in there, as it was also soaked through—and then moved into the adjoining guest room. Maybe there would be *something* I could wear until my own clothes dried. Or maybe Armitage had a hair dryer I could use to dry them or something—

But no sooner had I thrown open the empty wardrobe than the bedroom door opened, and I caught the reflection in the wardrobe mirror of the man himself tiptoeing in the room, dry clothes in hand.

He went to set the clothes down on the bed—and then realized that he wasn't alone.

So there we were. Me, naked under a towel. And Armitage, standing like a deer in the headlights at the foot of a very inviting bed.

"Fancy meeting you like this," I muttered.

"I didn't—I was just going to drop off some clothes. I realized—"

"So did I. Just a few minutes too late."

I gestured to the towel as best I could without letting it drop. His eyes traced a line from my eyes down to the place where the towel's two ends barely covered my breasts.

He licked his lips. Just barely. Just enough that I noticed.

"I'll just be going then," he said, dropping the clothes.

"Why?" I asked.

There were a million whys in that one. *Why won't you just say you want me? Why haven't you made me your real girlfriend or whatever? Why are we pretending we aren't falling in love? Why have you been comfortable having me as a study partner, sexual tension sharer, afternoon tea drinker, sky watcher, terrace enjoyer, sometimes hand holder? Why won't you just come over here and rip this towel off and show me that I'm not unwantable, that I'm sexy, that I'm yours and you're mine?*

He stopped in his tracks, not turning from the door.

"I don't know if I'd be able to stop once we started . . . whatever this is."

I knew he didn't just mean sex. If I wanted to stop having sex for any reason, I knew he would. This was about something bigger, something cosmic.

"Why would you ever want to stop?" I asked.

Truth was, I didn't want to know the answer. Not that it mattered then. Because in an instant, like a raging hurricane freed from a pillbox, Armitage had me in his arms.

Kissing me with a passion, a hunger, a need I'd only ever imagined.

He was right. When he wanted me in his bed, there was no question. I knew.

I'm not going to tell you what happened between us that night. It wouldn't be fair to him to share the details—and this book is already pretty unfair to him, so I'm not going to make it worse.

But what I will say is this: It was beautiful. It was special. It was real.

And, at least to me, it was undeniable.

CHAPTER THIRTY

WHEN EVELYN RETURNED TO THE BOARDING HOUSE THE NEXT morning, the entirety of Manhattan looked new. It was as if, overnight, someone had waved a magic wand over the dingy streets, washing away the grime and squalor and reimagined it as some sort of fairy tale. The motorcars and horse-drawn carriages played nicely together on the cobblestones. Children congregated in games of jacks instead of standing in line outside the sweatshops. Apple men and bakers handed out their wares to anyone looking mildly hungry and refused payment.

None of this was, strictly speaking, true. No magician in the world had the power to change the heart of a city like this one. But Evelyn still *felt* as though something—or maybe everything—was different today.

To her great relief, the boarding house was empty, which meant she could escape to her bedroom, run a brush through her hair and wash her face, replace her ruined wardrobe with one of the many modest rehearsal dresses she owned, grab a bit of stale bread from the kitchen that somehow tasted like Manna from Heaven itself, and dash off to the theater before anyone was the wiser.

Whatever magician had waved his wand over Manhattan must also have worked his way through The Empire, because as Evelyn walked down the House Left aisle, her skirt brushing the lush crimson carpet as though she were gliding over the clouds, everything gleamed. Here, she once again saw the possibilities of this holy place of creation. And in her ragtag company, she saw their potential to be its high priests.

A shiver took hold of her though the theater wasn't particularly cold. If she was getting this poetic and absurd over one evening with Thomas Gallier, there was no way she was going to survive their affair unscathed.

Her company was assembled with their usual breakfasts of apples and donuts, stretching their muscles and warming their voices as they nibbled and chatted. Yet the mood had none of its usual convivial charm. Jules's pale skin suggested he might vomit at any moment. Bea wrung her hands raw and red. Annie did her best to comfort. Nathaniel sniped with Betsy and Natia. Given the excellent, spare-no-expense acoustics in the Empire Theatre, Evelyn was treated to every other fragment of their conversation. Fragments like *ain't ever gonna see that little kraut girl again* and *prob'bly threw her under the jail.*

She smirked. She was under *something* last night, but it was not a jail.

"Morning, kids!"

Her voice reverberated through the hall, calling the attention of the waiting crowd. All at once, from the stage, the orchestra pit, the wings, and everywhere in between, nearly thirty heads snapped to face her.

A beat, a half-beat, even, and a tidal wave of relief and elation crashed over her.

They stampeded, and the bravest of them—Jules—even leapt straight over the pit and into her arms with enough force to nearly knock her over.

Annie, clapping her hands together in delight: "Evelyn! You're alright."

Nathaniel, lighting up a cigarette without a lick of concern: "Better than all right, I'd say."

Rose, annoyed: "What the hell happened to you last night?"

Melvyn, unable to help himself: "What happened to her last night? Well, the coppers wanted to talk to her, but she just couldn't finish her *sentence*."

Jules, his arms around her as though he'd never let her go again: "Akio and I were at the boarding house all night, waiting for you."

Bea, shooting him a look: "In the *parlor*, where non-residents are allowed, naturally—"

It went on like that for some time. It seemed everyone wanted to touch her, to talk to her, to see for themselves that she wasn't some ghostly apparition back from a jail-floor grave.

When the tide finally went out and she reemerged from the deluge, she glanced over at Bea. "So I suppose everyone knows I got arrested last night?"

A pause. Bea adjusted her spectacles. "Well, I couldn't tell them *nothing*."

Good God. Evelyn withdrew herself from Jules's embrace and clapped her hands together, bringing this rehearsal to order. Not only did they have too much to do today to waste their time on her, but she was in far too good a mood to speak about her time in the city's custody.

"Alright, everyone! Listen up and listen well. If I was beaten by the police last night and could still arrive on time and focus on my work, then I think all of you can do the same, yes?" Again, The Empire's good acoustics did their job, and she heard a creak all the way from the back of the theater. She bit the inside of her cheek. Thomas was up there. He was watching over her. She just knew it. "Now, let's show our ever-so-gracious employer spying on us from the back balcony that we are worth all the money he pays us, shall we?"

Good-natured grumbling broke out from all corners of the stage, but it meant very little of consequence. They were all performers, after all, and after a week of rehearsal on their new acts, they were eager to show off what they'd been working on.

Knowing Thomas was watching up in the balcony sent a flush of almost-exhibitionist heat beneath Evelyn's collar. She wanted to impress him. Wanted him to look at her now in public with the same awe he'd bathed her in last night.

But before she could call The Dancing Dozen to the stage for a demonstration of what was proving to be a suitably scandalous act, Bea ushered Nathaniel to center stage so the man might give a clinic on tap dancing.

Evelyn groaned. That meant Beatrice would want to *talk*.

"This is the part where you tell me what happened last night," the woman said, materializing at her side as Nathaniel lit up the stage.

Evelyn hesitated. "Am I telling my friend, or am I telling the land-lady whose job it is to make sure I don't get into any moral trouble in this big, bad city of ours?"

A gasp. "You didn't. You and Mr. Gallier?"

That scandalized tone, so disapproving, so worried, told Evelyn all she needed to know. Bea was not as thrilled by this turn of events as Evelyn was.

"I did *not* send him to save you last night so the two of you could fall into some sort of romantic disaster."

"Romantic disaster. Please. Give me a little more credit."

"I can't. Not when it's him. I've *never* seen you in this state over a man before—and certainly not a man like that. It's not like you to lose your head this way."

It was the sharp disapproval that rocked Evelyn back to reality. Yes. Of course. This was the afterglow of excellent sex. Nothing more. She couldn't allow it to be anything more.

"I haven't lost my head."

"You're delirious. I wouldn't be surprised if you fell in love with him last night, you absolute fool."

"I won't fall in love. Not with anyone. You *know* this."

"Evelyn. I don't trust him. He's just like the rest, and I don't want you to get hurt."

Biting the inside of her cheek, Evelyn shoved her feelings down into the depths of her and adopted a posture she'd perfected—casual indifference to romantic sentiment.

"And you, Jules?" she asked after a moment of consideration, glancing back at her friend, who wore a rehearsal gown and bold red lipstick. "I know you're eavesdropping."

Jules spun in a whirl of high heels and skirts. "Eavesdropping? Me? Absolutely not. I would never do anything so unseemly. I was just spying on you and waiting for a moment to insert myself into the conversation. So thank you for helping me in that endeavor."

"What do you think about this new development? Beatrice is clearly unenthused. I should like your opinion. And don't tell me you don't have one. It seems clear to me that everyone does."

Painted lips pressed together. Evelyn's spirit dropped. She'd been so certain Jules would be on her side. "I think I have known you since we were children and you have never let yourself get carried away before. I'm sure you won't let that change."

"It's just a fling," Evelyn said, hating the way it sounded. Like she was trying to convince herself more than anyone else. "Nothing different from any of the others I've had before."

Nathaniel's dance reached its clattering crescendo, a clattering storm of noise and fury so loud and passionate that Evelyn almost missed Beatrice whispering, "I'd feel a lot better if I believed you."

CHAPTER THIRTY-ONE

AFTER OBSERVING REHEARSALS FROM THE DARK SANCTUARY OF THE balcony—and trying his best not to call Evelyn to his office for a quick repeat performance of last night's pleasures—Thomas knew he had to go about the business of his day. As Evelyn ran her Dancing Dozen through new choreography, Thomas and Andrew left for a meeting with a new potential investor, one whose attention Andrew had encouraged at the party the night before.

They barely made it down bustling 34th Street toward the hotel where their meeting would take place before Andrew began in on the smart remarks.

"I trust I don't need to inspect your heart this morning. If you were able to keep up with Miss Cross last night, I assume you're plenty hale."

Thomas's steps stuttered. "You knew I was with her? Did anyone else?"

"Your sudden disappearance from the party drew the attention of everyone in attendance, and I was no exception. None of them could understand your departure, but when Miss Matterly informed me that Miss Cross didn't return to the boarding house last night, I realized I had a piece of the equation they didn't. It seems your secret is safe for the moment."

All around them, Manhattan did its dizzying dance. Despite the fact that he and Andrew soldiered on together, Thomas felt very much like the unmoving center.

Secret. That word stuck in his teeth—the Cracker Jack of words.

Andrew adjusted his spectacles. "And you *are* going to keep it a secret, aren't you?"

After last night? After realizing he was in love with her? "No. I have no intention of doing any such thing."

Another block passed them by. So many people in Evelyn's life had done just that—kept her as if she were some shameful secret. He would not be another one of them.

"I assume you understand the consequences of this decision?" Andrew asked gravely yet not unkindly. "I don't need to explain them to you?"

Thomas adjusted his collar. Yes, he'd thought through the repercussions last night, and again this morning as he dressed to face the day. He'd never thought he'd be willing to risk it all for anyone, much less a woman.

Yet, here he was. Standing on the brink and more than willing to jump.

"Crossing Nehemiah Alban, particularly where his daughter is concerned, will no doubt have some consequences," Thomas agreed. "Perhaps very serious ones."

"And?"

"I have always seen myself as a man thoroughly in control of my own faculties. My own destiny and future. You have seen how I've built The Empire. Not a brushstroke has been painted, not a stone laid, not a light affixed, without my approval and oversight. I've built my life much the same way. Until this business with the papers. Until this business with Alban. But no more. I'm not going to surrender myself to him." As he spoke, Thomas felt a swell of conviction. His pride has always rankled at letting Alban tell him what to do, but it was more than that. He was winning back his precious control, but he was also ready not to hold on to it quite so tightly, at least where a certain woman was concerned.

"How do you plan to combat the inevitable complications?" Andrew asked, almost like a teacher leading a student to a complicated problem's answer.

"Just because I have turned off the path of least resistance doesn't mean that I cannot reach my destination, Andrew. I have never met a challenge I could not face and conquer. And I'll have Evelyn at my side. Have you ever met anyone more equipped to handle this sort of risk?" It was true. He had seen it in her face the night before as she emerged from the crowd of cops at the police station, bloodied but uncowed. Alban was a force—no doubt—but they had both reckoned with bullies, and together, they could do it again.

The Hotel Manhattan loomed ahead of them, its red carpet rolling out toward them like a beckoning hand. Andrew relieved himself of his top hat and winced a smile.

"Then it is decided. I wish you the best of luck, my friend."

"I sense some hesitation. Are you doubting me?"

"Not in business. As you say, you've overcome a great deal. I'm sure this will be no different. It's only . . . You should be careful of Miss Cross's heart. And your own. As talented as I am in my chosen profession, there are certain wounds even I cannot stitch up."

PART SEVEN

IF YOU SEE MY SWEETHEART

A NOTE FROM THE HISTORIAN

This is the part where I'm supposed to tell you what happened after Armitage and I fell into bed together. The real love story part of the love story. The problem is—this book is about Evelyn's love story, and my not-a-love-story.

Just know this:

There was a time when I truly believed that what Armitage and I had was the real deal.

I believed that for so long.

And then, one day, I couldn't anymore.

But my story and Evelyn's—and Thomas's and Armitage's—are like vines climbing up the side of a stone wall. So intertwined, you can't pull them apart without ripping out the roots.

I can't pull at the end of my story without finishing theirs first.

Here goes nothing.

CHAPTER THIRTY-TWO

In what felt like the blink of an eye, Thomas's and Evelyn's existences transformed into one—a life jointly lived instead of two that happened to intersect. A cash infusion into The Empire, contingent on the place finally opening, necessitated a celebratory dinner at Delmonico's. Thomas's one-line daily logs included oblique references to his love ("*hosted a guest at home this evening* and *stopped by a shop window this afternoon to inspect rings—just to look*"). The days between their coming together and The Empire's grand opening were packed with business: rehearsals, preparations, paperwork. Amidst it all, they snatched half-moments and fragments, enough to stitch together a tapestry of a shared life, a lifetime's worth of romance crammed into only a few weeks.

There was that second night they spent together, when he kissed a trail down her spine, marveling at her softness and how it felt beneath his lips.

"*May I confess something, Tom?*" she asked.

"*You have all of my confessions. Sharing yours is only fair.*"

"*You said you wanted to court me, yes?*"

"*I remember. I also remember you rebuffed me.*"

Her voice went small. Almost timid. "*It's just that I've never been courted before.*"

"*Never been courted?*"

"*Never properly. My relationships are more . . . straightforward than that. They're exchanges, really, more than they are relationships.*"

Resolve settled in his bones. "Well, we'll just have to change that,. won't we? I would be some sort of cad if I let a beautiful woman go a lifetime without being courted."

⇒◆⇐

And then, there was the morning when she was called down to the sitting room of the boarding house, where he waited with his hat in his hand, surrounded by all the women with whom she shared her home.

"What's this?"

He adopted the posture and voice of a perfect gentleman. The kind of character she'd never seen outside of a playhouse. "Miss Cross, I have asked your most esteemed chaperone here if I might take you to a fine supper. She's agreed so long as I have you home by nine. Would you be so good as to allow me the pleasure?"

She bit the inside of her cheek to keep from smiling. She couldn't make it too easy for him, could she? She turned to one of her friends, adopting an air of her own. "What kind of man is this, inviting me some-where without flowers? I have half a mind to send him elsewhere, Annie."

"Ah. Yes. I nearly forgot."

He retreated to the boarding house's front door and threw it open . . . revealing a line of delivery boys twelve long on either side, each holding a bouquet of flowers—each more stunningly appointed than the last.

Evelyn lost her ability to speak—much less her ability to play her part in this drawing room drama of theirs. Tom, though, merely shrugged.

"You said you've never been courted before. I'm only making up for lost time. Giving you at last what you've always deserved."

⇒◆⇐

And that time they returned to Coney Island for an evening stroll along the water at sunset . . .

"*Why did you choose me?*"

"*You're the most confident woman I've ever known. Why are you suddenly so insecure?*"

"*I've just been wondering, that's all. You had so many reasons to refuse me. Why didn't you? Or what interested you enough to even think you might want me?*"

"*You are the most chaotic, unexpected, wild, thoroughly unsuitable woman the world could have placed in my path—*"

"*Tom, we really must work on your complimenting skills.*"

"*And when we're together, I feel, for the first time, that I'm actually living my life instead of breaking it into shape.*"

A pause.

"*What about me? Why have you chosen me?*"

Another pause. She leaned in to whisper close, and he thought he had finally extracted a confession from her.

"*Because you're the most spectacularly generous lover God ever put on this Earth. Shall we return to the Italianate Boat Ride and confirm my feelings on that point?*"

⇒◇⇐

And after that bank appointment, when a man with whom she'd once been associated cut her, pretending not to know her for fear of embarrassing himself with her acquaintance . . .

"*Thomas, I just want to leave. This is humiliating.*"

"*No. We're not going anywhere.*"

"*But—*"

"*Not until I kiss you and remind him what he's missing.*"

≡◈≣

And the day he drove to the back of The Empire, interrupting her fire-escape luncheon with the others . . .

"What are you doing?" she called, running down to the pavement.

He held out a white duster for her, helping her to shrug into it, leaving warmth everywhere his hands touched.

"Taking you for an afternoon drive."

She considered, then decided she was not interested. "No, I don't think so. But I will take you for an afternoon drive, thank you very much."

"But you don't know how to drive a motorcar."

"Then I hope you're a skilled teacher."

≡◈≣

And the Saturday when they visited their elephants . . .

"Why did you save them?" she asked, reaching down to feed a handful of peanuts to the baby, who gobbled them up with ticklish gusto. "You didn't have to. You're only getting one day of work out of them at the grand opening before you ship them off to that farm. So why?"

"I suppose I saw something of myself in them. Forced to perform tricks for others. Made to be something they aren't. Trapped."

"And do you still feel that way?"

"Not now. Not when I'm with you."

Evelyn wouldn't admit it. Not then. Perhaps not ever. But it was the same for her. The time they spent together was the only time either of them were allowed to really, truly, unashamedly be themselves.

≡◈≣

Perhaps most important, though, were the letters.

Dear Miss Cross,

I am given to understand that love letters are the cornerstone of any courtship. I am also given to understand that you do not believe in love and will then be unable to write a love letter of your own to me. I resolve, therefore, to write one every day until I have convinced you to love me in return.

To begin this correspondence, I will merely say this. You are the only person under Heaven with whom I am fully myself. And whether or not you choose to see this courtship through to its end, I will always treasure that gift. And I hope I can be that same refuge for you. Always. Let us love one another, then, as if we are the only two people who have ever had the pleasure of it. For, indeed, maybe we are.

Yours Most Sincerely,
Tom Gallagher

The letters came every day, one after the other, each containing such prose as she'd never read before. And every day, after she opened a new one and let the words flow over her like baptizing rain, she picked up her pen to write a letter of her own.

And every day, she forced herself to set the pen down again. She could not write love letters to Tom Gallagher. She couldn't write what she didn't allow herself to feel.

A NOTE FROM THE HISTORIAN

I don't know anything that happened during that time in Evelyn and Thomas's life together. It's all made up. But I don't care.

As a historian, I know that most of our work is often about misery. What went wrong, who caused it, and how that negatively impacted generations to come. I cannot remember the last time I'd picked up a nonfiction book that gave me a peek into someone else's quiet moments of happiness.

That's fine for some books. But I don't want to miss out on Evelyn and Thomas's joy in favor of a chronicle of their suffering.

As a person, too, and not just a historian, I couldn't handle that.

Once, Armitage accused me of being sentimental about their story. That I was reading into everything so I could imagine a fairy tale in the gaps. I don't think that I am now—and I don't think I was then either.

True, most of the stuff I imagine happened between Evelyn and Thomas during their courtship is made up. Influenced by my own experience. Stolen from real life and shoved into a historical costume tailored for their personalities and quirks and baggage.

I mean, I'm an adult. I was from the start. I know that every time something good happens, there's a horrible thing stalking around the corner to ruin it. Evelyn would probably agree with me that stories like her and Thomas's simply don't end in happily ever afters.

But I don't care. Let them be happy. Even if just for a few pages. For a few stolen, golden days in someone else's half-borrowed memory.

After all, if Nehemiah Alban had his say in it, their happiness wouldn't last very long anyway.

CHAPTER THIRTY-THREE

THERE WERE A GREAT NUMBER OF THINGS THAT COULD GO WRONG when building an empire. Revolutions and mutinies, lost battles and surrenders. And building The Empire was no different. As the day of their opening grew close at hand, the furious energy with which the rehearsals, the construction, and the entanglements were conducted grew ever more intense and frenzied. Most moments, unless she was pinned beneath Thomas or vice versa, Evelyn hardly knew which way was up. Her life was dominated by the counting shuffles of dancers, the tightening of modiste tape around her wide, fleshy hips, the tuning of the orchestra, Thomas's hand in hers . . .

And the drumbeat repetition of Bea's disapproving tuts in her ear.

But Evelyn ignored those.

Or, at least, she tried to.

"I won't be having this conversation again, Beatrice," Evelyn muttered. Onstage before them, Annie rehearsed her act with her usual aplomb, even briefly employing the help of one of the electrical workmen, impressing him with the escape-artist feats she performed in her wheelchair. "We have too much work to do, and this is absurd."

"I'm only saying that you have a chance to leave now. Before you get hurt even worse than you already will."

"I can leave him any time."

"And what if he leaves you?"

That won't happen. Evelyn knew that with an unshakable certainty. But she didn't dare say it out loud. Because it was such certainty that often led to those heartbreaks about which Beatrice always warned her.

The lights in the theater flickered. A symptom of the maintenance work, no doubt, but Evelyn wouldn't have been surprised if she'd caused the energy fluctuation with her own mind.

Evelyn excused Annie with a few notes about her act, then waved Betsy to center stage. Her act was not an elaborate one. Once the stage was set with a single table, two chairs, and a crystal ball, Betsy settled in.

"Evelyn?" she asked.

"Yes, Betsy?"

"My plant's not here," Betsy said. "With all of the construction going, they must not have let her in."

What a fortune-telling act lacked in the ability to truly foresee the future, they made up for in stagecraft. True talents didn't go in for indulgent props or effects, but that wasn't to say there wasn't plenty of strategy or style to be had. Betsy employed a rolling rotation of audience plants who made her mystical work possible. Evelyn checked her watch and glanced at one of the stagehands lingering in the corner.

"Will you please rescue Miss Washington's audience plant? Thank you. In the meantime, I'd like to work with someone else. Keep this train rolling—"

"I could work with *you*," Betsy offered. "Just for practice."

"I'm not an audience plant. I don't think that would be productive."

"She doesn't mean her act," Nathaniel Fry offered from the wings. "She means her *gift*, Miss Cross."

Betsy shuffled her tarot cards. "You don't believe in the magic, you're all the more likely to get cursed by it, Nathaniel Fry!"

"I'm a man of reason and science. I believe in fortune-tellers as much as I believe in God or demons."

"C'mon, Evelyn," Betsy said gamely. "Let me show him wrong. I'll read your palm—free of charge, too. Used to be three-bits when I worked down on the boardwalk."

Years in the theater had taught Evelyn the tricks behind this hokum. There was no real magic. There were no proper soothsayers. It was all smoke and mirrors and lies.

But it was her job to keep these rehearsals rolling.

"Very well, then."

They sat across from one another, and whether true prophecy was about to occur, Evelyn felt as if the entire room settled into a tense, watchful silence. The hand she offered Betsy was slick with sweat.

"I should warn you," Betsy began, low, "the future isn't always what we should expect or hope."

Evelyn's heart banged against her ribcage, though she wasn't quite sure why. This was, after all, complete bunk. "I think I can handle it," she said, before turning to the assembled parties all around her. "Everyone else! I want corner rehearsals. Dancing Dozen, drill that last sixteen count until you're moving like a perfect unit. Cansino, work with the orchestra on that aria of yours. Tyrone—"

Betsy gave her hand a small squeeze. "Miss. They know what to do."

"Right. Of course." Oh, why was she delaying? Why was her hand now *shaking*? Why did it take sincere effort to smile? "Let's begin, shall we?"

Needing no further instruction, Betsy rose and began her usual introduction, something about calling down the ancient magicks and uncovering the secrets of the future and the hidden lies of the past. Once she was done, she swept into her seat and collected Evelyn's hand once again, trailing her fingers along the fault lines in her palms.

"Let's start by establishing some facts—that's how *you* know *I* know what I'm talking about. You had a tumultuous childhood. Poor."

Evelyn nodded. The accuracy only served to soothe her. Nearly everyone in vaudeville—an art form of runaways and immigrants—had the exact same backstory. Not much magic in guessing that. Just a good cold reading. Betsy continued.

"No father. Mother did the best she could. You had a great trauma around the age of . . . thirteen? No, fourteen . . . that shaped the rest of your life. It ruined you, but also made you, didn't it?"

Evelyn thought involuntarily of the casting director and his private office. That . . . Anyone could have guessed that.

Couldn't they?

Betsy's grip tightened. Her words gained speed and intensity. She was no longer speaking to Evelyn, but to something deep inside her—the part of her that parsed out the truth from lies.

"You reached nearly the pinnacle of success, but now, you fear you are losing your grip. You have everything you could wish for—love, fame, fortune. But you worry that everything you hold now will be lost to you."

Evelyn's breathing went shallow. "How do you know that?"

"The same way I know that you *will* lose everything."

And with that, every light in the entire theater snapped out.

CHAPTER THIRTY-FOUR

In the darkness around her, chaos took hold.

But Evelyn did not breathe. Or speak. Or move except to withdraw her hand from Betsy's.

You will lose everything.

No. It was nonsense. Betsy's conviction must have been faked. Its ring of truth fabricated.

Evelyn would *not* lose everything. Betsy was no prophet. And—

A more troubling thought occurred.

Most women in Betsy's profession used deductive vagaries to make their predictions. The same way she knew that Evelyn had a rough, poor, fatherless childhood—by sheer probability given what Betsy *did* know about her past and her present—she might be able to deduce other things, too.

Perhaps Betsy *was* just cold reading. Maybe she knew that her love for Tom was doomed the same way Jules and Bea did.

The past was the greatest predictor of the future. Love stories like Tom and Evelyn's never worked out. They had no *happily ever afters*. It was a safe bet, then, that this one was destined for destruction too.

No. She rejected that. She would not allow herself to fall prey to such obvious parlor tricks and fancy. Evelyn Cross had never fallen in love and never let her life tumble into romantic turmoil.

She could leave Tom any time she liked.

She could.

And she would.

Eventually.

Yes. Yes, she would.

But for the moment, with the chaotic darkness all around her, all she wanted was to go to him.

Her cast had escaped through the stage door and into the bright sunlight of the street outside. She could follow, or she could direct her steps elsewhere. Why shouldn't she?

As quickly as the shadows and her skirts would allow, she retreated to Tom's office, and once her eyes adjusted, she lit the oil lamps, blushing the room in a glow of golden light. Tom was nowhere to be found; surely, he was helping the electricians bring the power back on. She resolved to entertain herself and wait for him, even as Betsy's and Beatrice's warnings wrapped around her like a winter chill.

Distraction. She needed a distraction. The stack of fresh newspapers—the afternoon edition—seemed as good a place to start as any. She picked the first up, grimacing when she spotted *The Manhattan Daily* across the banner, skipped the stock market news dominating the front page, and dove into the lowbrow pages beyond.

What she found there . . . it shocked her so thoroughly she wondered if she might have been dreaming it. If the oil fumes had gotten to her brain.

But no, when she stepped closer to the flame to inspect the pages by its light, she knew she was not imagining things.

Because there on the society page was a nearly half-page photo of the lovely, slender society *damette* Miss Constance Alban extending her hand to one Mr. Thomas Gallier in front of a positively picturesque flower shop. The headline above that chestnut of an image?

WEDDING BELLS FOR THE EMPEROR?

Evelyn didn't know how long she stared at the photo, committing every detail of it to memory and cursing herself for being such a fool.

A fool for believing him when he said he'd chosen her. A fool for feeling so betrayed by this flimsy piece of paper.

All she knew was that one moment, she was considering how best to rid herself of this terrible emptiness inside her, and the next, a set of strong, familiarly warm hands were reaching for her waist.

"There you are. My man says the power should be back on by tomorrow morning. Are you alright?"

"What is this?"

Shrugging off his touch, she spun and flashed the paper for his inspection. Thomas's face blanched, then reconstructed itself in a mask of casual indifference. He even had the gall to roll his eyes.

"Nonsense, that's what it is. Put it in the bin where it belongs."

No. This could not be happening. She could not have been lied to by him. She couldn't have fallen for this. "You told me that you chose me. That's why you rescued me that night. That's why you came for me—"

"I did. Of course I did."

"Then what the hell is this? If it's in Alban's papers, it might as well be a goddamned wedding announcement."

"Miss Cross . . . Are you jealous?"

Yes. Jealous enough to kick the teeth of his smug smile in.

But just as he had the moment before, she bottled her emotions, corked them tight, and threw them into the depths of her heart's ocean, never (she hoped) to resurface.

"Jealous? Why should I be jealous? We're not anything to each other. Just an affair. This dalliance of ours always had an inevitable Armageddon."

"You don't mean that. Not anymore."

This time, when he placed his hands around her waist, she didn't twist away. Nor did she reply to his obvious attempts to coax some sort of romantic confession out of her.

"Alban cornered me. Took the picture. Constance Alban is a fine girl, but I am here with you and that will not change. No one controls my fate but me. Not anymore."

For so long, Evelyn had known which feelings were safe and which were decidedly not. Friendship and affairs gave her access to a whole host of delightful emotions—joy and thrills and affinity and affection.

But this? Whatever it was she was feeling for Thomas? Whatever risks and vulnerabilities it exposed in her tender heart?

She hated it.

So she did her damndest to expunge it.

"We should go somewhere," she said, slapping on a grin as if the last few moments hadn't passed between them, as if Constance Alban wasn't staring at her from Thomas's desk. "The rest of the cast has decided to take the afternoon off. I don't see a clear way to get them back. It's no use rehearsing without the full lights, anyhow."

Thomas started, but clearly decided it wasn't worth arguing. "Where would you like to go?"

"Back to bed. Or we can stay here and fulfill a fantasy of mine."

His eyebrows knit. "You're upset. We should talk about this—"

"Fine then," she said, abandoning his embrace to collect her shawl and hat. "If you're not in the mood, then I want to dance."

CHAPTER THIRTY-FIVE

THERE WERE COUNTLESS THINGS TO DO BEFORE THE EMPIRE'S grand opening on Saturday. Thomas's task list numbered in the dozens of pages—interviews to give and inspections to conduct and large, ribbon-cutting scissors to polish to a mirror-shine.

But ever since meeting Miss Evelyn Cross, Thomas fancied himself something of a tightrope walker, balancing his work on one side and his life with her on the other. As the pressures around the grand opening mounted and he faced the very real possibility of finally having that which he'd worked his entire life to gain, that balance tipped dangerously, threatening to topple him.

The problem, though, wasn't the toppling.

The problem was that he didn't care. He *wanted* to let the rope slip from beneath his feet, wanted to feel that stomach-flipping thrill of flying.

He liked her. He *loved* her. And it was those simple facts that changed everything.

That's why Thomas had agreed to this silly expedition of theirs. She was doing what she did best: putting physical pleasures between them when things got too difficult. But he didn't care. Not today. Not after that spectacle Alban had pulled with Constance and the press this morning.

He craved the pleasure of Evelyn's company. And he would have it. What was the point, after all, of acquiring so much power if he were not allowed to indulge occasionally his basest whims?

Traveling through Manhattan at this time of day was never a simple business. Motorcars, carriages, horse-mounted gentlemen, walking ladies and apple men and truant children all fought for dominance of the street, meaning that Thomas had indulged Evelyn almost a full hour of carriage-hidden fumbling by the time their team of horses crept to its final halt.

The street to which she'd brought him couldn't have been abandoned—nowhere in Manhattan was properly *abandoned*. There were simply too many people for that. However, it certainly looked that way at first glance.

Like so many streets in this city of theirs, the building facades stretched up toward Heaven and then, by concrete steps, descended past the sidewalks toward Hell. Evelyn chose the second path, practically hopping down toward a basement door painted with the words ALFONSO MORETTI'S ITALIAN SWEET SHOPPE.

The curtains on the windows were drawn. From the street, Thomas could see no signs of life from within.

"All of Manhattan's wonders right at our fingertips and you've brought me to a *basement*?"

"It's not just a basement. It's a racket. Typically, rackets are run by lousy social reformers, but this? This is one of the good ones."

Nothing left to be done, Thomas followed her. "I thought we might take tea at a fine hotel or explore a museum. I hear there's a fantastic whale skeleton on display at—"

"You'd rather look at whale skeletons than go spieling with me?"

He hadn't a clue what spieling was. Not that it mattered. He knew he would do anything so long as it meant more time with her. So long as it replaced her false smiles and desperate hands with something real.

Evelyn knocked three times on the basement door. When three knocks answered back, she swung it open with practiced grace.

It didn't look like any Italian Sweet Shoppe he'd ever seen. Probably because it wasn't. It was an illegal, unsanctioned dance hall—the kind that regularly got raided for indecency by Evelyn's dear friends in the municipal police.

By the dim electric lighting supplemented by a mismatch of candelabras haphazardly screwed into the walls, Thomas could just make out some of the room's more noticeable features. A slapdash of furniture that now sagged under years of use. Along one wall, a bar had been constructed out of discarded shipping containers, the wood grain splashed with seawater and the packing labels from a dozen different countries. A heavyset bartender with a thick, scraggy beard— the eponymous Alfonso Moretti, Thomas could only assume—slung drinks into cheap tin mugs as a band played for dancers on a bare floor in the center of the room. All around, chairs and small tables had been set up I-style for the patrons, who alternated between low chatter and ecstatic dancing.

The crowd, too, was a strange one. Or it would have been if not for Thomas's recent vaudeville education in all things bizarre. Men and women, men and men, women and women, triumvirates and groupings and everything and everyone in between. Mixed races, mixed classes, mixed faiths, mixed languages—they all found their way to this place.

Still, that wasn't what made Thomas pause in the doorway. The strangers were harmless, after all. It was a flaw of his own that worried him.

"I'm not much for dancing."

Evelyn slipped her hand into his. Warm. Reassuring. Sweet. "Good thing you're with an expert. I'll teach you."

However, they barely made it two steps inside before a table of familiar faces waved them down.

Jules Moreau. His . . . partner? . . . Akio. And Beatrice Matterly. A trio whose excitement at seeing their friend vanished when they realized she wasn't alone. She was alone with *him.*

"Well," Beatrice said first, smiling tightly, "look who it is."

"Ah, great minds think alike, don't they?" Evelyn replied, leaning against a chip-paint wall. "Bea, shouldn't you be home supervising the residents?"

"If everyone else is taking a day off, I don't see why I shouldn't." Bea's attention shifted to Thomas, then back to Evelyn. "I'll have a glass of wine, if you would."

Jules slipped Akio some pocket change before Thomas could even offer. "Darling, will you treat us to a round, please?"

It was only a harried moment later, when Thomas was alone with Jules Moreau and Beatrice Matterly, that he realized he'd just been hustled. Evelyn must not have been aware of it, as she chattered with Akio all the way to the bar, but Thomas, on the other hand, spotted the grift instantly.

He had nowhere to run. He was now at the very particular mercies of Evelyn Cross's two best friends.

Who both looked beyond unenthused at his presence.

It didn't take three guesses to understand why.

He cleared his throat. "I take it you've read the afternoon edition."

Beatrice sniffed. "I don't need any further excuse to dislike you."

"But yes," Jules interjected. "We've read it."

Ah. This was a *talking-to.* "I suppose I should have seen this coming."

"A man like you doesn't have friends," Bea said. "You've made that very clear. It doesn't surprise me that you wouldn't anticipate what friends might do for one another."

The dig stung.

"And what is it that you're here to do?"

"Help make this decision easy for you," Beatrice replied, her face taut with deferred emotion.

"What decision?"

"To leave her."

"Leave her?" Thomas balked. "Why would I do such a thing?"

Beatrice tossed her head. "Because you're going to eventually. We've seen this story before, and Evelyn has gone out of her way to *avoid* being its main character. But here we are. In the middle of history repeating itself as farce."

"I'm not going to leave Evelyn. I love her."

The ease of that statement clearly caught his interrogators off guard. A moment of silence prevailed, broken up only by the wail of a mournful horn from the band across the room.

"You absolute fool," Bea said. "You fell in love with her?"

"You ask that question as though it's particularly difficult," Thomas replied. "It was quite easy, in fact. Denying myself for so long was the difficult bit."

Jules reached out across the table and took Thomas's hand, a consoling, almost maternal gesture. "Friend—may I call you friend?"

Friend. Thomas wasn't sure he'd had one of those since he was eleven years old. "If you like."

"Friend, you are, without a doubt, the biggest imbecile on the planet, and if the matter didn't concern our dear Evelyn, I might even adore you for it. However, as it is, it appears that Evelyn has profoundly broken her vow never to fall in love—"

Thomas's entire universe snagged on that accidental confession. Warmth flooded his entire being.

"She loves me?"

Jules's jaw dropped. "She hasn't told you as much?"

"You *just* informed me that she *couldn't* love," Thomas said. "Why would she inform me of something everyone thinks is impossible?"

"A simple *no* would have sufficed," Bea grumbled.

"No, then. She has not told me she loves me. Has she told you?"

"She doesn't have to tell us." Bea brushed imaginary dust from her gown. "Again, you don't grasp what friendship entails, do you?"

"If our feelings are in such accord, then I fail to see why I'm being interrogated here. Do you want my credentials? Should I show you my accounts and assure you I'll care for her the rest of our living days? Shall I read from the love letter in my pocket?"

Thomas might as well have just been crowned King of the World. He'd hoped—even suspected—that Evelyn loved him, but to have it close to confirmed opened up an entire galaxy of possibility.

Damn Alban. Damn the papers. Evelyn Cross loved him.

Beatrice didn't share his optimism. In fact, she seemed hell-bent on destroying it.

"Do you love her enough to sacrifice everything? To reject a woman with the power to change your life as Constance Alban could? To love forever a woman who has nothing to offer you?"

It felt as though the drums from the racket's band had taken up residence inside his own skull. His heart told him *yes*. Without question. He would marry her this very minute if she would say yes to such a proposal.

But years of trained feeling restrained him from answering out loud.

Bea took that as an admission. She laughed bitterly. "I didn't think so. You are one of the wealthiest men in this city. In my entire life, I've never met a man with sharper elbows than you, and I was a mistress to a Fifth Avenue millionaire for most of my younger years. Your ambition gives you away, sir. That ambition means you will do anything to acquire and keep power. Even at the expense of your own heart. Or someone else's."

Jules added, "Listen, friend. We loathe the idea of accusing you of anything untoward."

Bea snorted. "I do not."

"We hate it," Jules continued, sharper. "Because Evelyn has given everything for us, saved us from ruin and, to be frank, saved my life more times than I can count. She has been dealt such cruelties in this world. Please, don't be another one."

Bea nodded along, definitive. "If you love her, you should end this before it is ended for you."

Thomas swallowed dryly. "Ended *for* me?"

"When, inevitably, you get an offer too good to pass up and you must leave her behind. Or when she becomes an embarrassment to you and your reputation cannot bear it. Whenever your vanities and your ambitions once again outweigh your so-called love for her."

Bea said it as though it was all very natural indeed, as though she were reading prophecy.

This was it. The moment to decide. As he had decided to run away from England. As he had decided to reinvent himself. As he had decided to move to America. As he had decided that night to save Evelyn.

He understood the risks. He knew his options. And the choice was clear.

"I will say this and I will say this only," he said at last. "I have glimpsed true love only once before in my life. It was like seeing a ghost—something you believe one moment and then chalk up to an overactive, youthful imagination the next. But with her, I wonder how I ever could have doubted. Love is real. I know this now, and I know it because of her. Because I am nothing without this love I have for her.

So, no, Miss Matterly. Jules. I have no intention of letting Miss Cross go. My heart is hers as long as she will have me. I am not her father. I am not her endless string of lovers. I am not this world of ours that cast her aside. I am *hers*."

Just then, Akio and Evelyn arrived with the round of drinks, but Thomas's eyes never left Beatrice's. Her stare communicated everything she no longer had the space to say out loud.

Evelyn handed Thomas a glass of soda water. "And what are you three hens clucking about?"

"Dancing." He lied first, then told the truth. "And you."

"My two favorite subjects. Shall we?"

When she smiled, even a false one such as that, Thomas quite forgot everyone else in the room existed.

"I should ask you," he flirted, taking her hand and pressing his lips to her knuckles.

"Then, by all means," she said.

His heart caught in his throat. Good God, she was so beautiful. "May I have this dance?"

"I thought you'd never ask."

As he rose and led her out to the makeshift dance floor, the band struck up a raucous tune. The sound bounced off the domed underground walls—so loud Thomas feared for the structural integrity of the place.

But even so, he managed to catch Jules and Bea reflecting on what had just transpired.

"Do you think he's right?" Jules asked. "Do you think they'll last?"

Bea's response was as easy as it was grave. "No. Not a chance."

CHAPTER THIRTY-SIX

WITH A WHOLE TIN OF GIN INSIDE OF HER AND THE MUSIC HOT AS hell, Evelyn felt as though she were successfully outrunning her feelings. This was good. This was what she needed. This was what she was good at.

"I thought we might start with a slow dance—a waltz, perhaps," Tom stuttered as she dragged him toward the mass of swirling, shadowed forms. The spieling was in full effect, and she did not want to miss a moment.

"Absolutely not. What's the fun in that? Come along. Follow me."

Pulling him in close, she moved her body to the strong beat of some Irish dancing tune crossed with a vibrant African drum. This wasn't like any of the dances he would have learned in high society, but it was a joyous affair, and she wouldn't have them left out—no matter how much he protested.

"I don't move like this," he said.

She laughed—a sound that barely registered over the music. "You certainly do. I've seen quite a bit of this movement in your bedroom."

Fire awakened in her when their eyes met. Something in him turned dark, feral, and when she brought his hands to her hips, he did not retreat.

"See?" she called over the unfamiliar song. "I'll make a dancer of you yet."

Once, she'd heard a nun say that singing was the soul itself praying. And if that was true, then dancing was the soul sinning. And whether he believed it or not, Tom sinned *beautifully*.

Evelyn likewise threw herself into the dancing, letting the carnal nature of it whisk her away.

She and Tom were not strong enough to hold the universe back for very much longer, she knew that. And if she didn't evacuate herself from this shelter they'd built for themselves, she would inevitably be crushed. Betsy's and Jules's and Bea's and her own fears would come to horrible fruition.

But for the moment, this dance was enough. She lost herself in the rhythm—lost herself in his uncomplicated touch.

Just like their relationship, however, no song could last forever. The band turned their attention to a soft and painfully sappy song.

Tom's face lit up. Now *this* sort of dancing, he could do.

As soon as the waltz began, she expected him to take up a perfect dancing posture and sweep her around the floor. Instead, he pulled her in close and barely moved his feet to the music.

What they were doing could hardly be called dancing, really. Which was why she was so keen to leave.

"We should go, I think. I'm sure Bea and Jules gave you a devil of a time—"

"I'm happy to stay."

The waltz itched against her skin.

"Bea and Jules are, well, intimidating to say the least. But it's a wonderful thing, to have friends so devoted. To be loved so dearly."

There was something unspoken there. That he didn't feel as though *he* were loved.

It was an invitation for a confession. Evelyn silently declined.

She'd never told a man she loved him. Not once in her entire life. She knew the dangers of saying those little words out loud—they were a curse, one you brought entirely on yourself. Whether or not she felt for Tom, she could never bring herself to fall so low. It was too great a risk.

Especially after that little newspaper stunt this afternoon.

"Evelyn. I want to tell you the truth. Always."

"Oh, please. Not this. No confessions. No grand proclamations. I only want to dance—"

"I have wanted one thing my entire life. And falling for a vaudeville dancer could destroy it."

Her heart faltered. He continued:

"I think . . . I think I would be happy to be ruined. But I cannot do it for someone who doesn't love me in return."

With great force, he stopped their dancing altogether so he might catch and hold her gaze. Evelyn had nowhere to go, nowhere to run from all that he offered.

"Your friends have told me that I must choose between my ambitions—between Miss Alban, between her father's help and esteem, between the sympathies of society—and you. I will do so. Happily. But I must know that you would want such a thing."

Hot tears blurred Evelyn's vision. She had half a mind to leave him on the dance floor altogether. Her weak body, though, made that quite impossible. "Why should I make confessions? Why is it always the woman who is expected to—"

"I love you."

Those three words knocked her planets out of orbit. He put them all back together by placing his warm, big hands on either of her cheeks.

"I *have* loved you since the first moment I saw you, and every day, I have found something new, something deeper, something altogether more wonderful to love in you. I have never built anything so strong as my feelings toward you. I could never earn enough money to buy this sentiment. My life, my works, my fortune—they amount to nothing when laid out before my love for you, Miss Evelyn Cross."

His lips were so close. The urge to close the space between them was overwhelming. Anything to get him to stop talking. But when she tried, he pulled back.

"Please, don't. Don't say this."

"It's the truth."

"Why now? Why—"

"Because I am on the brink of something, Evelyn. And I need to know that I won't be alone if I fall."

She wanted to believe him. More than anything, she wanted to throw caution to the wind, tell him she loved him, and watch the world itself bend to the fairy-tale glory of their romance. After all, experience taught her that men's promises dissolved to ash after sex, but Tom was still here. Still loyal. Still faithful. Still as wonderful as ever.

But he wanted something from her she'd never given before.

It was too frightening. The risk too great.

Her voice hitched.

"You love me?"

"Yes."

"I don't believe you," she lied.

"Then I suppose I'll just have to prove it."

He kissed her, then. And though neither of them knew it, a figure in a darkened corner of the racket collected his hat and left. He had a report to write, and his powerful client would not be kept waiting.

A NOTE FROM THE HISTORIAN

I have to imagine that the sex that night was great. Evelyn would have spent the whole evening saying goodbye to Thomas with her body, wringing the last pleasure from him that she thought she would ever get.

After all, Evelyn was not going to stick around for love. That was the deal. And if she couldn't have love, then she would at least get very, *very* good sex.

Again, this is all speculation. When my last relationship ended, I would have given anything to know that our last night spent together was our last. I wish I could have kissed him a little harder, pulled his hair a little tighter, held him a little closer and longer.

I hope Evelyn got all of those things.

What I know for sure she got?

The proof Thomas promised her, in the form of two pieces of paper left on her bedside the next morning.

First, there was an invitation:

CHARITY BALL BENEFITING
THE SOCIETY FOR WOMEN'S SOCIAL
HYGIENE TO BE HELD AT THE
HOME OF GEORGE C. CONTHORPE AND
MRS. GEORGE C. CONTHORPE
ON OCTOBER 17, 1897

And second, there was a handwritten letter.

My Beloved Evelyn,

    I have attended a number of these affairs alone. It is my dearest wish to never be alone again. At a party or otherwise. Would you do me the honor of joining me?

Yours Always,
Tom Gallagher

CHAPTER THIRTY-SEVEN

By the time she arrived at The Empire to prepare for their final day of dress rehearsals, Evelyn had determined to ignore the invitation, the note, and all it implied. Ignoring it would send a message— no. *This affair has come to an end. We are through.*

That was for the best. Then, she could begin the process of recovery. She could nurse her inevitable sadness and damaged ego with champagne and sleepless nights and begin the search for her next lover. No society parties. No more public entanglements.

Just sex.

When Evelyn stepped onto The Empire's stage, though, she did not find it empty as she usually did. Beatrice was engaged in flurried chat with Andrew Samson, something intense and quiet that dissolved the second they both noticed her presence.

With a small bow and quick goodbye, the good doctor left. Evelyn didn't bother to ask what it was they were discussing—she knew it could only be about her and Thomas.

Let them gossip while they can, she figured.

Once Andrew was gone, she collapsed on the floor and began relieving herself of her boots. She needed to rehearse this morning. Needed to dance. Needed to focus on what she was good at.

After all, if she was going to throw Thomas over, she'd need a spectacular act. One that would find her a new paramour and one that might get her a new booking when he inevitably fired her.

Beatrice strolled over, her voice teasing.

"If you don't mind my saying so, Evelyn, you look like absolute hell. We have an investors' preview this afternoon," she added, as though Evelyn could forget, "so I hope you brought some heavy-duty grease-paint for those under-eye bags. Or better yet, some house paint."

"You know, that's what I love about you, Bea," Evelyn retorted, fussing with the laces of her boots. "You're never subtle."

A pause. Evelyn waited for what she knew was to come.

"What happened after you left the racket last night?"

"You've never been one to fish for erotic details, Bea."

From the corner of her eye, Evelyn caught Beatrice's hand flexing at her side. Ah, that's what she and Andrew had been fighting over. Whether or not Beatrice had managed to break up the two of them. "So. He didn't end your affair?"

"No."

"And you didn't either?"

"No, but I fully intend to. He has made things altogether too serious. It's untenable."

"How?"

He's fallen in love with me, and I don't have the first idea what to do with a man foolish enough to do that.

"He's asked me to accompany him to some party tonight at George Conthorpe's estate."

Evelyn braced herself for the inevitable rebuke. *You wouldn't dream of going, would you? I know those people and they're all snakes— Thomas included. Don't trust him. Don't attend the party. Don't let yourself be swept off your feet. Don't listen to your heart.*

But Bea surprised her.

Something deep and abiding shifted in her friend—a change so potent it electrified the very air.

"And you're going, aren't you?"

"Why on earth would I do that?"

"Because he's going to ask you to marry him."

Evelyn's mind filled with railroad screeching. The words from his letter came back to her. *It is my dearest wish to never be alone again.*

"*No.* No. No . . . No, he's not. He couldn't. He wouldn't—"

"That is *the* most important social occasion of the year," Beatrice interjected, her features sharpening. "It's where reputations and lives are made and broken. If he takes you there, it's because he's announcing, to the entire world, or *his* entire world, which is even *more* important, that he wants you to be his wife."

Evelyn's vision started to sway. Last night, he'd declared that he would prove his love.

Now, he was preparing to do the one thing her father had never done for her mother. The one thing no man had ever even considered doing for her before. The thing Beatrice had been so sure he wouldn't do.

He was going to tell the entire world that he cared, that he cherished her, that he chose her above all others—damn the consequences.

He was not only going to love her. He was also going to make that love *seen.*

"No," Evelyn snapped.

"No? I think I know a little more about this world than you do. That *is* what it means—"

"I mean *no, then, I'm not going.*"

"Absurd. Of course you are. You love him."

So matter-of-fact. So obvious. Evelyn couldn't stand it.

"You hate him," she protested, trying to force her world back into some semblance of order. "Why are you suddenly pushing me—"

"I know these people. You *know* what they've done to me, how I despise them. And as loath as I am to admit it, I believe . . . I believe

I was wrong about Mr. Gallier. He is different. What is happening between the two of you, it's different as well. I didn't think so, not at first, but this proves it."

"It's a piece of paper," Evelyn protested, but with less force than before. "It doesn't prove anything."

Slowly, Beatrice lowered herself until she was at Evelyn's height. And said precisely what Evelyn needed—and couldn't bear—to hear.

"My dearest friend. I have known you and cared about you longer than I have just about anyone in this ever-loving, God-blessed waking world. And you know what I have always loved most about you?"

"My sparkling personality? No, it's my ankles, isn't it? I *do* have very good ankles."

"You never let anyone or anything get in the way of what you want."

Unable to face her friend's no doubt kind eyes, Evelyn stared at her hands, those hands Betsy said prophesied a dark future.

"Well . . ." she said, her voice small, "I don't have a dress."

Evelyn could practically hear Beatrice's smile. "Leave that to me."

CHAPTER THIRTY-EIGHT

IT WAS AN EFFORT OF THE DANCING DOZEN, GETTING EVELYN TO THE party that day. After the rousing success of the investors' preview, they'd all rushed directly home to set about preparing her—and they did not disappoint.

Beatrice's dress fit perfectly. With the right pair of slippers (borrowed from Rose's small collection) to adjust for the difference in their height, the striking silver-blue gown laced by Natia clung to her body as though it had been made for her by magic. To complement the gown's effect, Therese also styled her hair in an appropriately fashionable manner while Debora ensured that her makeup conformed to the rules of the ballroom and not the theater. The ironing and pinning and bustling and polishing had been done by all the rest.

She looked as beautiful as she felt.

And she felt like the most beautiful woman who'd ever lived.

Yet, when she and Beatrice arrived by rented cab at the swirling wrought iron gates of the Conthorpe estate, Evelyn couldn't seem to move herself from the darkened safety of the carriage.

"Are you sure you don't want to come with me?" she asked.

Beatrice glanced through the glass window at the throngs of attendees lingering in the illuminated, gated garden.

"No," she said, without a trace of envy or disappointment. "I swore I would never go back, and I have no intentions of making a liar out of myself, thank you very much."

That was as close to a *get lost* as Evelyn had ever heard from Beatrice, but still . . . she twisted her fan in her silk-gloved fingers.

"I haven't ever done this before."

"What? Been in love?"

"Well, I actually meant *attend a party as fancy as this*, but yes. I suppose you're just as correct. I don't have the first idea what to do in this situation."

The cab lurched forward. Evelyn's stomach clenched. Only a few moments now and she would arrive at the most important night of her life.

"Well, when it comes to the love bit, I'm afraid I can't help you. I was always a failure in that department. However," Bea said, reaching across the small space of the carriage to tuck a lock of hair back into Evelyn's pins, "check your ankles in the mirrors. If you slip up and show one, they won't ever let you live it down. Never drink the punch given to you by a stranger. If you play cards, you *must* cheat, and when you cheat, you mustn't get caught. And . . ."

Their eyes met. Bea hesitated.

"And?" Evelyn prompted.

"Don't ever let them hurt you."

A chuckle—nervous. "Or don't let them *know* they've hurt me."

"No," Beatrice said in one of her famous *don't argue* tones. "Don't ever let them hurt you. Anything that's worth having, they can't take away from you. I promise."

The carriage door finally opened.

"Wish me luck."

"I would, but you don't need it."

And when Evelyn stepped out of the carriage and into her future, she held on to one simple truth above all. No matter what happened tonight, at least she was gifted with some truly remarkable friends.

Love of a different kind. But still. Love.

And it was that love that gave her the strength to press forward, ready to receive—and give—even more.

CHAPTER THIRTY-NINE

MISS EVELYN CROSS WAS NOT ON THE LIST.

A footman eventually allowed her inside when she insisted—to his confusion—that she was the guest of Mr. Thomas Gallier and that he would be expecting her, but the fact remained. She was not on the list.

Quite the auspicious start.

Once inside, Evelyn retired her cloak to one of the uniformed servants and joined the crush searching for alcohol and company and gossip.

Without companions or an escort, she found herself lost. She'd grown up on the busy streets of Manhattan, dodging strangers and navigating crowds since she'd learned to walk. Finding her way through a sea of tuxedos and gowns puppeted by slender rich folk shouldn't have been any trouble.

And yet, as she attempted to skirt whispering couples and scheming mothers and champagne-toting waiters, it occurred to her that in all her years on the stage, she hadn't ever encountered a spectacle quite like this. The wealth on display was ostentatious and tasteless. Every conversation she caught in passing was riddled with lies and half-truths—you could just tell by the way their voices slithered around the words. Fans hid blushes and kept confidences. Judgmental eyes followed her, but when she caught someone staring, they smiled as broadly as a friend would, only to go right back to questioning stares once she turned again. Whispers carried in these halls, too, and no matter how they tried to stifle their whispers about *Evelyn Cross—Thomas Gallier's tart—the bicycle of vaudeville benefactors,* that gossip followed her.

Her theatrical training kicked in. She mentally reached for the costume of Miss Evelyn Cross, Star of the World's Greatest Stages, but hesitated to fully put it on when she remembered Beatrice's advice: *Don't ever let them hurt you.*

So Evelyn kept her chin high and her eyes straight ahead. As she might with a complicated dance routine, she counted all the things she had that these people could never take away.

Her friends. Her career. Her self-worth. Her talent. Her reputation— at least amongst people who mattered. Thomas. Her lifetime of tomorrows with him.

In that moment, she almost pitied this faceless crowd of strangers. They had their gossip and their self-importance, but she had what really mattered.

"Tom!"

When he materialized in the distant center of her view, his name came to her lips thoughtlessly.

He rushed over to her faster than was strictly polite.

"Miss Cross," he said, tipping his head but never quite meeting her eyes.

"Oh, sorry. I forgot we're in civilized company now, *Mr. Gallier.*"

"What are you doing here?"

"I was invited." An attempt at a flirt. The firm set of his jaw didn't shift. She let out a nervous little laugh. "*You* invited me. Did someone drop a piano on your head today?"

"Ah. Yes. The invitation. Well, someone should have—"

Evelyn cut him off. "Aren't you going to ask me to dance? Or tell me how lovely I look? Or give me flowers? I don't know—what do men do when they want a woman's attention but want the rest of the room to stop talking about them?"

A glint of recognition lit his face as he scanned the ballroom as if for the first time. *Indeed. We are not alone*, he seemed to think.

"Yes. A dance," he said. "Very well."

This time, he didn't ask. He simply swept her onto the floor without a word.

Instinct agitated the hairs on the back of Evelyn's neck. This wasn't her Tom. This was the *old* him, Thomas, all business.

She shrugged it off. This change in behavior made sense when she considered their change of backdrop and costume. *She* may have been unwilling to adjust her attitudes to fit this stuffed-shirt soiree, but that didn't mean he was.

There was also the matter of the proposal to consider. Evelyn was given to understand men were never quite themselves when approaching the subject of marriage.

Yes. That was it. He was nervous.

"As I understand it," Evelyn said, "the purpose of an exercise like this one is so you might talk intimately with your partner. And yet, a cat's got your tongue."

Tom bore holes into the wall behind her head. "I have quite a bit on my mind."

"Yes, I suspected as much."

His grip tightened at her waist—the first sign of life in his otherwise dead hold. "Really?"

"Beatrice told me what's going on here tonight. You don't need to play coy about it. Unless you wanted me to be surprised?"

Thomas's eyes narrowed. "Miss Matterly? How does she know? Did Andrew tell her?"

"No, I believe it was pretty obvious. To everyone except me, that is."

"So you knew and you still came?"

"Did you not want me to come? Mr. Gallier, I've heard that men get anxious before they propose to a woman, but this is—"

"*Propose?*"

Thomas Gallier had spent too many hours practicing the waltz alone in his room to stumble.

Still, his feet got the better of him, and he faltered.

"Yes, propose." Evelyn laughed, rather enjoying that dumbstruck expression toying with his handsome features. "Fine, then. If you're so nervous, allow me to do the honors."

"*No—*"

The band picked up the tempo. He led her through the dizzying paces. A watchful audience spied from the sidelines. Evelyn clutched him tighter, white-knuckling her courage so it wouldn't abandon her. "Don't speak. Allow me to say this. I believe I owe you this before you do what you're about to do."

He followed her instructions.

Evelyn's head swam. The ballroom blurred. Were those phenomena from the dance or from something else?

No. It didn't matter. It had to be said. If he was going to marry her, he needed to know how fully and completely he'd captured her—and how willing a captive she was.

"From the first moment I saw you, I felt as if I were seeing another half of myself. As if I'd found a piece I'd lost so long ago I'd forgotten I ever had it in the first place. I just knew. It was as if my very being were saying *Oh, yes. I've found you again. Please don't ever leave me as you did before. I don't know how to be complete without you.* And what's more, Tom, I don't *want* to be complete without you."

She received no response but the wail of her heart in her ears.

"You know," she continued, "I never used to believe that anything could last. I was always moving. New city, new train, new show, new bed, new man. But . . . with you, it's like . . . for the first time, I see what forever could look like. And what's more, I'm not afraid of it. Because I know you won't hurt me. Because I know this is real, what's happening between us. Thomas, I—"

"Mr. Gallier! There you are! I've been looking for you everywhere."

Evelyn fully planned to ignore that velvety feminine voice and finish her confession. Thomas had other plans. Like a dog called to his master's heel, he halted at the edge of the dance floor, sending Evelyn nearly crashing into several onlookers.

When she found her feet, Thomas was grinning down at a petite blonde woman in a white gown that might have passed for a wedding dress in the right light.

Not just any woman.

Miss Constance Alban. The most eligible young lady in Manhattan.

The same one Thomas had been photographed with just yesterday. The one he'd told her not to worry about. The one he said he didn't want.

The woman wasn't alone, though. Strangers flanked her on either side and Dr. Samson, who sternly schooled his usually smiling face, rounded out the group.

"Miss Alban," Thomas said with a little bow, ignoring the rest of their newfound company. "Your mother *was* encouraging me onto the dance floor earlier this evening. I was only trying to appease her."

"Very well, then. I suppose I can forgive you." Her little button nose crinkled and she placed a gloved hand upon Thomas's. "You're a very fine sport. Now, who might this mysterious partner of yours be, then? Aren't you going to introduce us?"

"Yes, Thomas," Evelyn agreed, asking a question to which she already fully knew the answer. "Who is this?"

In almost perfect unison, the woman and Thomas snapped to attention.

"Yes. Well. Miss Alban, please meet Miss Cross. Miss Cross is the star of The Empire's vaudeville show. And Miss Cross?" The slightest hesitation. The briefest show of his cards. And Evelyn felt herself crash against the rocks. "Please allow me to introduce Miss Constance Alban. My fiancée."

A NOTE FROM THE HISTORIAN

I should probably rewind a bit.

But first . . .

Present Day

A BIG PART OF BEING A HISTORIAN IS MAKING SURE THINGS MATCH. The difference between the truth and a lie can all come down to a matter of a few mislaid lines or figures, and exposing those little fibs—and why someone may have wanted faulty information out there—can result in a career-making find.

Thomas Gallier was a treasure trove of mismatches. His secret identity, his love affair with Evelyn, his entire life lived in the gaps between what he told people and how that differed from fact. The more of these discrepancies I found, the more I revealed about the man, and the more I revealed about the man, the more I wanted to know. It became a game for me, in some ways. Trying to expose a person who'd spent his entire life desperate to hide.

But for all my dogged pursuit of Thomas's hidden depths, I almost missed a crucial one.

Thomas's personal financial ledger on the day of The Empire's investor preview noted one particularly interesting entry.

Purchase: Engagement Ring, sapphire sideset by diamonds
Purchase Price: $375.00
Cash Upon Receipt
Payable To: Charles Lewis Tiffany, 15 Union Square West

By this point in American history, Tiffany had already made its name as *the* jeweler of choice for the swell set. In 1885, the company redesigned the seal of the United States of America, for crying out loud. Just two years later, it would buy a significant portion of the French crown jewels. Everyone who was anyone got their most important jewelry from Tiffany, and it wasn't a surprise that Thomas Gallier would gift his wife a piece of hardware like that upon the occasion of their engagement. The woman he married was, after all, from one of the wealthiest families in the city. Of course he would gift her something that cost in the ballpark of fifteen grand in today's money.

"Ah, yes. Constance's ring," Armitage said when I presented him the receipt during one of our study sessions.

And he should have been right. It should have been Constance's ring. There was only one problem with that assumption.

"It doesn't match."

He let out a little laugh of confusion. "What do you mean by that?"

I gestured him over to the fireplace, where the imposing portrait of Thomas and Constance hung overhead. Hands daintily folded in her lap, the painted Constance showed off a truly remarkable yellow diamond on her ring finger.

"I don't know what you're getting at," Armitage said, at length.

"That's not a Tiffany engagement ring," I explained. "That ring is the same one her mother *and* great-grandmother have in their wedding portraits. It's an heirloom, not something new. It doesn't match the purchasing records."

With a shrug, Armitage returned to his favorite chair. "Maybe he bought Constance a ring, but she wanted to wear a family piece. Or maybe it was a prop for one of his vaudeville things. Or maybe it was an investment. Or maybe it was improperly catalogued, just a normal ring. Not an engagement ring at all."

"Or maybe Thomas Gallier was going to give someone *else* an engagement ring that day, but something stopped him," I countered.

"A little fanciful, don't you think?"

I didn't think so. Not after everything else I knew about Thomas and Evelyn's relationship.

It felt like he was lying to me. Like he knew something he didn't want me to know.

Like I was Evelyn, a breath away from being caught unaware by some world-shattering piece of news.

But considering Armitage wanted as many facts as possible, I pushed. If he had even an inkling of where I could find an answer, he needed to give it to me.

I wasn't going to be caught like Evelyn.

"Does your family keep any records of their jewelry collection? Chains of custody or something like that? It'd be pretty easy to figure out if Constance got a ring from Thomas around the time of their wedding. We might be able to track it down, too. I'd love to see what it looks like."

"I don't think we keep track of things like that."

Once again, I was staggered at the ineptitude of rich people. *Oh, we have so many priceless jewels, we don't even care if a few go missing.*

"But you'll look, right?" I asked, taking my place in his lap and cuddling into his embrace. Admittedly working a little of my feminine charm to get what I wanted. "Please? For me?"

"Sure. Of course I will."

He nuzzled my neck and somehow the rest of the night just got away from us.

I never got those chains of custody. I don't know if he ever looked.

Which means I'm well within my rights to go with my gut here.

We return to that morning, before the ball. Evelyn and Beatrice had just had their talk. And Thomas walked into The Empire completely, thoroughly, and unapologetically un-fiancéed.

CHAPTER FORTY

THE DAY BEFORE THE EMPIRE'S GRAND OPENING, THOMAS ENTERED his pleasure palace with a heavy pocket. He'd told Evelyn he would prove his love. And he intended to do just that. The ring he'd purchased would go a long way to help him in that endeavor. Tonight, he would meet Evelyn at the party, declare his love, and ask her to marry him in full sight of high society. As he bound himself to Evelyn, he would throw off the control he'd let the Manhattan elites have over him. In a matter of a few short hours, his entire life would be different.

Freer. Better.

So perhaps we can understand why, when he arrived for the investors' preview of the vaudeville, he was too distracted to notice that the crowd of well-heeled men had not just one decidedly uninvited member, but an entire posse of them.

"Good morning, gentlemen," he said, withdrawing his key to open the front of house.

"Ah, there's the man of the hour."

Thomas turned to find Mr. Alban's pale, tight face and his usual attaché of fine gentlemen—as well as, for reasons unknown, the unusually sour-faced Smith and a push-broom mustached police officer.

What any of them were doing here, Thomas hadn't the first clue. But with the eyes of his entire investor corps upon him, he had no choice but to play along.

"Mr. Alban. It's wonderful to see you again. Welcome to The Empire."

"Pleasure's all mine, boy. I've heard of nothing else around Manhattan but your delightful vaudeville program—to say nothing of the rest of this fine facility. I'm thrilled to see the object of so much gossip with my own two eyes."

The meaning was clear to all. Alban would be judging this theater—and their work, their time, and the investors' money hung in the balance. Thomas had held off the newspapers until now, but only because Alban had allowed it.

Very well, then. If he wanted to play, they would play. Evelyn had built something marvelous with this show. Even Alban, jaded as he was by Thomas's as-yet-unspoken rejection of Constance, would see that.

"Very well, then. Gentlemen—allow me to introduce you to The Empire. In all of her glory."

A tour was first on the agenda, and after the appropriate awe had been extracted, Thomas ushered his crowd into the theater, showed them to their seats, and took his own as the orchestra tuned up.

Alban took the liberty of seating himself directly to Thomas's left, separate from the rest of the audience. Which meant that instead of focusing on the show, Thomas spent the entire bill clocking Alban's microexpressions and twitches.

While Alban remained eminently stoic, the rest of their audience fell perfect prey to Evelyn's show. The men laughed at all the appropriate bits, clapped after each performance, and even gave Evelyn and her Dancing Dozen a brief standing ovation.

It was a smash. Just as he'd known it would be. Pride swelled within him, and it took a considerable amount of energy not to smirk. *Take that, you pompous moralist,* he wanted to whisper to the man next to him. *You overestimated your regressive hold on this city. But you can't destroy the undeniable. Not with a million newspapers.*

However, he held his tongue and when the final curtain fell, the assembled men slipped into uncomfortable silence. Waiting, Thomas knew, for the unelected leader of their pack to place upon the show his own seal of final approval.

"Mr. Gallier," came the eventual summons. "I should like to speak with you. Alone. It won't take a moment. I'm sure Mr. Samson—"

"Doctor."

"Of course. *Dr.* Samson can take your guests to luncheon, and you can join them directly."

Power moves on top of power moves. Thomas steeled himself for the inevitable fight to come.

Once their companions were gone, ushered by Andrew to the third floor, where they would be taken on a culinary odyssey through The Empire's seven restaurants and bountiful food stalls, Thomas started for his office.

"Shall we—"

"Don't talk," Alban said, low and unmoving. "Just listen."

"I beg your pardon—"

The man scoffed. "Can't even follow simple instructions. *Really.* Makes me wonder if I should be going to all this trouble to make you my son-in-law."

Son-in-law.

Thomas had thought he'd been clear that was not his fate.

But with The Empire and its success hanging in the balance, Thomas walked a tightrope.

"With all due respect, sir—"

"You have built something wonderful here, Mr. Gallier," Mr. Alban said, waving his walking stick at the grandeur all around them, the masterpiece that had been the work of Thomas's adult life. "It would be such a shame if it all crumbled down around you."

"Ah." It was as Thomas had feared, and he found himself almost relieved by this inevitable turn in the conversation. "So we've arrived at the threats portion of our program."

"We had an agreement, you and I. You've disappointed me and you've disappointed Constance. She was positively heartbroken when she heard about you and that fat little charity girl."

Thomas highly doubted that. Perhaps she'd played the wounded lover for her father—but he knew that her interest in him would never hold a candle to her affection for Edward Langmore.

"I'm terribly sorry to have disappointed her, but—"

"Excellent. If you're sorry, then I'm sure you'll endeavor to correct the mistake."

"What does she like? Flowers? Chocolates? A box seat to our premiere on Saturday?"

"Engagement rings."

There was no way Alban could have known about such a ring currently occupying Thomas's pocket. But Thomas's hand went to brush it just in case—a privately defensive posture.

"My boy, we do not have to be at cross-purposes. I can forgive this folly of yours, this chorus girl diversion. I do not wish to make your life a misery. Please. Come to your senses."

He was all friendliness now. Almost more dangerous for his amiability.

"I am perfectly in my right mind," Thomas said.

"Then why can't you see clearly to marry my daughter?"

"Because I do not love her. And what's more, she does not love me."

"Love," Alban snarked. "As if that ever mattered. Marriage is just like any other business deal you've ever struck, Mr. Gallier. A map of concessions and trade-offs and sacrifices to get what you really want."

"What I really want? What I really want is Miss Evelyn Cross. Now, if you have nothing further to say, sir, I will have my leave of you—"

"You *will* marry my Constance."

"I stopped taking orders when I was eighteen years old. Forgive me if I don't change my stripes for you now."

Retiring to one of the theater's front row seats, Alban adopted a relaxed, almost bored air. "It wasn't an order. It was a fact. You will marry her, you stubborn boy."

"Don't call me *boy*."

"Would you prefer *son*?"

"You have some confidence for a man who has been refused at every turn."

"The refusal won't stick."

"And why not?"

The tone Alban adopted now was both condescending and pitying. As if he were explaining all this to a child. "Isn't it enough that I could destroy this show with a few strokes of my typewriter? Thomas, the vaudeville you've slapped together isn't fit for Christian eyes. Fat women dancing about with barely any clothes on? A man fashioned as a lady? Mediums and magicians? Negroes and queers and flagrantly un-American displays of foreigners? *Socialists*? You couldn't possibly expect me to allow decent, god-fearing Christians to take in such lascivious entertainments."

Thomas laughed in his face. "You severely underestimate the people who read your newspapers. You have tried to wipe out my performers time and time again, but you saw how the investors reacted back there. The people can be swayed by your writing, but in the end, they all just want to be entertained. I'm not afraid of you anymore. And those people back there? Those stars who just gave the best show of their lives? They never were."

Mr. Alban's lips pulled back over his teeth in what must have been a misguided attempt at a smile.

"Mr. Gallier, you're breaking my heart."

"You'd have to have one first," Thomas muttered.

Damn him. Damn him to hell. Thomas tired of this endless rotten-go-round. He was getting off—no matter the consequences.

But then, Alban tutted and pulled something from his breast pocket, just as he had at their first formal meeting.

"I don't want to publish this story. But it will be going out in the paper tomorrow if we can't reach some sort of accord."

Thomas had half a mind to ignore it. Another threat. What was the worst that could happen? What could possibly . . .

But that *what if* eventually won out, and Thomas snapped up the neatly typewritten story.

Only halfway through the first paragraph, and the words blurred.

An entire life built on hiding his past. And here it was, written out in plain newsprint for the world to see.

"How . . . how did you find all of this?"

"My man Smith is an exceptional bloodhound. But I don't think that's the right question, sir. The right question is what are you going to do if it gets out? You'll be ruined."

"It's America. Everyone reinvents themselves," Thomas defended, voice hollow.

"Yes, but not so many people do it while engaging in what might be considered criminal fraud. You've lied, Thomas. You've lied to investors who have put up unfathomable sums of money for this building. They believed in Thomas Gallier. They signed their money over to Thomas Gallier. And that means you took them in under false pretense. If my friends in City Hall get ahold of this . . . I'm afraid the consequences would be dire."

The bars on the cage around Thomas's heart tightened. He couldn't breathe. He couldn't think. He didn't need Alban to spell out the way this would utterly wreck his life, everything he'd ever fought for. But the old man did it anyway.

"As I'm sure you can imagine, you would be put under immediate arrest. That's all very well and good, you'd say. You could handle it. Perhaps hire a lawyer to make sure you're looked after in prison. But as the investigation begins, your personal effects will be collected for evidence. What might an officer find in such a collection? I'm sure there's evidence to be found of all manner of crimes. Dr. Samson performing medical interventions on degenerates in your home. Chaperoning infractions at Miss Matterly's boarding house that could see her license revoked. Homosexual acts involving that female impersonator and his attaché. Prostitution by Miss Evelyn Cross."

"She isn't—"

"I don't think the courts will see it that way. And even if they don't get her on that charge, she could at least be charged with conspiracy in your fraud. I'm sure all the little citizens of your Empire had some hand in it."

"They didn't know," Thomas protested. "None of them knew."

"What proof will they have? How will the fat, crippled, socialist Negro queers that populate your social circle convince a judge in this city, my city, that they're innocent?"

The walls were closing in. Thomas felt as if he'd been transported back to Coney Island, at the top of the roller coaster.

"I could protect them."

"Well," Alban said, so civilized, so controlled. "Let's assume that's true. Unfortunately, we come now to the worst of it. When you are arrested for this fraud you've perpetrated, your assets will be seized. And when you are inevitably found guilty, the city will auction them off to the highest bidder. I will be that highest bidder, Mr. Gallier. While you are rotting alone in a jail cell for the rest of your days, I will spend every last second ensuring that, as president of The Empire, everyone you care about is destroyed. Not only will I own this building, I will own the future of each soul within it."

He rose and offered Thomas his hand to shake—as if this were a business deal instead of the end of his life.

"Now. I'll ask again. Will you marry my Constance?"

God, no. Please. Please don't make me make this terrible choice. I only wanted Evelyn. I only wanted her. I can't . . . I can't live without her. Please—

"It is a simple question, Mr. Gallier. I expect an answer."

Evelyn always told Thomas how good it was to love people. For so long, he had questioned that judgment. Now, he was reminded why.

Evelyn had taught him how to love without fear. And this was the consequence. He loved too deeply and too unselfishly to do anything else but save her.

This choice would break him. To marry Constance Alban and forsake Evelyn would mean the end of all things good and true. But it wasn't so much a choice as a moral imperative. Loving Evelyn meant protecting her. It meant giving her up, breaking both their hearts, so that she and her friends could continue to live in peace and freedom and security.

His life for all of theirs.

Thomas brushed his fingertips over the ring box in his pocket. One last goodbye.

So. There it was.

Yes, Miss Cross would be allowed to return to her life without him. Their friends would relish their newfound stardom that The Empire brought them. The Empire would be allowed to continue, flourishing through the years and leaving his mark on this world, proving that his small life had meant something. Dr. Samson would continue his lifesaving work, protected from the prying eyes of small-minded, conservative, hateful society gossips. All would be well for those he loved more dearly than himself.

And Thomas . . .

Thomas would be married.

Thomas would have a beautiful wife.

Thomas would have a fortune.

Thomas would have power.

Thomas would have prestige.

Thomas would have influence.

Thomas would have it all.

Thomas would have everything he ever dreamed of.

Except the one thing that really mattered.

Which meant that Thomas would also be very, very miserable.

"Yes. I accept."

CHAPTER FORTY-ONE

THE DETAILS OF THROWING HIS LIFE AWAY WERE IRONED OUT EASILY enough.

That night, Thomas would propose to Constance. They would exchange vows tomorrow afternoon during The Empire's grand opening. What better way to drum up press, Alban no doubt thought, than for the pleasure palace's owner to be lawfully wed onstage in front of God and all his twisted little subjects? Constance would then move into Thomas's house, and he and her father would begin the intertwining of their businesses early Monday morning. A honeymoon across Europe would be delayed until the summer, naturally.

Such a neat and tidy coffin Thomas prepared for himself.

He did not mention the ring in his pocket. He would not be giving it to Constance. When the subject of a band was brought up, Thomas suggested Mr. Alban find some family treasure in their stores for that purpose. The older man happily agreed.

Considering a formal proposal was not necessary, Alban left to give his daughter the good news—and inform Edward Langmore that his attentions would no longer be endured.

As soon as Alban disappeared through the brass-plated doors, Thomas caught his reflection in the polished metal. He revolted at the sight. Vomit rose up the back of his throat. He heaved. He couldn't breathe. He couldn't think. He couldn't—he couldn't—he couldn't—

He had to.

"Thomas?" Dr. Andrew Samson's voice reached him. Arms hauled him up from where he trembled, doubled over. "Thomas, what's wrong? Are you quite alright—"

"No."

Andrew blinked. Thomas collapsed onto a bench.

"What's happened?"

"I'm to be married."

"I suppose it's not to Evelyn."

Even saying the words aloud scalded his throat. "No. Constance Alban."

"I see. That's why he was here."

"Yes."

"And you . . . You agreed?"

"I don't have a choice."

Andrew scoffed. "Of course you have a choice. You don't *have* to marry anyone. There's no law binding you to her just because her father wants it."

"He's threatened Evelyn."

"You could protect her."

"Not against this. He's . . . discovered something about me. If it gets out, we're all ruined. My own ruination, I could stand. But if I don't give him what he wants . . . you all will go down with me. And I couldn't live with myself knowing—knowing—"

He choked again. Damn it. He cared about them. Even the ones who hated him, like Jules and Beatrice. And now, he had to sacrifice everything for them. Maybe he would light himself and The Empire on fire if it meant being with Evelyn, but he would not pull her, or Andrew, or any of the rest into the flames just to secure his own happiness. This had to be done. He was the only one who could protect them all.

"Fight him, then," Andrew encouraged. "Stop him."

"I can't. I'm not strong enough. Not powerful enough. A lifetime of fighting and I'm exactly as helpless as I was—"

"When you were . . . ?"

As I was when my parents died. When my name was stolen from me as a child. When my fake life was ripped away from me as a young man. When I was abandoned by everyone I knew and cared about and cast away, never to return home again.

Only—he wasn't helpless, was he? He had strength and power enough to do this. To save the woman he loved and all those they cared about. That was something. He would hold on to that.

"When you were what, Thomas?" Andrew repeated.

He turned to stone. A gift to himself—returning to his old ways, his old self, his old costume. It was the only way to keep from breaking down.

"Never mind that. I have made my choice. I must now get on with living it."

"You don't have to—"

Thomas snorted in a sharp breath, trying to shock his body into working properly again. "Dr. Samson, you once told me you do not have the medical capabilities required to fix a broken heart. Do not exceed your mandate by attempting it."

The clock on the wall ticked—too loud and too long.

"What will you do now, then?"

"I will get married. But first, I must write a letter to Miss Cross."

No more protests or speeches from Andrew. For that, Thomas was grateful.

"What will you tell her?"

"The truth."

"Which is?"

"It's over."

It was all over.

CHAPTER FORTY-TWO

EVELYN RECEIVED NO LETTER REVOKING HER INVITATION TO THE Conthorpe ball. Perhaps the letter was lost, perhaps some calamity had befallen the messenger Andrew dispatched to get it to her, perhaps someone at the boarding house had forgotten to give it to her. The history on this point was unclear.

Some things just don't make any sense. Sometimes letters don't arrive. Sometimes people fail you. Sometimes hearts get broken. Sometimes people just can't love you the way you want them to.

Fact, unlike fiction, gets messy. And this part of the story is just that. Messy.

So it was that Evelyn found herself at the Conthorpe ball that night, dressed to fall in love but finding herself falling in a very different direction indeed.

Fiancée. A simple enough word. Three syllables. Seven letters. One simple definition. But when shaped by Thomas's perfect lips, it was as if Evelyn had never heard it before in her life.

Her universe hung crooked now, knocked off balance by the sight of Thomas's hand around another woman's waist.

This couldn't be happening. He couldn't be with another. He'd invited her here to propose to her. He loved her. He'd said it. He'd made her *believe* it.

No, it had to be a joke.

But then . . . no. It wouldn't be a joke, would it? Or rather, it *could* be a joke, but a cosmic prank played on her, not one pulled by Thomas Gallier.

The universe had handed her the only man she would ever love, convinced her to fall for him against her better judgment, and then ripped him away from her just when it seemed like she might break the terrible cycle of poor women having their hearts broken by wealthy men.

She'd worked so hard to never become her mother. And yet . . . there she was. Standing in her shoes. Repeating her mistakes. Fitting the role all too well.

Evelyn's throat went tight as she asked, "Your fiancée?"

"Only for a few minutes yet," Constance Alban said, her eyes sliding over Evelyn's shoulder, apparently seeking something, or someone, she didn't find. "It's no wonder you're surprised. I can't quite believe it either."

"I offer my most hearty felicitations. Surprise or no."

It was only her years of training that saved Evelyn's voice from wavering or her smile from faltering.

Awkward silence reigned. All around them, the partygoers pretended not to watch the confrontation, but there was no ignoring the weight of their sidelong stares. Still, Evelyn would not be the one to buckle first. She stared at Thomas, waiting for him to say something, *anything*, but he focused his attentions on his new fiancée.

Ultimately, it was Dr. Samson who couldn't bear the discomfiting quiet any longer. "Miss Cross, would you care for a dance? I haven't been out on the floor all night."

"No, thank you," Evelyn replied, never once taking her eyes from Thomas's guarded face. "My escort for this party seems to be otherwise engaged. I should take my leave before I look like a third wheel."

Please, say something. Stop me. Tell me it's all a ruse. Tell me it's a joke. Save me from this heartbreak.

But Thomas did nothing of the kind. Once again, it was Dr. Samson who came to her rescue.

"I'll walk you out, then," he said, offering her his arm.

When she took it, her hand was shaking. "Thank you."

And she turned her back on Thomas for what she was sure was the last time.

She and Dr. Samson proceeded through the party without passing a word between them. It wasn't until she'd collected her cloak and started for the door that he finally said something.

"It's a rotten play," he said, his signature smile sad now. "One of the worst I've ever seen. The hero didn't even get the girl."

Evelyn gripped her cloak. "Hero, Doctor? I don't see any heroes around here."

And with that, she left, carrying the last scraps of her pride along with her.

Outside, she passed the cabs lingering on the sidewalk and elected, instead, to walk.

Just in case.

Just in case he might follow and need to catch up with her.

But he didn't.

She walked the entire way home alone.

CHAPTER FORTY-THREE

THE NEXT DAY, ON THE OCCASION OF HIS TRIUMPHANT GRAND opening, Thomas Gallier was married.

Andrew handled all the details. After receiving Evelyn's letter of resignation, he facilitated the collection of Evelyn's things from her dressing room, ensuring that no traces of the woman would remain in the theater. He shuffled the vaudeville bill so that Jules Moreau was the headliner. Dr. Samson handled the press admirably, too, informing them that Thomas was so swept off his feet by this whirlwind romance with Miss Alban that he could hardly think straight, much less give interviews.

Nehemiah Alban was busy with Thomas's elephants, to which Constance had evidently taken a liking. The newspaperman overruled Thomas's original plan to facilitate their retirement, instead granting a parcel of parkland in the Bronx from his considerable holdings, from which they could be brought out as an entertainment for The Empire's most special events.

Alban also arranged for a popular performer from down the street to pad her body and lead The Dancing Dozen, and her act was as big a hit as the good old city had ever seen—a very funny joke at the expense of all the *truly* fat women in the chorus line.

The ceremony and The Empire's grand opening were all lovely and perfect and everything Thomas could ever have wished for. Thomas became the toast of the town before the evening ended. The lines to enter the pleasure palace circled around six city blocks and tickets for the vaudeville were impossible to get for the next three months.

And Thomas walked through it all like a dead man.

That night, he retired to his home—along with his wife and her servants. The ghostly manor had first been his haunt, and then, for a short time, become his and Evelyn's nighttime hideaway. Now, it pulsed with the signs of someone else's life. Laughter. Chatter. Heeled shoes tapping against wooden floorboards. Perfume clouding the air. Trousseaus being unpacked.

As his bride made herself well enough at home, Thomas retreated to the darkness of his study, with its unlit lamps and barren fireplace. The shadows matched his mood. He closed the curtains to shut out even the streetlamps.

This was his life now. An eternity of this empty room. The companionship of a woman he could never love and the well-earned hatred of the one he could never stop loving.

Eventually, the pain of it grew too much to bear. He glanced at the whiskey decanter on his bookshelf, the one he only kept for guests.

He uncorked it in one swift move. Not even bothering with the dusty snifters, he slammed back his first sip of alcohol in ten years.

That burn was the first time he'd allowed himself to feel all day. It was a delicious pain, one completely out of his control. Liquid self-harm.

He took another sip. And another. And then the sips turned into swallows which turned into glugs and by the time he resurfaced, he had no idea how many drinks he'd had. He only knew the decanter was empty.

On his wedding night, he did not retire to Constance's bed. Instead, he waited for the sunrise in his office, letting the alcohol deaden the blow of his last, most bitter revelation.

He had spent most of his life lonely. Meeting Evelyn had changed that. She'd taught him the beauty of community, of companionship, of love.

It was appropriate, then, that failing her brought him back to that horrible first state. He had begun lonely, and he would die that way, too.

Except for the bottle. That would keep him company.

It was what he deserved.

CHAPTER FORTY-FOUR

She knew better than to delude herself. But until the ship bound for France pulled away from its mooring, freeing itself into the river that would lead out to the wild, untamed sea and an uncertain future, Evelyn clung to her last wisps of hope.

Hope that Thomas would leave his sham of a marriage and come after her. Hope that Dr. Samson would bring everyone else to their senses. Hope that her friends would all quit the show in solidarity. Hope that they would forgo their stardom and salaries to stand with her. Hope that they would get on this ship with her and run away to France, where they could all dance at the Folies Bergère, drink themselves silly with champagne, and relish their new lives away from this damnable, pathetic scene.

But her hopes were dashed against the rocks as the tide carried the SS *Hibernia* off on her timely departure. Thomas would not come. Dr. Samson could not move him. And her friends were too poor and disenfranchised to have morals or sentiment—they couldn't afford them. Not in this economy.

Evelyn stayed leaning against the banister of the top deck for a long time—perhaps longer than was healthy. She supposed she was searching the dock for anyone who might have been late, anyone who might have wanted to say goodbye or run away with her.

But when the dock dissipated into the distance, she remained, bidding a final farewell to Manhattan, the only home she'd ever known.

To her surprise, someone said goodbye right back.

Miss Banting's—painted so tall she and Evelyn were practically eye to eye—stood victorious against the wall of a warehouse overlooking the river. She waved farewell . . . apparently to her missing weight, but as far as Evelyn was concerned, the woman might as well have been waving at her.

She thought back to the last time she'd seen this great lady. Back then, she'd been so afraid of change.

But she knew better now.

Nothing changed. Not really.

And that's how the story ends.

PART EIGHT

THE CIRCUS IS CLOSED AND THE SHOW'S AT AN END

Present Day

It's pretty self-indulgent, right? To keep interrupting someone else's story with your own? "Hey, Thomas and Evelyn, I know you have a whole thing going on in 1897, but I'm getting some billionaire dick here in 2023, so if you could pause for a few pages and let me fill the people in—that'd be great."

But I swear, this is important. Maybe not to anyone else, but to me. And to Thomas and Evelyn's story—to their ending.

As previously discussed, Armitage and I agreed that I would work independently. He would only read my final report upon completion of my research.

So . . . I put off the completion of my research. It wasn't that I was just stalling—there was still plenty to read and plenty of documents to cross-check, but I wasn't exactly speeding toward next steps. Why? Well, I would say it was a lot like our relationship. On the one hand, I felt like we had been together forever, but on the other hand, Armitage had still never mentioned any future beyond what we would order for dinner that night. And so, I worried that maybe everything would be over the second I turned in my research.

I wanted it to be undeniable, our love. But I was terrified it wasn't. That I was living a fairy tale while he was living in a horny lit professor's terrible first novel.

Then one day, I was sitting in the park (finishing my totally normal winter snack of ice cream, as one does), and I couldn't help but watch the couples walking past me. Usually, I wouldn't have paid them any attention. I tried not to look too closely at other people's relationships—it made me too jealous and way too insecure.

There's something so romantic about New York as the weather turns from fall to winter, though, and on that day, everyone seemed more in love than usual. Beneath the waning moon, each couple glowed with their own halo of radiance. A special spotlight that hit each one in time, declaring to the universe that these two people were meant for each other. They all walked closer, nuzzled cozier, held hands tighter.

They made me think of Thomas and Evelyn.

And then, they made me think of me and Armitage.

My hands felt empty without his.

That's when I knew I couldn't delay writing out Thomas and Evelyn's story anymore. I had to know the truth: Was it just this research project, or was there something more happening between us? The only way out was through. Finish the report, turn it in, and see where our relationship went from there.

So I told him I was going to a conference (a lie), locked myself in my shitbox apartment with all the Domino's I could eat, and wrote until my fingernails started to chip. It wasn't quite like the book you just read. I don't want to get ahead of myself, but in light of what happened next, I've gone back and made some revisions.

In the version I delivered to Armitage, I wrote in plain, clear terms about Thomas Gallier. His true origin—an origin he'd tried desperately to hide. His business association with Dr. Andrew Samson—a business partnership that became a real friendship. His elephants. His appearances in the newspapers. His almost, not quite, never-could-be love story.

I wrote about Constance Alban and their marriage of convenience/blackmail. Family lore would describe her as *Thomas Gallier's one true love*, but I laid out how the sudden increase in orders of whiskey to the Gallier house after their nuptials indicated a descent into alcoholism that can only be described as Tennessee Williamsian in nature. I even scrapped my note about the erection thing, hoping a straightforward account would convince him how important this story was.

When I finally gave the report to him, I was a woman on the brink. For one thing, now that I had spent so long with Evelyn and Thomas, I knew this couldn't be it for their story. I wanted to share them with the world. On my blog, in a book, in a goddamn Netflix series—I didn't care. I just wanted Evelyn and Thomas's story to come out of the shadows.

As I sat on one of Armitage's many brocade couches watching him page through my report, I realized there was another, more selfish, reason that my stomach was in knots. It had nothing to do with my work, and nothing to do with the fact that I hadn't eaten a vegetable in a week. It had to do with us.

Because as I had finished writing Evelyn and Thomas's story, I had becoming increasingly aware of the parallels—sure, I was no vaudeville star, but I was certainly fat, fabulous, and responsible for bringing a certain amount of spontaneity and joy to a certain rich man's previously rigid existence. Historically speaking, that hadn't worked out so well for Evelyn, and now, I wanted Armitage to tell me that our story wouldn't end like theirs.

I needed him to tell me that, actually.

But when Armitage finished reading my report, he merely said: "Thank you, Phoebe"—like I'd just given him the newspaper.

"Thank you?" It was a December afternoon, and I had curled up next to him as he read, but now I found myself shivering despite the fireplace and the warmth of his body.

"Yes. Thank you. Now, what do you want for dinner? Thai?"

"What do you mean, *what do I want for dinner?*" Maybe it wasn't the cold that was making me shiver. Maybe I was shaking—with shock, and the beginnings of anger.

He chuckled. "Dinner's the final meal of the day. When you eat, you generally need to pick something *to* eat—"

"I want to talk about this."

"Oh. Yes. Um. It's very well done. You're a keen researcher." A pause. I felt every muscle in my face tense, and he must have picked up on my disbelief—not that I was hiding it. "Is . . . is that what you're looking to hear?"

"No. I mean, thank you, but that's not really what I meant."

"What did you mean?"

He fixed me with a look of slightly narrow-eyed amusement. It was like we were communicating on two different frequencies. I was serious, maybe more serious than I'd ever been in our entire relationship. He treated me like this was just a silly lark.

"I . . . I think people need to know about Thomas and Evelyn," I said. "We shouldn't keep this story to ourselves."

"Phoebe," he said, my name almost a tut, "that wasn't the deal."

"I know it wasn't the deal, but I want the deal to change. This is different. *Everything* is different now."

We're different now.

He set the research dossier on the table, shrugging as he did so. "I had a curiosity. You satisfied it. Now, what about dinner?"

I couldn't believe how chipper he was. How *normal*. As if he couldn't possibly understand why this mattered to me.

"We're not talking about dinner."

"Oh, yes, we are. I'm starved."

"This is important."

"Okay, then." He breathed in and focused on me. "Go ahead. Tell me why."

I thought he was being reasonable then, hearing me out.

"It has real historical significance."

"Maybe, but people are going to ask where you got the story. The documents and everything. How are you going to explain that?"

"I'd tell them the truth. It all came from you."

"Those are my family's documents. I wasn't exactly at liberty to offer them up for public consumption. Come on, let's be serious about this—you know what my father is like."

His father. A few months ago, I might have let him have that. Might have been so desperate to be liked that I would have made some bad joke, locked Evelyn and Thomas away forever, and gone about my life. All so Armitage would like me more.

Not anymore. Not now.

"Who cares? Who cares if anyone knows you gave me access to those papers?"

"My family will care. They'll tear you apart before they let this out. Thomas and Constance are the reason our company exists. No one wants their dirty laundry aired out in—what? Your newsletter? Some book?"

I recoiled. Dirty laundry? Was that how he saw Evelyn?

Was that how he saw *me*?

"It's not dirty laundry. It's a love story."

For the first time, he seemed flustered. There it was—the understanding that I was not going to be talked down.

"You're under an NDA," he reminded me.

"And you could let me out of it with a wave of your pen."

"It's not—I'm not going to—" His neck flushed red. He tried another tactic. "Listen. You're right. Evelyn and Thomas were interesting. No doubt. But we can put this little story behind us. File this away, clear those old boxes out of the attic. Too much clutter anyway."

That "clutter" was the sum total of Thomas Gallier's contribution to the original version of "this little story." To erase it would be, effectively, to erase Evelyn Cross altogether.

He smiled. "And we can finally be together without those two dead people hanging over us all the time, hm?"

I glanced up at the portrait of Thomas and Constance Alban. The husband and wife whose portrait had presided over almost every research and writing session I'd yet conducted.

It seemed to me that there were *always* two dead people hovering over us, just not the two I would have preferred.

"But what about Evelyn?" I asked, my voice small.

"What about Evelyn?"

"You can't just let the world forget her."

"I get that it's a love story, and I get that you've invested a lot in this, but honestly. They're two dead strangers. Why do you *really* care—"

"Because they're us!"

I don't know why I said it.

No. Fuck that. I *do* know why I said it. I said it because it's true and because I felt it in the long bones of my body.

"What was that?" Armitage asked, as if he hadn't heard.

"Never mind. Forget it."

"No. Explain yourself."

He stood up, leveraging his height against me. I turned to my research dossier.

"It's just . . . how could you read all of this and not think there were at least *some* similarities between what happened between them and what's going on between us? Don't you see it?"

"No."

The word, one syllable, two letters. To me, it was a blow. He said it like it was a kiss.

"Excuse me?"

"If I see a similarity, it's because you wrote it there. You with your editorializing—"

"This is *facts-based research.*"

"God, why are you pushing this? You want to be like them? Phoebe, he *left her.* He threw her away like she was nothing. Not exactly the model for a great relationship."

He gestured between us. For a split second, I thought he was reaching out for me, so I flinched back. Hurt, his gaze softened.

"Unless . . ." he trailed off. "Unless you don't think this is a great relationship."

I said nothing.

"We're not going to end up like them," he promised.

"Then prove it."

Do something, say something—anything at all to make me believe you. His hands came up to cup my face. I didn't fight them.

"Phoebe," he started. "I—"

This was it. I could almost see his perfect lips shaping around the words. *I love you.* But instead, he just offered:

"I don't want this to come between us."

But I knew it already had. For some reason, I thought again about that night on the park bench, watching the happy couples walk by under the drifting snowfall. How my hands had felt empty without his, how those same hands felt like irons around my face now.

I thought about how I'd been sitting on that park bench alone because he rarely left the house in my company.

I thought about how he'd never said it. Never said *I love you*. And still, six months into our time together, couldn't bring himself to do it now.

Love was a series of choices. A role you step into every day, a part you play through ovations and heckles.

Maybe, I bargained with myself, he didn't have to say the words if he could just show me.

I gave him another chance.

"Then let me have the story. Risk something for me. Forget what your family will think. Forget what *anyone* will think. For once, just do something because you want to."

"I can't," he said.

Can't was not the same as *don't want to*.

Clearly upset, Armitage raked a hand through his hair. "If you go public with this, then you know you can't have me too, right? Don't make that choice. *Please.* Don't do this. I've always stood by you. I *want* to always stand by you—"

No, you haven't. And no, you don't.

The thought was immediate, a lashing out from a bitter cavern I didn't even know existed within me.

It was true, though. I hadn't realized it until that moment, but with that one idea, it all settled in with blistering clarity.

"Do you remember when you said you were afraid of me?" I asked, voice shaking.

"That's ancient history. I said that before we—"

"Why?"

No answer.

"Why are you afraid of me, Armitage?" I repeated.

He dropped his cowardly head. Ran a hand across his mouth, then through his hair. He quivered beneath my stare.

He didn't have to say it. I knew.

He had never been seen in public with me. Dinners at home. Cocktails in his private, walled garden. Long hours in his study. Nights in bed with the curtains drawn.

Did his parents know about me? Did his friends? He'd locked me in a pantry rather than tell his dad about my existence.

How many parties had he been invited to over our time together? A hundred? How many times had he invited me to go with him? Zero.

He was all over the society pages. Speculation ran rampant about his love life. Inset photographs of him and luridly thin women abounded.

God, I was going to be sick.

I loved this man.

And this man was ashamed of me.

To him, I was good enough to fuck. Good enough for wonton soup and cold medicine and limoncello spritz and movie night and T-shirts. Good enough to waste time with. Good enough to rehearse being a real man with a real heart. Good enough to use.

But not good enough to be a part of his real life.

Not good enough to love.

He was afraid of me because I wouldn't fit into the world of his fancy friends, wouldn't win his asshole father's approval. I knew then that if it came down to it—*when* it came down to it—he would not choose me.

That's why he would rather burn a great love story than share it with the world. He was vain. Cowardly. He was one of the most powerful men in the world, but terrified what people would think if he didn't fit their expectations.

Not only could he not bear anyone thinking that *this* Gallier liked women like me . . . he couldn't bear the thought of anyone knowing that another Gallier did, either.

That's why he was scared.

He reached for me. "Let's just sit down. Forget about the book. Forget about everything. Start over."

No. I wouldn't.

I started for the door.

"*Please*," he said, his voice breaking this time. "Why can't we just go back to the way it was?"

"Because I deserve better than the way it was."

From the moment I started working on this research, I knew that Evelyn Cross shouldn't be a footnote in someone else's story. A long-buried secret no one uncovered for over a hundred years. Doomed to be erased.

Deniable.

I wouldn't let that happen to her.

And after studying her courage, her confidence, her unflinching sense of self-worth for months, I now knew how to make that choice for myself, too.

All this time, I'd been thinking I wasn't good enough for Armitage.

But he wasn't good enough for me.

I left without another word. I didn't listen as he shouted my name, begging me to come back like I was the last lifeboat abandoning him on a sinking ship. I didn't answer his calls. I didn't return his texts. Didn't buzz him up when he rang at my shitty apartment.

The choice destroyed me, but it was the only one I could make.

When he did finally break through, it was with an unsigned, unmarked letter. No Gallier letterhead, no flouncy signature. Just a plain white envelope filled with ripped-up scraps of paper. It took me a minute to reassemble the page, but when I did, I realized two things:

1. It was our NDA. Torn up into a dozen pieces. Ready for the garbage.

2. It was the official end of whatever Armitage and I had together. He'd said if I went public with the story, we were over. And by giving me the freedom to do just that, he might as well have waved me goodbye.

So I took the hint. And I wrote.

I gathered up the copies of my research from the Gallier family archives and my own trove of documents from the Manhattan Historical Preservation Society and all the notes I'd scrawled over the last few months. Between shifts at the MHPS, I devoted every spare minute to writing this book, this new story of Evelyn and Thomas. I leaned into the similarities between their story and mine and Armitage's. History repeats itself, you know, and I was stupid to think I could escape that.

But when I finished it, when I left Thomas in that sad study and that sadder alcoholic stupor—when I left Evelyn on that ship bound for an uncertain future—I knew I couldn't let that be the end. Not after everything they'd been through.

Not after everything *I'd* been through.

As I'd been researching their relationship, I'd wanted nothing more than for them to have a happily ever after. With this manuscript in my hands, I realized that I had the power to give them one. Their story could be a fairy tale. In the end, the man could be a hero and the heroine could get the guy. Their friends could be saved. The pawn in her father's matchmaking schemes could be with her true soulmate. The close-minded villain could get what was coming to him.

Love could win.

Like any rich douchebag, Armitage was obsessed with classical studies. He went around quoting ancient dead guys all the time, and one of those quotes stuck with me.

A man called Menander once wrote:

We live, not as we wish to, but as we can.

I know I'm not anybody. Who is Phoebe Blair to question a playwright whose work has lasted since the third century BCE?

Still. Fuck that. I will live as I wish to. And if I can't, then I will *write* as I wish to.

Maybe this story is not historically accurate. Maybe I will never be allowed to show my face at academic conferences again, and maybe the Gallier family will use their entire fortune to make sure that my life is ruined for this.

But I don't care.

Because . . .

One day, I will be nothing more than a story, too. And when that day comes, I hope someone writes me a fairy tale.

≡◆≡

And so, we turn back the pages, turn back time. It is the night of the ball. Evelyn has just been told that Thomas is getting married. And now, they are on one final collision course.

CHAPTER FORTY-FIVE

SHE'D MADE IT NOT TEN STEPS OUTSIDE OF THE MANSION BEFORE his voice reached her.

"Miss Cross? Miss Cross?"

Miss Cross. So they were back to it, were they? Pretending.

A shaky breath. Then, she stopped and turned. "Yes, Mr. Gallier?"

He flinched at the sound of that name. His false name. But she didn't care. Let him hurt.

"I . . . I don't know what to say."

"Say?" She laughed, though it clattered through the air like a poorly crafted joke. "What is there to say?"

Thomas straightened to his full height. Evelyn watched as he took firm control of his emotions and settled back into that dead-eyed coldness of his. "You couldn't have expected us to last forever, could you? We were both using each other. You needed me to save your career. I needed to sow my wild oats before I became a real gentleman. You are not fashionable, accomplished, rich, wholesome, or connected enough to last. This relationship always had a natural conclusion—you always said so yourself. This just happens to be what that conclusion looks like."

Evelyn had been hit by many men in her life. Once, she'd been beaten so badly she lost a month of bookings because she couldn't even spread her lips to sing.

She'd never been hurt by a man as badly as she was in that moment. Looking at the man she loved, wondering if it had all been in her head.

"You have made your choice. You've made it very clear why. In a contest with your ambition, I couldn't win," she said, voice wavering. "You don't have to hurt me."

"I'm not trying to hurt you. If the facts hurt you, then that is entirely your problem. I'm simply laying them out. You cannot ever crawl back here—back to me."

Oh. It was so obvious now. She knew what he was doing.

Trying to break her heart. Trying to make it seem like he hadn't ever cared. Because if he was a heartless cad who'd manipulated her, then she wouldn't see him for what he really was, what he'd always been, what she'd always feared he was:

A coward who cared more about his status than his heart. Just what she'd always feared—a rich man who abandoned her the second she fell for him.

In that moment, her pain ignited into white-hot rage.

"Crawl back to you?" She let loose, no longer concerned with anyone overhearing. Let them hear. Let them know what kind of man he was. "You think I would *ever* crawl back to *you*? You love me and you're throwing it away and now you suppose I could *ever want you again*? You are a spineless, weak, pathetic man who has everything and still traded it for an illusion. You think these people have power? You think they're worth a damn? You think they'll make something out of you? You're wrong. It's smoke and mirrors. What we do at The Empire is fake as cardboard trees and *still* we're more real than the whole lot of them put together. And that's what you've traded our love for, Thomas. You bargained away something real for a lifetime of *fake*. That mask you wear, this character you play? That's all you will ever be now—all they'll ever let you be."

In her speech, she'd subconsciously stepped forward until they were almost nose-to-nose. Even then, he didn't blink. Evelyn's heart collapsed in on itself.

"You know what?" she breathed, her words vanishing to clouds in the cold air. "I actually don't think I'm hurt. I think I feel sorry for you."

Thomas's hands flexed. "Why?"

"Because you showed me how to love. How to *really* love, not just play-act at it. And now that I know how, I have years ahead of me to love again. But you? You couldn't really love someone if you had a thousand hearts to give and a thousand lifetimes to try."

"You don't understand. And you never will," he growled.

"Then explain it to me," she challenged.

For a moment, she thought he might slap her. Or kiss her. Or explain himself.

But then, a sweet, thin voice rang out from the steps of the mansion. The voice of his fiancée.

"Mr. Gallier? Mr. Gallier?"

He turned at that sound. And Evelyn knew it was all over. "You'd better run, sir. That's your future calling."

His shoulders tensed, and she knew she had his attention. "I really am happy for you, you know. I'm sure the two of you will be very rich together."

CHAPTER FORTY-SIX

THAT NIGHT, SHE'D FALLEN ASLEEP SOBBING. EVELYN COULDN'T have been unconscious for very long, though, because when she did wake up, her pillow still squelched with tears.

At first, she didn't open her swollen eyes. She lay there for as long as she could stand it.

The trouble was that once she fully awoke, everything would change. This would be the last morning she rose from her lumpy mattress. The last rays of Manhattan sunshine warming her skin through her window. The last breaths of hardwood lacquer and powdered soap and cheap perfume. The last brush of familiar, clean sheets against her skin.

She had to say goodbye. Sad as that was. But she had no reason to rush. She heard almost none of the boarding house's usual echoes and groans—her fellow residents must have been at The Empire already.

"Good morning, beautiful."

Bea's voice interrupted her silent farewell. Evelyn pushed herself up to sitting. As if this were just another one of their casual morning chats, Bea perched on the edge of Evelyn's trunk and flipped through the morning newspapers.

Evelyn averted her eyes. She did not want to read anything about The Empire or its Emperor's wedding to its new Empress. In a few hours, she would be crossing the ocean, and that was all the seasickness she could endure, thank you very much.

"Yes, I'm sure I'm quite beautiful this morning," she said. "Absolutely peerless."

"You look well enough to headline an entire vaudeville bill. The tears bring out the natural sparkle in your eyes."

One could always count on Bea to make the most of any disaster.

"Where are the others?"

"Some all-hands meeting at The Empire before the opening. Jules called it very early this morning. Sent messengers for everyone and everything."

"And you stayed behind to say I told you so, I suppose," Evelyn muttered.

"That is the trouble with being a caretaker, Evelyn. I get infinite opportunities to say *I told you so*, but when those opportunities come around, it never tastes as sweet as I hoped."

Well, at least Evelyn's worst fear wouldn't come true. She didn't have to hear any gloating. Still, she couldn't help but dig. "Quite a lengthy way of saying *no*."

The pair slipped into comfortable quiet then. There was nothing to say, really. Evelyn had confessed the whole sorry story to everyone last night before collapsing in bed.

Bea hummed as she scanned her newsprint. Evelyn wedged herself into a front-lacing bodice, then proceeded with the rest of her dressing and toilette. It was only when she requested Bea's help with the buttons along the back of her gown that they spoke again.

"Will you see me off, then?" Evelyn asked.

"I actually came to ask you something. Something serious."

"Yes?"

"Do you love him?"

Evelyn stared down at her hands. "I never said it."

"But you do. Don't you?"

Evelyn's lips trembled to answer, but when she realized that she would go the rest of her life without *ever* telling him, all that came out was a broken sob. She gripped the back of a chair for support, leaning forward as Bea's hands lithely commanded the last of her buttons.

"Ah. I see," Bea said.

Oh, why didn't Bea rub this in her face? At least then, she could be angry at Bea instead of angry with herself.

"I should have listened to you. In the beginning, I mean," Evelyn said. "I should have better protected my heart."

"Maybe. But now, what's done is done. And what do you intend to do about it?"

Dressing complete, Evelyn swept her hair up into a simple chignon.

"I thought that was obvious when I packed all of my belongings and said *I intend to move to France.*"

"You aren't moving to France," Bea replied in that commanding, *I know all* way of hers.

"What do you think *I intend to move to France* means? Is it a euphemism I haven't heard of?"

Bea flattened her expression. "There isn't *any* euphemism you haven't heard of."

"Then draw your own conclusions vis-à-vis my intentions to move to France," Evelyn snapped.

She couldn't take this emotional tennis match any longer. She wanted this chapter of her life to be done. She wanted a new challenge, a new adventure, a new Evelyn.

She wanted to be as far away from the man she loved as possible. That way, it might be harder to miss him.

"He loves you too, you know."

"I know."

She knew. And that's why it hurt so much.

He loved her. And he still chose someone else.

"Love is rare, Evelyn," Bea implored. "You know this better than anyone. If he loves you, if you love him, then you should fight for it."

A humorless laugh. Another crack in Evelyn's heart. "Funny, Bea. Because he couldn't seem to muster the same strength to fight for me."

PART NINE

THE CURSE OF THE DREAMER

A NOTE FROM THE HISTORIAN

I've done a lot of interrupting at this point, so I'll try to move things along here. To that end, I hope you'll allow me a little table-setting.

Imagine, if you will, the machine of that morning, each part with its own particular function:

- Beatrice and Evelyn, leaving for the boat that would take Evelyn to Paris.

- Thomas and Andrew, preparing for the wedding and readying The Empire for its opening.

- Jules calling a meeting of the entire vaudeville company—for reasons unknown.

- And Miss Constance Alban, in a dressing room backstage at The Empire, trying not to think about Edward Langmore, the man she really loved.

CHAPTER FORTY-SEVEN

IN THE WINGS OF THE EMPIRE THEATRE, THOMAS AWAITED HIS FATE as if it were the guillotine. All morning, he'd been shuffled around his pleasure palace, hobnobbing and shaking hands, giving interviews and pretending that his world wasn't shattering all around him, but now, in the darkness, in these last few moments of freedom, he could no longer pretend.

Dr. Samson flanked him, playing the role of the best man to Thomas's groom. He seemed as enthused to be there as Thomas did—which was to say, with all the excitement of a man awaiting execution.

At length, a stagehand approached Thomas and whispered that it was time. The orchestra pit overflowed with the music of some grand number and, as they'd rehearsed this morning, the performers filed out onto the stage to the awe and applause of every member of their sold-out audience. Thomas and his groomsman followed the bishop, landing in their assigned places last.

Thomas knew he wasn't doing particularly well at performing the part of the happy groom. He fought to force some kind of smile, anything to convince the world he hadn't been bullied into this fantastic match of his.

But then, Andrew had to rob him of that smile.

"Thomas?"

He didn't move his eyes from the back door of the theater, where Constance would, in a moment, make her grand entrance in front of their thousands of close, personal friends.

"Yes, Doctor?"

"How is that old heart of yours?"

A difficult question. So easy to answer. "Don't have one anymore."

And just like that, the orchestra began their rendition of Pachelbel's Canon. The bishop stepped forward.

The wedding began.

And Thomas's life ended.

CHAPTER FORTY-EIGHT

AT THE SOUTH STREET SEAPORT, THE HORN OF THE SS *HIBERNIA* blew several warning calls, loud and clear as a firing squad's shots.

"Ah. This is me. The next grand adventure awaits."

Throwing her arms around Bea, Evelyn tried to squeeze into that touch everything she couldn't bear to say out loud. *Thank you* and *I'm sorry* and *I would never be the same without you* and *I'll never have another friend like you as long as I live how will I bear to be without you please won't you write to me please please please.*

"There will be another boat tomorrow," Bea muttered into her shoulder. "Your ticket can be exchanged."

More of this? Why spoil a perfectly good scene with an encore? Evelyn busied herself with her gloves.

"And why would I do that? If I leave tomorrow, that's another day I'm not in fabulous Paris."

"You aren't *really* going to let them open The Empire without you, are you?"

"Yes," Evelyn said. "Yes, I am. I have to."

Because if I go back, I may never rid myself of this cancerous love for Thomas Gallier.

Once again, the ship's horn signaled its imminent departure. Panic—sharp and stinging—gripped Bea's soft features.

"Evelyn," she said, her voice breaking. "Are you really going to let that man rob you of your dream? Are you going to let him deny you? Please. Don't betray yourself that way."

357

The boat screamed another whistle, and with every intention of turning her friend down, she peered up through the sunshine from under the brim of her traveling hat. Somehow, the angle was just so that she stared head-on at an advertisement painted on the brick wall of a nearby warehouse.

Miss Banting's, smiling smugly down at her, waving her hands as if to say, *Oh, yes, run away with your tail between your legs. I've won this round—and every one that will come after.*

Her mind changed then and there. Maybe she could have let Thomas win. Maybe she could have run away from his world, from his sharp end of society that would never accept her the way she was.

But she couldn't abide losing to a damn weight-loss advertisement. Under no circumstances.

Evelyn checked the small watch she kept tucked into the skirt of her traveling dress.

"How fast do you think we can make it to 34th Street?"

CHAPTER FORTY-NINE

MANHATTAN, THE CITY OF SPECTACLE, HAD NEVER SEEN ANYTHING quite like the opening of the Empire.

If only Thomas could have enjoyed it.

As Constance's wedding march filled the acoustically perfect hall, Julia Moreau stepped to center stage, cheekily positioning herself directly in front of the bishop, who looked none too pleased at suddenly receiving a face full of feathers from Julia's extravagant plumage.

Thomas might have laughed if it weren't taking all his strength to keep from crying.

"Ladies and gentlemen! Loyal denizens of the Empire!" Julia called, settling the audience down. "Today, you will see wonders beyond your wildest imaginations! You will worship at the temple of Bacchus and Thomas Gallier! You will marvel at the modern world and peek through the curtain that separates fantasy and reality."

Wild applause. At least Evelyn had been right about one thing—the audience truly loved the spectacular she'd put together.

"But first, you will witness that most sacred of human rites—marriage!"

Applause, applause, applause. They might as well have been applauding Thomas stepping up to the hanging block. Julia continued:

"Now, this is not a normal marriage. This is the marriage of two of this city's most famous children! Thomas Gallier, the Emperor himself, and Miss Constance Alban—the Princess of Manhattan! All rise for the procession of the wedding party!"

The doors at the rear of the theater opened. Six identical, slender women in softly colored gowns marched up either of the aisles. Thomas wanted to scream. Alban must have been so certain of their nuptials that he'd prepared all of this in advance—such coordination would have taken weeks.

Control your breathing, Thomas. Don't let them see you suffer.

Once the bridal party was in position, the trumpets wailed. The doors opened again, and Julia's voice chimed out to the back of the house. "Remain standing for the arrival of the bride."

There she was. The soon-to-be Mrs. Thomas Gallier, sweeping down the aisle to adoring sighs and cheers. Constance—with her perfect hair and willowy body and gown that must have cost more than most in this theater would see in their lifetime—should have radiated sunshine on her father's arm. However, when she arrived at Thomas's side and was handed over, he pulled back her veil to greet someone very gray indeed.

Once the audience settled, the bishop began the ceremony.

"Dearly beloved . . ."

As the bishop spoke of marriage and sacrifice, Thomas focused on his gold crucifix—a distraction from his present circumstance. Sacrifice indeed.

He didn't even acknowledge his future wife again until she whispered his name.

"Thomas?"

"Yes, my dear?" he asked, the words catching on his tongue like tender fingers on sandpaper.

"On the night when we danced, you said that I made you realize something. What was it?"

"That doesn't matter now."

"It matters to me."

"*. . . the holy bonds of Christian matrimony . . .*"

He glanced down at her, only to realize she wasn't looking at him at all. Constance was staring out at someone in the audience.

Edward Langmore. Hat in his hands. Stuck in the middle of a long row of people, trapped as he watched her marry someone else.

"Thomas, I don't think I want to marry someone I don't love," she said, her voice barely carrying above the roar of his hammering heart, but her hazy eyes possessing a surprising confidence. "A lifetime is such a long time to be alone in a marriage, don't you think?"

"*. . . vouchsafed by the state . . .*"

"You . . . you don't want to marry me?" he asked.

Her ringlets bounced as she shook her head. Tears leaked onto her cheeks, leaving tracks in her white powder, but she was smiling all the same—a real smile. "No," she said. "And I don't think you want to marry me either."

"*. . . and made sacred by the watchful blessing of the Lord our God . . .*"

It was both the best and worst thing Thomas had ever heard. Best because he might now be free—if he hadn't lost the one woman he'd wanted the freedom to choose.

He didn't have time to make a decision.

"Mr. Gallier. Miss Alban," the bishop said. "Will you two turn and face each other?"

They did so. Neither of them with any certainty.

"Please repeat after me," the bishop intoned. "I, Thomas Gallier—"

"I, Thomas Gallier . . ."

If Thomas hadn't been so attuned to the noises of The Empire, he might not have heard it. The slight, echoing *pop* in the back of the house—the sound of the doors opening when they weren't meant to be. Against his better judgment, his attention swiveled to that one noise—

Evelyn.

Watching him marry someone else.

The great doors framed her and even the dim theater lights didn't dull her shine. Her bottom lip trembled. Her hair had come loose from her simple bun. Her hat sat askew on her head.

Still. The most perfect woman he'd ever seen.

And when their eyes met, he discovered the gods and poets were right. They were two halves of a single whole, and their combining was the only thing that mattered in this universe. The only thing that could right all the wrongs they'd suffered.

Thomas found himself smiling at her. Lost in the magic.

The bishop continued. ". . . do take Miss Constance Alban to be my lawfully wedded wife."

The reply came quickly, thoughtless, natural.

". . . do take Miss Evelyn Cross to be my lawfully wedded wife."

CHAPTER FIFTY

THE CHAOS WAS IMMEDIATE. EVELYN DIDN'T KNOW HOW IT HAD happened—had everyone planned for this?—but all at once, Julia whistled, and the audience, the performers, and various members of the wedding party turned on each other. Constance Alban fled the stage, gathering up her skirts in a big, unseemly heap. Her bridesmaids chased after her in scandalized horror. The coppers, who had been stationed at every exit for the purposes of crowd control, immediately sprung to action, unsheathing their clubs and waiting for their orders. Mrs. Alban spiraled into a huffy tantrum. Mr. Alban shouted at Thomas from his place in the audience, red-faced from rage. Alban's suited goons, positioned in seats around the theater, sprang up, ready to quell this minor riot. The audience rustled their confusion. Thomas walked toward the edge of the stage—toward Evelyn—as if in a trance. Dr. Samson shuffled down the aisle to head off Mr. Alban.

In short . . . madness.

And in the midst of all that visual and emotional mess, darling Julia stepped forward with her usual grandiose aplomb.

"Ladies and gentlemen and other assorted characters along and beyond that duality, I am most pleased to announce a change in program!"

A roar echoed through the crowd. It *must* have been planned, somehow, because as soon as Julia spoke, the performers leapt into action. The orchestra *oompahed* to life. Julia led a song. The audience, diverted from the drama for a moment, focused their attention on the show.

This, of course, could not be allowed to stand. Dr. Samson's interventions must not have been compelling because at Alban's spluttering direction, his men and the officers of the law surged forward.

"Order! We will have order!"

Vaguely, Evelyn had to wonder what he thought would happen when the dust settled. Say the police were able to quell this. What then? Would they hold Thomas down and force him to marry Constance? Would they toss Evelyn out on her ear and imprison her so she would never darken Thomas's doorstep again?

Evelyn found herself caught in the middle of it—the cheering audience all around her, the coppers pressing in from behind, the dancers marching down the aisles like a coming army, Thomas's eyes meeting hers above it all.

It was only when Bea grabbed up her hand and started her down the aisle that Evelyn realized just how difficult actually *getting* to Thomas would be.

"Come on!" Bea shouted.

"Where do you think we're going?" Evelyn asked, struggling to keep up.

"To get you to Thomas before Alban's hit squad takes him out."

"Might be too late for that," Evelyn muttered, an involuntary shudder rocking through her as she realized just how many coppers there were.

Boxed in, Bea looked helplessly down the rows of audience members. Nothing that way but a row full of folks avidly taking in the spectacle. Still, without hesitation, she charged forward, forcing Evelyn to mutter *pardon me*s and *excuse me*s as they navigated their large skirts over knees and tucked-away handbags down the row.

Once free of the tangle of seated theatergoers, Bea tugged Evelyn into one of the Romanesque alcoves built into the far house left wall.

Covered today with a celebratory banner, it provided the perfect dark, hidden place for the two of them to catch their breath outside of the fray.

"Oh, damn," Bea breathed. "I was worried about this."

"What is going on out there?" Evelyn hissed.

"We all decided this whole thing with you and Thomas was no good. Soul-rotten. So we all decided to change it. I would make sure you got here. Akio would work on Constance Alban. Dr. Samson would convince Thomas. And Jules would prepare the performers, make sure that nothing got in the way of your reunion."

She said it as if listing out who might bring what snacks to a picnic.

Evelyn cringed as a cymbal crashed beyond their thin banner-curtain. It sounded as if someone had just crashed a human skull into the thing rather than a normal drumstick.

"*This* was your grand plan?"

Bea winced. "I believe Thomas may have gone rogue. Now, if you will, let's go this way. I think I might know of an opening—"

Throwing back the curtain, Bea slithered down through the tiniest of gaps between the wall and the seated patrons at the far side of the theater. Evelyn had no choice but to follow.

However, when they reached their halfway point, it became apparent that this would *not* be their ideal choice of escape. Because at the end nearest the stage stood Mr. Alban, his face uglied with rage. Evelyn backpedaled, only to find her *other* escape similarly blocked—this time by the coppers chasing her from the opposite direction.

The charge was led by none other than Officer Push Broom Mustache himself—the same one who once promised to destroy her.

Terror coursed through Evelyn's bloodstream. She was trapped.

But then, over the cacophony, a slight, feminine voice reached her ears.

"Miss Cross! This way!"

The voice came from Miss Constance Alban, who had reemerged from the wings, still in her wedding gown, and waved over her father's shoulder. *Come this way.* Evelyn balked.

Constance seemed insistent, but Evelyn would absolutely *not* be going that way. Mr. Alban looked prepared to kill her.

"Coppers! Arrest this woman!"

Constance protested. "Father, please—"

"Quiet, you useless girl! Get back on that stage. Do as you're told."

Of all the remarkable things Evelyn had seen today, there was none more remarkable than what came after Alban spit those words in his lovely daughter's face. Tossing her bouquet carelessly over her shoulder, she hauled back one fisted hand and smashed it into his left eye.

The crowd went *wild*. And if Evelyn was being honest, she did, too.

A sensation that only increased when Constance Alban practically dove over the crowd and fell into the arms of a very portly, very plain, very, very happy man—and kissed him.

"I can't believe it!" Evelyn cried.

"Really?" Bea smirked. "I don't think it's so outlandish."

Not so outlandish? The Dancing Dozen were heading off lines of policemen in the aisles with their fabulous fan kicks. Betsy Washington blew a fistful of her magic dust in the eyes of a handful of Alban's guards, causing them to stumble back uselessly as the glitter embedded itself into their sclera. Mrs. Alban had been scooped up by Caruso, who belted sweet nothings directly into her scandalized ears. Annie made a big show of getting caught in a policeman's handcuffs, then freeing herself from them with her usual illusionist's flair. Nathaniel left a tap shoe–sized kick mark on the face of at least one man who got too close to the stage—an act that received thunderous applause from the second balcony. Dr. Samson assured anyone close to him that this was part of the act—all while Natia slipped pamphlets about her various socialist causes into their unsuspecting pockets.

It was mayhem. It was anarchy. It was spectacle. It was glory. It was theater in its finest, purest form.

Through it all, Julia conducted the small army from center stage, breaking up the choruses of her song to shout marching orders at them.

And the audience, perhaps against their better judgment and all the rules of decency and decorum, ate it up with their bare hands. The entire theater had turned into a pantomime. Prim ladies loudly casting their boos against the long arm of the law and Alban and anyone else attempting to set the original wedding back to order. Stiff-mustached gentlemen waved their canes to assist the beating back of the security forces. Folks stomped their boots in time with the riotous music coming from the orchestra pit and joined their off-key voices with the familiar refrain.

Tomorrow, they would all write off the scene as a huge publicity stunt. Alban's place as the most powerful man in Manhattan would be secure—as would his daughter's reputation—by virtue of the fact that this whole farce had been nothing but that. A farce. The papers would have a field day regaling the masterful performance put on by Thomas Gallier's grand Empire players and their high-society compatriots. What a lark! What a scene! What a fabulous opening!

With the path finally cleared, Evelyn made one final cross to the stage steps.

As the orchestra's song slid into its final chorus and the audience reached the height of its emotional splendor, Mr. Alban collected himself from the bloodstain that had disappeared into the crimson carpet and hollered a hasty retreat.

There were other words thrown about as he called off his brute forces and led their exodus. *You'll regret this. I'll have you all. You'll never work in this town again. You'll be ruined.* Evelyn believed he meant that. But when she looked across the stage, the crowds finally parted and every other thought left her mind.

There was nothing left there but Thomas.

Before Evelyn knew it, she was running. And he was running. She thought they might collide, but as if they'd been choreographed to do so, they both skidded to a sharp halt just before they managed it.

A vague part of Evelyn's subconscious acknowledged that the full house watched them with hushed anticipation. The orchestra traded their bawdy barroom singalong for something classical and sweeping.

She and Thomas weren't just players in this show now.

They *were* the show.

But for maybe the first time in her life, Evelyn didn't have any interest in performing.

CHAPTER FIFTY-ONE

After surrendering his identity for so many years, Tom Gallagher never thought he would be himself again. Thomas Gallier was too ingrained in him, the mask and costume too vital to his survival. If he met his true self on the street, he was not even sure he'd recognize him.

However, as the woman he loved crossed the stage toward him, he realized how foolish a fear that was.

Tom Gallagher was always there inside him. Just waiting to be seen.

And Evelyn Cross had seen him.

He'd been undeniable from the start.

CHAPTER FIFTY-TWO

EVELYN HAD BEEN FIRM, DEVOUT, EVEN, IN HER RESOLVE TO PER-form at The Empire's opening, drink gobs of celebratory champagne, and leave without ever even seeing Tom again.

But then . . . their eyes had met across the busiest room in all of Manhattan. And he'd said her name.

Now, they stood not even a step apart from one another, and she knew in her heart that her entire life led up to this moment.

"Why, hello there, stranger," she said, her voice trembling. "Do you come here often?"

"I should be asking *you* that question," he said, his lips quirking in that familiar smile of his. That smile that looked like home.

"Well, I was in the neighborhood, and—"

"I heard you were leaving for Paris."

"The damndest thing, wouldn't you know it? I almost got on the ship, but then I remembered! I get seasick. So I decided to walk."

"Walk? To France? Across the ocean?"

"I never had a head for geography. Anyway, I was walking down 34th and it occurred to me . . . I still had something to say to you."

"Even more than you said last night?" he asked.

"Yes."

All hint of a joke abandoned her tone. She could not humor her way out of this. She'd almost lost him once. Now that the fates had given her another chance, she could not mess it up.

Thomas cleared his throat. "I have something to tell you, too."

"Oh, I got the feeling when you destroyed your big society wedding for me," she replied.

A strong hand cupped her cheek. A few traitor tears threatened to slip when she thought of how she'd nearly gone through an entire life without this. Without Tom.

"I'm sorry. You didn't deserve last night. You didn't deserve any of this. I didn't want to leave you, and I didn't do it for my ambitions. Alban found out about my past. He threatened you. He threatened all of your friends, Dr. Samson. I was afraid if I didn't break your heart, that you wouldn't believe me. That you would keep putting yourself in his path, that he might take any excuse to hurt you—"

"You . . . you were protecting us?"

Her mind tripped over that. Protecting them. Protecting *her*.

"You taught me a great deal about how to love people. I thought my life and my heart were a small price to pay if it meant that you could be safe and happy—"

"Happy? You think I could be happy without you? You absolute fool of a man."

He had the audacity to look sheepish. "You are the strongest person I've ever met. Of course you could be happy without me."

No. She couldn't accept that. She was strong, but that didn't mean . . . "No one could be happy without the man they love."

Light flooded his face. Evelyn was certain the same happened to her. "You—you love me?"

"Yes, Tom Gallagher. I love you."

"And I love you."

How could something so simple fill her with such spectacular joy? Such peace? Such security and warmth?

She didn't know it was possible to be this happy on the day the man she loved was set to marry another.

371

No, she didn't know it was possible to be this happy—period.

"This is quite the publicity stunt you pulled," she breathed against Thomas's cheek.

"Do you really think so?"

"Mm-hm."

He smirked. "Well . . . I'm about to make it even better."

And with that, he dipped down and—to thunderous applause— kissed her as she'd never been kissed before.

The kiss of an undeniable love.

A FINAL WORD FROM THE HISTORIAN

And, unlike some of us . . .

No. Actually . . .

Unlike most of us, they all lived happily ever after.

The End

PART TEN

HIS LAST THOUGHTS WERE OF YOU
(EDITOR'S ADDENDUM)

A RESPONSE FROM
ARMITAGE GALLIER

It is customary, when one becomes the subject of a book, to be contacted by the publisher for both comment and fact-checking purposes. Typically, this means that the subject and their team of lawyers will comb through the book and reply with a detailed list of confirmations, "no comments," and statements regarding the lack of support for any unsubstantiated or incorrect claims.

Against the advice of my counsel, against the recommendation of Gallier Entertainment and Telecommunications' Board, and against the wishes of my family, I am providing the following statement, to be printed in its entirety in all editions of *A Showgirl's Rules for Falling in Love* by Phoebe Blair.

The claims made in *A Showgirl's Rules for Falling in Love* are, to the best of my knowledge, entirely factual.

Thomas Gallier, the founder of Gallier Entertainment and Telecommunications, did use a false identity to build his life and career in the United States. He did engage in an illicit affair with the notorious chorine Evelyn Cross. He did enter a marriage with Constance Alban, daughter of newspaper mogul Nehemiah Alban, without any pretense of genuine affection. He did nearly drink himself to death.

And he did love Evelyn Cross.

Similarly, Miss Blair makes entirely accurate observations about my own person and character. I do concern myself entirely too much with what people think. I did get food poisoning from one of the Gettys' weddings. I did leave an ambassador's ball to bring her wonton soup. I am afraid of my father. I am afraid of losing my power and influence and money. I am afraid of what others think. I have no idea what it's like to be a normal person. Or to feel like normal people do.

I was a coward for not loving her in public.

I was a coward for letting her go.

I was wrong for trying to erase Evelyn and Thomas.

I was wrong for letting my fear get in the way of the only thing that has ever brought me real happiness.

All of this, I concede to be true.

However.

There are certain elements of Miss Blair's account that cannot go uncontested.

I wasn't paranoid or micromanaging in the beginning of our partnership. I simply wanted to be near her. I have never *quivered*. I don't recall rigging any ticket system to help her win third baseline seats at a Yankees game. I was afraid of losing her. I didn't send her the NDA as a goodbye; I sent it as a gift. She was good enough—too good for me. She had nothing to be insecure about; she was the most beautiful woman I'd ever seen. Singular.

Above all, though:

She claims that I did not love her. This is incorrect.

I did love Phoebe Blair. Ever since she sent me her first email, riddled with too many exclamation points. Ever since the first time I saw her—in that dingy basement, with marshmallow fluff on her face. Ever since she squealed with delight over finding an original Jules Moreau poster in Thomas Gallier's personal effects. Ever since she cried in my arms while watching *Groundhog Day*. Ever since her favorite pink sweater turned my best white shirts salmon. Ever since she fell asleep on my shoulder in front of the fireplace, since she wrote that ridiculous erection line, since she took the endless cups of tea I offered her between her perfect lips, since we first made love, since I failed her, since she walked out of my life forever. And I imagine I always will.

This is as good a time as any to clarify one more point. No, I didn't ask my family about our jewelry collection. But not out of malice. I didn't ask because I didn't have to. The Tiffany ring Thomas purchased on that fateful day was among the first things I discovered in his personal effects. It had been hidden under lock and key in my top desk drawer ever since. I should have told Phoebe about it the second I trusted her, but . . . I couldn't. Not even when I began imagining what it would be like to propose to her with it someday.

The ring may not seem like much to anyone else, but to me, it is the only way to understand how I could break the heart of the woman I loved.

In Phoebe's telling of their story, Evelyn Cross accuses Thomas Gallier of being a magic trick—most of him, the best of him, is hidden. There was no way Phoebe could have known how true she struck there. To be a Gallier is just that: to hide as much of yourself as possible. There are expectations a Gallier must meet, a certain image that must be upheld, a reality that must be maintained if we're going to keep the banks and the boards and the business partners happy. No deviations are allowed.

As a boy, my father threw my collection of comic books into the fireplace because they weren't a "worthy pursuit" for the man who would one day take over his company. I learned to keep my comics under a loose floorboard in my bedroom. When I made fast friends with the kids at my school who were on scholarship, he kicked them out of the house the first time they visited. I started sneaking out to see them in their neighborhood instead. When I proved an inadequate sneaker, he shipped me off to boarding school in Switzerland. We stayed friends by streaming video games online—a habit I bribed my Swiss roommate into keeping a secret when my dad came to visit. I stored Halloween candy in an old vase because he never let me have sweets. I gave our staff Christmas gifts in January when he wasn't paying attention because he didn't believe in "bonuses." I tipped our waiters under the table and our cab drivers on Venmo because gratuity was beneath him. I went to the movies at midnight because he refused to watch anything made or distributed by our competitors. I once told him I was out of town so I could go incognito to some tacky, touristy Broadway show (he only went to the opera and the symphony) and played sick so I could watch the *Umbrella Academy* finale instead of going with him on a golf trip with potential business partners.

He wasn't the only culprit, of course. He was just the loudest. I was the heir, which meant I got it in varying degrees from the board, from my mother, from the rest of my family whose fortune depended on me, from our friends, from investors, from the press, from anyone who had any interest in the company I would one day lead.

My entire life, I learned that the only way to protect myself was to hide myself. Anything I exposed to the world was fair game for other people to dissect and dismiss and ruin and steal away.

So anything that was important to me, I tucked away in a box. Metaphorical *and* physical.

Thomas and Evelyn's story? If I let Phoebe give it to the world, then everyone I knew would tear apart this beautiful thing that had been ours. It had to be kept secret.

The ring? If word got out about it, my family would want it appraised and sold off to the highest bidder. It wouldn't be mine to give to someone I loved. I had to lock it away in my drawer.

My own heart? If I let Phoebe see that, she might have realized the only thing in there was her. Phoebe on the back terrace looking like bottled sunshine. Phoebe near the fireplace, biting her lip as she considered a weathered document. Phoebe standing in the kitchen, pulling apart the two golden halves of a grilled cheese sandwich. Phoebe kissing me like I was someone worthy of love. Like I was someone worthy of finally letting the world see me—all of me, not just the pieces I allowed it to see.

And Phoebe herself? Our love? I didn't hide that because I was ashamed of her. I hid it because I didn't know how else to keep it safe. I'd lost everything else I loved. I couldn't bear the thought of losing her, too.

Ironic, isn't it? I was so afraid. And in the end, that fear was how I lost her. But I'm not afraid now. I want the world to know. Because the risk is worth it. *She* is worth it.

I *do* love Phoebe Blair. It's undeniable.

And I have no right to ask, not after what I have done to her, not after how thoroughly I ruined us. But if she is ever so inclined to rewrite our story . . . if she ever wants to reclaim us the way that she reclaimed Thomas and Evelyn . . .

Then I will be here, waiting between the pages for our own Happily Ever After.

Signed,

Armitage Gallier

ACKNOWLEDGMENTS

When I first learned about Billy Watson's Beef Trust, a famous vaudeville act featuring a chorus line of women over two hundred pounds, I instantly knew I would someday write a book inspired by them. Before I had read a piece of historical reference material, before I understood how vibrant and diverse the vaudeville scene was, before I grasped the depth and complexity of America's fatphobia, something about these women clicked with me, stayed with me, and sustained me through the arduous and joyful writing process to come. That was 2021. Now, as we prepare to release this book into the world in 2025, I can't begin to express my gratitude for all the people who have shaped Evelyn, Thomas, Phoebe, Armitage, and all the rest—but I will make my best attempt.

To begin, I have to acknowledge the real vaudeville figures who inspired this book. Not just the women of Billy Watson's Beef Trust, but trailblazers like female impersonator Julien Eltinge, tap legends like Bill Robinson and the Nicholas Brothers, disabled artists like Jules Keller, political activists like Emma Goldman, comedians like Morey Amsterdam, and fearless women like Sophie Tucker—to name a few. Without their tireless efforts to create great art in the face of overwhelming injustice and prejudice, not only would this book not exist, but American art as we know it would be a wholly different and duller landscape. I thank them, and I hope my tiny attempt to shed some light on this diverse, forgotten American artform inspires more people to explore this small section of our shared past.

After researching and writing this book came trying to get it published. I once, in a fellowship application, described my agent Maggie Cooper as someone I would go to war for—and I stand by that. Maggie is one of the most remarkable people I have ever had the pleasure of meeting, and I am so grateful for the patience, care, creativity, and passion she brought to this process. Whether called *Hungry Women* or *The Fat Lady Sings* or *A Showgirl's Rules for Falling in Love*, she championed Evelyn, Phoebe, and me—and I will forever be grateful. Thank you to Laura Schreiber, who pulled the book out of submission hell and gave it a home. The entire team at Union Square & Co. has been a dream to work with. Juliana Nador, you are a queen, and I bow before your editorial prowess. Erin McClary, you are one of the best editors I have ever worked with, and I'm so grateful for the heart and knowledge you brought to the process. Barbara Berger, Amanda Englander, Christina Stambaugh, and the entire staff at Union Square from the copy editors to assistants to marketing personnel, I am forever in your debt, too. Christine Heun, Decue Wu, and Patrick Sullivan, thank you for making this the most beautiful book I've ever held. Decue, thank you in particular for making Evelyn so stunning.

I also can't let this opportunity pass without thanking the Manchester Women's Writers Group, who welcomed this little Southern American weirdo while she camped out in the great English North for a few months. I can still remember sitting in the Central Library reading room, typing out the first page of what would become this book, and feeling so nervous about bringing it to the read-around. But you all welcomed me and embraced me with open arms. I can never repay you for the kindness, the generosity, the expertise, and the laughs you shared with me for those six months. I only hope you all know how much every minute meant to me, and to the development of this book. Meg and Jo, you two are legends. Thanks for the hours of wine-soaked chat while I lived in Manchester and long-distance social media friendship since. You two are the real deal.

Occasionally, I get my head out of my books, and when I do, I'm lucky enough to have a coterie of exceptional friends who make non-work life worth living. There's Sara and Alex, who were unfailing companions during the writing of this book and who kindly gave me their blessing to borrow the name Armitage. Vieta, Andy, Jana, Keara, Hannah, Shea, Charles, Mary Kate, Sophie, Ioana—all of whom, in their own way, have made my life richer. The Blue Cypress Book Club, who remind me every month how lucky I am to live in a world where there are romance novels; thank you, Jodi, and everyone there. Mom, who is the best friend a girl could have—and an even better mother. Derek, who didn't mind when I talked story problems at him for car rides on end. Mere, who believed in this book from the start. Nia, Lila, and Elizabeth, the best sisters in the world. Shaely, the greatest therapist known to man. And, of course, the Birdies, who have had to listen to me talk about this book for almost four years now. I hope you're all happy to never hear a tipsy vaudeville anecdote from me ever again.

Adam. My entire job is words, and yet, I can't find any that capture the love I have for you. Maybe one day, when we finally meet the aliens that I'm sure are out there, they'll have the language for it. But for now: thank you for taking this journey with me. I love knowing that tomorrow and every day after, there will be more adventures waiting for us. And I love you.

To myself. While editing this book, I developed a severe eating disorder. I lost my inner Evelyn Cross. I fell out of love with myself. I hope that one day, when I look back on these pages, I'll fall in love with me again. I hope I'll find the strength to rewrite my own future. And if you're struggling like me, if you've lost *your* inner Evelyn, I wish the same for you. If you or someone you know is struggling with an eating disorder, you can find support at the National Eating Disorders Association; see nationaleating disorders.org.

And finally, thank *you* for reading *A Showgirl's Rules for Falling in Love*. It's the book of my heart. I hope it finds a small place in yours.

ABOUT THE AUTHOR

ALICE MURPHY is the pen name for a prolific Hallmark screen-writer and romance author from the Deep South. She collects secret recipes, secret admirers, and secret histories.